Winter's Child

by Christine D. Shuck

Also by Christine D. Shuck

Benton Security Services
Hired Gun
Smoke and Steel

Chronicles of Liv Rowan
Fate's Highway

Gliese 581g
G581: The Departure
G581: Mars
G581: Earth

War's End
War's End: The Storm
War's End: A Brave New World
Tales of the Collapse
War's End Omnibus - Books 1-3

Standalone

The War on Drugs: An Old Wives Tale
Get Organized, Stay Organized
Winter's Child

Watch for more at christineshuck.com.

1. Now

- Nichole -

September 18th, 2019 - Brisbane, Australia

All I ever wanted was a family to love. A family of my own. Children. A husband. Love. It's all I ever wanted.

I struggle to get ahold of myself on the drive to the police station. It isn't easy. Tears keep running down my cheeks and my nose is dripping. I know I look a sight.

But all I can think of is what if Jhon dies? What if his brain is swelling and bruising as we speak? Or he's hurt so bad that he isn't Jhon anymore? He was so still on the gurney. His face gray, bloodless. The EMTs walked, no spare seconds for small talk, their entire focus on Jhon's care. The ambulance roared away, sirens screaming, lights flashing.

I fear so much. I fear being alone and fear Jhon passing from this life, from our lives.

Will our unborn child ever meet his father? This man who may have paid the ultimate price, his life, to be a father to our children, and a husband to me.

Elizabeth. They wouldn't let me talk to her. Not that it would have helped. This is just what she was hoping for, after all. A group of paramedics checked her over. One watched me, her eyes slitting, jaw set in anger. And then they had placed Elizabeth in the back of a police car, wrapped her in a blanket, and gave her a stuffed bear. They don't know what she has done. They don't know who she is and what she is capable of. No one does. Only Jhon and me - we are the only ones who have seen it, who know her for what she really is. Everyone else, well, they're all dead or long gone.

I hit her so hard. Seeing her fall limp to the carpet keeps replaying in my mind's eye.

I hadn't had a choice, but that didn't make it any easier, seeing her lying there, limp on the floor as I dragged Jhon out of the bedroom and down the hall. No time to worry about the trail of blood. He needed help *now*, not after I had secured her inside of her room with lock and key. As if I even could, with the house in flames. All I could do was stop her and get to Jhon. Save Jhon. Save the father of my baby.

Jhon was right. God, he was so right. He said it was too big a secret to keep, that something like this would come out. And of course they will think the worst. I can't even blame them for that. It *looks* terrible. The locks on the door, bars on her windows, the ketamine in the fridge, and her unconscious on the floor. She looked perfect, lying there, her red curls framing her face. Ignore the blood on her nightgown and hands.

What could I have expected?

I breathe in and out. I concentrate on self-calming. As the car turns, slows at lights, and speeds up - I remember my therapist's words. *Breathe in through your nose and deep into your belly. Feel your stomach rise. Purse your lips and exhale through your mouth.*

I do this for what feels like forever. We are miles and miles from the police station. This was intentional, but now, in the thick of it, it all feels like a mistake. Jhon could die. Might already be dead. All because of me. All because I couldn't have a normal pregnancy. My deficiency. My shortcoming.

The breathing does the trick. At least for now. My tears have dried on my cheeks. Only their salty tracks betray the fact that they were ever there. I want to wash my face; it feels... crusty, and my skin is taut. There's blood on my nightgown. Is it mine? No, Jhon's.

The baby's head presses hard against my cervix and he is quiet right now. Earlier, he was kicking in tandem with the rise and fall of the sirens as the ambulance carrying his father raced away.

I can't help but wonder if our son will be a musician. He has a good sense of rhythm.

I push that from my mind. Thoughts of the future are a bad idea, a walk down a path that creates more questions than answers, more fear than solace. What will happen to me? Will they blame this all on me? I feel the voices rise inside my head. They question, they accuse, they warn. I'm no different from her, no different at all. And I'm terrified they will see it, that they won't believe the truth.

What is the truth? We riddle truth with lies. I'm living proof of that. And perhaps, perhaps, she was right. I think about that often. It wakes me up at night, heart pounding, throat tight, remembering, while wishing I could forget. But I don't. I can't.

During the day, it's easier. Life is full of distractions, of work, of its challenges. But at night, when the world is quiet, when darkness descends, the voices start. The memories flood back. And in my dreams, I'm right back there, with her, helpless.

My former therapist knows a lot about it, but she doesn't know everything. Some of it is, well, unbelievable. Impossible. And I know better than to mention it. The complete story is far too unbelievable. No one could look at all of it, the entire picture, and walk away thinking I was sane.

I often wonder if I'm sane.

The only time it feels okay - or that all is right and well with the world - is when I'm sculpting. The clay, cool, thick, turning warm and slick beneath my hands. Everything else drops away. The world stops. I forget to eat. Eventually, my legs tap out a rhythm that breaks through my focus enough to tell me I need to pee. That's what sculpting is, a frantic dash to rinse the clay from my hands in time as I try not to pee down my leg. All that I am, with my fingers in the clay, is the operator. The voices guide me, help me, or berate me depending on my progress. I feel as if I have purpose. And isn't that what we all want? Some kind of purpose?

I wonder if it was the same for her. Maybe it was. Perhaps she and I are more alike than I wish.

The night is chilly, dark, and it is raining. Typical winter weather for Brisbane and not so different from living in Seattle. I have steel handcuffs on my wrists. The police officer who put them on my wrists tightened them an extra click. He did it on purpose. I could feel the anger rolling off him. It felt hot. If I were a painter, I would have painted his outline in reddish-orange, maybe even a dark purple. He thinks he understands what he sees. That I hurt her on purpose, and that I was the one who hurt Jhon. He thinks he sees the whole picture. It is a perfect little package, wrapped up neatly with a bloody bow. I can see it in his hard eyes, the flinty glances in the rearview mirror as he looks back. He thinks he knows what happened, but he doesn't. No one does. Only Jhon, and me, and Elizabeth.

I almost hate that name. Elizabeth.

Now, Isabel, Lizzie, those names still fill my heart with such love. Even Elsa. I can live with Elsa. But Elizabeth?

My face is a map of my emotions. I know it must be, as I feel the officer staring at me in the rearview. I look up and he holds my eyes for a second before glancing away. What does he think he sees? Anger? Contempt? Hatred?

Elizabeth. She stared at me from the police vehicle twenty feet away. There in the gloom, for just a fraction of a second, a tiny smile appeared on her face. No one else saw it. Only me. She's so damned smart like that. Too smart for me. Too smart for Jhon. We were fools to think this would work. That we could make it another winter with her. She's grown smarter, harder, more slippery, and so very dangerous.

I don't blame him. This angry officer, his back rigid, his hands clenched on the wheel as he takes a turn hard and I slide across the slick plastic seat. If it makes him feel better to do it, to cause me this extra bit of pain for the drive from here to the station, so be it. They don't know what I know. I keep repeating that to myself. It helps remind me I once would have reacted the same way.

It would serve no purpose to argue, to explain. I know better now. In some ways, I wish I didn't.

They won't understand. But somehow, somehow, I must try to explain it all. Or, at least the parts that aren't too crazy. Somehow, I have to convince them I'm not a danger to Jhon or Elizabeth.

That will be hardest. Convincing them I love my child. Because I do. I love her. That might seem strange, and these police would be quick to point their fingers and tell me how my love is twisted, and wrong, but they don't understand. I can't make them understand either. I will tell them the story of it all and hope to God that they listen to me. That they believe. Everything we have done has been to protect her, to love her, and to provide a safe environment for her. Somehow, I have to make them believe that. Hell, I need them to believe *me*.

The rain keeps falling, hard, not soft. The rain in Seattle is far gentler, but here, on the outskirts of Brisbane, it feels like an attack. It pours down, swift and heavy. There is a sharpness to it. A thousand needles hitting all at once.

And there have been so many attacks in recent days that I don't react as I once did. When they pull me out of the vehicle, I'm soaked. The rain is cold and my fingers and toes are already ice-cold, stiff. The officer does not try to shield me from the rain, despite the obvious baby bump. He's angry, so angry. If you want to piss off an officer, hurt a child. I want to tell him that if there had been any other way to stop her, I would have done it. But there was so much blood, and I panicked. After I hit her, she fell so still I was sure she was dead. Instantly I thought of Isabel, Lizzie, and Elsa. That I would never see them again. And I love them. Even as I fear Elizabeth. I can't help but love her in some small way, too. I see the others in her. And even if *she* is dangerous, they are not.

The portico on the side of the police station is empty. The officer parks fifty feet away on purpose. He's soaked too, but his anger rises. It looks like steam at the moment. Maybe the rain will cool him. I shiver, my body aching and stiffening until I feel as if I am waddling about on two frozen logs for legs. My baby shifts, kicking into my bladder, which is full, as usual, given my pregnant state.

An officer at the side entrance stands under the portico and yells at the officer holding my arm. "Searles, get her in here, for fuck's sake. We don't need the DHA up our ass. This is going by the book. Now get her in here. The room is waiting."

The officer holding me growls, his teeth set on edge. His beefy hand tightens on my arm, and he pulls me towards the building. I'll be sporting bruises tomorrow, without a doubt. I can't help thinking that they would pair well with the older bruises on my back and shoulders. The rain pelts us, running in rivulets down my front, my legs, and puddles into my shoes as we escape it under the portico and they hustle me inside.

"I need to use the facilities," I tell the two other men waiting inside, trying not to let my teeth chatter. One of them, a short, heavy, balding man, stares at me with open contempt. The other, younger, in his mid-thirties, nods and points toward the desk where there is a young female officer.

"She'll take you."

They remove the cuffs but hold onto my arm, the arresting officer bruising it further in his iron grip as he walks me towards the restroom, the young woman matching our steps. She takes over from there. First, she holds open the door for me, then enters the bathroom, stopping just inside of the door. She watches as I use the toilet. There is a trail of water that drips from the door to the toilet and a puddle is forming at my feet. At least it is warm inside of the precinct. Outside it is bitterly cold. How cold, I don't know. I hadn't been down under long enough to move from Fahrenheit to Celsius. I'm hopeless at the conversions.

I shiver uncontrollably. I'd done my best to control it outside in the rain, but now, in here, I feel safer. Foolish, I know. As if hiding it was my way of toughing it out or something. I just hated how the first police officer looked at me. I hated the thought of him seeing any weakness. After all, I survived her. And I survived losing my first two babies. I'd fought to keep this little baby boy alive inside of me. I wasn't weak, I was strong.

"I'll get you a change of clothes," the woman says. "Get you out of those wet ones." Her uniform has a name tag, but from my angle I can't read anything more than the first few letters, HENN... She sticks her head out of the door and speaks to someone out in the hallway. A few seconds later, a knock on the door and a hand shoves a green prisoner's uniform through.

A prisoner. I am a *prisoner*. The voices rise, a cacophony of panic ricocheting through my head.

They're going to lock you up, Nichole.

Throw away the key.

Jhon's dead. Or brain-damaged or worse.

All because of you, Nichole. All because you had to have your way. You just had to be a mom.

As if you could do any better.

As if you ever could be a mom.

I want to reach inside my skull and pull out the voices, one by one. I want to scream at them to be silent, to be still.

Instead, I thank the woman. Hennessey, A. - that's what her name tag reads. Did A stand for Amber? Angela? Or Astrid, a favorite of mine since I binged all five seasons of *Fringe* on Netflix as I lay there in bed trying to keep my baby alive. If our baby had been a girl, I would have insisted on Astrid.

As I fumble with my sodden shirt and skirt, I imagine reaching in with razor-sharp fingernails, rifling through the gray folds of my brain, and pulling each trash-talking loop of brain-flesh out with cold precision.

The color of the prisoner uniform isn't ugly. Dark green is one of my favorite colors, but the fabric is rough, abrasive. My skin chafes, first from the wet and the cold, and now, from the tough, canvas-like material.

Hennessey sucks in a breath as I stand there in my bra and panties and slip on the pants. My back is to her, so I'm guessing the bruises have ripened to a lovely purple-black by now. What must she think? That my husband had beaten me, that was for sure. How many times did she see it in her line of work? Beaten, cowed women - terrified, shaking, maybe even soaked to the bone like I was. But to think my husband beat me. Gentle, kind Jhon? Not likely. Not if she spent a handful of minutes in his presence. He might get crabby, even snappy if woken too early, but never, *ever* would he have even dreamed of violence towards me. Not a chance.

I pull the shirt over my head, wincing as it passes over bruised flesh. I pull the end of my ponytail out of the collar and walk over to the sink. If I could just squeeze out the water, the sodden mess would dry easier. Hennessey stops me. "Sorry, but the detective needs those as evidence, Ma'am."

"Of course." My voice is raspy, no doubt from screaming. No actual surprise there. I hand her the sodden, dripping clothes. And she slips them into a clear plastic evidence bag with blue latex-gloved hands.

Two by two, hands of blue. The line from River Tam in the show *Firefly* echoes in my mind. A small puddle of pink water is already forming in the bag. An image of Jhon on the floor, lying so still, his breaths shallow and ragged, and the blood from dozens of stab wounds hits me then. So much blood.

"I'll take you into the interview room now. This way, please." Hennessey's voice seems kinder. The bruises have changed her mind about what this is. She thinks she understands. Thinks it's Jhon. She isn't right, though. None of them are. They hadn't seen what I had seen. And even if they had, they would have explained it away.

I walk with her, no handcuffs on my wrists. There aren't many here, not at night. Or was it morning? Yes, early morning. The few that are there, stare. Their faces are tight, eyes flinty, full of anger and distrust. I'm sure I do myself no favors by staring back at them, meeting their eyes. Now I am branded as something else, something far worse.

Mothers are expected to be soft, kind. Mothers are not dangerous, except when in protection of their young. And mothers, the good ones, don't beat their children or try to kill their husbands. To these men, I am a monster. Will that change when Hennessey speaks to them? Maybe. But they still wouldn't understand.

She removes my cuffs in the interrogation room and leaves me, saying that the detective will arrive soon. I can see from the hooks on the seat and the table bolted to the floor that handcuffing a prisoner is the norm. And from the raised voice in the hall from my arresting officer, I assume she is catching hell for taking them off of me.

I stare at my wrists. The tight handcuffs have chafed them and they are red and swollen from the ride in the back of the cruiser.

There is no clock in the room. No way for me to tell time. I should be tired. The past few months have been nothing but constant exhaustion, no matter how much I slept, but not now. Not in this moment when everything is dependent on whoever they send through the door. I need for them to understand, for them to believe me, for them to see how hard I tried. How hard Jhon tried.

In my head, the seconds turn to minutes and then hours. Days, even. The voices tell me how worthless I am. That I have been a fool. That I will spend the rest of my life in a place like this. Metal walls, rivets, and cameras watching my every move. This is what I have to look forward to. My child will be born in a place like this, and they will rip him from my hands. He will grow up wondering what he had done to deserve such a terrible mother.

I try breathing. Tears fall, and I rock, hands on my belly, trailing gentle fingers along until I identify his tiny butt pressing outward, his head positioned at my cervix.

We had been so close. So close to spring and Isabel's return. To meeting our son.

Had it all been for nothing?

No one will believe me.

My eyes are closed when the door opens. I fear opening them, expecting nothing but hostility and hate. I wasn't expecting to see a familiar face. Not at all.

Vincent Gallagher stands there staring at me, a note in his hand, his back to the camera and two-way glass. I focus on the scribbled note in his hand. Then back up at his face. His eyes warn me even as the tone in his voice sounds indifferent.

"Good evening, Mrs. Staunton, I'm Detective Gallagher."

I nod.

More tears come. They blur his handsome face, a face I have kissed more than once. My best friend and my first steady boyfriend. My first lover. What the hell was he doing here in Australia? I haven't seen him in, what, ten years? Not since the day I told him it was over. The day before I left for Seattle, never to return. I'd left him behind in Kansas City. My life in the Midwest over, buried. So much pain, loss.

The years have passed and Vincent is even more handsome than I remember. Mature now. No longer the boyish, youthful face I remember. My mind flashes on lazy Sunday afternoons in the backyard of Andy and Hannah's house, Vincent and me and half a dozen others swimming in the pool and soaking up the sun. Stolen moments at theater rehearsals and soft kisses. Our last day together and the hurt on his face when I said I was leaving. I had wondered about him over the years. Imagined him dating, starting a family, going to the police academy. So many memories. He'd been a friend first, the only one in a new school and new neighborhood. We'd grown up together. Next-door neighbors. Friends through elementary and middle school. Lovers by our junior year at Northeast High School. And here he is. Here we both are. Thousands of miles from our childhood homes in Kansas City. In a different country, half a world away from our childhood home.

He sits down. His body is graceful, lean, his dark hair cut short now, so different from the ponytail he had sported through senior year.

"Mrs. Staunton, I understand that there was a fire at your residence and that your husband and your daughter," he starts as he looks down at the opposite side of the note, "Elizabeth, both injured. I'd like to talk to you about tonight and the events that led up to the fire and the injuries that your husband and daughter have suffered."

I swallow hard. Of all the people in the world to be interrogating me, Vincent Gallagher is the one man, aside from my husband, who knows me, truly knows me. If I had any chance to avoid spending the next decade of my life in prison, it depended on convincing him I wasn't crazy, that I hadn't tried to murder my child and my husband and set our house on fire. The note in his hand, now crumpled and shoved into his pants pocket, changes everything. He is taking a chance. A dreadful, yet miraculous chance on me. In mere seconds, my fear has turned to hope. I will tell him the truth. All of it. Vincent, my childhood sweetheart, is my only chance at saving my family. But even he doesn't know everything about my past. To understand it all, I need to tell him everything.

I steady my breathing, dry my tears, and speak. "I met Jhon in Seattle while volunteering at a soup kitchen. We married the year after graduation."

Vincent opens his mouth, but I hold up a finger. The nail on it is short, ragged. I have chewed it down to the quick.

"Please. I'll tell you everything. Maybe you'll believe me, maybe you won't, but you have to let me tell it to you from the beginning. Please."

I don't know if it is the look on my face or our shared past, but he closes his mouth and gives a nod.

"It all began on December 21st, 2013, the day I gave birth to my daughter."

Incident/Case #: 18-02521

Classification: Assault/Arson
Date: 2018-20-09
Location: Rush Creek, Raaen Road
Victim (s): Staunton, Jhon and Elizabeth
Suspect: Staunton, Nichole
Evidence ID#: 18-02521-005 (page out of handwritten journal)

A LITTLE GIRL. J SEEMS excited. Although not as excited as he was when he talked about us having a boy in the house. I suppose I should be too. Instead, I just feel as if I'm on the edge, not scared, but as if something terrible is coming.

I know, I know, the voices aren't helping. One minute they are warning me that this baby, this child, could be my undoing. Other times, they are silent. Ominously so. Such a simple question I have asked from the universe: Am I meant to be a mother? The voices always have something to say, a string to pull, a button to push, and yet, at this moment?

They say nothing.

- N -

2. Before

- Nichole -

December 21st, 2013 - Seattle, Washington

Jhon's feet disappeared into the crawlspace of our rented home. He was crabby, and I already wished I had said nothing about the noise I heard. The fluffs of insulation rained down from the opening in the ceiling. The tufts of spun glass looked like cotton candy. I groaned. My vacuum was on the fritz and with it being right before Christmas, I dreaded going out at all. I'd have to get it up with a broom and dustpan and hope I missed nothing and not find it later with my big, swollen feet.

Some creature, most likely a raccoon, seemed to be up there. It walked around in the crawlspace above my head, no matter where I went in the house. And of course, it only happened in the early morning, when I was the only one awake to hear it. Jhon was not a morning person, not at all. Especially not now, when he was working sixty, sometimes eighty-hour weeks for an understaffed non-profit. He slept soundly, too, especially back then. Like a rock. When we had lived in California for a year, he slept through an earthquake that shook the dishes off the rack and broke three plates on the Moroccan tile floor. He didn't so much as crack an eyelid. So it wasn't any surprise that the creature climbing up the inside of the wall before dawn didn't wake him. For me, however, it was a different story. I woke up wondering if it was tearing a hole in the walls. The strangest part was hearing the creak of the floors as it followed me from room to room in the attic above my head.

Raccoons are curious creatures. My adoptive parents fed a troop of raccoons every evening on their back porch. But with our baby coming anytime, the last thing we needed was some wild creature loose inside the home we were renting from Jhon's boss. And I knew for certain that the boss's wife would not want a raccoon in her attic. I shook Jhon awake with difficulty and as soon as he stopped grumbling, he heard it as well. A few minutes later, he'd pulled the ladder out of the back shed and shoved the lid aside, disappearing into the crawlspace. All I could think about was the tiny glass slivers Jhon would get.

It did not prepare me for the sudden explosion of sound and fury as Jhon came face to face with the raccoon.

What had I been thinking? A swath of loose fiberglass rained down as Jhon's feet reappeared, the rest of him following. The deep growls and snarls the raccoon was giving off got my heart hammering. He slid out of the attic crawlspace, fiberglass sticking to his pajamas, catching in his hair, and he almost missed the top step of the ladder in his panic.

"Christ!" he sputtered, wild-eyed, fiberglass falling all around us as the raccoon rampaged through the crawlspace above. "I thought you said the raccoons at your parents' house were nice! That one looked like he was going to rip my throat out!"

I picked at the pieces of insulation. Jhon looked like someone caught in a demented carnival experience that had included a pink cotton candy explosion. Above us, the raccoon rustled up to the edge and peered down at us. When our gazes connected, it growled again and backed into the shadows.

I couldn't help laughing. It started with shaking, my shoulders and mouth twitching as I picked the pieces of insulation off of Jhon, the ones in his hair, and down his back. He glared at me as I stifled my giggles, snorting. Every so often the raccoon would move back to the opening, as if hoping we had left, and peer at him with its beady black eyes before retreating with a growl.

"Christ," Jhon growled, and above them the raccoon growled in return. I dissolved into laughter then, laughing so hard my belly hurt. Jhon joined in, even as he picked at the insulation that was clinging to his pajamas.

I ran my hand over my now enormous belly, surprised the baby hadn't moved. She was often more active in the mornings. At over eight months, I was counting the days until our due date. I was also counting the days until Christmas, just four days away.

"I think we need to find a wildlife specialist or something," Jhon said, peering at the opening in the ceiling. "Maybe I should call Jacob?"

Jacob was both a mentor and boss for Jhon, and also our landlord. When he and his wife flew out of the country to head up the new Peruvian office of ULSC (Using Loans for Social Change), we had been struggling with finding a place to stay. Our lease had been up in our one-bedroom apartment, and prices in the housing market had begun to rise, making our search for a place big enough to house us and our soon-to-be-born newborn, difficult. Jacob had known he would be away for at least six months, and then another month, maybe two, in Australia, working with the Aborigine population. He had offered us his house at half the rate we had been paying for our one-bedroom apartment and we had jumped at it.

"No, we can handle it. He's given us free rein of this place at a steal, Jhon. I'll look up who to call." I peered up at the hole in the ceiling. A growl came, as if on cue. "Yeah, I'll go do that *now*."

As I turned away, a sharp pain knifed its way through me. I'd had a few Braxton-Hicks contractions, but this was nothing like that. This was something far different, more painful. I sucked in a breath just as another one tore through me.

"Oh." I reached for the banister, digging my fingers into the wood.

"Is it the baby?" Jhon was at my side, his arm curving around me, steadying me as I wobbled in place.

Another stabbing pain, then another, and another. Was this labor? Was I in labor? All the books I had read had described labor as being like painful menstrual cramps. I was wondering if perhaps they had understated things, when I felt dampness on my legs.

"Oh, wow, I think my water just broke," I wheezed in between the agonizing stabbing pains.

Jhon, who didn't have a giant watermelon in his belly and could see my feet, turned a shade of gray as he looked down at the floor.

"I'm calling 9-1-1."

"It's just my waters breaking," I gasped.

"No, no it isn't." He picked me up then and from his arms I could see a small puddle of bright-red blood spreading across the fine oak wood stairs. That was when I screamed.

The pain was overwhelming. I felt the tears coursing down my cheeks long before I realized I was crying. There was something terribly wrong.

Fifteen minutes later, my screams and the siren of the ambulance rose and fell together and felt just as urgent. In all of my life, I had never felt such agony. The paramedic's face was professional, but I could see the urgency in his eyes. His lips were moving, but all I could hear were the voices banging about in my head.

Your baby is going to die and so are you.

This is the way it should be. You don't deserve to live.

Jhon wasn't inside of the ambulance, but I knew he was following behind. He had looked furious when they said he couldn't ride with me, and I knew it had to be fear. Jhon never got angry. He grabbed my hand and told me he would meet us there. I shivered, the terror running through me. Tears blurred my view of his face as they loaded me into the ambulance and closed the doors.

I tried to breathe through the agony. I tried to ignore the voices. As I did, their cacophony rushed in.

Something's wrong and it's all your fault. You are going to die. You can't even grow a baby. What kind of a woman are you? You can't be a mother. You can't even carry a baby to term properly.

They went on and on. Endless.

The first paramedic raised my feet, stuffing a cushion under them, and I could see the splashes of bright-red blood on my legs. The paramedic near my head was keeping up a steady stream of information as he radioed ahead to the hospital.

"Incoming OB patient, age 24 years, with placental abruption. BP is eight-seven over 42 and pulse is at 149. We're starting an 18 gauge and will need two units of Type O at the ready. Administering O2. We're going to need the OB on call to meet at ER. ETA five minutes."

I could feel the jerks and twists of the ambulance as it sped around corners, slowing only when necessary for traffic outside. I fought the dizzying pain and a growing wave of exhaustion crept over me, darkness turning my vision into a long, dark tunnel with only a dim, dwindling view of the paramedics and inside of the ambulance. Something was happening to my hearing as well. Where there had been the loud siren, the voices of the paramedics, now it felt as if they wrapped everything in thick padding.

"Nichole... Mrs. Staunton..." The paramedic near my head was speaking, but it was so far away, and I was so tired, so exhausted, so...

Blackness descended, the sounds and light and motion fading. I remember lights moving past overhead, a face above mine, voices. And then nothing.

The steady beep of machinery was my first conscious memory. The sounds of feet and voices moving outside were the second. And the warmth of Jhon's hand holding mine, the feel of his hair against my fingers.

I opened my eyes to a darkened room. It took me a moment to process it, to realize where I was, to estimate the time of day.

I am in a hospital. It is nighttime. And Jhon is here with me.

I could see a spot of drool escape from his mouth. His hand was curled around mine and his head leaned against my hip. The rest of his body was in a chair by the side of my hospital bed. He couldn't be sleeping in that position, and yet his steady breathing showed he was.

It was at this moment that the memories came flooding back and I reached with my left hand for my belly, no longer taut and full of a child. The skin was deflated, empty. I winced as my fingers found the incision. They had taken her via Cesarean section. I gasped then, my eyes searching the room for the bassinet and seeing nothing. Was our baby in the NICU?

"Jhon. Jhon, wake up."

He stirred and raised his head, wincing in pain. One hand went up to his neck. His eyes opened, and I could see dark shadows under them.

"Nichole, oh thank God." His face crumpled. "I was so scared you wouldn't make it, that you wouldn't wake up. I've been here, ever since, ever..."

He stood then, wincing again, and pulled me against him. "Oh, Nichole." The sadness in his voice sent a thick rope of fear running through me. Where was our daughter? Why wasn't she here in the room with us?

"Jhon, where's our baby? Is she in the NICU?"

Jhon froze and pulled back. Up close, he looked wretched, and I couldn't help thinking that I had never seen him look so bad, not even when the news of his mother's death from a stroke had come in.

Tears welled in his eyes. And he shook his head, dropping his gaze. His shoulders slumped. My gut twisted. I felt the panic rise in me.

"She was stillborn, Nichole. They say she must have died within the previous 24 hours. The um, the umbilical cord got knotted up, stopped delivering nutrients, and..." His voice petered out and he looked up at me with such a look of agony and despair that I felt as if my heart was being torn asunder.

You killed your baby.

"No," I whispered.

You killed her. What kind of mother kills her baby? What kind of monster kills her baby while it is still inside of her?

"She's in the NICU. She has to be."

Jhon shook his head, tears sliding down his cheeks. "They tried. But she was gone. Long gone. They tried anyway, even while the team worked on you."

His voice faded. I could still see his lips moving, but the voices, God, the voices seemed to get louder and louder, a rushing thunder of them, repeating the words over and over.

You killed your child.

You killed your baby.

You killed her.

You killed her.

I put my hands over my ears, closed my eyes, and tried to blot them out, tried to not hear them anymore. But it didn't matter. They wouldn't stop. I began screaming. It sounded like a wounded animal. It brought the nurses, the doctor on call, and the room filled with people.

I kept screaming, if for no other reason than to blot out the voices. They wouldn't stop, not for a single second. One decisive yank and I had the IV out. Another and I'd ripped the heart rate sensors off of my skin and tried to move my legs off of the bed. I needed to find my baby. If I could just find her and hold her and kiss her. If I could just see her, just once, somehow I would make it better. I'd breathe life into her. She wasn't dead, she couldn't be dead.

Jhon had tried to take my hands, to calm me, but I flailed and I fought. This was not the time for quiet, for acceptance, or inaction. The nurses pushed past him, their mouths moved, but I couldn't tell you what they were saying. It felt like a movie with the sound turned off. Worse, they had substituted the sound with an endless unwavering howl of an animal in distress. Something primal, guttural, wordless.

I felt hands on me, pushing me down into the bed, holding me still, and the flash of a needle before it sank into the meat of my arm. As an icy rush of heaviness surged through me, my scream ended. The voices too. And then I was back to myself. I realized my throat was raw from screaming. That there was a track of blood coursing down my arm where the IV had been. My hospital gown rent to one side, testament to my struggles, an errant milk-swollen nipple showing. They held me there, immobile, until my body relaxed under them, unable to fight the powerful sedatives they had injected into me.

Time slowed. My mouth worked, but my tongue was heavy, my words drawn out.

"I waaannt my baab..."

My eyes slid shut and with them, my consciousness slipped away.

I woke the next morning to find I was in restraints. Jhon was nowhere in sight. My arm was clean, no blood in sight, although where the IV had been, there was now a dollar coin-sized bruise.

This time, I didn't scream and fight them. I lay there and waited for them to take off the restraints, to bring me water and leave a tray of food that I had no intention of eating. When Jhon arrived, his clothes were clean and his hair was still damp from a shower. Other than that, he looked just as bad as he had the night before. I still felt lethargic, but I suspected they were continuing to drug me. It wasn't the massive dose they had given me the night before, one that had knocked me out, but it was enough to keep me calm.

I found out that I had been unconscious for two days after the delivery. I had hemorrhaged, and it had taken almost four pints of blood to save my life. At one point, they had to resuscitate me when I flatlined. Jhon would later tell me he held our daughter for a few moments. By the time I woke up, the autopsy was complete and our little girl had been cremated.

"She was beautiful, Nichole," Jhon said, his voice breaking, "so tiny and perfect."

Later, far later, when my body had healed enough for me to go home, even if my heart had not, the doctor told us we would be better off "considering other options." I tried to wrap my head around the words, tried to find a positive in them, but the voices had other ideas.

You can't even make it nine months without killing your child.

Jhon wants a family. Guess how long he's going to stick around if you can't give it to him?

Mother was right. Everything you touch dies. You can see that now, can't you?

They woke me up at night, haunting my dreams until I jumped out of bed, sheets flying, a scream on my lips.

I had carried my daughter for eight months, only to lose her. But I wasn't a mother. I wasn't... anything.

Incident/Case #: <u>18-02521</u>

Classification: Assault/Arson

Date: 2018-20-09

Location: Rush Creek, Raaen Road

Victim(s): Staunton, Jhon and Elizabeth

Suspect: Staunton, Nichole

Evidence ID#: 18-02521-006 (page out of handwritten journal)

I dreamed of death last night and pulled the Death card this morning. Everyone, everyone was dead. Everyone except for me.

Alone again. Just like before.

I sat at the dining room table. It was Thanksgiving, but no one had cooked anything. The turkey sat on a large serving plate, feathers still on it, uncooked, dead eyes staring at me. J sat in his customary seat, and I in mine. I remember thinking it was inappropriate for him to be dead and still here in the house.

I wasn't pregnant either, not really. Although my belly was round and full. I put a hand on it and knew, absolutely knew, that there was no life inside.

I was hungry for Thanksgiving dinner. Instead of eating, I just sat there and waited for the scene to change. But it never did.

- N -

3. Living With It

- Nichole -

October 29th, 2014 - Seattle, Washington

“Come on.” Jhon’s voice was calm, but I could hear the frustration buried beneath. It had been building for months. A slow burn. It was a painful departure from the first days of our grief, when nothing helped except to hold each other and cry. But we had split in our paths. Jhon had held our baby for a moment, whereas I had carried her in my body, feeling every kick, every flutter. She had been alive inside of me. And there she had died, in the one place she should have been safe.

Jhon wanted to move on, but I didn’t. I just wanted to close my eyes and wait for death to take me. At the most basic level, I had failed, and our child had died inside of me.

“Nichole, you promised you would do this.” He paced back and forth in the living room. He didn’t have far to walk, just a few steps in each direction. The space was tiny, far too tiny for me to have a place to sculpt. But that didn’t really matter. I hadn’t touched clay in nearly a year now. The muse was gone, vanished into the earth along with our baby girl.

I felt hung over, drained of energy. Why couldn’t Jhon see that?

“Can we just go next week?”

He scrubbed his hand over his face. “No, no, we can’t. You promised you would go, Nichole. You *promised* me.”

He sounded like a little boy asking for a trip to the park or a candy store. And I resented the hell out of him for it. Why couldn’t he understand I didn’t want to go out? That I felt like I *couldn’t* go out?

I didn’t want to sit with a bunch of miserable, grieving people and tell them my story. I didn’t want to share my grief. It was *mine*, and mine alone. Mine to keep close, and wallow in if I felt like it. I had spent almost nine months growing a child inside of me, only to lose her.

As if he were reading my thoughts, Jhon said quietly, "It wasn't just you who lost a child, you know."

The wound was still raw. It didn't matter that nearly ten months had passed. Every day, week, and month was time I was supposed to have spent holding our baby. Our baby.

Our baby.

Every day after returning from the hospital empty-handed, I had looked in the other book, the one I never got to use or chart progress in. I kept it in the drawer of my nightstand. When my fingers moved over the words, "Within the next week, your baby should turn over for the first time," I had cried. The same had happened when I read about the milestones for smiling, sitting, and crawling.

The book had disappeared shortly after that. I looked for it everywhere. But it was gone. And I knew Jhon had taken it, tossed it out with the garbage. I hated him for it, even though I knew what I was doing to myself was nothing better than torture. Reading about the little girl she would have been, could have been, if my body hadn't failed in its duties - it was a cruelty. But that didn't mean that I didn't want it back. It was something to hold on to. Especially now. When everything else, including my marriage, felt unmoored.

Jhon waited, and the moments stretched out. Empty. Lonely. Begging to be filled with something, anything.

"My hair looks like shit." I sniffed my underarm and winced at the sour smell. When was the last time I had used deodorant? Or taken a shower? "Tell me I have enough time for a quick shower."

I ignored the look of relief in his eyes, in his voice. "Yes, but only if you get in there now."

An hour later, sitting in the flimsy plastic and metal chairs among a handful of people in a large semi-circle, I struggled to ignore the voices. My hair was still damp in places, and there was a snarled knot of hair near my scalp. I'd struggled with it the entire drive over before finally giving up in the parking lot.

I fought to sit still, to not run from this place and escape to our car. Jhon must have sensed it. He glued himself to my side, his hand in mine. I hated hearing the stories, the sadness. There was a mousy woman with more white than brown in her hair who talked about losing her only child to leukemia. Another couple were trying to figure out if their marriage was worth saving after a string of miscarriages and stillbirths. There were more, far too many more. Their voices blended together, their stories were the same, and I hated every one of them.

I itched to leave. I wished they would shut up. Each miserable story reminded me that the world was full of loss and heartbreak. And yet, it felt as if I were having to share it with others when all I wanted was to be left alone. Why couldn't I hold it close? I had earned my misery; I had carried our child inside of me and not even known she was gone. For two whole days! The doors breathed in another couple, both of them spattered with the rain that had begun seconds after we entered the building.

The nervous young man who I thought had been leading the meeting perked up. "Kate! You made it!"

Kate and the man by her side looked as if they had stepped out of a Calvin Klein ad. Kate had brown hair that fell halfway down her back. Her face, her eyes, gave off a sense of innocence and wholesomeness. My mouth dropped open. This was the facilitator? She looked like she was barely out of her teens!

"Sorry, Leon, the rain came in from the west and there was a fender bender on the highway." Her eyes landed on me, and she smiled warmly. "I see we have some new faces. Welcome!"

I'm sure she would have said my name if I hadn't slipped my coat off. I had plastered the adhesive name tag onto one lapel and then took it off, folding it and draping it over the back of my seat.

I nodded, not bothering to smile, and mumbled my name. Jhon, however, wasn't letting me off that easy.

"I'm Jhon Staunton, and this is my wife, Nichole. We lost our unborn child last December, right before Christmas. It was a stillbirth."

The way he said it felt so casual, so dismissive, and anger flared through me.

"She."

Jhon half turned towards me. "Hm?"

"Our child wasn't an it - *she* was a girl."

Jhon's pale cheeks bloomed with two crimson spots. He pulled his hand away, hurt and embarrassed. It was a shitty thing for me to do. I realized that much immediately. I know he hadn't meant it like that and I'd deliberately misinterpreted it, and probably embarrassed him too.

Kate had looked from him to me and back again before saying, "Welcome, Jhon, Nichole. I'm glad you are here."

The rest of the meeting felt like some kind of fucked-up AA meeting. Or at least one you would see in the movies. Some people shared, others didn't, and Kate, who had to be older than she appeared, handled it all with aplomb. Her words smacked of the mental health field and I wondered about her background. She barely looked old enough to be driving, and yet she was running this meeting and saying words and phrases that professionals used.

I couldn't help but head straight for her during the break. I still had a chip on my shoulder, and Jhon moved to the opposite side of the room, which told me all I needed to know about how he felt. My husband was good at controlling his feelings, far better than me. When he needed space, he took it, and he wouldn't say anything until he had time to analyze it.

I was so focused on finding out more about Kate that I nearly ran right into her as she walked out of the bathroom.

"So what's your story, anyway?" I blurted, smooth as ever. "You don't look old enough to be out past curfew, but you sound like a therapist."

Kate smiled then and gave a small, rueful laugh. Several others standing within earshot turned and stared. "Believe me, I get that a lot." I waited, eyes narrowed, and she said, "I'm twenty-three, and I actually entered college when I was sixteen. It was part of my school's advanced classwork for the gifted and I basically had no friends at that point, so I blew through college and earned my Ph. D. by the time I was twenty." She smiled warmly at the man she had come in with when he walked up and handed her a bottle of water. "I met Rob that last year of school and, well, the hospital had a position open that included running this class and I specialized in Family Counseling with a focus on loss and the grieving process and here I am."

Twenty-three. A year younger than me. What did she know of loss? What did she know about anything other than what she had learned in books and college?

"So you help people get over their loss?" I might have bared my teeth as I asked it. I didn't want to get over losing my baby. All I had was an urn buried in the ground with her ashes. A damned plaque with her tiny footprints. I wanted my baby in my arms. Nothing else, and certainly no empty platitudes, helped right now.

Her eyes were direct, her voice compassionate. "No, Nichole, I don't believe we get over loss. I help people *live* with loss. It isn't up to me to tell you to get over it, or to move past it. We each grieve differently. I'm just here to help anyone who needs tips on *living* with the loss they have experienced."

Her voice was soft and her eyes were so kind that I felt like punching her. I struggled with this for a moment and then, finally, having no words to say, I nodded and walked away.

Each week it was the same struggle, the same discussion with Jhon.

"Nichole, please, group is in an hour."

To which I invariably answered, "I don't want to go."

Sometimes I would win, and sometimes Jhon would. I hated stepping outside, though. I hated talking about our pain, our loss. It was something that felt personal. Pain shared didn't feel like a burden lifted. It just felt like a miasma of grief had settled into my bones. I wasn't me anymore. I was someone else, something else. A woman who had lost her child before she could even become a mother. I was bereft and alone. Jhon's presence didn't help; it only reminded me that my body had failed us, failed him. And that I was less. Less than he deserved, less than our innocent child had deserved. I couldn't get past it. Hell, I didn't *want* to get past it.

Get past it.

The words infuriated me. I hated the very idea of them. As if our child, our tiny baby, was something to get past. She had been beautiful in the photo, despite the waxy gray skin and the stillness that screamed death, not sleep. They had let Jhon hold her, just for a few moments, after her birth. I had pored over every single picture they had taken of her. I searched her tiny, still face for markers of me, of Jhon.

They were too busy saving my own worthless life, pumping damn near a liter of blood into me, that I lost my chance to hold her.

I had refused to return to Jacob and Mary's house. When they released me from the hospital, I'd begun walking upstairs and found a spot of blood that Jhon had missed cleaning up. I just turned around and walked back out. I couldn't even bring myself to go up there to the second floor where it had all begun. After a two-day stay in a hotel room, we'd found an overpriced one bedroom in the city. I'd crawled into bed and stayed there.

Today it was raining. Not unusual for Seattle. It was a torrential downpour outside, and the eve of the year mark since our baby was born, when Jhon insisted I get up.

"We're going to group, Nichole. Get up. Get in the shower."

I think I might have told him to fuck off.

He raised an eyebrow and pulled the blanket off of me, sniffed it, grimaced, and headed for the hall where the laundry closet was.

The cool of the December day rushed in and my bare feet were cold. Jhon slammed the lid on the washer and I could hear the water pour into it.

We only had one set. The other, a quilt I had purchased at the Farmer's Market for an exorbitant price, had been covered in blood and ruined. I had the choice of lying in bed with no blanket or getting up. One sniff of my body odor decided it. I levered my unwilling body out of bed. It had been days since my last shower, maybe even a week, and my hair was stringy and matted on the right side. I stared at my reflection in the mirror as the water heated. It disappeared in a fog of steam. I stepped inside and the hot needles of water abraded my skin. I watched a wall of fog climb up the opaque shower doors and roll down over the other side.

Outside, it was a chilly 43 degrees. My hair, still wet, clung to me like a chilled helmet and I hunched in my coat, shivering and pissed off. Of all the days for Jhon to insist we attend a meeting, this was not one of them. I glared at him and pulled away when he tried to put an arm over my shoulders.

Inside of the building, the heater's warmth dispelled the cold air, but not my chilly attitude. Part of me felt bad — I knew I wasn't being kind to Jhon — but in some ways this made me even more angry. I didn't need a guilt trip. I had a right to my misery. To my grief. One year ago, I had it all. One year ago, I was counting the days until my baby was born.

The room was empty, save for me and Jhon and Kate. Kate stood up, a smile on her face. "Glad you could make it!"

I glanced at the clock on the wall. We were ten minutes late. Where were the others? Were we literally the only ones there? There was no way I could get out of talking if there was no one else here. I turned to leave and ran into Jhon's chest.

"Nichole, we're staying."

"There's no one else here, Jhon," I hissed at him through gritted teeth. The thought of sharing with this girl, who had never seen a moment of pain, was unacceptable. My grief, my pain, it was my own. No one else's. Not even Jhon's.

You didn't carry our child for months and months. Your body didn't betray you or fail to feed our baby, and you didn't give birth to a dead child. You have no idea how hard this is for me.

"You're right, Nichole. I didn't. I can't. And I wish I could take your place, take this hurt from you. I wish you would let me share it with you."

I gasped, my hand flying to my mouth as I realized I had spoken those words out loud. Jhon took my hand and gently pulled me over to a seat in the circle. I didn't fight him. I sat, wishing I could take back my words, my thoughts. They were mine, not something to share or spill out into the world.

Somehow, whether it was the empty room with just Kate and me and Jhon, or that I had finally spoken my mind - something changed.

I changed.

I talked, and I listened, and I cried. All the hurt, all the fear, it didn't go away all at once. And Kate was right. I didn't move past my loss... *our* loss. But I found a way to live with it. It was as if in that moment, everything, all the overwhelming, debilitating pain of it, slid aside enough for me to do more than just exist. To do more than be alone and isolated in my misery. And it was there, in a basement room that smelled a little like mold and had really shitty coffee, that I learned to live with my grief.

Incident/Case #: 18-02521

Classification: Assault/Arson

Date: 2018-20-09

Location: Rush Creek, Raaen Road

Victim(s): Staunton, Jhon and Elizabeth

Suspect: Staunton, Nichole

Evidence ID#: 18-02521-007 (page out of handwritten journal)

I should be happy. I should be in love.

E. was supposed to be everything I needed. Everything that completed me.

I'm a mother now. So why do I imagine what it would be like if I tossed her down the stairs? What sound would it make? Would she bounce? Would the solid concrete suddenly turn to rubber? Suck her in and hold her? Or would there be blood?

I was careful not to say that to J. He reacted badly to my dream. The voices say he can't be trusted. No one can.

- N -

4. Steak and Margaritas

- Nichole -

July 18th, 2015 - Seattle, Washington

Kate handed me a margarita, a huge grin on her face. The day was warm, and the sun shone down, the warm rays threatening to burn my pale skin. That was one thing I missed about the Midwest, the sun. Or at least, I appreciated less rain. Seattle was inevitably raining or dreary. I had read once that it had the highest rate of suicides in the state, and most blamed the weather for that. Today, though, it was in the mid-80s and the glass was sweating, the coarse salt slipping off the rim and sliding down in slow trails towards my fingertips. I sipped it and smiled.

"This tastes amazing."

"The secret is a splash of amaretto liqueur. I interned in Las Vegas counseling gambling addictions and paid the bills tending bar at Carrabba's. This is my special version of their Carrabbarita."

"I'm afraid of how much I like this," I told her, and sipped more of the citrus sweetness with a hint of amaretto up through the straw.

Kate laughed. "Don't worry, I'll run out of booze after three or four of them." I shook my head in response, sipping again. I seldom drank. My body just couldn't handle it. I'd be loopy after one and sloshed after two. I needed to slow down or Jhon would have to sling me over his shoulder and take me back home before the steaks were done.

The men were talking by the grill. Rob turned and asked, "I just have one question for you, Nichole. Do you like steaks done the right way or cooked until they are shoe leather?"

"Don't listen to my husband. He's convinced that anyone who doesn't eat steak when it's still oozing blood and just stopped mooing is doing it *wrong,*" Kate fired back, laughing.

"I'll take mine medium-rare, please."

Rob sighed and shook his head. "At least it is better than *well done* and long dead."

Kate rolled her eyes. "Whatever, you raw-meat-eating barbarian!" She took a sip of her own drink. "It might be tried and true, but my favorite drink is a margarita on the rocks with salt."

It had been seven months since the day at group. I guess you could say I had a breakthrough that day. All I know is that once I'd started talking, things changed. We went home that day and I changed the sheets and cleaned our tiny apartment from one end to the other. I'd even reclaimed a small corner of the room and put together an area to sculpt in. Miniature versions of bigger pieces came first, anyway. I felt compelled to create a series of children in various stages of childhood. I'm sure Freud would have had a field day with that, but all I knew was I wasn't spending my days in bed sleeping or crying. I gained back a little weight and my clothes no longer hung on me. My arms and legs no longer looked like sticks.

As the winter had slipped into spring, Kate had asked me to take over the meetings. She had a new position, one that worked with children in the foster care system and took up a lot of her evenings. By then, I had gone from huddling in my shell to being great at drawing out others, especially the newbies. Life has the stunning capacity to change on a dime, and there were always people leaving and others coming in for the first time.

"How's group?" Kate asked, sipping her margarita and then reaching for one of the spinach and cream cheese pinwheels I had baked. She popped it into her mouth and closed her eyes, a blissful smile turning the edges of her mouth up.

"Pretty good," I said. "I heard from Lenore Halloway. She just crossed into the third trimester with no difficulties, so, yeah."

I tried to be happy for them, but I was also jealous. What can I say? I'm far from perfect. "And a new couple showed up last week and they were back again this week. Wife's talking, husband isn't. They lost their twin daughters in that ten-car pileup a few months ago."

Kate grimaced. "I remember them coming in to the hospital. I was there for an incoming consult and saw the ambulances arrive with the girls. It was hard to see."

I didn't want to talk about the group. It was one thing to facilitate it, but I had also learned a powerful lesson soon after Kate had handed the responsibilities of facilitating the meetings over to me. And that was to leave those sad stories behind each night. Doing so made it better for Jhon's and my relationship. He couldn't take hearing them like I could. Hearing others' stories - it was a reminder that I was still alive, and that even if I never stopped missing her, I had to live in the now. Kate had been right. I hadn't learned to get over it, I'd learned to live with the loss, and my sculptures were living proof. I had recently won a commission to create a set of sculptures. The finished pieces would be cast in bronze for a local park. It had meant an upgrade in my workspace, and I had settled into an enormous warehouse that was divided into shared workspaces on the outskirts of town and spent my weekdays and even some weekends there when Jhon's work took him out of town. High ceilings, tons of light when the rainy Seattle weather cooperated, and a place to focus on my work.

I looked up and realized Kate was staring at me. "What?"

"You just looked lost in thought there and..."

"And what?"

"Well, I wanted to tell you that Rob and I are becoming foster parents."

I blinked in shock. "Oh my God! That's... *amazing*, Kate!" A grin spread over my face.

I guess it was the memory of Andy and Hannah, and my years there in their house, but I could already see how wonderful Kate would be. My own adoption at the age of seven had been fast. Once the authorities had established that I had no next of kin to contact, it had sailed through court. I couldn't tell you *why* I had never called Hannah and Andy Mom and Dad, but they had never asked me to, and I hadn't thought of it until high school when a girlfriend of mine had asked. I remember shrugging. Hannah and Andy were everything I could ask for in parents, and I loved them, but it would have felt weird to call them something different after all the years I spent in their home. It felt like the words Mom and Dad were a minefield I didn't want to explore. I like to think that they understood that and that's why they never pushed me to call them something different.

Imagining Kate and Rob fostering and even adopting a child sounded fantastic, and I could see the excitement in her face.

"We start the classes in a month. Rob will be hard-pressed to attend, what with his work schedule, but he's promised me he will find a way," she added and popped another pinwheel in her mouth. "These are sooo good. If I keep going, I'll be too full to eat any steak!" Her eyes sparkled. "Will you give me the recipe? Rob is hosting a barbecue for his boss and I want to serve these."

I grinned and reached for my sketchbook and ripped out a page to write down the recipe. I never knew when inspiration would strike, so I carried my sketchbook everywhere.

Our relationship had changed from facilitator/attendee, to one of peers, and from there, a deep friendship had blossomed. We had a lot in common. We were both younger than our husbands. Several years, in my case, and a decade stretched between Kate and Rob. She was struggling to find a place in her husband's world where everyone was older and jaded by court cases and more. She had told me that some men in the firm were on their second or even third wives and she had struggled with finding equilibrium, while continuing to pursue her own dreams of counseling children in the foster care system.

And of course, we both wanted children. I hadn't let myself think about it for most of this year, but the longing was creeping up on me again. A big part of me wanted to prove the voices wrong. I knew I hadn't failed. That I had done everything I could - prenatal vitamins, no alcohol, healthy diet. Everything had been in place for our child. I'd read the books, bought the safety equipment. Fate had had other plans. If I had learned anything in a year of group therapy, it was that fate twists and turns like a snake. It is cruel and kind, and it is everything in between. It doesn't care how you feel, or how much you want something, and it sure as hell doesn't mind your tears.

"That's it?" Kate stared at the recipe. She looked up at me. "Nichole, you make it look so perfect, though. How can something with only four ingredients taste so darn good?"

I grinned and shrugged as I sucked down the rest of the margarita and reached for another pinwheel and popped it into my mouth. I was going to be loopy if the menfolk didn't hurry and serve up some of that red meat. I could see the shish kabobs of fresh vegetables we had bought at the farmer's market earlier in the day were browning nicely.

My thoughts strayed back to motherhood. After the doctor had sat us down and suggested we consider alternatives to me becoming pregnant again, I had questioned everything. Even with our breakthrough there with Kate on the one-year anniversary, it had still been hard, damned hard. I couldn't help wondering if maybe we could foster and adopt.

"I think I'll talk to Jhon about taking the classes too. If Rob is on board, Jhon will be as well. He's brought up the idea of adopting, but we just don't have the financial resources for that." I swirled my straw in the remains of my drink and frowned. It had shocked me to learn how much it would cost. A minimum of $15,000 dollars to the agency and up to $50,000 per child. It was simply impossible with our current income. Jhon's work was in the non-profit sector, and he made peanuts. My sculptures were unknown, and if it hadn't been for a former teacher referring a client to me, I still would have been making tiny sculptures in our cramped apartment and selling them at the farmer's market for peanuts. As it was, my commission was half eaten up with the space rental and the supplies I would need to complete the commission.

Kate let out a squeal of excitement and clutched my arm. "Ooh yes! We could go to the classes together! They said there was room for at least three more couples. You've got a few weeks to convince him, if he even needs convincing, and we could catch dinner or drinks afterwards!" She took my empty glass. "You need another."

I giggled in return and let her take the empty glass from me. Jhon walked over, a plate of steaks in his hand, and kissed my cheek, "You are looking happy." His free hand slid down my back and fondled my rear, winking as he did. Our sex life had come raring back a few months ago. "It's good to see."

I kissed him, the taste of margarita still on my tongue. It mingled with the malty taste of the beer he was drinking. Later that night, long after we had said our boozy farewells and driven home, we kissed again, deep and hungry. We made love and after he had slipped away for a quick shower, I felt him snuggle up to me, our bodies curving together. We fit together well.

"I love you, Nichole."

"I love you, Jhon."

There was silence then, and I could hear his breathing slow, deepen.

"Jhon?"

"Erm, yeah?" Sleep fogged his voice.

"I think we should try becoming foster parents."

There was a long silence. I wondered if he had fallen asleep. Outside, I could hear the sounds of the city all around us. In the distance, a car horn, and nearby, a group of girls laughing as they walked on the sidewalk below our second-floor apartment. They giggled, then shrieked as a car filled with male voices passed by, catcalling and whistling at them. A cat fight, likely in the back alley, came next. The growls and shrieks of two toms fighting over territory or a female. After what seemed like forever, Jhon spoke.

"Rob said he and Kate are going for it."

"Yeah, Kate said the classes start in a month," I answered, keeping my voice as neutral as I could.

There was another silence. But only for a few seconds this time.

"You were a foster kid."

"I was." Again, I thought of Andy and Hannah. "But I never felt like one, though. That might sound strange since I never called them Mom and Dad, but they adopted me pretty soon after I came to live with them. After... after my mom died."

"You never talk about your birth parents."

I felt my gut twist. I had only a few reminders of her: the scar that was hidden by my hairline and the box full of photos and miscellany. The memories, well, those ran deep, dark. They haunted my dreams.

"There's not much to say, is there?"

"Isn't there? I know your dad died when you were young, but weren't you six or so when your mom passed? Don't you remember her? I mean, she was your mom, and..." His voice petered out and he pulled me closer, his body warm. "I'm sorry. You just never talk about it."

"Hannah was my mom. Andy was my dad. And they were wonderful, Jhon. They were everything I could ask for in parents, and I loved them as much as they loved me. The first six years of my life, it doesn't matter compared to the love they gave me from the day I walked into their house."

I said it without crying, which was an improvement. Losing them two months after my eighteenth birthday had been hard, devastating, and it had taken a long time for me to even say their names without breaking down. Knowing they had died, asleep in their bed, without ever waking to the fire that had taken their lives was at least a small kindness to my broken heart. But losing them in a fire, just as I had lost my mother, was haunting.

That was when the voices had started back up, louder than just the murmur I had heard throughout my childhood and adolescence. Louder and louder, until they rang in my head and refused to be silent. It had taken leaving everything I thought I wanted and going away, far away, to create a new life for myself. It had also taken a lot of counseling and plenty of anti-depressants to shut the voices up.

Every time I felt loss, back they came, determined to pull me down deep into sorrow, self-blame, even madness. It was at those moments that I felt closer to my birth mother than I liked. My mother had been tormented by her demons, but she had also succumbed to, and even embraced, them. I couldn't help fearing it would be my fate as well.

The silence had closed in on us, thick and dark, but it reminded me that I was loved, simply by the warmth of Jhon's presence, his body spooned against mine. Our love had started as dazzling fireworks and magical nights and smoothed into an easy companionship spiced with intense bouts of lovemaking. Especially now, as I came out of the deep depressive funk I had fallen into.

My thoughts drifted to our baby girl. Jhon had named her Patricia on the death certificate. I hated the name. I hadn't told him that. I couldn't. I had been catatonic at first, robbed of all happiness, silent with grief. If it hadn't been for Jhon, they would have filed her as nameless, or Baby Girl Staunton. A nothing. A child devoid of any name. Still, I hadn't liked it. If I had thought to speak in those first few days, I would have named her Elizabeth. I had always liked it; it meant oath of God. And even though I wasn't religious, it had felt right somehow.

"We are doing better now, aren't we?" Jhon asked. He ran a hand down my arm, soft, comforting.

"Yes, I think so." And I did. We were better. I was better.

"If you want to try fostering, I'm willing."

My heart swelled. "Yeah?"

"Yeah."

"I'll ask Kate for the info to sign us up for the classes. We can get them in now before you have to go out of town again." I know my voice betrayed my excitement. I felt his hands move again, reaching first for my nipples and then, when they had hardened in response, sliding his hand down my front to the sensitive nub between my legs. I turned towards him, my own hands moving over his body. After a few adjustments, our bodies fit together again.

"I love you, Nichole."

"I love you too."

By the time we finished the second round, the moon had escaped the clouds and its cool light streamed in the window. It felt like a promise, a good one, of things to come. We lay there together, and I slipped into sleep with a smile on my face. Children's laughter filled my dreams.

Occasionally, the thought strikes me. If I had known what was to come, would I have smiled? Would I have signed us up for those foster care classes? Sometimes I tell myself, if I had only known, I would have run like hell for the hills.

Despite everything, I'm not sure if I would have or not.

Incident/Case #: 18-02521

Classification: Assault/Arson

Date: 2018-20-09

Location: Rush Creek, Raaen Road

Victim(s): Staunton, Jhon and Elizabeth

Suspect: Staunton, Nichole

Evidence ID#: 18-02521-008 (page out of handwritten journal)

Considering a series of pieces. I'll call them the Children of Ruin. The thought is percolating in my head, thanks to the dreams and the voices.

Always the voices.

Maybe it's not real, like Doc says; nevertheless, I can't help thinking the voices are both warning and guide. No one understands. J can't seem to, and E is too young. I'll figure it out. What's real and what's not.

The art will help. At least on that, we are all in agreement. Even the voices say so.

- N -

5. Forever Home

- Nichole -

March 24th, 2016 - Seattle, Washington

My phone chimed as I finished cleaning my hands free of the clay. I saw it was a message from Kate.

Exciting news. Call me!

I smiled as I dried my hands. We had finished with the fostering classes, and we both dipped our toes into the foster care pool. Jhon had convinced me to try out respite care first, now that several offices were opening in South America and other locations. We had moved to a two-bedroom apartment in Ranier that we were subletting out until we flew to Peru in a few months' time. With several departmental shakeups, they had tapped Jhon to lead an office and he would need to serve for a six-month stint before returning to ULSC headquarters in Seattle. He had promised once we returned, he would push to stay in Seattle, thus paving the way for us to foster and adopt a child.

I looked in the mirror and noticed I had missed a spot of clay. A smear of gray ran along my cheek. The new commission, one that was twice the price of the trio of bronze children I had completed late last fall, was well underway. A director of an arboretum in southern California had found my work in the park and insisted on hiring me to create a series of bronze statues for the entrance to the children's garden section of the arboretum. She had gushed over the trio of statues for twenty minutes before telling me she could find me more work, work that would keep me busy for months, even years, if I wanted it.

Now, with the trip to Peru hanging over our heads, I was rushing to complete the commission in time, then sublet the warehouse space while we were away so that the rent didn't gobble up all of my profits while we were south of the equator.

Kate and Rob had fostered a sibling set of three for two months while I had seen a steady stream of a dozen children come through respite care, ranging in ages from a few months to age twelve. The certification worker we were paired with, the one who had handled our application and given us stacks of paperwork to fill out, tests to take, background checks, and more, had warned me I would be better off accepting a wide range of children.

"Everyone wants babies, Nichole. Everyone. And they rarely stay because a family member comes along and gets them. Now, once you are all approved, if Home Finding calls you and you aren't interested in that age, just tell them that. It won't affect your chances or take you off the list."

She had a plain, round face framed in a fashionable pixie cut. She also was an adoptive mother to more than a dozen children she had taken in over her twenty-year tenure of working in the foster care system. The van she drove could seat twelve more if she didn't mind breaking a traffic rule or two.

I had nodded, saying nothing. I'd heard the spiel several times. Sometimes it felt as if the parade of social workers and teachers were trying their best to talk us out of fostering. One teacher who ran the fostering classes had spent one entire class period recalling nightmare scenarios about the children she had fostered. Jhon had summed it up one night as we had drinks with Kate and Rob. "The joys of foster parenting we get to look forward to! Where the children will never love you, they will pee in your shoes, break your most prized possessions, murder your pets, and set fire to your house. What's not to love about that?"

Kate and I had laughed, but Rob had looked uncomfortable. "I don't know whether or not to believe that woman."

That had launched a debate about the merits of telling potential foster parents horror stories just to weed out those who might be on the fence about the whole fostering thing, anyway. In later classes, the same woman told heart-rending stories of her own fostered and adopted children. Peed in shoes or not, she had kept going.

I dialed Kate, and she answered on the second ring. "Hold on, sweetie, let me get that for you," she said in a happy singsong voice certainly not intended for me. "Nichole?"

"Hey, I got your text."

"Oh my gosh, come over and meet this little angel who was just dropped off by the worker! Are you busy?"

"Just finishing up," I said, rubbing the spot of clay off of my cheek. "I'll be there in twenty."

"Can't wait for you to meet her!" Kate squeaked. I didn't have to see her face to know she was grinning from ear to ear in excitement. Her voice gave it away. This one sounded special. I hung up, picked up my purse, and fished around for my keys before heading out the door.

I tried calling Jhon on my way over, but it went to voice mail. He was snowed under in meetings and committees and had been for most of a month. I had already scaled back on the respite in response to his busy schedule, as well as my increased workload and deadlines. My to-do list included completing the clay models, getting a go-ahead from the client, and then pouring the bronze. I left a short message on his phone and sped up onto a busy roadway full of traffic. Fridays always seemed far more hectic and drivers seemed far more short-tempered and unforgiving of others on the road. As if they had more than enough of everyone and just wanted to return home. I waited for the light to change and for the car in front of me to go. Behind me, another car honked, which was ridiculous, since there was nothing anyone could do except wait for the light.

Twenty minutes later, I pulled into the driveway of Rob and Kate's modern home.

Their subdivision was new, less than five years old, and Rob's income, even as a junior lawyer in the firm, had ensured the best when they went house-shopping. The last on the street to be built, it was a sprawling McMansion, with five bedrooms, five and one-half baths, a manicured lawn, and plenty of room for a large family if they wanted it. Rob had paid for the basement to be finished out, complete with pool table, air hockey, a bar, and an enormous television that covered one entire wall. Kate called it his man cave and, when not busy grilling, the men would disappear into it for hours.

Kate had decorated three of the smaller bedrooms, alternating between pastels and bright primary colors. She wasn't afraid of color, yet another thing that we both had in common, and we had spent several Saturdays shopping at Pottery Barn and IKEA for child-centric furniture and decor.

The sibling set they fostered for a month had been adorable and sweet, and she had cried for a full day after they ended up going home with next of kin. The aunt had promised they would get to visit and then cut off communication a few weeks later when the youngest threw a tantrum and cried that she wanted to "go home to Mama Kate."

It was an aspect of fostering that they all knew could happen. The primary purpose of fostering was reunification, but having a child in your home, in your life, well, even providing respite for a few days forged a bond. There had been several, including an adorable little girl around the same age as our daughter would have been, that had found a way into my heart. Saying goodbye to her had been hard.

I knocked on the door and let myself in, calling out as I walked into the large entry hall. "Hello there!"

There was no answer, and I headed for the back door. It was a lovely day, and the first sunny one in a while. It had rained for two weeks straight and when the skies had been clear this morning, my heart had lifted. Seattle's rainy weather got to me.

I crossed into the enormous open-concept space that incorporated the living room, kitchen, and dining room and then headed toward the back door. I could see Kate's dark hair and a tiny head of red curls bouncing on the trampoline. Kate had gone all out on the backyard, filling it with a trampoline, swing set, and play structure besides the landscaped terraces that were raised up into a tall wall that surrounded the backyard on all sides.

As I stepped through the back door, it set into motion the chimes, and Kate turned and grinned at me.

"You made it!" She walked over and gave me an enormous hug, whispering as she did, "She's perfect. Such a sweet girl. She was *abandoned*, if you can believe that. Why would anyone want to give up a beautiful little girl like that? It's nuts. Anyway, I'll tell you more later. Come meet her!"

Kate turned to the little girl. "Elizabeth, sweetheart, I'd like you to meet a friend of mine. This is Nichole."

The girl was tiny, but I could see she was out of diapers already. I guessed she had to be at least two years old, but not over three. Her hair was a riot of red curls that fell to just past her shoulders, and her eyes were the most brilliant crayon-blue I had ever seen. A small spray of freckles splashed across her nose and cheeks.

She stopped jumping and stared at me before skittering off of the trampoline and over to Kate. She hid behind her, peeking out to stare at me again before ducking away, back to the safety of Kate's skirt.

"Hi, Elizabeth!" I said, smiling down at her. She peeked again and managed a tiny smile before vanishing back into Kate's skirt. I heard her mumble something then.

Kate heard it too. "What's that, sweetheart? What did you say?"

"I Isabel," came a tiny whisper. "Not Izbeth."

Kate blinked, and we traded looks. Kate was right. I couldn't help but feel shock at the thought that anyone would abandon an adorable little girl like this.

"You want us to call you Isabel?" I asked, leaning down and smiling at the single blue eye I could see peeking around Kate's skirts.

"Yes, pwease," the little girl lisped.

Kate's lip quivered. "Oh my God, Nichole, those are the first words she's spoken since the caseworker dropped her off two hours ago."

It wasn't unusual, or so we had been told. Especially with the young ones. No matter how terrible the circumstances they had come from, being thrust into a new place was terrifying.

Jhon and I had hosted a three-year-old who stayed mute the entire three days he was with us. And he had been with his foster family for two years. Changes, especially that young, were traumatic and overwhelming.

I smiled at the little girl. "Well then, Isabel it is. Right, Mommy Kate?" I put out my hand. "I brought something for you. Would you like to see it?" I could see just the edge of her head nod in response. "Okay, well, reach your hand out and get it."

A tiny bronze statue, a miniature replica of the model for my first commissioned project, lay in my hand. At three inches in height, the little girl had curls in her hair just like Elizabeth's. In fact, she could have been her twin.

Kate gave a little gasp. "Oh Isabel, *look*. It's *you*!" She glanced up from the statue at me, a look of wonder on her face.

"How in the world, Nichole?"

I shrugged, as surprised as she was. When I had gotten her text, I had grabbed two figures, one boy and one girl, and put them in my pockets. It was downright eerie to compare the little girl statue with the very human child in front of me.

"Tank oo." Elizabeth's tiny hand lifted the bronze statue from my hand, and it disappeared behind Kate.

I'd cast it with the leftover bronze as a keepsake. It was the perfect size to take with us everywhere since we would vacate the sublet furnished two-bedroom flat and would already have put our furniture in storage when we moved from our one-bedroom apartment. I had more samples, of course, but not of this statue. I had only made one copy.

"The resemblance is..." Kate's words petered out.

"Children look a lot alike at this age," I said, knowing it wasn't true, shocked myself at the eerie resemblance between Elizabeth and the statue.

Elizabeth seemed enamored with the statue, and it broke the ice. While still shy, she no longer hid behind Kate's skirts. It seemed that the mini Isabel statue had distracted her from her fear or nervousness. She wandered over to the swing set with it and climbed to the top of the slide, sitting there, holding the statue, her lips moving.

Kate slipped away for a moment, and I watched Elizabeth playing on the swing set.

"Here." Kate pressed a glass of ice-cold sweet tea into my hand. I had taught her the recipe I had learned from Hannah, my adoptive mother, and Kate had loved it and now made it daily.

"Thanks."

We sat down in the deck chairs. We could see Elizabeth but weren't close enough that she could hear us talking. I turned to Kate. "Okay, tell me everything."

"They found her on the steps of the Blessed Sacrament Church in Seattle. Someone had tucked her birth certificate into a small backpack on her back and nothing else."

"Oh my God, Kate, I saw that article! She's the girl in the news from last week!"

"I know! When they called me to ask about placement, I freaked out." Kate shook her head.

"So then we know who her birth parents are," I said, my eyes still on Isabel. "Have the authorities contacted them?"

"Birth parent. There was no father listed on the birth certificate," Kate corrected and took a sip of her sweet tea. "Her name is Elizabeth Pazza, and her mother is Gail Pazza. According to the records, Gail was in her late thirties when Elizabeth was born."

"So, were they able to find an address on record for this Gail Pazza?"

"Not so far. She's no longer at the address on record. Elizabeth, or, well, Isabel, if that's what she prefers, is almost two and a half years old. She was born on December 21st, 2013."

I blinked and struggled to keep the shock from showing on my face. Elizabeth was born on the same day as I delivered our stillborn daughter. I swallowed hard. What were the odds?

Kate continued, oblivious to my reaction. "I'm trying not to get my hopes up, Nichole. It's been all of, what, three hours in our home? But if they can't find next of kin, and they've been looking for four days..."

I leaned over and hugged her. "Kate, you know the drill."

She sighed and leaned into the hug. "I'm being ridiculous, aren't I?"

"Remember," I said, "They will pee in our shoes..."

"Destroy our most prized possessions," she chimed in.

"Kill our pets and set fire to our homes," I added.

"And never love us," Kate finished, laughing and shaking her head. "Well, there was that closet-peeing boy Silas who was afraid of the dark."

I shook my head. "That boy was *not* afraid of the dark. Not at all. Remember how he hid in the closet and leaped out at me wearing Rob's old hockey mask? Scared the crap out of me."

Kate snorted. "Oh God, how could I forget? You screamed and Jhon came running and Rob looked so ticked off." She giggled at the memory. "And who could blame him? He'd kept his high school letter jacket in the closet of the bedroom Silas was staying in. It was ruined! Our one adventure in respite care and Rob almost wanted to quit fostering altogether!"

We sat there, sipping our tea for several minutes. Kate was shaping up to be my best friend. I knew it by the silence. We could sit in silence for minutes without feeling the need to fill it with words. I was going to miss her when we went to Peru for nine months.

"She's so quiet. So shy," Kate said. Elizabeth still sat there at the top of the slide. The bronze statue hopped back and forth in the child's hand. I could see the little girl's mouth moving, but we were too far away to hear what she said.

"That will fade," I assured her. "She needs time to get used to you, to figure out how to deal with the trauma of being abandoned. She's been in the hospital all this time?"

"Yes. It was raining, of course, and she was ill from the exposure. She's still recovering from an upper respiratory infection. High fever, the works. But it went away overnight and her caseworker said I was the first number on the list, so..." Kate shrugged her shoulders, grinning with excitement. "Here she is."

She looked so excited that I couldn't help but worry about my friend's heart and the potential heartbreak that would follow if this adorable little girl didn't end up staying. And what were the chances of that? Even if her mother didn't return, which she might, there was likely extended family somewhere out there. She was beautiful, young, sweet - all the traits one could hope for in a child.

No, Elizabeth — or Isabel, as she was asking to be called — would not be here for long. Family would come looking for her. Without question. I only hoped it was sooner rather than later, because I feared Kate would be heartbroken if this beautiful child stayed for more than a few days. I knew my heart would have a hard time with it. It already was. I looked at her and thought of our child, born on the exact same day. With Jhon's ginger hair and my blue eyes, would this have been how our child would have looked had she lived?

Wondering that made me sad all over again. Kate and Rob had a beautiful little girl in their lives, but Jhon and I would have to wait another year or more until we returned from South America.

When we did, I swore I would throw myself into finding us a cute house on the outskirts of the city, where we would fill the spare bedrooms with a passel of children. I smiled, thinking of creating a workshop in a barn, one that would ensure I could work and live in one place and that we could raise a family in.

That evening, as the sun slipped lower in the sky, I said goodbye to Kate and Elizabeth, the latter of whom smiled and gave me a tiny wave. I wanted to be out of the way for when Rob returned home to meet Elizabeth for the first time.

My heart ached as I navigated the evening commute and wove my way into traffic. Who would leave a sweet little girl alone in the dark and the rain like that? What kind of monster leaves their perfect little girl on the steps of a church? And why?

Incident/Case #: 18-02521

Classification: Assault/Arson

Date: 2018-20-09

Location: Rush Creek, Raaen Road

Victim(s): Staunton, Jhon and Elizabeth

Suspect: Staunton, Nichole

Evidence ID#: 18-02521-009 (page out of handwritten journal)

Tired, so tired. E has a cold. J won't help. Says he's too tired from working the long hours. The voices say he's lying. That he gets off work and goes somewhere else.

Or to someone else.

He said he wanted E but now? Now? He leaves me alone for hours on hours with only the voices and a little girl for company. And the way she looks at me, sometimes. As if she knows just what button to push. Always PUSHING. Never a moment to myself.

- N -

6. South America

- Nichole -

July 5th, 2016 - Arequipa, Peru

I stared out of the window of the plane, my eyes registering the Nazca Lines, but my mind was elsewhere.

"Amazing, aren't they?" Jhon's head bumped against mine as he tried to see the lines out of the narrow airplane window.

"Hm?"

"The Nazca Lines down there."

"Oh yes," I said. I shook my head and stared at the window, noticing them for the first time. "They are."

His hand stole over mine, his smile gentle. "You are a thousand miles away, aren't you? Or maybe closer to four thousand eight hundred and seventy miles away, I'm guessing."

Jhon knew me far too well. Thanks to needing to vacate the sublet apartment sooner than we thought, and our flight to Peru scheduled for early July, Kate and Rob had welcomed us into their home. They had the room, and the offer had been a lifesaver. While Rob and Jhon were both at work, I had spent the past several weeks with Kate and Elizabeth.

Our belongings were in storage, I had sublet out my warehouse space to another artist, and we were all set to go. My heart wasn't, though. I wanted nothing more than to stay at Kate's and spend time with her and Elizabeth.

"Sorry," I said, squeezing his fingers.

"Don't be." Jhon smiled at me, met my lips with his. "Let's face it. Kate and Rob struck gold. They have a beautiful little girl in their home, with no family popping up out of the woodwork to whisk her away. She's amazing, cute as a button, smart as a whip, and everything we want in a child. But you know what? There are others out there. And we will do this stint in Peru, go back, and stay in Seattle. And we will find our own perfect little girl or boy. We will."

I kissed him and laid my head on his shoulder, suppressing a sigh. I adored Kate and wanted her to be happy. But I couldn't help but envy her. On our last night at their house, we had grilled out and waited for the sun to disappear behind the horizon and had set off a few of our own fireworks while enjoying the show. Their house was in the perfect spot for viewing the city's annual display and Elizabeth had loved it. She had climbed onto Jhon's lap and clapped and giggled at each fresh burst of light in the sky.

They had looked so alike that it was eerie. Their red hair matched and Jhon held her with the ease of a man comfortable in his own skin, one who finds parenthood a welcome and easy thing.

The shy little girl who had arrived at the end of March was now a giggling, warm, vivacious little girl. She seemed advanced too. Her speech was already moving from the telegraphic toddler speech to now incorporating more words and descriptors. Kate had been excited, saying that a recent evaluation had shown Elizabeth was functioning at the level of a three- to four-year-old.

The name change had been the only oddity. One day, she appeared happy with being called Isabel and the next it was Lizzie. It had taken Kate by surprise, and she Googled "child wanting to change name" one summer afternoon.

"Everything I'm seeing shows it is more of a tween and teen thing," Kate said, as she browsed on her phone. Elizabeth was playing with two other girls on the playground. They were giggling and running from two boys. "I wonder it if is any of her playmates who have older siblings or something."

Kate had joined a mom's group, and they met several times a week at the park. I had finished up my projects and had plenty of time on my hands, so I had tagged along, playing the honorary aunt to the hilt when I arrived with bubble wands and unicorn cupcakes from my favorite bakery.

"You know, Jhon pointed out that Isabel and Lizzie are both derivatives of the name Elizabeth," I said, nibbling at a cupcake.

"That's a good point. I hadn't thought of that. I guess it doesn't hurt anything to indulge her," Kate had said.

I couldn't help thinking of Elizabeth now, as we flew further away from her. She had blossomed at Kate and Rob's. The shyness had stuck in there for months and then in late June, it felt as if it had changed overnight. As if a switch flipped and she realized that she was safe and loved. Once she did, her true happy self had emerged. It was right around then that she had asked to be called Lizzie. By that point, none of us could deny her anything. I know I felt as if I were trying to soak up the energy and happiness Elizabeth put out as if it were fuel. Perhaps I just hoped it would keep me going during the long months we were in Peru.

Jhon would be busy, non-stop, with the start-up of a new office. *It's for a good cause,* I told myself, *this will change hundreds if not thousands of lives.*

As if on cue, the middle-aged woman on the other side of Jhon asked him what brought us to Peru.

"I'm coordinating opening a new office for ULSC," he responded and handed her a card.

"Using Loans for Social Change," the woman read out loud. "So, like a bank?

"Micro-loans geared toward the single entrepreneur, with only a 2% interest rate. That 2% rate, it doesn't pay for much. A majority of our funding comes from self-made entrepreneurs who want to give back some of their good fortune, like the Gates family, Warren Buffett, and plenty of others who prefer anonymity." Jhon smiled. He excelled at this. His boss said he had an honest face, which he did, but it was Jhon's passion that won others over.

"So who can get these micro-loans then?" the woman asked, her eyes sparkling with interest.

"Anyone. We have provided loans to someone as young as fifteen years old to age eighty. And for pretty much anything you can think of - we once helped a young man born without legs to purchase a hand-powered cart he uses to sell fresh fruits and vegetables at the local market. Instead of staying home, helpless, he is helping his family make a living."

"Wow, that's amazing!"

"We established an office in Lima in 2013 and now I'm hoping we can offer this same opportunity in and around Arequipa."

He launched into his latest focus, getting common citizens to kick in funds. While Jhon talked, I thought again of Elizabeth. Kate had seesawed up and down for the past three months, certain that at any moment a relative would pop out of the woodwork, or even Elizabeth's mother, and derail Kate's hopes of keeping the little girl. It was the hardest part of fostering and one they had warned us about over and over. At any moment, things could change on a dime, and a child you had grown to love and care for might return to family. During one class the four of us had attended, a panel of foster parents showed up to answer our questions. One woman had said, "A D- bio parent will trump an A+ foster parent any day of the week. If they are making any progress, no matter how slow, they will get their child back. Prepare yourself for that."

Kate's moods had alternated between hope and despair. It was impossible not to love Elizabeth. When she walked into a room, it somehow felt brighter. And when she smiled, well, I envied Kate and Rob. It was a joy just visiting and spending time with her, and I tried to temper it by imagining her as a sulky teenager and just couldn't. We all waited for the call from the caseworker, hoping against hope that this gentle child would stay.

There had been nothing. Not a whisper. Not even with the police looking for Elizabeth's mother, Gail Pazzo. Wherever she had disappeared to, Gail Pazzo didn't seem to want to be found. The police reported that the small, yet well-appointed middle-class house they had lived in was still full of furniture, clothes, and more. The only thing amiss was an errant bloodstain in the bathroom. Elizabeth's caseworker told Kate and Rob that the case had been on the edge of being upgraded to a missing persons investigation when there had been a verified sighting of Gail Pazzo in Spokane. A week later she was seen again at a traffic stop outside of Billings, Montana. After that, the authorities stepped back, shrugged, and ruled it child abandonment. Kate and I spent hours wondering what kind of mother would abandon such a beautiful and sweet child. It made no sense.

When we left, Kate and Rob were still waiting to hear if the case would now be fast-tracked to adoption. Even in the cases of abandonment, the wheels of justice moved at a snail's pace.

I crossed my fingers for them. Elizabeth was special. But Jhon was right, we would find the perfect child too. He had promised, and had the home office promise as well, that there would be no more traveling after this. There were plenty of opportunities for Jhon right there in Seattle. In another year or two, we would take our nest egg we had been saving up and put a down payment on a house. Meanwhile, we could rent a two-bedroom when we returned next year. It would be enough space to allow for one foster child, maybe two.

I stared out the window at the Nazca Lines, marveling at the engineering it must have taken to create them. I settled back in my seat and closed my eyes. We would land soon, but the journey here had been long. I didn't mind a catnap before we had to make our way through the long lines in customs or find a cab into the city.

What felt like seconds later, the plane jostled, hopped, and bucked as it pushed its snout through an unexpected cloud layer. My eyes flew open, pulling me out of a memory from the past. I could still smell the acrid smoke, as if the fire were here on board the plane. It wasn't though. That fire happened decades ago. *You are safe and you are loved.*

"Hey, you okay?" Jhon squeezed my fingers. "It's just a little turbulence. What were you thinking about?"

I blinked, reconciling what was here and now with what wasn't.

What wasn't now was the fire. I wasn't a small child any longer. Nor was I alone, or at the mercy of my mother. I was here, on a plane, headed to Arequipa. When the memories came, they sometimes took over, and I was there in the past, instead of here in the now.

I shook my head as if the act would clear the lingering vision of smoke curling up and inching its way along the ceiling, spreading oily and dark, a monster all on its own, growing, feeding.

"I, uh, I'm fine."

Jhon didn't look convinced. I couldn't blame him. My memories, nightmares, could get pretty intense. Waking up from them was always stressful. In the first years after I had gone to live with Hannah and Andy, they had made sure I saw a therapist. When I had described some memories, he had suggested visualizing an exit door or way out. I had thought about that, and one night, in the middle of a bad one, I had imagined a rainbow whirlpool. In the dream, I had leaped into it. I had woken, back in my bedroom, my heart pounding, but at least I was out of the nightmare. In later years, I learned to force my way out of it. No rainbow whirlpool needed. I had been on the cusp of doing just that when the plane banked to the left, dropped, and then shuddered.

Jhon squeezed my hand as the plane plummeted, rising again and swooping to the right. It was winter here, and the dry season, but Mother Nature had other plans. As we dropped further into the clouds, the entire cabin grew dark enough that the interior lights activated.

We listened as the captain announced first in English and then repeated it in Spanish. It was the standard, "Fasten your seatbelts, stay in your seats, we've got turbulence." Around me, I could hear the clicks of seatbelts being fastened. I didn't bother; mine had been on the entire time.

Landing in Arequipa was a nail-biting, white-knuckling ride. Jhon's pale white skin had paled even further as he clutched the armrests. For me, it was the seconds after landing, when the engines thrust into reverse to help brake the metal bird, that was the most unnerving. The sound of the engines shrieking set my teeth on edge. As we arrived, the sun had disappeared beyond the horizon and the freak storm was upon us. Wind howled, rain pummeled the plane, and water ran across the tarmac in a wash.

"This is unusual for this time of year," Jhon commented as he stared out the window. "It's dry as a bone this time of year. Cold too."

I groaned. The last thing I wanted was to deal with the cold. I wished I had stayed with Kate and Rob while Jhon handled the newest ULSC office opening. It would have given me more of a chance to spend time with Elizabeth. I stopped myself there.

This is why you should not *be there. Elizabeth isn't your child. She isn't even Kate and Rob's yet. But if she's going to be anyone's child, it will be Kate and Rob's. Be the fun aunt all you like, but that's it.*

Sometimes the voices in my head could be reasonable and even something to pay attention to. I knew I loved that little girl. But Kate and Rob got the call, not us. I felt a flash of resentment flood through me. If Jhon had a job that kept him in Seattle, we wouldn't be rootless right now, and I might have been the one who had welcomed Elizabeth into our home instead. If not her, then at least I could have a little boy or girl to distract me from thinking about her. The memory of Elizabeth sitting on Jhon's lap as we watched the fireworks returned to my thoughts. The same shade of red hair and sprinkle of freckles. If we had been chosen as her foster parents, no one would look at her and ask if she was ours. There would be no question.

It might have been wrong of me to think that. In fact, I'm sure that it was, but the thought returned, over and over. I even caught myself wondering if Hannah and Andy had ever felt that way. Probably not. Their funeral had been well-attended. I had met many of Andy and Hannah's other foster children over the twelve years I had lived with them. They had fostered dozens, kept in touch with as many of them as they could, and I had been the only one they adopted. I had asked why one day, and Hannah, her hands digging deep into the soil of her garden, had looked up at me, smiled, and said, "Just when I thought I couldn't stand getting my heart broken by so many wonderful kids coming in and then leaving us, you came along. And we are so glad you did."

I tried to imagine what it would be like to have that many kids come and go. Some of them had spoken at the funeral, remembering their time with Hannah and Andy as a quiet respite, a haven amid such turmoil. They weren't wrong. Hannah and Andy's house had been an older house, sprawling, with six bedrooms over three levels. By the time I got there, the three of us sort of knocked about in it, with several of the bedrooms ready and waiting for children to come and stay. They had closed their foster license the month after my adoption, and then sold off or gave away the extra furniture, clothes, and toys. The upside of it was that I had a room dedicated to toys and art. By the time I turned ten, Hannah had bought a pottery wheel for me and it took over one corner of the room. I had been sculpting ever since. Andy showed me what he thought I needed to know in life, but Hannah fed my interests and encouraged me to fly. Hannah had excelled at that.

I wanted to do that for a child. I wanted to be that kind of mother, the mother I had found in Hannah. Thanks to her, my love of art wasn't just a side passion, it was a part of my everyday life. Well, almost. It would be hard to work on my full-size projects there in Arequipa, but I could still manage smaller projects. The smaller pieces were easier to work with in our tiny rental, and later I could use the best of them as models for my larger commissioned pieces.

As we made our way off the plane and headed toward customs, I daydreamed of our future foster child and our return to Seattle. Jhon had promised, and I was holding him to that promise. We would return and start our family. I would connect with each child - watch what interested them and then feed it and encourage them to grow up and follow their dreams. Just as Hannah had done for me.

Jhon nuzzled my neck. I shivered and felt goosebumps rise on my arms. "We're going to have a great time here, love. Time will pass quicker than you can imagine."

I hoped so. I hoped Elizabeth didn't forget us in the next nine months. And I hoped that, somehow, when it was all said and done, I would get to be a mom.

Incident/Case #: 18-02521

Classification: Assault/Arson

Date: 2018-20-09

Location: Rush Creek, Raaen Road

Victim (s): Staunton, Jhon and Elizabeth

Suspect: Staunton, Nichole

Evidence ID#: 18-02521-010 (page out of handwritten journal)

He's... gone. Not even a note. Not a whisper. No explanation.

Perhaps it is what I deserve. Things would be different if E. had been the boy he had been hoping for. Perhaps he would have stayed. Maybe even loved me.

No.

- N -

7. We'll Do It

- Nichole -

September 18th, 2016 - Arequipa, Peru

It felt as if winter would never end. The days were cloudless, but it was still cold. I hadn't gotten used to Fahrenheit to Celsius conversions, so I did not know what temperature three degrees Celsius was, but it certainly wasn't what I would consider warm. We had left Seattle at the height of summer, my favorite time of year, and found ourselves entrenched in winter, my least favorite season. I kept busy, first with helping Jhon as he set up the office in Arequipa and later through daily walks to a local farmer's market. I would have done more sightseeing, but it wasn't warm enough. Most of the tourist-oriented activities - the tours and city events - were closed for the season. In another couple of weeks, they would open up again as the days warmed, but for now, I had little to do.

It had been two months since we had left Seattle and I missed it. Someone else willing to pay twice the rent snatched up the apartment we had planned to get in Arequipa, which forced us to stay in a cut-rate room for rent until something else came available. Internet was spotty, and I hadn't been able to check emails in a week. Jhon was ill-tempered, a sharp departure from his normal self, thanks to delays in the delivery of several computers he needed in order to get the ULSC office up and running.

Arequipa was an enormous city. I hadn't known what to expect, but it wasn't the sprawling metropolitan city that greeted me. Jhon had explained it was a city and not a rural area that many of the ULSC offices were placed in. It was far larger and more modern than I had envisioned. Despite this, they blocked us at every turn from getting what Jhon needed to create a successful outpost for the ULSC program.

With the internet at the office spotty, I had hunted down an internet cafe to check in on my business and personal emails, rather than suck up any of his narrow bandwidth. Seated in The Gaming House, pimpled, overweight teens with headsets and rigs that told me teens' obsession with video games wasn't limited to the United States surrounded me. Most had Monster drinks tucked into the beverage holders of the plush gaming chairs, as well as enormous bags of snack chips. The guy next to me had an extra-large bag of Lays potato chips that read "Sabor a Pollo a la Brasa." The flavor of grilled chicken in potato chips. I'd have to find some for Jhon. My husband was a potato chip junkie, and a random gift of potato chips might curb his grumpy mood. The large room was dark, the computer screens and LED strip lighting on the floors the only light inside. The guy next to me turned and gave me a once-over. He looked at my thin laptop with a puzzled frown and then returned to his game, barking commands over his headset. I spared a moment's glance at his character, something big and armored, and guessed at the game.

"Mundo de Warcraft?" I asked, giving him a quick smile as I waited for my computer to boot up.

He eyed me and smiled back. "Si." His eyes slid back to the game as a new battle began.

Hearing Spanish, day in and day out, was helping take my meager high-school Spanish classes to a whole new level. As I walked through the city or listened to the radio stations that played in the taxicabs, the words had gone from a mash of nonsense to resolving into snatches of recognizable phrases and words, even basic ideas. I had taken to walking each day on the busy city streets, running even simple errands, in order to practice the language and improve.

The laptop whirred and the Windows sign-on box appeared. I entered the code and waited for the next screen to load, typed in the internet cafe code I paid for, and waited for my messages to download. It had been two days since I had been online and my laptop seemed to groan in protest as 128 messages appeared in my Gmail.

I sighed. Why had I signed up for so many shopping apps?

It took time to go through each one, find the Unsubscribe at the bottom, and then delete the message. One after the next. I could see a message from Kate far down the list and wanted to hear her news. The last I had heard, they were fast-tracking the adoption after learning that Elizabeth's biological father was a sperm donor. With no other family coming forward, and Gail Pazza either missing or intent on not being found, the courts were in favor of permanency in Kate and Rob's home.

I itched to read the message, but I continued going through the list. It felt like a promised reward, like one of those sea salt caramels Hannah used to buy for me from the Aldi on Paseo. The ones with dark chocolate. Reading Kate's email would be my reward for getting rid of all of this junk mail.

I arrived at hers and clicked on it. She often included pictures, and this email was no exception. I gave a whoop of excitement when the photo appeared. It was of the three of them, but also the judge standing behind them, smiling. Elizabeth looked so happy. She had bright white teeth and a broad smile. Kate had placed a bow in her hair. Elizabeth's dress was a white bespoke frock that Kate had found in Flora and Henri on First Avenue the last time we went shopping.

My heart hurt. My smile dropped, but only for a quick second.

I'll find a little girl to love too. I know I will. And I can always be Elizabeth's honorary aunt and spoil her rotten.

I clicked on the message, which I had ignored in favor of the picture attached.

To: artistnichole1990@gmail.com

From: thegr8k8@gmail.com

Subject: Surprise!

Attachments

So this happened. Wasn't sure they would go through with it until the last second, but they did! I just have one question. Will you and Jhon be Elizabeth's godparents?

-K-

Godparents? My heart leaped again. Kate had mentioned once or twice that she was a lapsed Catholic, or something close to it.

"I grew up without it, except for Baptism and Confirmation." She had rolled her eyes. "The nuns hated all of my questions. And catechism was boring as hell." She had laughed then. "The weird part? I kind of want that for my kids too. Call it a just in case or something. God, that sounds stupid, doesn't it?"

I had laughed with her and told her about my history with church. Hannah and Andy had gone every week to Unity Village in Lee's Summit and I had loved it there. The grounds had been beautiful, full of flowers and landscaped walkways and places to sit. The people seemed warm and welcoming. It had been a pleasant experience for me, and while I had not sought out a church since leaving, nor felt the need to, I believed that religion, faith, had its place. As a reassurance, or a way to guide us in kindness and love.

That had been my experience. Jhon, who was also a lapsed Catholic, hadn't felt the same. Many discussions back and forth, most of which had been while I was pregnant, had ended with a wait-and-see compromise. I could see how a church like I had attended could be a place of solace, but Jhon was against organized religion, vehemently so.

And here we were, being asked to serve as godparents. What would he say to that? As I could remember from television and movies, it involved baptism of the baby, or young child in Elizabeth's case, with the parents and godparents present. They would wait, I guessed, since we couldn't be back until early spring of next year.

That meant I had time to convince Jhon. It was for Elizabeth and Kate and Rob. He didn't have to do anything more than stand there and agree to be her godparent, right?

To: thegr8k8@gmail.com

From: artistnichole1990@gmail.com

Subject: RE: Surprise!

Oh my GOD!!!! Tears in my eyes, so happy for you!

Yes, yes, a thousand times yes! We'll do it! I would be honored to be Elizabeth's godparent and I know Jhon will too! Um, dumb question, but is it okay to put off the baptism until spring? Or can we do this over a video call?

I miss you guys soooo much.

Arequipa is friggin' COLD right now and I can't wait for spring to start soon. Of course, after that, the wet season starts. Torrential rains, fun, fun!

How did she do? Is she happy? Was she excited?

Hug Rob and that beautiful, sweet girl for me. You were right, that dress looks PERFECT on her!

-N-

I went back to eradicating the rest of the emails I didn't need - auto insurance, a sale at Zulily, and so many more. I had paid for two hours' access and the clock was ticking down with just twenty minutes left when Kate's reply popped up on my Gmail.

To: artistnichole1990@gmail.com

From: thegr8k8@gmail.com

Subject: RE:RE:Surprise!

Thank you! I wish you could have been there!

The judge was so grim, and then when they issued the ruling, she hardly looked at us. But we were the last case heard that day. She dismissed the court, jumped up from her seat, and had the biggest grin on her face. It was surreal.

I called the Blessed Sacrament and asked if we could do it via an uplink and they said, "No." Luddites! But it's okay; it can wait until you return. We already listed you as our respite provider and emergency contact, and this is more of a formality than anything.

Oh my gosh, Elizabeth was so cute during the ceremony and the judge gushed over her. After they took the picture, she shouted, "Hoo-way!" The entire courtroom started cheering!

I think she's doing well. She's never asked, not once, about her mom. Perhaps she will later, who knows.

Rob's got a big case. That Ponzi scheme that hit the papers right before you left? The guy hired and then fired his first lawyer and then called Rob. I'll be a law widow for the next few months. Wish you were back, I'm counting the days!

-K-

She had attached a few more pictures of Elizabeth and I clicked on them and sighed. Kate had taken the photos at the local playground and Elizabeth was running and playing with another little girl, the photo catching her in mid-leap, her mouth open in a joyful shriek, her red curls flying behind her.

I wished again that I was there, with Kate, watching Elizabeth grow. At this young, they changed daily. Would she even remember me when I returned?

The guy next to me leaned over and stared at Elizabeth's picture. "Ella es tuya?"

I shook my head, "No, soy su madrina."

"Ah, si. Ella es muy bonita." He reached for his flip phone and the screen showed a laughing little girl that looked nothing like him on the screen. The photograph had caught her in mid-squirm. "Mi pequeña niña."

He didn't seem old enough to be a father, but appearances could be deceiving. I nodded and said, "Adorable," which was the same in Spanish as it was in English.

He would have said more, but there was a blast of frenzied voices over his headset and he turned away, his focus back on the game at hand.

As my internet minutes dwindled to single digits, I smiled and waved goodbye to him. He nodded and managed a return wave before I walked away. It was time to return to the small office Jhon was in and bring him some butifarra for lunch. We were in love with the local street food. I was partial to the ceviche, and Jhon was obsessed with the butifarra, a sandwich filled with ham, lettuce, radish, and chilies. The salsa criolla, which was made from sweet onions, was the crowning addition that brought a simple sandwich to the next level.

The next two months passed a little faster as I filled my days with routine. I had become a regular fixture at Biblioteca Municipal after learning that I could access the Wi-Fi there for a better price. Then there was the bonus of being surrounded by books. A surprising number of them were available in English.

Jhon and I would leave at the same time each morning. He would head to the office and I would take a bus to the library and be waiting as the doors opened. If I couldn't be in my studio, creating art, my second-best option was reading and exchanging emails with Kate and other friends. I was becoming proficient at reading Spanish, but my speaking skills were still rusty. One librarian had asked me if I would consider reading to schoolchildren in Spanish and English and I had jumped at the chance. Anything to occupy my time.

"Hola, Señora Nicholetta!" the middle-aged librarian caroled as she opened the door wide. She was five feet tall, round, and her face creased in a perpetual smile.

"Hola, Señora Adolfa!"

I walked down the hall to a room set up with tables for laptops. I wasn't the only one. There had been a small crowd waiting at the door. Most were students, some in their teens, others just a few years younger than me, their book bags heavy with textbooks. A few smiled in my direction.

I entered a large room filled with bulky wood tables and set up my laptop. I'd check emails, surf the internet, and then read in the children's library and head back to the office with Jhon's butifarra. He was getting things in shape in the office and had stopped being such a grouch. We'd been together long enough that I knew it had nothing to do with me and I just kept my distance until it passed.

As usual, once my laptop booted up, and I connected with the library's Wi-Fi, I found an email from Kate.

To: artistnichole1990@gmail.com

From: thegr8k8@gmail.com

Subject: I'm worried

The weirdness has gotten a little weirder and I'm getting worried about Elsa. Yes, Elsa. She insists on it, says she isn't Isabel, or Lizzie, that she's Elsa.

First thing I did when she said that name? I looked it up. Just like the rest, it's a derivative of Elizabeth. How weird is that? I mean, if she were older, it would make sense, right?

She's been having dreams, nightmares, and they are getting worse by the day. She woke up last night sobbing and screaming, "She coming!" When I ask her who is coming, she says, "Her!" and points at her photograph on the wall, the one the investigators found of her in her mother's home. That one of her in the pink onesie? It was as if she didn't recognize herself.

At first, I thought maybe it was post-adoption blues. They warned us of it in the Adoption Prep class we took after you flew south. But now I'm not sure. This feels different. It feels like dissociative identity disorder more than anything else. And I suppose that is possible, but I've had zero experience with it.

I wish you were here. I could use a sympathetic ear.

-K-

I frowned and typed in dissociative identity disorder into a search bar. The first result read:

Dissociative identity disorder (DID), also known as multiple personality disorder (MPD), is a mental disorder characterized by the maintenance of at least two distinct and relatively enduring personality states. The disorder is accompanied by memory gaps beyond what would be explained by ordinary forgetfulness.

Elizabeth having some mental disorder? That couldn't be right. Kate had to be overreacting. I remembered it was never a good idea for doctors to treat family members. Half of the time they missed important clues, the other half of the time they saw illnesses when there weren't any. That had to be the case here. Elizabeth, or whatever name she wanted to go by, was perfect. Kate and Rob had won the kid lottery.

I sat in the large room and stared out the window as a storm rolled in, rain falling in heavy sheets, obscuring the view of the other buildings across the street and beyond. I searched my memories for anything that would make sense, any way that Kate might have misinterpreted an innocent action or words from Elizabeth, or Elsa, as she was now calling herself.

In the spring, Elizabeth had been shy, tentative. It must have been terrifying for her. She had taken some time to get used to her new environment. Then summer had unfurled, and so had the little girl's true personality. The fun-loving, merry girl had been a treasure to behold. It had been a little strange that she wanted to be called Lizzie, but hey, she was doing fantastic, better than anyone had hoped, after being abandoned on a church doorstep.

Could a little backsliding be normal? She'd been through so much and no one knew what she had been through in the first two years of her life. A person who would abandon a small child, they might have been abusive as well. It wasn't a stretch to assume that. And I remembered Kate mentioning that Elizabeth had a baby brother who had died of SIDS in his first year. The trauma of that was there as well.

To: thegr8k8@gmail.com

From: artistnichole1990@gmail.com

Subject: RE: I'm worried

I wish I was there. Between Rob working nonstop and Elizabeth/Elsa feeling blue, I'm sure it feels overwhelming, but you've got this, Kate. You, of all people, know what she needs most: patience and love. And, I don't know, maybe a therapist? I mean, I know YOU are a therapist, but perhaps you should get some distance and another perspective on this. Do they see kids this young?

Surely it isn't as bad as DID. I looked that up and sure, the name changes make it look bad, but... this is *Elizabeth* we're talking about here. You hit the lottery, sweetie, you know that you did. I'm sure to end up with the ones that pee in our shoes!

Hugs!

-N-

I pressed send and watched as it whizzed off. It had to be a phase. After all, she had gone through so much. Her mother had abandoned her, and who knows, likely abused her. Even in the best of circumstances, even in a loving home with two adults who loved you, it wasn't as easy as flipping a switch.

Kate was worried, of course she was, because she cared so much. It was one thing I loved most about my friend. Kate had such an enormous heart. She had admitted to me, long after my breakthrough on the anniversary of the stillbirth, that seeing me as I had been before the breakthrough had hurt her heart. She had wanted to help me, wanted to see me pull myself out of the place of suffering and back into life, even as she knew things like that took time.

"Each of us has to work through our traumas in our own ways, our own time, and our own space," she had said. She was too close to the forest with Elizabeth and she couldn't see the trees.

Kate will figure it out. She just needs to step back and let her beautiful little girl process her emotions and move through the trauma that she has been through. It will all work out.

I felt a tentative tap on my shoulder and looked over to see Maria, one child who came every day for my reading class. "Buenas días, Señora Nicholetta." Maria had huge brown eyes and she was missing one of her top front teeth. She had lost it last week just as I finished reading *Kevin and the Tooth Fairy*.

I smiled at her. She was one of my favorites. She always sat in the front row and held so still, her eyes rapt, never squirming, never talking.

"Hola, Maria! ¿Es hora de clases?"

"Si, Señora."

"Muy bien. Lidera el camino!"

I shut my laptop down and stood, reaching out to take Maria's hand. It was time for reading class.

Incident/Case #: 18-02521

Classification: Assault/Arson

Date: 2018-20-09

Location: Rush Creek, Raaen Road

Victim (s): Staunton, Jhon and Elizabeth

Suspect: Staunton, Nichole

Evidence ID#: 18-02521-011 (page out of handwritten journal)

Sometimes I wake up and, for a moment, I'm not sure if reality is a dream and dream is reality.

I feel like I am alone, miserably alone, struggling to raise this girl on my own.

Some days I'm sure he's gone forever, others that he has returned, that it was all a mistake.

- N -

8. A Tragedy We Cannot Comprehend

- Nichole -

March 21st, 2017 - Seattle, Washington

The rain was hitting the roof of the boarding ramp as I stepped off the plane. I'd spent the past two days in transit, an airline strike stranding me in Mexico for a day before I could board a nonstop flight to Seattle.

It was impossible to sleep in the busy terminal, but I had tried. Every time I closed my eyes, I pictured Kate and Rob and my heart broke all over again at the loss. And Elizabeth, sweet Elizabeth, what she must be going through as well. It was beyond comprehension, and it reminded me of how inconstant life can be, that things can change on a dime when we least expect it.

Their loss felt impossible to accept.

I will admit that, despite my own losses, I *still* do not understand death. I can't wrap my head around it. It seems unreal, and somehow, incomplete. Where does life go when it flees a body? The spark, the indomitable uniqueness, that vanishes in an instant, it all feels so inconceivable.

Chalk it up to too much television, but I always imagined that a phone call from overseas, or in this case, a continent over 4,000 miles away, would be garbled. Or filled with static. Instead, it was crystal-clear. They didn't even know how far away we were.

Kate had listed us as her and Rob's emergency contacts and when the call came in at three a.m. on Jhon's cell phone, we were both slow to wake. The ULSC had made sure that his phone had GSM, which allowed for out-of-country calling, which was our saving grace. Without it, the police would not have reached us. As it was, they ended up leaving a voicemail as we hunted in the dark for the phone.

"Who is it?" I asked, yawning and rubbing my eyes. Jhon reached out and turned the overhead light on. He was frowning.

"The Seattle Police Department called on a next of kin for Elizabeth. They left a callback number." He pressed the speaker button and replayed the message while I scrambled for a pad of paper and a pen.

Seconds later, he had dialed the phone number, and I drew close so I could hear as well.

"Yes, this is Jhon Staunton. I'm returning a call from a Sergeant Cummings regarding Elizabeth Long."

A series of clicks, one short ring, and a man's voice. "Cummings speaking."

"Yes, this is Jhon Staunton. You called and left a message regarding Elizabeth Long?"

"Yes, thank you for returning my call, Mr. Staunton, considering the early hour. I have you and a Nichole Staunton listed as the next of kin for Elizabeth Long. Would that be correct?"

"Yes, we're her godparents," Jhon answered. "She's the adopted daughter of our friends Kate and Rob Long. Has something happened?"

"Mr. Staunton, I regret to inform you that Mr. and Mrs. Long perished in a house fire late last night. Their minor child Elizabeth escaped unharmed through an open window and is here at the South Precinct."

"Oh my God!" A wail of sorrow burst out of me. "Oh no, no, NO!"

Jhon stood up, phone in hand, and paced the length of our tiny studio apartment. He held up a hand to me, and I did my best to choke back the sobs.

"How? I mean, you're sure? How did this happen?"

"I'm sorry, Mr. Staunton. I don't have any additional details. The fire is still under investigation. All I can tell you is that we have Elizabeth here at the station and with you listed as next of kin, I can release her to you, or if you cannot take her, we can place her with Children's..."

I jumped off the bed and yanked the phone from Jhon. "I'm out of town, but I'll catch an early flight and return to Seattle right away."

"Where are you flying in from, Mrs. Staunton?"

"Mexico City," I lied and Jhon stared at me, mouth agape. "I'll book a flight and fly home to Seattle. I'll be there as soon as I can."

"All right, well, we will get her into emergency foster care until you arrive."

I wrote the phone number he gave me down, recognizing the name. It was the same caseworker Elizabeth had when she arrived at Kate's house. I thanked him and ended the call.

"Here," I said, tossing the phone back to Jhon, "get me a flight out this morning. I'll shower and then pack."

By six a.m., I had showered, packed, and was shoving a humita around on the plate, a cup of brewed coffee gurgling about in my stomach. Just as I was leaving, I remembered to ask Jhon to call the Biblioteca Municipal and let them know I had to leave the country and couldn't continue the classes. Grief over Rob and Kate and worry for sweet Elizabeth, alone and back in foster care, consumed me. I wished that I had the chance to say goodbye to Maria and the others there in my reading class.

Jhon kissed me and hugged me tight.

"Go home. I'll follow as soon as I can. I need at least a day or two to wrap everything up. The office is on its feet and will do just fine without me," he said, his eyes stricken. "Go take care of Elizabeth. Poor kid, she needs us more than ever right now."

The flights down to Peru had been straightforward, with short layovers. The way back was not as easy, especially with it being the last minute. I found myself crowded into what Jhon referred to as the cattle-car section. Even as a non-profit, we had traveled business class, and sometimes, first class. The return trip was a lesson in just how miserable air travel can be on a last-minute, cobbled-together set of flights.

By the end of the first day, I had flown from Arequipa to Lima. On the way down to Peru, we had flown from Seattle to Los Angeles and then from Los Angeles to Lima. After arriving in Lima, however, I could only find a connecting flight to Mexico City. And that landed me in the middle of an airline strike. I sat in the terminal waiting for a flight out for over 16 hours. Exhausted, my eyes burned, and yet, I could not sleep.

Kate, sweet Kate, was gone. And Rob, with his amiable smile and love of grilling and disc golf. How could their house have burned? It was brand new, with the latest of safety equipment in a safe neighborhood with a reputable architect and builder. Kate had shown me all the safety features on one of my first visits, giggling over how impressed their certification worker had been.

The enormity of the loss staggered me and I know it showed. The other people in the terminal stared at me with curiosity and pity. I must have looked a sight with my red-rimmed eyes, tangled hair, and wrinkled clothes.

By the time I landed in Seattle, there was a woman from the ULSC headquarters I recognized waiting for me. Brandy Lippert was well-known as a whiz at organizing. She handled the office parties and fundraiser luncheons and so much more. I realized Jhon must have contacted her to help pick me up from the airport and held back tears of relief. She was a social butterfly, but put her on a task, and she was like a dog with a bone. She could move mountains and had, with plenty of organizing challenges in the past. Brandy waved at me, rushed forward, and hugged me.

"Nichole, Jhon emailed and asked me to meet you. I am so sorry to hear about your friends." Her eyes traveled over me. "Oh honey, you've been through the wringer, but I've got some good news. Come on, let's get your bags and get you out of here."

While we waited at the baggage carousel for each of my three stuffed-to-the-brim bags to slide down the ramp, Brandy told me they had found a two-bedroom house for us, moved our furniture out of storage into it, and even found a bedroom set for Elizabeth.

"The office took up a collection, and we have filled it with toys, clothes, everything she needs." Brandy smiled. "Everything is waiting for you and Jhon and little Elizabeth, even a company car." She held out the key ring, and I took it, tears gathering once again. My head ached. I felt sandpaper dry, inside and out. My vision blurred as my eyes filled with tears.

"Oh, sweetie." Brandy's forehead furrowed. "Don't cry. I'll cry too if you do!" Tears sprang into her eyes and she reached out and hugged me again. "It's going to be okay. You are here now. A little rest, a shower, and some clean clothes and you will be right as rain to take that sweet little girl home."

I took a deep breath in and nodded.

An hour later, she had parked in the tiny driveway of an adorable post-World War II era bungalow, helped me haul my bags inside, showed me the layout, and hugged me again. The woman was a hugger. And for once, I didn't mind at all.

"Thank you, Brandy. Please thank everyone else for me, for us, too."

She'd grinned, eyes sparkling. "Anything for you and Jhon and little Elizabeth." She winked. "Your husband is one of my favorites. Now get some rest!"

She slipped into a scarlet-red Nissan Leaf and drove away, calling out as she did, "If you need anything, you just call."

The sun had disappeared, and the clouds were promising rain as I dialed Sergeant Cummings and left a message on his voicemail, and another message for Elizabeth's caseworker, Cara Aubergine. I slipped out of my clothes, showered, and fell into the bed, my mind shutting down, exhausted from travel, and from grief.

It was past ten in the morning when my eyes opened again, and only because my cell phone in the other room was ringing. It rang four times and went to voicemail. I needed a moment to center, to wake up, and have a cup of coffee. I had been operating on nerves and stress for three days, and my stomach growled an angry objection to anything that didn't at least include a coffee and a bagel. It felt as if I'd had enough peanuts and sweet cookie things to last a lifetime. Looking down, I realized I'd fallen asleep on top of the covers, my bath towel still wrapped around me.

Brandy had thought of everything, down to unpacking and putting away our stored clothes in the dressers and closet. Even my favorite deodorant was in the bathroom, new and unopened. I stopped in the middle of dressing and sent a mental thank you to Brandy and everyone else in the head office. This was the work of more than just Brandy, and it spoke volumes about the people Jhon worked with. They had taken the time to organize everything, and in our darkest hour, we were lucky to have them.

I found the coffee with little trouble and turned the hot water kettle on, readying the French press. I peered into the refrigerator and smiled. Brandy had stocked it full of Trader Joe's. There was milk, my favorite soy creamer, and even packs of kids' yogurt and organic juice boxes. Tears pricked my eyes, making everything blurry.

I reached for my phone and listened to the voicemails. One was from Cummings. He wanted to interview Elizabeth. The second was from Jhon, checking in. The third was from Cara, Elizabeth's caseworker, asking me to call as soon as I could.

I dialed her first, adding the creamer to the coffee until it was a creamy mocha. I sipped the rich sweetness of it and savored the feel as it slid down my throat. Cara picked up on the second ring.

"Hi, Cara, this is Nichole Staunton. I'm Elizabeth's godmother."

"Nichole! It is so good to hear from you! I've tried calling you several times and just got your voicemail. I was getting worried!" Cara was in her late forties, round, jovial, and she wore diamonds on each of her fingers. We had met twice, both times at Kate's, when Cara came by for a visit. She had outlived three husbands and joked that she had married poorly yet outlived them all. Considering she drove a five-year-old Mercedes, it looked as if she had married far better than she let on. Kate had told me once that Cara had worked for Children's Division as a caseworker for over twenty years.

"There are few like her," Kate had commented. "You know how high of turnover the caseworker positions can have."

I sighed. "I'm so sorry, Cara, I was in Peru. I got here as quick as I could."

"Peru!" Her rings clanked against her phone. "My goodness, I didn't know! The police officer, Cummings, said you were out of town and headed home, but I didn't realize you were that far away!"

"We were scheduled to return soon, anyway," I said, taking another sip of the heavenly coffee. I loved the Trader Joe's dark roast. Whoever had filled the kitchen with food had picked all of my favorites and thought of Elizabeth, too. There were four different children's cereals in the cabinet, as well as steel-cut oats. "I flew in late last night."

I wasn't about to tell her I had cut my part of the trip short by two full months or that Jhon had promised to do whatever he could to get back to Seattle within the next couple of weeks.

"Well, the temporary placement we have has been calling me nonstop. I swear I received three phone calls yesterday and two the day before that." She sighed. "They're new, but it's getting ridiculous. Elizabeth is a sweetheart. I can't see how they can have this much trouble with her."

I frowned. What kind of trouble could a three-year-old little girl be?

"Well, we have set everything up for her, and her room is ready to go. I know she will feel better once she sees a familiar face. How soon can she come home?"

Cara's relief was palpable. "Honey, I'll go get her this morning and have her to you by lunch. How does that sound?"

My heart leaped. "Cara, that would be amazing."

By the time the car pulled into the driveway, I had set some of the Trader Joe's mozzarella sticks to bake in the oven and set out a few fruit cups and called Jhon to update him. He told me the ULSC was sending out another staff member to take over the last details of the rollout.

"I'll be on a red-eye and home in time for the funeral."

My breath caught. "Oh God, I hadn't even thought of the funeral." My stomach churned. Rob's parents were both elderly and lived in Florida. Kate's mother was dead of cancer and her father was a kind, sweet man. I'd met him once.

"You've had a lot of other things on your mind, Nichole. How's Elizabeth?"

"She'll be here any moment, any minute, in fact. I love you and I'll see you soon."

As soon as I saw the car arrive, I ran to the door to open it. Elizabeth looked just as I remembered, if taller now. I dropped to my knees, remembering what the instructor had said about how big and intimidating adults can appear when a small child looks up at them.

She was wearing an ill-fitting dress that was faded. One sleeve had a tear in it. She had nothing with her, no bag, no toys, nothing. Of course she didn't. The fire had taken it all.

"Hi, sweetheart, do you remember me?"

Elizabeth stood there and stared at me for a moment. She looked shell-shocked, pale, scared. My heart felt as if it might shatter. Thank God she had made it out of the house unharmed. I couldn't imagine the horror and fear and pain she had endured over the past few days. I smiled at her. She nodded then and took a tentative step towards me.

It was killing me, seeing her so close yet wounded in spirit. Back to the shy, frightened girl I had first met a year ago. I opened my arms. "Would you like a hug?"

She nodded, and I slid my arms around her, tears filling my eyes, my heart aching at the loss of Kate and Rob. I shared her sadness in the very depths of my soul. She curled against me, hiding her face in my neck, and I picked her up. She was still so light, a tiny wisp of a child. I wondered if her bones were hollow, like a bird. She snuggled closer, and I stood, crying, holding her. I was making a scene for any curious neighbors looking out their windows at the moment. I didn't care. Not one whit. She was here with me, and I wrapped this precious little girl in my arms. She had been through so much in her young life, but I was going to make sure she felt loved and safe from now on.

I felt a hand on my shoulder. Cara stood there, her eyes sparkling with unshed tears. "Come on, let's get her inside. It's a new address, so I'll need to do a quick walk-through."

We walked inside and the oven timer dinged. "Mm, that smells good!" Cara chirped, her voice bright and cheery. "I'll bet you are hungry, aren't you, Elizabeth?" She reached for the oven mitts. "I'll get them. You have your hands full." As she pulled the baking sheet out of the oven, she turned and smiled at Elizabeth, who had turned, her nose following the smell. "Miss Lenore said you didn't eat a bite of breakfast and no dinner either!"

My stomach grumbled just at the thought of missing two meals in a row. "Oh no, you must be so hungry!"

I felt Elizabeth's head nod.

"Here, let's sit you here." I set her in one of the two tall chairs that rested at the breakfast bar and set the food and juice in front of her. The sweet little girl said nothing, digging into the food, starving. I suppressed a flare of anger. Had the emergency placement refused to feed her?

Cara saw the look on my face and chirped, "Okay, sweetheart. Miss Nichole and I need to talk, so you just stay right there and eat, okay?" She turned to me, touched my arm, and said, "Will you show me around, dear?"

In Elizabeth's bedroom, she nodded and smiled, and then closed the door and stepped close. She pitched her voice low. "The emergency placement said she has been having some emotional issues."

"Of course she has. Her parents died!" I hissed in return, then, "Why haven't they fed her?" Just thinking of it made me want to march over there and give the woman a real talking-to.

Cara held up her hand. "Lenore said that Elizabeth has been violent and threatened another child in the home. They have a six-year-old who was placed with them two months ago, and the two girls were sharing a room. I guess it didn't go well."

I opened my mouth and Cara raised her hand again. "Also, Elizabeth threw her dinner yesterday, which is why she didn't eat. She threw the plate at the emergency placement, and it hit her in the face. They put her in her room by herself. They moved the other little girl to another room, and they felt it necessary to lock the bedroom door. I will deal with that, believe me, because that is unacceptable. The emergency placement stated that Elizabeth threw a screaming fit, destroyed the bedroom, including most of the toys in it, ripped the curtains to shreds, and defecated on the other girl's bed. This went on for hours. By the next morning, she was over it and they said she was quiet and withdrawn all morning. She tried to get her to eat, but Elizabeth seemed to be afraid. I'll admit, the emergency placement was plenty upset over the state of the room, but I can't see her denying Elizabeth food. I'm telling you this because you need to be aware there will be a lot of work and time before this little girl feels safe again. If you don't think you can handle that, it's best that you tell me now."

I felt a wave of dark depression wash over me as I imagined the level of trauma Elizabeth had gone through in her brief life. How much of her anger was actual pain and fear? How frightened she must have been! First by the fire and then by the unfamiliar environment and an older child. Who knows, maybe the older girl bullied her. She was twice her age, after all. The suggestion that a child twice her size was afraid of Elizabeth was ludicrous.

"Well, she's here now. And I'll work on finding her a therapist as soon as possible."

"I know she is in good hands with you, Nichole." Cara smiled and squeezed my hand. "The room is beautiful, by the way; you've done a lovely job with it. I know Elizabeth will be happy here!"

Half an hour later, I watched through the large picture window as she drove off. Elizabeth had devoured everything on her plate and I had shown her the bedroom. She had reached for a stuffed penguin and looked up at me, a shy, questioning look on her face.

"This is all yours, Elizabeth. All for you."

She cuddled the penguin close and looked at the floor, then she mumbled quietly to herself.

"What did you say, sweetie?" I leaned closer.

"I'm Isabel," she said in a tiny voice, peering up at me, the penguin held in front of her face so that just her curls and one bright blue eye showed.

Isabel. Of course. I thought of how much she had been through, how hard it must be for her. She had reset herself back to the shy little girl I had met almost a year ago.

"Isabel, of course." I smiled, patting her shoulder gently as I pointed at the penguin. "And what is this one's name? And is it a boy or a girl?"

There was a moment of silence as she held the penguin away from her face and regarded it. Her face was solemn, and serious.

"His name is Thomas. He's a boy."

We were waiting hand in hand for Jhon at the airport the next day. He looked rumpled and exhausted from his flight, but as soon as he saw Elizabeth, he sank to his knees and held out his arms. She didn't run into them like she had the last time he had seen her, but after a moment she approached him and laid her head on his shoulder. As he stood, with her in his arms, I was struck again by their similarities. The same red hair and freckles and pale skin. Were strangers to be looking at us, they would see my curls and wide smile in her. She looked like our natural-born child. My stomach churned at the sudden realization that I had gotten what I wanted - but at the cost of two dear friends' lives.

Jhon drew close and kissed me. We stood there, while others moved frantic and quick around us. I nestled my head on his shoulder and we stood without moving for a minute, perhaps two.

"Come on. We have enough time for you to shower and change before the service."

We took Elizabeth with us. I had scheduled an emergency consult with a therapist and also finagled a regular follow-up for the following week. I had asked him if it would help for her to say goodbye to Kate and Rob and he gave the go-ahead.

"Even small children need the ritual of being able to say goodbye," he had said. I liked him already and looked forward to him helping Elizabeth.

As we stood by the graveside with a dozen others, I held Elizabeth's hand and listen to the pastor speak.

"Losing Kate and Rob is a tragedy we cannot comprehend. It is hard to see two in the flush of youth and happiness struck down in such a way." The pastor's voice faded into the background as I noticed a police officer standing at the edge of the group.

The service ended a few moments later and we said our goodbyes. Most were strangers, but a couple of them were familiar. Rob and Kate had hosted a barbecue the previous June and we had met several of Rob's co-workers then. A tap on Jhon's shoulder was my only notice of the police officer's approach.

"Mr. Staunton, Mrs. Staunton, I'm Detective Cummings of the Seattle Police Department. Would it be possible for me to speak with the two of you?"

"Perhaps you could just speak with my husband, Detective. I don't want to leave Elizabeth alone right now."

"Of course." Cummings nodded and he and Jhon stepped away to speak. Their voices pitched low. They spoke for only a moment, and I saw the detective hand my husband a card and walk away. We drove home from the service and changed out of our black clothes. I set Elizabeth at the breakfast bar with a snack, and Jhon and I slipped outside. The lawn was patchy and brown, a stark contrast to the neighbor's lush green turf.

"What did he say?"

Jhon's lips tightened, his expression grim. "He said it was arson. Also, he said that both Kate and Rob were dead long before the fire spread. Blunt force trauma. This wasn't an accident; someone murdered them."

Horror rushed through me. Had Elizabeth seen anything? Heard anything? What if she had witnessed the murders? Tears sprang to my eyes and I could feel a headache gathering.

"Oh God, Jhon."

"They want to question Elizabeth."

Anger surged through me. "What? Why? She's a little girl who has been through terrible trauma! Have they even thought about what that will do to her? No!"

"I told him we would talk to her therapist and see what he recommends. Cummings says that they have trained professionals there at the station who would handle it."

"I don't know if I like the sound of that," I said, drying my tears, anger and dread at the thought of her being questioned unsettling my empty stomach.

"Nichole, they aren't asking, they are telling us. We're only her foster parents."

I glared at him. "We'll see about that."

Elizabeth was in our home now. My heart mourned for my friends, but I was going to make damned sure that Elizabeth felt protected and loved, just as Kate and Rob would have wanted.

Incident/Case #: 18-02521

Classification: Assault/Arson

Date: 2018-20-09

Location: Rush Creek, Raaen Road

Victim (s): Staunton, Jhon and Elizabeth

Suspect: Staunton, Nichole

Evidence ID#: 18-02521-012 (page out of handwritten journal)

I've been feeling upbeat, despite the nightmares and the voices, always the voices. "Stay busy," I tell myself, and it helps, it does.

But a few moments ago, it hit. The sense that I am, and perhaps we all are, inches from the dark abyss. It rises, dark, oily, and corrupt. It rises and I find myself sure that life can, and will, turn against me.

I don't know what to do when it hits and, frankly, it's terrifying.

I keep lying to myself and saying it isn't real, and everything will be fine. "Clean the house, care for E, save a little into the rainy-day account I set up at the end of last year."

But then the voices slide in and say, No rainy-day fund will ever protect you from the darkness that is coming.

Smile. Pretend I'm fine. While deep inside, in my lizard hindbrain, the panic sirens are blasting.

- N -

9. Second Forever

- Nichole -

June 21st, 2017 - Seattle, Washington

The first moment I heard Elizabeth stirring, I knew something was different. I had been awake for an hour, seen Jhon off to work, and was enjoying a second cup of coffee when I heard her feet touch the floor.

There was a thump instead of a soft creak of the floorboards. It sounded as if she had leaped from her bed onto the floor. Her tiny feet stomped down the hallway, halting only when her smiling face appeared at the entrance to the kitchen.

She stood there, curls scattered and messy, her *Frozen* nightgown cockeyed, with Elsa haughty and alone on the front of it, and she grinned at me and caroled, "Morning!"

I opened my arms for a hug and she ran toward me, jumping at the last second as if she had a booster rocket attached to her feet.

"Oh, my goodness! Aren't you in a fine mood today?" I laughed and gave her an enormous hug. "Did you sleep well?"

"Uh huh. I eat panquakes for breakfast? Pwease?" She took my face in her tiny hands, her blue eyes inches from mine. "I soo hungry for panquakes, Mommy Nichole."

My heart lurched. She'd called me Mommy Nichole twice now, and it felt so amazing and good. It also filled me with such guilt. To think that Elizabeth had given my sweet friend this honor, and now she was gone. I remembered how Kate had burst into tears the first time she had called her Mommy. Elizabeth had looked so confused. And now I knew how good it felt. I did my best to hide the sudden moistness in my own eyes.

"You are sooo hungry?" I kissed her little button nose and bent my head down to tickle it. Her little nose, with its splash of freckles, turned up at the end, and I loved to hear her giggle.

"That tickles like a buwerfly!"

This past weekend, Jhon and I had taken Elizabeth to the Tropical Butterfly House at the Pacific Science Center on Second Street. The butterflies had entranced her. They had flitted about, and she had stood still as a Starry Night female butterfly had landed on the tip of her finger.

I had taken picture after picture with my phone while we were there. But that one had stood out as magical. I had zoomed in and the other people blurred to indistinct shapes and colors. Her red curls were held with a ribbon and her white dress was edged in red, matched by her little white shoes with a red buckle. As I had snapped the picture, a woman had stopped beside me and said, "Your daughter is so beautiful. Look how well she is holding still for the butterfly!"

I hadn't corrected her, just smiled and thanked her. An enlarged photo of her and the butterfly was already on order. I would frame it and hang it in the hallway. The first of many photos. I couldn't help but daydream of a home of our own with a long hallway filled with family photos.

It had been just over three months since our return and every day felt better than before. Each day felt as if we grew closer and closer, becoming a family.

"Panquakes? Pwease?"

I laughed, and she grinned up at me. Today, it was as if she was a new person. As if the switch had flipped and she had moved out of her sadness, her fear, and dove straight into living her life again. That had to be a good thing, right?

She will backslide. No one can take that kind of loss, heartbreak, and worse and be okay. We joke that kids are made of rubber, adaptable, and able to bounce back. But that doesn't mean they are immune to trauma.

"Do you want chocolate chips in them?" I asked, knowing what the answer would be.

"Yes, yes, yes!" Elizabeth said, jumping up and down.

"Okay. You go get dressed and I'll make you pancakes."

"We go to see the buwerfly again?" she asked, her face lighting up.

"How about we go to the arboretum instead? There are butterflies, flowers, and even *hummingbirds*."

Elizabeth gasped, her eyes getting round. "Like the picture?"

I nodded, and she shrieked with excitement. "I get dressed right away!"

She ran down the hallway and I chuckled. For such a tiny child, she could make plenty of noise. She had been obsessed with a delicate painting of a hummingbird on her wall. I had caught her climbing up on her dresser last week so that she could see it better. When I found her there, she was standing there so still, staring at it with such intensity. She had ducked her gaze away when she saw me, a look of fear crossing her face, as if she thought she was in trouble. I had picked her up in my arms and returned her to the floor. Then I'd set the picture on the top of the dresser where she could see it without climbing and falling.

I pulled the pancake mix down from the shelf and reached into the refrigerator for some chocolate chips. Hannah would make these for me every Saturday morning until I hit my teens. I smiled at the happy memory. Andy slept in on the weekends, but Hannah would be up at the crack of dawn, same as me. It had been our time together, when the rest of the world was sleeping off hangovers, or just plain sleeping in, and it had been special. The world was quiet, even the street outside was silent until mid-morning. Hannah would cook the pancakes and I would set the table in the sunny breakfast room that had windows running along its entire length. We would plan our day, just the two of us, although the plans usually included Andy. Long after morning soccer or nights spent at friends' houses had become my dominant Saturday morning activity, I would ask Hannah for the pancakes. I think that she loved that time with me just as much as I enjoyed spending it with her.

As always, I felt the bittersweet joy of memory run through my heart. Most of my best memories were that way, a moment of happiness, bordered and framed with loss. I kept the smile, though, because I knew Hannah would smile if she could see me now.

I had whisked the mixture and heated the pancake pan by the time Elizabeth returned. She had dug out a new dress I had purchased the other day. It was a pale green and a gauzy, transparent top layer embroidered with flowers lay over the solid satin-smooth shift.

"I need help," she said, reaching behind her for the zipper.

I wiped my hands off and reached for the zipper as she turned her back to me. "Of course, sweetie. There you go." She twirled back around and smiled up at me. A wave of love ran through me. "You look so beautiful in that dress, Isabel."

She twirled again, climbed up onto the stool with no small amount of effort, and said, "I'm Lizzie now, Mommy Nichole."

Lizzie.

When had she asked to be called Lizzie last year? It had been at least two months, maybe three, after Kate and Rob took her in. And it couldn't have been more than a week, maybe two, before Jhon and I left for Peru. I blinked at her and said, "Okay, sweetie."

As Elizabeth stuffed herself with pancakes and drank a cup of milk, I pondered it.

Isabel.

Lizzie.

Elsa.

Elizabeth.

I thought of Kate's email about the personality shift in fall and her startling concern Lizzie might have dissociative identity disorder. I wasn't saying it didn't exist. Of course it did. And there were people out there who suffered from it. But a preschooler? That didn't seem possible.

Kate had sent only a handful of emails after the one in mid-November. They had mentioned Elizabeth, of course, but after my tepid response to her concern about DID, she'd said nothing more. I hadn't thought about it, but now I wondered if I should have been more understanding, not as dismissive.

I opened my laptop on the counter and Googled "dissociative identity disorder in preschool-age children."

Sure enough, it was a thing. In fact, DID formed *no later* than ages six through nine. I clicked on the question, "How do you know if your child is dissociating?"

Regressed behavior—the child might act much younger than they are through their voice, language, and behavior. You might have the sense that they 'look and feel' younger. Saying "we" or "they"—dissociative children feel as if they are 'multiple.'

Well, she sure wasn't doing that. Not at all. It had to be a response to her trauma, but DID? I wasn't a psychologist, but that didn't sound like the behavior that Elizabeth was evidencing. Not at all.

I would bring it up to the therapist. We had formed a great relationship. Marcus, who Elizabeth referred to as Mistah Marcus, was a gentle giant of a man. As a play therapist, he was part of a group of therapists at Seattle Play Therapy on 9th Avenue. Therapy was every Tuesday at 11 a.m. Elizabeth and I would meet Jhon at Panda Master for lunch afterward. The staff there loved Elizabeth and would bring her a special pair of child chopsticks and an intricate folded napkin in the shape of an animal, different each time.

It was odd, this name change, and also rather timely. It wasn't just a name change, but a personality change at the same time. Such a marked difference. Isabel was shy, quiet, almost reserved. Lizzie was boisterous, fun-loving, and anything but reserved.

Marcus would have an idea or two with how to deal with it. I wasn't too concerned. In every way, this seemed like an improvement. Elizabeth seemed happy, sweet, obedient, and excited about her day. What more could I ask for?

"Mommy Nichole?"

"Yes, Lizzie?" I looked up and laughed at the sight. Elizabeth's mouth and face were covered in streaks of chocolate. So were her hands. The pancake had vanished. Streaks of chocolate covered the outside of the bright green plastic milk cup.

"I need a napakwin."

"Oh my, yes you do." I suppressed a laugh and reached for a clean dishcloth. "Don't move. I'll get you cleaned up."

Nope. There wasn't anything wrong with my beautiful little girl. She was perfect.

Four hours later, after Elizabeth had run up and down the paths, laughing and giggling, we had eaten lunch and I had insisted she nap, we headed out one last time to a park I hadn't been to since last year. It had been Kate's favorite spot. Roxhill Park was a little farther out than we usually ventured, but it had a broad range of play equipment that catered to the little ones and up through to the older pre-teen crowd. There was even a skateboard park off to one side. Kate had met with a group of moms there, and I knew Elizabeth would enjoy seeing her playmates again. In a few more weeks, she would enter daycare part-time so that I could begin work on another commission that was due in late fall.

I had avoided going for months. Partly because of the memories — we had gone there several times before I left for Peru — and also because I was worried about what the other mothers would say. Would they look at me and compare me to Kate? If so, I was sure I would fall short. In some ways, it felt as if I had stolen Elizabeth from her. It was ridiculous to think like that, but when the voices reared their heads, it was with messages like that.

I had resumed my own twice-monthly therapy sessions on Marcus' gentle suggestion. It helped keep the negative voices at bay and gave me some mental distance when they couldn't be silent. My therapist, Lois, was in her late thirties, and she was teaching me to dig deep into my fears. It had been her who had suggested we return to Roxhill Park.

"Don't let loss stop you and Elizabeth from remembering the good times," she had counseled.

I had sat there, my hands twisting in my lap. "It's more than that. It's... guilt. I feel guilty somehow. Because I wanted Elizabeth for my own so much. It's awful how much I envied Kate. And now I have this beautiful little girl. I sometimes feel as if I had stolen her."

Lois had nodded and asked, "Did you bludgeon Kate and Rob to death?"

"What?" I gasped in horror. "Of course not!"

"Did you start the fire?"

I just stared at her. "No!"

She had leaned forward, met my eyes, and asked, "Do you feel you deserve happiness?"

Tears had sprung to my eyes at that question. The losses I had seen. The memories of my birth mother, of Hannah and Andy. I thought of Vincent, of my stillborn baby, and of Kate and Rob — all of it lined up in what felt like an endless string of grief and loneliness. And in that moment with Lois, I had realized she had hit the nail on the head. After all of it, through all of it, I could feel the voices crowding up to whisper the darkness into my ears.

That I wasn't worthy.

Of love.

Or happiness.

Or joy.

I hadn't been able to answer her question that session, or most of the next. But it had turned the tide. It was time to return to Roxhill Park. To the memories I had of sitting and talking with Kate and the other moms. Of watching Elizabeth run and play.

Parking, as usual, was difficult. On the third circuit, I caught a break and maneuvered my Honda Accord into a spot. As I did, I waved at the woman leaving. I couldn't remember her name, but her face was familiar. She smiled and waved, then her eyes drifted to Elizabeth, and the smile vanished. Her expression hardened as she drove away.

How odd. I had to have imagined it.

The rain had stayed away for a week, and Elizabeth and I had made the most of it. Earlier today it had been a perfect, sunny day. The wind was picking up now and I could see clouds gathering in the distance. The temperature had dropped at least ten degrees since noon. *Perhaps it would have been better to wait,* I thought. I opened my mouth to suggest it might be better to come another time, but Elizabeth had already spied a girl she used to play with.

"Let's go! Let's go!" she cried, squirming in her car seat, her small feet kicking the back of passenger seat in front of her.

The second she was out of the car, her legs were in motion, her smile wide and happy as she flew down the path towards the playground. I followed at a trot and could see the gaggle of mothers in their customary place in the shade of several massive oak trees. Just twenty feet away was one of the main play structures, and I could see the children swarming over it. Elizabeth made a beeline toward the play structure and the other children while I raised my hand in greeting and walked over to the other women. A couple of them ignored me, but the rest gaped in shock. Two of them looked hostile. It was not the response I expected. The women were on the granola-crunching side of parenting, and while Kate and I had both agreed that television and sugary cereals were both in our lexicon, we had fit in well. The last time I had visited the park, one of Elizabeth's friends was having a birthday party and they had hired a magician. I looked for that mother and realized she had been the one who had driven away.

Sharon, a round, jovial mother of three, plastered a sickly smile on her face, meeting my eyes for a moment before her gaze flew to the playground, searching for her two older children. Her youngest, an infant boy, was at her feet, mouthing on a teething biscuit.

"Nichole! My goodness, what a surprise to see you! What are you doing here?"

I was trying to smile, but there was something wrong. I could feel tension; the air was humming with it. Forcing the corners of my mouth up seemed at odds with the vibes I was getting off of all the moms.

"Hi, I, um, I just thought I'd bring Elizabeth by her old stomping grounds to see all of her friends."

Sharon nodded again, her smile slipping. "Gosh, Kate stopped coming a while back. What was it, early January?"

A mother who didn't even bother to smile answered, "Yep, right after Elizabeth broke my Edy's arm in two places."

My mouth fell open. My Elizabeth? Kate's Elizabeth? There was no way. No... way. A scream sounded behind me and the women surged as one, Sharon pushing past me as she ran towards the children fleeing the playground. Elizabeth stood at the monkey bars and watched the other children go. One or two were still there on the play structure, their bodies still, their eyes trained on their friends and mothers. They made space between them, giving Elizabeth a wide berth.

Sharon collected her two children, and Marjorie had Edy by the hand. I could see that the girl's left arm was thinner and paler than the right. She didn't have a cast on now, but then, she wouldn't some five months later. Edy was crying, and Marjorie just glared at me before hustling her child away.

"Nichole." A quiet voice behind me spoke, and I turned to see Brenna, who I had found vivacious and funny. There was no humor or smile on her face. Instead, she wore a look that spoke of extreme discomfort. As if they forced her into a role she did not belong in or wish to endure.

"Nichole, you seem like a nice person. And Kate was a wonderful person, too. We were so very sorry to hear about her and her husband. It was a tragedy, truly it was. Nichole, I know this is a public park and you can go where you want, but..." She looked at the other mothers who were listening, their faces tight, stressed. "But I think it would be best if you didn't bring Elizabeth back here. We won't allow our children to be treated that way. She needs help, Nichole."

I tried to make my mouth work. Tried to understand, to question it, but it was as if all the growth and progress we had seen, and Elizabeth's transformation from a shy, frightened girl to a happy, healthy one, meant nothing. That it was nothing more than a mirage.

Ask them what in the hell they are talking about.

Do something; you're supposed to be her mother.

What is so wrong with her they would act like this?

Maybe it's you, Nichole. Looks like you can't hack it as a mom. That's why your baby died. It was a sign. One that you can't seem to listen to.

I should have said something. Anything. But in that moment, the voices were too loud, too harsh, too... too much. I just turned away and walked back to my precious little girl. She stood there next to the monkey bars, her smile gone. By now, the rest of her former playmates had been called away and I could see the mothers packing up their blankets and folding chairs and strollers.

I took her hand. I didn't know what to say or what to do, but I found a section of stairs and sat down and pulled her onto my lap. Elizabeth cuddled against me, nestling her head against my chest, one hand reaching up to play with my hair. She smelled like the strawberry shampoo I had used in her hair last night. I wrapped my arms around her.

"I didn't do anything, Mommy. They just sqweamed and ran away."

"I know you didn't, sweetheart."

"I didn't do it," she insisted, tears forming in her eyes. "It wasn't me."

"I know." God, I knew she hadn't hurt Edy. She wouldn't. She *couldn't*. I thought of the photograph of her with the butterfly on her finger. So gentle, so calm, so respectful of a life far more delicate than hers. Elizabeth couldn't have done what they said. It was impossible.

Whatever had happened here, it had been an accident. Why couldn't they see that?

"Come on, Lizzie, let's go get a snow cone and go home. It looks like it might rain soon."

A ghost of a smile returned to her lips and within a few minutes of snow cone noshing, she was back to her happy self. It reminded me again of how lucky we were.

Long after dinner and a bath and story time and bed, Elizabeth well and asleep in her bed, I had sat with Jhon in the living room and told him everything. Like me, he had shaken his head.

"There's no way she would hurt that kid. No way. It had to be an accident. It had to. Damn, for a bunch of granola-crunchers, they sure are judgmental as hell." He tipped a bottle of Johnny Utah Pale Ale to his lips, his teeth baring in anger. I smelled a wash of grapefruit, citrus, and resin. He squeezed my knee. "Babe, you'll find a better mother's group in our area. Screw those women."

He turned and looked at the closed door at the end of the hall. "She's different today. Better. More like I remember her right before we left. It's obvious that she's happy and doing well. Don't let those women derail you, Nichole. Don't let them tear down the life we are building together. Elizabeth is where she needs to be. And she's the wonderful little girl we remember so well."

I nestled against him, snagged the bottle from his fingers, and took a gulp. Jhon was right. Whatever had happened at Roxhill Park, it had been an accident. My heart hurt at the memory of Elizabeth's confused and hurt look. I felt a surge of resentment and anger towards those mothers. How could they accuse her of something like that? What was wrong with them?

We had been told in the classes, warned, that our children would face a myriad of challenges. Foster children had it rough. They didn't come into care because of excellent parenting, after all. All I could think of was that they had misinterpreted the situation, and that the other mothers had jumped to the wrong conclusion, especially after such a serious accident. They had turned on Elizabeth because she wasn't from an intact family. Because she was a foster child. I had seen it happen. Lived it. Watched as parents in my new neighborhood discouraged their daughters from playing with me. It had hurt, and I hadn't understood it. Vincent's mom hadn't been like that. She'd encouraged our friendship. She'd been kind. Curious, to be sure. But kind.

My heart hurt and my blood boiled at the thought of the parents rejecting Elizabeth just because she was a foster child. I took another pull of the beer and Jhon laughed, got up, and grabbed another beer from the fridge.

"Fuck those granola-crunching, judgmental, foster kid-blaming bitches," I said.

Jhon blinked. He opened the second beer, returned to the couch, and clanked his bottle against mine.

"Exactly. Fuck 'em."

We sat in silence for a moment longer.
"Nichole?"
"Yeah?"
"You are an exceptional mom. Never forget that."

Incident/Case #: 18-02521

Classification: Assault/Arson

Date: 2018-20-09

Location: Rush Creek, Raaen Road

Victim (s): Staunton, Jhon and Elizabeth

Suspect: Staunton, Nichole

Evidence ID#: 18-02521-013 (page out of handwritten journal)

I pulled the Ten of Swords today. Reversed. As if the upright card wasn't bad enough.

She's sneaky. Manipulative. She's messing with my head. I look in her eyes and she's full of guile. The voices tell me she isn't to be trusted. That she is out to get me.

I believe them.

- N -

10. An Odd Request

- Nichole -

July 10th, 2017 - Seattle, Washington

When Father Daniels called from Blessed Sacrament Church, I answered immediately. It was early afternoon and Elizabeth was away at daycare. I remembered Kate mentioning him, and he and I had traded voicemails back and forth since the week before. Now that Elizabeth was in daycare three days a week, I had stopped subletting out my studio and gotten back to work. I was hard at work on a new commission, and the check they had written to cover the supplies sat folded in my purse for over a month. I had just deposited it at the bank and was reviewing the supplies I needed to order when my phone rang.

"Mrs. Staunton? I'm Father Daniels with Blessed Sacrament. I was hoping I could meet with you this week."

We talked for a few minutes and agreed to meet on Wednesday. I hung up, frowning. He had asked for me to *not* bring Elizabeth with me. It felt like such an odd request, and I couldn't help wondering why. Weren't priests supposed to like kids? I wondered too if he knew I wasn't Catholic.

I mentioned it to Jhon that evening and he raised an eyebrow. Being listed as Elizabeth's godparents was rather a moot point now, since, according to Cara, we would finalize the adoption by mid-September. After all, the state had already gone through the motions of finding any extended family for Elizabeth and come up empty. The only reason it was taking as long as it had was that the court wanted to be sure we were ready to commit to a permanency and that Elizabeth appeared happy and healthy.

"Why bother?" Jhon had asked, not interested in baptism or any of the rest.

"It was important to Kate and Rob," I said weakly, and he grew silent.

"In honor of their wishes, then? I can get behind that, as long as it ends there. We can raise an ethical child without religion, Nichole."

It was a line he had held from early in our relationship, one that I agreed with. You could raise a child with morals and ethics without religion or faith - but I recognized that faith was reassuring for many - and that it had its place in our lives. Jhon was against it, whereas I believed that nearly all faiths served a positive purpose. Perhaps that is why Kate had asked me to consider being a godparent to Elizabeth. She knew Jhon was an atheist, but I held the firm middle ground between organized religion and atheism.

I nodded and Jhon looked relieved. Elizabeth piped up then, "Father Danweels was nice. I 'member him."

"I will tell him you said hello if you like, love."

"Can I come?" Elizabeth asked.

"It's on Wednesday, at the same time you are going on the nature walk with your daycare. You don't want to miss that!"

Her eyes lit up at the mention of the nature walk. The daycare had arranged for a school bus and they would walk along Discovery Park, along the shores of Puget Sound. "The one with the lighthouse?"

I nodded, and she wiggled in her seat at the table. "When? When?"

"In two days. Not tomorrow, but the next day."

This seemed to satisfy her and the thought of visiting the priest fell from her mind, replaced by the far more exciting promise of an outing to Discovery Park. She was doing well, in every aspect, and the odd behavior from the other moms' group faded to a niggling itch at the back of my mind. I will admit that it had stung. Perhaps their rejection of Elizabeth was, in some indirect way, of me. More than that, I didn't understand it. Not at all. I'd joined a group that met in a park near our house. And I'd watched Elizabeth like a hawk, interacting with the other moms for over two weeks before I let my guard down and relaxed a little.

By then, there were three other girls competing for best-friend status. The other moms just smiled and exchanged knowing looks when I told them I was her foster mom and that we would adopt soon. Angela Tompkins, Jemima's mother, had said in response, "Classic new-mom moves. She's fine, she gets on great with the others. Come and sit with us. Let them play." She had two older children, one a teen, another just entering middle school, and they were both away at camp.

After each visit to the park, I had asked, "Did you have fun, Lizzie? Was everyone nice? Were *you* nice?"

In return, she had looked at me with her big, blue, innocent eyes. "I always good, Mommy. I *love* my friends." And she would launch into a long description of whatever game the girls had been playing.

By the third week, the other moms had taken me under their wing and allayed my fears.

"Lizzie wouldn't hurt a fly. She's so sweet with Kenzie."

"Stop worrying so much, Mama Bear. Those girls are doing just fine."

When one child came screaming from the playground, bleeding from a minor scratch on her knee, my heart missed a beat, until I saw Elizabeth trying to help her friend walk, her tiny face full of worry and concern.

"Mommy, we need a Band-Aid!" Half a dozen mothers reached for their purses in response.

My worries slipped away with time. We had settled into calling her Lizzie, and Cara had shrugged her shoulders when I mentioned it during her monthly visit.

"Nichole, in the decades I've spent in this job, kids do some crazy things. Believe me, they do. Changing her name? That's just typical kid stuff. Don't sweat it." She had reassured me and then turned to Lizzie when she came in the door, Jhon a step behind her. "Hi, Lizzie! How are you doing, cutie-pie?" She had opened her arms for a hug and Elizabeth had bounded into them, hugging her caseworker with infectious joy.

Cara had eaten dinner with us, visited Elizabeth's room, and memorized all of our child's Barbie names.

"I love this part of the job," she said, standing outside next to her car. "She's been through so much, and yet, her spirit is so warm and open. She's lucky to have you and Jhon, and, dare I say it, you are lucky to have her. The judge set the adoption date for September 13th. I hope that will work for you?"

"We wouldn't miss it for the world," I answered, my heart full of joy, of thankfulness.

I thought of all of this as I drove to Blessed Sacrament Church. On a normal day in an upscale area like this, I would gawk at the expensive houses and wonder about the people who lived in them. But today my thoughts were occupied with a litany of questions. What was it that the priest wanted to talk about?

I knew Jhon was against organized religion of any kind, and with good reason — his mother had dabbled in different churches and groups, at least two that were considered by most to be cults, and it had caused his childhood home to be filled with arguments and worse while his parents disagreement grew more and more heated.

In the end, his mother's obsession with religion had resulted in a fight while their family was driving along Highway 101 in Oregon. Jhon and his two younger siblings had been in the back, their parents in the front, and whether it was the fight that led to the distraction, or the deer bounding across the road, it mattered not. The car had gone off the road, went airborne, and then crashed into the shallow surf. Jhon had been the only one to make it out alive.

His paternal grandparents, estranged from their only son, had taken him in and finished raising him. They had died within months of each other, before Jhon graduated college, but not before doing their best to force faith into him. Was it any genuine wonder he showed such a disdain for religion?

I had grown up with a far gentler version. The Unitarian faith was so open and accepting, and as many times as I had tried to describe the peace and love I had found in the walls of Unity Village, Jhon could not understand. His experience had been different and interlaced with trauma and loss.

I parked across the street from Blessed Sacrament and stared at the building. Should I just go in the front door? What was the protocol for entering a church when it wasn't for worship? I hoped the priest didn't expect me to go to Confession. The limited amount of knowledge I had of the Catholic Church came from what I read on the news or saw on TV. Not much.

I sat there in the car, contemplating not going in. Perhaps I would just call him and tell him something had come up, anything. I jumped out of my skin at the soft rap on the passenger-side window.

A middle-aged man in a black shirt and pants with close-cropped gray hair smiled at me through the glass. "Hi, are you Nichole?"

"I, uh." I cast around the car, discombobulated. Should I roll down the window? Get out of the car? I chose the latter, stepping out as a car flew by, inches from hitting me. "Oh crap!"

Father Daniels appeared at my side, his hand on my arm, a warning hand raised at another oncoming car. He was tall, far taller than Jhon's six-foot frame, and he towered over me. "Let's get out of traffic, shall we? They fly down the road here."

The car had braked, coming to a stop, and the other direction also slowed and stopped as the priest held up a hand of warning or benediction. For all I knew, his hand was lighting up like a neon sign from Jesus telling them to slow the heck down. I wasn't sure I was too far off, because I've never been able to get Seattle drivers to slow down. Even with a child in tow.

We walked across the street, his hand cupping my elbow, his other hand directing traffic, which resumed its fast pace as soon as we crossed over and stepped onto the sidewalk.

"Well now, safe and sound." He opened the massive front door. "After you."

Entering the sanctuary was like entering a different world. It was massive. For one, the ceiling had to be fifty, maybe even seventy-five feet tall. Stained glass windows lined the sides. The exposed brick walls combined with the rich wood and painted red brick pillars. The overall look was impressive. I knew they had designed the building to inspire awe in the power and might of God, but I was busy drooling over the architecture.

The door closed behind us and the sound of the traffic outside disappeared. In this place, every footstep on stone was muted. If I listened, I could hear faint whispers of the busy world outside, but it felt removed, and peaceful.

"I'm sorry for yelling like that," I said, feeling like I was twelve years old. "That car took me by surprise."

"Don't worry at all about it," Father Daniels said, his eyes twinkling. "I coach basketball to a horde of wayward youth every Tuesday and Thursday. I've heard far worse."

A priest coaching basketball? Well, he was tall enough for it, that was for sure.

He extended his hand, gesturing toward the long row of pews. "Please, step into my office."

I laughed and followed as he led the way deeper into the sanctuary, picked a pew five rows back, and gestured for me to sit. I stared again at the building, noting more details.

"This church is beautiful."

He nodded. "Yes, I enjoy it here. They assigned me to a newer building in Phoenix for several years. It didn't have the same presence or atmosphere as the older ones do."

We sat for a moment. I stared at the structure, the details of martyrs or saints in the beautiful stained glass, before I turned to him. "Sorry, I get distracted by architecture. It was my minor in college. Silly, I know. What could I do with a minor in architecture, anyway?"

"Isn't the point of college to explore your interests and find your life's work?" he asked.

"I guess you have a point."

"I have a plethora of them. I keep them hidden with my robes for Sunday Mass." He smiled and I couldn't help grinning in return. He changed the subject. "How is Elizabeth?"

"She's well. Amazing, as a matter of fact." I pulled out my phone and found a recent photo of her on the playground, her three friends clustered around her, a group of smiling children. "I joined a group of moms that meet at a local park, and the other kids love her. It's been a change for her, but she is so full of love, and her personality is starting to shine through."

Father Daniels leaned close to see the pictures better. I recognized the aftershave. It was the same as Jhon's. I hid a smile. A priest who wore Burberry Brit Splash for Him. Huh.

"So, no conflicts, no acting out?" he asked.

"No, none. She's... perfect," I answered. "Just as we remember her from last year." I thought of the granola-crunchers at Roxhill Park. "We had one run-in, but that wasn't Elizabeth's fault, not at all."

"Will you tell me about it?" he asked, tilting his head and settling back into the pew.

I shrugged and wondered where this was heading. When would he tell me why he had asked me to stop by? And would it include an admonition that children deserved a proper religious upbringing?

"Um, sure. It was a few weeks ago. I took Elizabeth to a park that Kate had taken her to last summer. There's a mom's group that meets there. I thought she'd enjoy seeing the group of children she had played so often with." I described the way the children had acted and what the moms had said, especially Ida's mother and Brenna.

Father Daniels nodded, his face thoughtful. "I remember the incident. After it, Kate came to me and asked for my help."

"To have Elizabeth baptized?" I asked, thinking that perhaps they had done it without us, not wanting to wait.

"No, they had gotten that done right away, the second week in January, if I remember right."

"I don't understand," I said, feeling rather dense. "If they had already had the baptism done, what more did they need from you?"

He arched an eyebrow, a smile playing across his lips. "The church serves in many more ways than baptism, Mrs. Staunton, not just as a source for holy water."

I could feel my cheeks heat up.

"I'm sorry, I didn't mean..."

"Please, it's fine. I gather you don't attend church?"

I winced. "Not really. I mean, my adoptive parents attended an, um, more laid-back church. Unity Village." I said it in a whisper. I was sitting in a Catholic church. Was it considered blasphemous to mention another faith? Was I going to piss this guy off, irk him, or annoy someone higher up the ecumenical food chain? I didn't know, but I also didn't want to know.

Really, what are you doing here?

What does this priest want, anyway?

I blurted out, "I'm sorry. I realized I don't know what to call you. And ever since we talked on Monday, I've thought and thought and *thought* about it and I don't know what you want. Maybe Kate and Rob were less lapsed and more religious than I thought. But I'm not. I don't even know if I believe in God and, well, if you thought I'd join the church and bring Elizabeth to church on Sundays or something... um, I've got to tell you in all honesty that church is not my thing. I've got nothing against it, it's just not my cup of tea, and my husband is one hundred percent atheist. He's a nice guy, but yeah, complete atheist."

I wasn't sure what he would do. The words had just come out in a rush, my head bobbing in unison with my words, and I felt like some ditzy bobble-headed doll. I wished I could take the words back. Did priests take offense if you told them you weren't into going to church? Did they throw non-Catholics out of their buildings while dousing them in holy water and chanting scripture? I had no idea.

The priest had the indecency to look amused. "Okay, let's start with the easy one. I answer to Father Daniels or Father Isaiah, but Isaiah seems to be a mouthful. My boys call me Father Iz."

I blinked. I knew little about Catholics, but I was pretty sure priests were supposed to be celibate. "Your... *boys*?"

"My basketball kids," Father Daniels clarified with a grin. "Ruffians, the entire lot of them, with big hearts and even bigger problems at home and school. As for the rest, let's see, I wouldn't be doing my job if I didn't encourage you to attend church, but I know better than most that it isn't for everyone. And as for why I asked to meet with you..." His face lost its smile, a serious look replacing it. "Kate approached me soon after the baptism. It surprised me when they asked for it, the baptism that is, since Kate had been quite specific when she first met with me and asked if we would perform it for a child who was not a member of the congregation. She had also been very clear that she wanted you and Jhon present as Elizabeth's godparents."

"They asked if we would serve as Elizabeth's godparents, and we love Elizabeth. It was a simple decision for us, even though neither of us is religious." I shrugged. "It was important to her."

"It grew even more important as the winter wore on," the priest said cryptically. The way he said it reminded me of the first weeks after my return from Peru, when the detective investigating the fire had insisted on questioning Elizabeth. He'd been cryptic too, but in a far more devious way. It had started innocently enough, but as the questions continued, I had seen a pattern emerge. I'd insisted on ending the interview right there and then, infuriated. As if a tiny girl could actually be responsible for their deaths. Rob was a criminal defense lawyer, for God's sake. If someone had killed Kate and

Rob and then set fire to their house, it was someone he had dealt with or represented, not a three-year-old girl!

"Explain, please." Again, I felt uncomfortable. Had I just ordered a priest to explain himself? If there was a hell, I was pretty sure I was going there, whether or not I believed in the place.

Father Daniels paused. He seemed to search for the right words. His frown deepened. "I don't know how to say this any other way, so I'll just say it. Kate asked me if I would consider performing an exorcism."

"A *what*?!" I didn't give him a chance to answer. The question was rhetorical. Exorcism? I had watched the movie *The Exorcist* with my adoptive father Andy. He had been a fan of horror flicks, especially those from the '80s and '90s. The movie had given me nightmares for weeks.

I stood up. "I'm sorry, but no, we are not having this discussion. Elizabeth is the sweetest, most gentle child I have ever met. I've spent months with her in my home, as well as months last year when she lived with Kate and Rob, and I don't believe Kate would ever ask for something like that. You either have the wrong family or, or..." I shook my head and backed out of the pew, bumping against the kneeling bench in my haste.

Father Daniels raised his hands. It looked like a cross between an attempt to calm and a benediction of sorts. "Nichole, please hear me out, please."

I stopped at the end of the pew. Perhaps this is what Jhon had been trying to say all along. That organized religion was a dangerous thing.

After the way the moms had treated me, how they had stared at Elizabeth like she was some freak, I didn't want to hear anyone out. Instead, I wanted to drive to the daycare and pick up my perfect child. Because that's what I had. I had a little girl who looked like a delicious blend of Jhon and myself, with her red curls and bright blue eyes. A little girl who ate her vegetables even if she didn't like them and who hugged me and kissed me and snuggled close when I read a bedtime story to her. She was perfect. She was everything I had ever dreamed of. And she needed me just as much as I needed her.

The silence hung between Father Daniels and me, thick, tense. I wanted to run, but I stilled and waited, praying he wouldn't tell me something that would further unsettle me. I didn't need that, and I sure didn't want it. When you receive a gift of the magnitude that we had, the last thing you want to do is look for the darkness.

Father Daniels sighed. "Kate first called me in the fall, after the adoption. She was worried about Elizabeth. It started with nightmares and then a depressive fearfulness had set in."

"She wouldn't have called you. Not for that. She would have called a therapist." The words sounded defensive, snappy even.

"She had. They'd explained it away as post-adoption blues and they had brought up the concern that it was, hm, a possible mental issue."

"Dissociative identity disorder, or DID, yes, she mentioned as much to me in an email." I nodded. "But she said nothing more, past that one email. She would have said something. I was her closest friend. And an exorcism? Seriously? Didn't those go out with the Spanish Inquisition?"

Once the words left my mouth, I wished for them back. Had I just attacked his faith? Something he had devoted his life to. Something he believed in. Now I really wanted to run. I imagined myself spinning around and digging in and pushing off, my legs stretching, my feet pounding, and the enormous building sucking up every squeak of sound.

He stared at me with what I could only interpret as pity. "Nichole, all I can tell you is what I saw. At first, in the fall, Kate was worried. By January, I could see she was *afraid*. And by early March, she was visiting daily, terrified of what was happening in her house. A few weeks later, she and Rob were dead and Elizabeth was with you. I half-expected you to contact me as well, but you didn't. After Detective Cummings reached out to me with questions, well, that's when I first called you."

"Scared? Terrified? Of what?" I asked, even though I didn't want an answer.

"Kate feared Elizabeth. I think she might even have been afraid for her life," the priest answered, his hands fisted together. "And after seeing what I saw, I feared for Kate as well. Fears that were realized."

I couldn't tell you why I walked away then. But I did. I didn't want to hear what this man had to say. I didn't want to believe anything was wrong with Elizabeth. Instead, I turned and fled.

He called after me, "Call me, Mrs. Staunton. If you need anything. Anything at all."

I didn't answer. My legs carried me outside, down the steps, and back to my car. As I slid into traffic with a squeal of my tires, heart and mind racing,

I told myself to stop talking to priests, or listening to granola-crunching moms. I shoved all the voices rising in my head like a scream into somewhere deep in my brain. To hell with them all. Every one of them had an agenda, whether or not I could see it, and I'd be damned if I was going to them ruin the joy that the three of us had made together.

Incident/Case #: 18-02521

Classification: Assault/Arson

Date: 2018-20-09

Location: Rush Creek, Raaen Road

Victim (s): Staunton, Jhon and Elizabeth

Suspect: Staunton, Nichole

Evidence ID#: 18-02521-014 (page out of handwritten journal)

My thoughts are muddled. Feels like thick syrup is clogging every part of me. I can't focus. Can't work. E skulks about. What does she want from me? Can't she understand I have nothing left to give her?

J comes and goes in my dreams.

I wake up each morning, unsure whether he is even real. Sit up, heart hammering, words on my lips unspoken.

"Are you here?"

"Or have you left me again?"

The silence in this house speaks louder than any words.

- N -

11. She's Coming

- Nichole -

September 21st, 2017 - Seattle, Washington

The scream woke me from a dead sleep and I was on my feet before I knew what was happening. There in the darkness of our bedroom, I wobbled toward the hall, my vision bleary. Jhon, as sound a sleeper as I normally was, was already in motion. "Lizzie screamed." He opened our bedroom door and dim light from the night-light on the wall seeped in, allowing me to get my bearings. He was already down the hall, Elizabeth's door open. I could hear the pitiful sounds of her sobs then, which sent me lurching down the hallway, reaching out towards the walls to steady myself as I shook the cobweb tendrils of sleep from my brain and did my best to put one foot in front of the other.

Jhon turned on the lamp shaped like a carousel. Pink stars danced across the walls and ceiling as the lampshade wobbled. Elizabeth launched herself into his arms, huddling against him, still sobbing.

"Hey," he said, and rubbed her back, leaning against her bed and rocking her. "Shh. You're okay, sweetheart. I'm here. So is Mommy."

Long before we had attended that last, emotional day at court, Elizabeth had dropped the awkward Mommy Nichole in favor of Mommy." And a few days after, Daddy Jhon had become Daddy. She still talked about Mommy Kate and Daddy Rob, but not since late July.

Marcus, Elizabeth's therapist, had pronounced her the healthiest, most adaptive child he had ever seen and told me I was welcome to return if there were problems down the line, but he didn't see a reason to continue with another therapist.

"She is a beautiful, happy child, Nichole. You won the jackpot." He had said it with a smile. "But then, I'm guessing you already know that." He'd shaken my hand. "Take her home, be her mom. And," — he drew closer, meeting my eyes — "I can see how hard this has been for you, that your fortune comes at such a price, and losing two good friends. But don't let your sadness overshadow this gift. Elizabeth is precious, and she is in the hands of two people who love her. It is what you all need. Never forget that."

I had wished him well. He was returning to New York, and he'd made it sound like a transition to another therapist was unnecessary, despite all that she had been through.

I joined Jhon, leaning in close, my lips grazing the tops of her curls. Elizabeth was damp, sweaty. Her tiny body shook with sobs and she said something, but the words muffled, absorbed by Jhon's shirt.

"What did you say, sweetheart?" Jhon asked, pulling away, and Elizabeth said it again. My sleep-tired brain wasn't functioning well. To me it sounded like nonsense, but Jhon frowned.

"What did she say?"

"I think she said, 'she's coming,'" Jhon answered.

"Who's coming?" I asked. Jhon gave a confused shrug.

I yawned and my jaw popped. "Come on, let's bring her back to our bed."

"We aren't supposed to co-sleep," Jhon protested.

"Well, it's a good thing we aren't foster parents, then." I grinned, and he chuckled.

A moment later, we shuffled down the hall, a many-limbed, odd-shaped lump of sleepy awkwardness. I lay down on my side of the bed, Elizabeth snuggled close against me, nestling her head full of curls against my chest, her small body curving into mine until I was the big C and she was the little one. I wrapped my arm around her. Jhon reached over and laid an arm over both of us. Together we formed a protective shield, and soon her whimpers and sobs ceased and her breathing smoothed, slowed, and deepened as she slipped back asleep.

"Her first nightmare," Jhon whispered.

I was already slipping into sleep. I replied with a mumble that probably wasn't actual words and returned to the dark abyss of sleep.

The sun wasn't even up when Jhon slipped from bed. I listened to the floorboards creak as he ambled down the hallway and into the kitchen. They were getting geared up for another location opening. We were staying put, the three of us, but Jhon would handle most of the details remotely, rather than going out of the country like he had before. He had been putting in twelve-hour days for two weeks now. I slipped back asleep and woke to the weak sunlight making its way across the room. Both bedrooms were east-facing, which meant the morning sun, if there was any, would shine in the rooms. This wasn't a problem for me. I was up long before the sun's rays kissed the edge of the sky. Today, however, I had slept in. Elizabeth remained curled against me, asleep. This was surprising as well. The two of us *both* sleeping in? I couldn't remember it ever happening.

I slipped my arm out from under her, and she mumbled and burrowed deeper into the covers.

The aroma of coffee greeted me. That and a burned-toast smell. Jhon never could remember to monitor the toaster oven. He burned a round of toast each morning, especially if I wasn't there to monitor it. I poured the coffee, took a sip of the lukewarm concoction, and frowned. Thirty seconds in the microwave and it tasted better.

"Mommy?" Elizabeth's face pressed against my leg, her eyes little more than half-open. She rubbed the sleep from her eyes with one fist, holding tight to my leg with the other.

"Hey, sweetheart! Good morning!" I set my coffee cup down and picked her up, holding her tiny body close to mine. She cuddled into me, quieter than normal, not her normal exuberant morning self.

"We both slept so late. My goodness! But that's okay, because today is Tuesday, so it's a you and me day. What do you want to do today?"

She didn't respond at first. Just cuddled against me, her fingers lacing into my hair and twisting it around her finger. Reserved. Quiet.

"Are you feeling okay?" I asked. She shrugged and nodded. I reached my hand up and felt her forehead. It felt normal.

"Hey, how about pancakes? We could go to CJ's, maybe even see if Daddy wants to join us."

"Okay." Elizabeth's response seemed muted.

I frowned and felt her head again. "Does your tummy bother you?" She shook her head. "Well, okay. Go get dressed and I'll call Daddy, okay?" I set her down and gave her a kiss on the top of her head.

Elizabeth nodded and padded down the hall to her room. Normally, the suggestion we go to CJ's was greeted with a shout of joy. The staff there loved her and would bring her one chocolate pancake, decorated with a whipped cream smile, blueberry eyes, and a maraschino cherry nose. Something was off.

She's just tired. That nightmare was a real doozy.

I resolved to ask her about it later, finished my coffee, and got dressed. The air outside felt cool, on the edge of chilly, and it was raining. Fall in Seattle was beautiful, rain or not.

It was a hectic drive to get to CJ's. In the last few years, the population in Seattle had exploded. An influx of California price refugees were now pushing real estate prices up to an almost unaffordable range for Jhon and I. Between that and the increased amount of traffic, we had talked several times about moving to a smaller town outside of Seattle, especially once we had accrued enough savings to buy a house. As it was, the urban sprawl was growing, and now the smaller towns inland were also getting expensive.

I was lucky to find a parking spot on my third circuit around the block and parked, waving at Jhon, who waited for us under the eatery's awning with a smile. His smile turned to a look of concern when he noticed Elizabeth's muted demeanor.

"Hey, sweetheart, are you feeling okay?" He scooped her up and gave her a kiss on the cheek. Whereas yesterday this would have elicited a giggle or an exuberant kiss back, today she leaned in and cuddled against Jhon. I smiled at the sight. They looked so perfect together, two redheads, one big, one small. I noticed a middle-aged female diner staring out at us through the large window, a broad smile on her lips. Even now, with her quiet behavior, Elizabeth drew attention and smiles.

"She's been like this all morning," I said. "She doesn't have a fever. I think she's just having an off day."

Jhon shrugged a little and then smiled. "Well, I can't complain about more cuddles from my little princess! Come on, let's go eat some pancakes and French toast!"

As we entered, the server, Leah, waved at us, gesturing for us to take the empty table. A moment later, she approached, a bright smile on her face for Elizabeth. "Lizzie! How's my favorite chocolate pancake-eating girl?"

Elizabeth looked up, her customary grin absent from her face. "I'm Elsa, not Lizzie."

Elsa? Yet another name change? Where had this come from?

Then Leah's grin faded a bit, and her eyebrows raised. She aimed a quizzical glance in my direction before she replied, "Oh, well, okay, *Elsa*. Do you still want a pancake?"

Elizabeth nodded. "But could I have a blueberry pancake instead? Please?"

Jhon and I exchanged glances, and I raised my hands, puzzled by the new name and behavior. It was odd.

Be thankful she's still her polite little self.

"I'll have my usual," Jhon and I said at the same time. We were creatures of habit, the three of us.

"Brilliant!" Leah caroled and zipped away. The restaurant was busy as ever, despite being later in the morning.

I leaned towards Elizabeth. "So, did you want to be called Elsa like the princess in the movie?" I searched my memories. We had introduced Elizabeth to several Disney movies. My favorite had always been *Beauty and the Beast*, and Jhon had been a fan of the classics - *Pinocchio* and *Snow White*. I couldn't remember us watching *Frozen*, but even if we hadn't, she could have seen it at daycare or even at a play date. Some moms I had made friends with had their televisions on all day. They were a far cry from the mom's group we had been booted out of back in June. And while Jhon and I were not big television watchers, it was possible she could have seen it at one of their houses on the days when rain stopped the group from meeting at the playground.

Elizabeth blinked and looked confused.

"I thought maybe you would have seen the movie *Frozen*, with Princess Elsa and Princess Anna. Maybe at Twyla's house?" I persisted.

"No."

"So what made you want to be called Elsa, then?" Jhon asked, looking confused.

"It's my name." She stared at us, shrugged, picked up a crayon, and began drawing on the paper placemat. Her lines, usually a mad bird's nest of squiggles, were clearer, more controlled and intentional. She concentrated on drawing. On a normal day, she would wave to the other diners and smile.

Today, she seemed withdrawn, quiet, and small worry lines appeared on her forehead and mouth.

The rest of the meal, and the rest of the day, was a muted, quiet one. The rain cleared, and we drove to the park after I saw on the group chat that several other moms would be there. Elizabeth continued to act off, so much so that the other moms noticed.

"Is she feeling all right?" Angela Tompkins asked.

"I don't know. She's been acting off all day." I watched as Elizabeth swung on the swings, keeping to herself.

"She's so quiet. She's never this quiet," Lydia D'Araujo noted. "Marisel thought she had done something wrong."

"She told the server at CJ's today that her name was Elsa, not Lizzie," I added, frowning.

"Oh God," Angela laughed. "Well, that explains everything."

"Does it?" I turned toward Jemima's mother, my eyebrows raised.

"Well, sure. I mean, think of it. Princess Elsa is moody and withdrawn, afraid of letting her powers hurt others. She self-isolates after losing her parents and locks herself in her room for, what, six, ten years?" Angela laughed again. "Classic defeatist strategies, severe depression, with a touch of narcissistic self-indulgence thrown in for good measure." Angela had been two semesters away from graduating with a doctorate in psychology when she learned she was pregnant. I liked her, but her constant psychoanalyzing got on some of the other mother's nerves.

"Okay, but I don't remember her *ever* watching the movie. That's the weird part. How could she be acting it out without having seen it first?"

Angela waved her hand. "Nichole, honey, *Frozen* is *everywhere*. There are ads for it, *Olaf's Frozen Adventure* just came out, and God, that was an *awful* sequel. There are a metric crap ton of books, coloring books, and more. For crying out loud, Lydia decorated Marisel's room in the full *Frozen* motif. Even if she didn't watch the movie, which she likely did at one of our house meet-ups, she has heard about it ad nauseum. Jemima is *obsessed* with that movie and can scream-sing every miserable song." She lowered her voice conspiratorially. "I misplaced" — her fingers traced quotation marks in the air — "the CD with the *Frozen* soundtrack last week." She giggled. "It's been the most peaceful week I've had in a long time."

Several other mothers laughed as well.

"Don't worry about it. Kids are always changing. Just wait until she is a teenager. Sheesh, we'll all be in for it then!" Lydia advised, and the other mothers clucked and groaned at the thought of the teenage years.

I sighed. "I hope you're right. It is so strange to see her like this."

"You won the kiddo lottery, Nichole, don't you forget that," Jan Bartholomew interjected. Her face was full and round, as was her petite frame, now that she was pregnant with her third child. Her younger son, who had just begun walking, had fallen asleep on the blanket, his thumb in his mouth. A tiny string of drool painted his rosy, fat cheeks. "She makes me wish I'd been lucky enough to have a girl." She winced then, as Aiden, her four-year-old, came roaring past, a foam sword clutched in his fist. "As it is, I'm surrounded by boys who refuse to put the seat down and won't pee straight, not even the *adult*!" The others groaned, commiserating with Jan's plight.

The discussion turned to the annoying things that men do, and how they each handled it, or didn't. I said little. I didn't have those issues. Jhon sat down to pee or aimed straight. He hung the toilet paper roll the right way, hanging over, not under. He squeezed the toothpaste from the bottom, rolling it up as he went. Jhon didn't scatter his dirty clothes everywhere. He even helped with cooking and chores and errands. And he was better at dusting than I was.

As the others bemoaned their men being handy but slobs, or hopeless at fixes but great at helping around the house, my thoughts continued to circle around Elizabeth.

There's something wrong, you know there is.

First Isabel, then Lizzie, and now Elsa. Each different in personality.

What if Kate was right? Could Elizabeth have dissociative identity disorder?

And what if she actually had *hurt Marjorie's daughter?*

I half-listened to the others talk, the voices rising, becoming louder, more agitated. I could feel my anxiety levels rising. And just as they were hitting a crescendo, Elizabeth's cries of pain snapped me back to present. Lydia was on her feet first. "Oh dear, it looks like someone ended up with a booboo!"

Elizabeth came towards me, sobbing. “Mommy, I hurt my wrist!” And indeed she had. Her left wrist was already swelling. “I fell off the swing.”

I gathered her in my arms and she melted into me, tears soaking my shirt. “Oh sweetheart, let us see.” Angela had worked as a nurse until last year. She examined Elizabeth’s wrist as Elizabeth whimpered in fear and pain.

“Well, Mama Bear,” Liz said after a moment, “I think a trip to the ER is in order. It could be a sprain, but with the swelling, I’m concerned that she might have a hairline fracture in the radius.”

Six hours later, Elizabeth lay asleep in Jhon’s arms, worn out, her tiny wrist encased in a small pink cast. She had picked at her dinner, unused to using cutlery with her right hand.

“How did I not even notice she is left-handed?” I asked Jhon after he tucked her into bed and closed the door. The wait in the emergency room at Seattle Children’s Hospital had been a long one. A bus full of children returning from a school outing had slid out of control and landed on its side. Most were just bumps and bruises, but they had taken the more serious cases to SCH. One of them Life Flighted in from the scene. We had sat for hours waiting our turn.

I felt awful. I should have been watching her, should have stayed closer. The voices in my head were reading me the riot act, and I felt awful, guilty, as if I had been the one to jostle her off of the swing. The staff at the hospital hadn’t made it better. They had questioned me, as if it were rare, this kind of fracture. I couldn’t help wondering if they thought I had hurt her on purpose and was just fabricating a playground injury.

“Babe, stop beating yourself up. Kids fall down. Kids get hurt.” Jhon’s voice was low as we returned to the living room. “I’ve heard the hospital can get a little nuts, almost aggressive, when they get a kid in with a broken bone. Don’t you remember the article in the *Seattle Times* when we were taking the foster care classes? About the foster parents they accused of child abuse? It turned out that the kid had RAD and was self-harming.”

“Elizabeth didn’t do it on purpose!” I protested.

“No, of course not,” Jhon soothed, reaching out to hug me. “She fell down, she got hurt, it happens. The hospital was just doing their job. Didn’t you say that they backed off when you offered to give them names of the other moms that were there?”

I nodded. Tears filled my eyes.

They thought it was your fault because it is. You weren't watching her close enough.

You are a terrible mother.

They can see you aren't her actual *mother. You are just a poor, inattentive substitute.*

Jhon kissed my forehead, his arms still encircling me. "Sweetheart, you are a wonderful mother. Elizabeth is happy here with us. She will be fine."

I wanted to believe that. And I wanted the voices to stop saying all the negative, awful things they were saying. If only Elizabeth would smile again. I wanted her to return to the sunny little girl I had spent the summer with.

But I didn't get that. Not that night, nor the next day, or for any of the days remaining in September, October, or November. As we moved into December and we made plans for Christmas, my happy little girl had vanished along with the sun. Her demeanor became as overcast as the sky outside.

The nightmares continued. First it was a couple here and there, and soon, at least three a week. By the time December rolled around, they were happening every single night. Our nerves felt frayed, our sleep cycles in shambles. Each night became the same. Screams. The screams were so loud there was no sleeping through it, no ignoring it. And always the same words, over and over.

"She's coming."

"She's coming."

"She's COMING."

Incident/Case #: 18-02521

Classification: Assault/Arson

Date: 2018-20-09

Location: Rush Creek, Raaen Road

Victim (s): Staunton, Jhon and Elizabeth

Suspect: Staunton, Nichole

Evidence ID#: 18-02521-015 (page out of handwritten journal)

I stare at the pieces of my life.

I no longer recognize myself.

The doctors can't help.

I'm alone in this.

Surrounded, yet alone.

I want to lock myself in the bathroom and scream. She's all I have, and God help me, I don't want her. Sometimes I wonder if I have ever loved her at all.

- N -

12. Winter's Child

- Nichole -

December 21st, 2017 - Seattle, Washington

If it hadn't been for the new therapist, and her suggestion to take notes of any developing behaviors or changes, I might never have put it all together. As it was, I still didn't figure it out immediately. Instead, it was a chain of smaller events, over time, that, when examined with the clarity of hindsight, told us everything we needed to know. By the time it all made sense, it almost cost us our lives.

Have you ever tried to put together a jigsaw puzzle that's been reversed, the blank cardboard side up, your only clues the shapes you are trying to match? You can't see the picture you are constructing. It felt a lot like that.

Elizabeth's most recent therapist was this warm, energetic woman in her mid-fifties. Elizabeth met with Zenzie every Tuesday at three in the afternoon, without fail. It was the same time she had met with Marcus before he had left to cross the continent and return to New York. After every fourth session, Zenzie would meet with me and ask questions, give suggestions. It was early on that she suggested a journal, one that would track things, changes in behaviors, and my own feelings.

"You don't have to share it if you don't want to, but it could help if we could look back and see if there were any specific events that inspired these changes in attitude or behavior," Zenzie had said.

What she said made great sense, and I got to work right away, working backward and referring to my journal to note specific dates. I added everything to a Google calendar, with Jhon's crazy schedule, appointments for Elizabeth, my own sculpting projects and more. It made sense to put it all in the calendar. Even our mommy/daughter outings went in there now that Elizabeth was recognizing letters and words. Once I had reviewed from March forward, I tried to jot down notes at least two to three times per week, but they had stayed the same since late September. The nightmares, first once-nightly occurrences, had increased in the last month to multiple nightmares in a night.

We had created a routine through the nightly disturbances. We would tuck Elizabeth in at night in her own bed, and, depending on whose turn it was, one of us would lie down with earplugs while the other stayed up and read a book or watched television.

As if she were stuck on some subliminal alarm clock, each night, at the stroke of midnight, she would wake from a nightmare, screaming. The one on duty would gather her up, calm her, and bring her into our bedroom, and we would cuddle up and go to sleep. It was a little harder now that there were multiple nightmares in a night, and both of us were feeling the effects.

Zenzie had assured us that in a situation like this, co-sleeping was helping, and who was I to argue? It felt right, and she was her sweet, cuddly self. If it were possible, I found she was even more willing to cuddle with us than she had been during the spring and summer.

And so the months wore on. We coped. And just when I was sure that this was it, the way things would be for the foreseeable future, it all changed on the evening of December 20th. Jhon was asleep when I was on duty for the night. I had just finished a chapter in the *Warrior of Kragdon-Ah*. I sat up, closed my Kindle, and stood up and stretched. My shoulders and arms ached. I had been working at the warehouse studio any day I could spare on the newest commission, a set of fairy children in various poses. The initial design had been approved. Now I would reproduce them in the full-size models. The last step involved using the lost-wax method in a nearby foundry. I was ready for Elizabeth to wake with her first nightmare so I could soothe her and then tap Jhon for his turn at the helm.

I stared at the clock on the wall, confused. It was three minutes past midnight and I had heard no screams, no nightmare.

Was it over? Had this stressful, anxiety-ridden time passed? Was she past the trauma?

Fool, no one just gets past *trauma. You know that.*

I turned off the living room light and padded down the hall, stopping at the split and listening for a moment. I could hear Jhon's even breathing, the clock ticking the seconds, without drama or hiccup.

And... nothing. No screams, no sobs, no crying out.

I nearly opened Elizabeth's door, but I didn't want to wake her. She had a big day ahead of her. She officially turned four years old at midnight. And miraculously, we seemed to have won a temporary reprieve.

She's sleeping. Open that door and she will wake up.

Take this as a win.

I heeded the voices and slipped into the bedroom Jhon and I shared. I slipped into bed and fell asleep, telling myself that maybe, just maybe, Elizabeth was returning to normal.

Later that morning, once awake, she asked for crepes, Jhon's specialty. He had blinked at her in surprise. The last time we had given her crepes, she had taken one bite and pushed the plate away.

"It's not my favorite."

Today, however, she dug in and the crepes disappeared. Jhon grinned, first at my whispered news that there had been no nightmare last night, and then at her sudden interest in his mad crepe-making skills. We celebrated her birthday with a group of friends from the mom's play group I had joined. The only other surprise of the day was her insistence that she was now Elizabeth, not Elsa.

The evening of her birthday passed in silence as well.

At first, I was excited. Maybe the therapy had worked. Maybe Elizabeth had grown out of it. I wasn't sure, but she also didn't seem as anxious or wracked with insecurities. There was no more waking from nightmares in the night and instead a calm, collected child appeared. The anxiety was gone, but so was the easy affection I had seen in Lizzie and the desperate clinginess I had endured with Elsa.

More and more I thought of them as different, these aspects of Elizabeth. When she called herself Isabel, Elizabeth had been timid and shy, yet sweet. As Lizzie, full of energy, vivacious, exuberant, and wildly affectionate. Elsa was anxious and fearful, but so affectionate. Who wouldn't want to cuddle a small child? Cuddles were one of the main perks of parenthood.

It was as if we had a taste of every flavor of a child in Elizabeth. Had I known then that we were about to experience something so dark, so terrifying, I wonder if I would have done what her birth mother had. Would I have left her on the steps of a church and run? Possibly.

But honestly? It was far too late. I loved her. It was no different for me than if she had been born of my body. I can tell you that truthfully. She was the same age, the exact same age, as our stillborn daughter Patricia, or Elizabeth, as I continued to think of her. It was as if fate had brought her to us, given us space in our hearts, and etched her into our family. We belonged together. The way here hadn't been easy. I still mourned Kate and Rob. I still felt a weird, uncomfortable guilt that they were gone and I had gotten my dream child. In my heart, Elizabeth was my child. I dreamed of our future together, and while I mourned the loss of Kate and Rob, I wanted nothing more than to wrap my arms around Elizabeth and never, ever let go.

These many months later, there had been no movement in the case, none. No leads. No new findings. Nothing. Classified as a homicide, it remained open on the books, but the police had stopped calling, which suited me just fine. The thought that a four-year-old child, well, three at the time of the fire, could have anything to do with it was insane. I was sure that, once they had thought about it, considered it, they must have thought the same thing. And Elizabeth? Our little girl? Not a chance.

Christmas followed on the heels of Elizabeth's birthday and we wanted it to be special. With everything she had been through, it wasn't hard. One of Jhon's co-workers showed up dressed as Santa with a stack of presents that the office staff had collected. Elizabeth had given one of her brilliant smiles in return, laughed and clapped, and tore into them. I already filled the space under the tree with piles presents - from us, from a toy drive through the foster agency, and even several of the moms in our play group. I worried about where we would store everything, but we had begun house-shopping and recently received a pre-approval for a loan that, given luck and good timing, could net us a larger home. Perhaps one with room for more children. I had been poring over several newer home designs where the smaller upstairs bedrooms opened out into a common space, perfect for a playroom. We would have room for all the toys, plus plenty more, when we moved. Until then, I would rotate them between Elizabeth's room and the storage shed in the yard. I hoped, too, that we could find a home big enough that we could welcome another child into our family. As an only child, I still remembered the isolation and loneliness. Hannah and Andy's former foster children often dropped in, and when they did, it only reminded me of how lonely it would be when they were gone again. We had such a perfect life. Another child for Elizabeth to play with sounded like bliss. Even watching the siblings in the playgroups fighting and quarreling didn't deter me. I wanted that for Elizabeth. Another little girl, perhaps close to the same age, would be perfect.

It was early January when the cracks in the façade first appeared. Oddities, words, and actions that just didn't jibe right. Elizabeth's behavior was atypical. Once more, we had a name change. The first time Jhon had called her Elsa, her lips had puckered, as if tasting something sour or disagreeable.

"My name is Elizabeth."

Jhon had blinked, shrugged his shoulders, and glanced over at me. "Well, okay then. Elizabeth it is."

Then there were the small things. Things that seemed to build bigger with each passing week. Her tastes in food had changed and she was fighting eating any vegetables at all. She'd also refused to use any of her Disney comforters and sheet sets. "Those are for babies. I don't like them."

She no longer wanted to go to the park, or the butterfly exhibit she had loved so much in the spring and summer. But then things took a darker turn.

There was a stray cat who showed up at our door asking to be fed. She was black, sleek-furred, and I would have adopted her if we hadn't been renting and the landlord had a strict no-pets policy. The cat had appeared in mid-summer, right after a wet week of rain, and Elizabeth had begged and begged until I relented and bought a stack of cat food tins at the grocery store. Each morning, she would carry out a half-can portion of the wet food and set it on the far corner of the stoop where the eaves gave protection from any stray raindrops. "She says her name is Clementine," Elizabeth had said, her eyes sparkling with excitement when she returned inside.

Jhon, sitting on the couch with his laptop, arched his eyebrows and gave me a look. I was a schmoo for kids and animals. I had fed a small army of strays in our first apartment. It had been located in a less than desirable part of the city and overrun with dumped or unwanted pets.

"She can't come inside, sweetheart. We aren't allowed to have pets," I had told her. And I had stuck to it, even if I had also continued to buy Clementine cat food each week at the grocery store.

"You promised to take Clementine with us when we find a house, didn't you?" Jhon asked at the end of September.

"Maybe." I avoided eye contact and focused on scrubbing the kitchen sink clean of all spots, real and imaginary.

He laughed, slipping his arms around me and nuzzling my neck. "And here I thought we were going to get a puppy."

"Dogs and cats can do well together. Especially if you get the dog when it is young and impressionable." I wiggled out of his embrace. His nuzzling had raised goosebumps on both my arms.

He followed, pulled me back into his arms, and kissed me on the mouth. "You are such a wonderful mom."

Clementine had done her best to convince us all that she needed to move *into* the house. And if I wasn't so desperate to get all of our security deposit back to help with the purchasing costs, I might have broken the rules. Instead, I bought a small, heated cat house in late November and Jhon had run an extension cord to it, shaking his head the entire time.

"It doesn't even freeze here. It says on the box the cat house is rated for up to minus ten degrees. I think it's overkill."

"Elizabeth is worried about her. This is a small price to pay."

Jhon shook his head. "Well, it's only for the winter, so..." He shrugged and rolled his eyes, holding back laughter.

"Oh, shut up." I laughed. "It makes her happy."

And it had. Until mid-January.

Each morning I set the can, or partial can, on the corner of the countertop for Elizabeth to take outside. That afternoon, after we had returned from errands out, I saw it was still there. Elizabeth sat at the breakfast bar, a brand-new coloring book and a box of crayons in front of her. She paged through the book, looking at every page.

"You didn't feed Clementine?" I asked, surprised. She hadn't missed a day, not even when she had a miserable summer cold in late August.

"She's not there," Elizabeth answered, still focused on the coloring book.

"Well, did you call to her?"

"No."

"Well, honey, take the food out and call to her. I'll bet she comes running."

Elizabeth shrugged, and a look of annoyance crossed her face, her lips flattening into a thin line. "Fine." She slipped off of the stool, snatched the can off of the corner, and opened the front door, closing it with more force than usual. Seconds later, she was back, climbing her way onto the stool and focusing on the coloring book.

"Did you see her?" I asked.

"No."

"Well, did you call to her?"

Elizabeth shrugged and turned the page. "I'm going to color this one." She reached for a black crayon. She had pointed to the coloring book in the bargain section and asked for it, and I had been too surprised by her choice to say no. It was marked down to fifty cents. Small wonder, it was a Halloween-themed coloring book, complete with creepy mansions and graveyards, and it was a far cry from her standard princess-theme choice.

I gaped at her. Every day, *every single day*, she had gone to the door and called to Clementine, a tin clutched in her tiny hand. The day before, I'd seen her crouched over the tin, adding something. When I had asked, she had said she was sprinkling catnip on the food. I had explained it wasn't like the herbs and spices I added to our food when we cooked, and Elizabeth had shrugged and walked inside to wash her hands. She doted on the cat. Now she didn't care?

I stepped outside and bent down to peer into the cat house. No cat. I looked over at the street. It was a busy street, but Clementine kept to this side of it. That likely had something to do with a large tom who had claimed the far side of the street as his own.

"Mrs. Staunton?" I looked up to see Jacob Matthews, our next-door neighbor, beckoning me to his side of the hedge. "Could you come over here for a moment? Just you, not the little one."

Jacob and his wife Fina were retired, and they'd put in an above ground pool the year before. They'd issued Elizabeth a standing invitation to come over whenever their grandchildren visited, which was often. He and Fina adored her, but at that moment, his face looked troubled. I called in to Elizabeth, "I'll be right back, sweetheart. Stay here, okay?"

Jacob meticulously maintained the hedge between our properties. He handled the landscaping for the landlords who had retired to Georgia, where their eldest daughter lived. He shaped every bush and tree with a careful eye. They trimmed the grass weekly and woe to the rare dandelion that pushed up from the perfect green turf. Jacob even went to the trouble of removing sticks, rocks, or other debris from both properties. Elizabeth loved to run barefoot through the grass and, considering the great care Jacob took with the properties, I felt safe allowing it. I made my way around the hedge and joined Jacob on his side. His face was grim. He nodded at a small lump on the ground covered with a piece of tarp. Clementine's fluffy bottle-brush thick tail was poking out.

"I found her here this morning."

I covered my mouth in horror, tears gathering in my eyes. "Oh no!"

"Didn't want the child to see it. It'd break her little heart. I saw how she was with the cat. I can bury it in back. But Fina thought you should know. Wanted to see if you thought Elizabeth would want to have a little funeral for her."

Tears leaked from my eyes and Jacob turned away, uncomfortable. "Was she hit by a car?" I asked, trying to stop from crying. I had to get it together before I told Elizabeth.

Jacob frowned, wiping his hands on his jeans. "No. I heard her. I was taking out the compost first thing after coffee and she was there, having a seizure. She'd thrown up too from the looks of it, and she had labored breathing."

"What in the world..." I knew nothing about cats. "Maybe she was sick, and we didn't know it?" She had seemed so healthy. Her coat was so sleek, and Clementine had been on the heavier side. I suspected we weren't the only ones who fed her.

"Looked to me like she'd ingested poison."

"Could she have eaten a poisoned mouse? Or, or maybe a poisoned mole?" The neighbors up the way had complained they had moles.

Jacob examined his hands, flexing the gnarled joints. "It's possible. But I saw her out just last night and she was fine. This came on pretty fast and, no offense, but that cat was the worst mouser I've ever seen. I watched a mouse run past her once and she didn't so much as blink. There's some black-hearted folks out there that don't like cats none. I've always preferred animals to people. Seems like they are more honest, but, yeah. Poison."

My heart ached for Elizabeth. Tears welled up in my eyes at the thought of someone doing that to such a sweet cat. "I'll tell her and get back to you soon. Thank you, Jacob."

I walked back inside. "Elizabeth, sweetheart, can you stop coloring for a moment?"

Elizabeth looked up from her coloring book reluctantly, a small frown on her face.

I took her hand. "Honey, sometimes sad things happen, and today, something happened to Clementine, and she died. Mr. Matthews found her and just told me."

I waited for a storm of tears. Elizabeth shrugged and said, "Okay." Then she returned to coloring.

I gaped at her. She had adored the cat. Was this the way trauma expressed itself? Was she internalizing it all? I wrote off Elizabeth's lack of response as shock. What else could it be? She had loved Clementine. I had seen that day in and day out for months.

I sent a text to Fina Matthews and asked her to tell Jacob that Elizabeth was too upset for a funeral and thanked them. Later, perhaps, Elizabeth would want to visit Clementine's grave.

That evening, when Jhon returned home from work, Elizabeth was already asleep in bed.

"I'm so worried about her, Jhon. She hasn't even cried. She must have taken this hard. I mean, she was even trying to give the cat treats yesterday, sprinkling catnip on her food."

Jhon frowned. "We have catnip?"

I blinked. "Um, yeah, I guess. That's what she said it was. It was in a bag. Pellets of some kind. She put it back in the pantry."

Jhon sat up from where he had sprawled on the couch, beer in hand. He frowned. "Catnip doesn't come in pellets, Nichole." He stood up, walked into the kitchen, and rummaged around.

Seconds later, a bag of RatX appeared in his hand, pulled from a dark recess of the pantry. "Holy shit, Nichole. Is this what she put in Clementine's food? How in the hell did this get here? Why would you buy something like this? This is poison!"

I gaped at him and the bag, my mouth working silently as I tried to put it all together. Separate memories slipped into place. Clementine had scratched Elizabeth a few days before as she slipped from Elizabeth's arms. I remembered being surprised when she slapped at the cat, which sent Clementine skidding out of sight. Later, at the grocery store, Elizabeth had slipped away for seconds while I stood at the meat counter, returning with what I had thought were cat treats. She'd put it into the cart. I hadn't looked at the bag, but it was the same bag Jhon was now holding.

"Oh my God, Jhon! She thought they were treats for Clementine! Remember when Clementine scratched her and Elizabeth swatted her? She told me she felt bad and wanted to give her a treat to make up for hitting her!"

"Christ. I'm getting rid of this right now. We're lucky she didn't eat it. Kids can do the craziest things."

We wrote it off. Excused it. After all, it was *Elizabeth* we were talking about. A little girl who had cried a bucketful of tears this past spring over a dead baby bird. The same girl who adored playing dress up and running a brush through my hair at night.

Elizabeth, whether she was called Isabel, Lizzie, or Elsa - was kind, sweet, and thoughtful. She didn't have tantrums, her playmates loved her, even the other moms commented on how sweet and kind she was. This had been an accident, nothing more.

Except that it wasn't an accident. Not at all. Neither of us knew what Elizabeth was truly capable of because we hadn't seen it firsthand. But we were about to find out.

Incident/Case #: 18-02521

Classification: Assault/Arson

Date: 2018-20-09

Location: Rush Creek, Raaen Road

Victim (s): Staunton, Jhon and Elizabeth

Suspect: Staunton, Nichole

Evidence ID#: 18-02521-016 (page out of handwritten journal)

The Devil card. I asked for guidance with E and pulled the Devil card. It is enough to make me want to get in the car and drive away. Leave her here. Maybe then I could sleep through the night without a nightmare, without fear.

She will be my undoing.

I feel like the string in a sweater, unwinding.

When it is all said and done, who will I be? Will I even know myself any longer?

- N -

13. Darkness Resides Here

- Nichole -

March 20th, 2018 - Seattle, Washington

Darkness, evil, it slips in. It isn't brash or obvious. It's... insidious. It creeps in and takes hold. When you realize it for what it is, well, it is far too late to go back.

Opening my eyes in the darkness, I was disoriented for a moment. What had woken me? For as long as I could recall, sleep was an elusive, inconstant thing. The therapist I had seen through my elementary and middle-school years said that it was due to the trauma. After all, the darkness held terrors, violence, dread. It held fire, too. I woke at the slightest sound and often could not return to sleep afterward, my brain firing a shot of adrenaline at the first rustle or thump, and my body was flooded with it.

Something had woken me. But what?

My eyes adjusted to the dark and another shot of adrenaline shot through me when I saw a figure standing on Jhon's side of the bed. A half-second later, I realized it was Elizabeth.

"Hey, sweetheart. Did you have a bad dream?"

For a few seconds, she didn't respond. Instead, she stood there unmoving, her gaze fixed on Jhon. He slept on, oblivious, his breaths low and slow. Then, just as I was about to speak again, Elizabeth bent over and set something on the floor. Then she turned and walked to my side of the bed. She rubbed her eyes and leaned against me. Her curls tickled my nose.

I put my hands around her and pulled her close. The last few weeks had felt especially off, and Elizabeth had been distant, quiet. At times, it had felt as if she was harboring a deep anger as well, though I had no idea why or where it was coming from. Jhon, with the latest expansion into an office in Venezuela, was exhausted and on edge. Elizabeth's mood seemed more temperamental, less sweet, and she had clashed with Jhon over dessert the night before, her lip pouting as he told her no to a second helping of ice cream.

"I don't like you anymore!" she had said, and marched into her room, closing the door behind her. She had even refused to hug him good night. It was a first, to be sure.

"Did you have a bad dream?" I asked again, and she nodded, wrapping her arms around my neck. I slid out of bed, lifting her up into my arms, and she cuddled into me. My heart expanded in my chest. This was the girl I knew. The one I loved.

How often had they said it in the classes? Trauma was part and parcel of this road we had found ourselves on. Even when they were smiling and laughing, even after they were adopted and welcomed into a healthy and happy home, every single foster child had oodles of trauma. And Elizabeth was no different. She had been abandoned by her birth mother, lost Kate and Rob in that terrible fire, been blamed by that first mother's group for her friend's broken arm, and lost a beloved cat. Loss and trauma. Trauma and loss. Abandonment.

"Come on, I'll get you back to bed."

She wrapped her legs around me and I carried her back to her room and slipped into the full-size bed beside her. We cuddled close. *Just until she goes to sleep,* I told myself. *She needs reassurance.* Under the fluffy blue comforter, the warmth and the early morning hour felt like lead, pulling my eyes shut. And despite the best of intentions, to stay with her until she was asleep and nothing more, I surrendered to sleep.

A yowl of pain followed by "Sonuva... what the hell is this doing here?" Jhon's voice interceded on my dream of a Mad Hatter's Tea Party, with Elizabeth playing the part of the Mad Hatter and me as Alice. I was yanked from staring down into my cup suspiciously to weak morning light with Jhon in the doorway holding a claw hammer, a disgruntled expression on his face. "This was on the floor next to my side of the bed," he said, and he reached down to examine his foot. "I stepped onto it and raked my skin against the claw of the damn thing."

Elizabeth sat up beside me, looking sleepy and perturbed. She stared at Jhon for a moment, frowned, and then pulled the covers up over her.

"Elizabeth, were you playing with a hammer yesterday?" I asked, wiping the sleep from my eyes, the last of the dream lingering with the disquieting vision of a bag of RatX sitting next to the teapot and the Red Queen shouting for me to drink the tea.

"No," she answered, her voice muffled under the thick covers.

I struggled to remember where I had seen the hammer last. Had it even been inside? It must have been. I had asked Jhon to hang a picture in the hallway. The order for a large canvas of the three of us had come in two days earlier, the best of a professional photo shoot the weekend after Elizabeth's adoption was finalized. We were lucky to have a small shed on the premises and to have access to it. It was far too small to park a car in, and far too dark and damp for me to use as a studio, but Jhon had quickly filled it with tools and totes filled with off-season clothes. I looked forward to us finding a home of our own that wasn't quite so small. The bedrooms in the post-World War II bungalow were cramped and there was virtually no closet space.

"I must have not put it back in the shed," Jhon said, wincing as he examined his injured toe. He didn't sound convinced. I remembered her bending down last night. Had she had the hammer in her hand? Could she have picked it up while half asleep? A feeling of disquiet crawled through me for half of a second before Elizabeth poked her head out of the covers.

"Mommy? Can we go to the park today?"

The breaking dawn looked gray and miserable. "We will have to see, sweetheart. Maybe we could go to the butterfly exhibit instead. Callie's mommy was talking about going today if it rained."

"I don't like Callie anymore." The edges of Elizabeth's mouth turned down into a grumpy frown.

I blinked in surprise. "Since when?"

Elizabeth shrugged and disappeared back under the covers.

"Get on out of there, kiddo," Jhon said as I slipped my socks on. "I need to help Mommy strip the bed. It's laundry day."

"Don't wanna," she said, her voice muffled.

Jhon's eyebrows raised, and he frowned. His mouth opened as if he wanted to snap off a retort.

I flapped a hand at him. "Don't worry about it. Who knows, maybe she's coming down with something."

Elizabeth was incredibly healthy compared to her playmates. I couldn't think of a single instance when she had been ill. The others, at least a half dozen of them, rotated through various illnesses, while Elizabeth sailed through unaffected. Perhaps one of the viruses her friends seemed to share with regularity had finally landed on her.

Jhon was on edge, but I wasn't going to let it cause a dust-up between the two of them.

"Sweetheart, if you want to sleep a little longer, go ahead. I'll make the bed later," I said to the Elizabeth-shaped lump in the bed. She didn't respond.

An hour later, she appeared, silently, in the kitchen. I was sketching out a new design and smiled at her as she clambered up onto the tall stool next to me.

"Are you hungry, sweetheart?"

She nodded. "I want peanut butter cookies and ice cream."

I stifled a snort of amusement. "I see. Well, I think that is more of a dessert item. You can have oatmeal, an egg sandwich, or yogurt with fruit. Which would you like?"

Elizabeth's expression soured. "I don't want any of those things."

I remembered the fostering classes, which had included some fantastic parenting tips. One night we had a substitute instructor. She was a young, bubbly woman who had tossed the dour instruction plan out of the window and given us gems to use in conversations with our future kids - such as giving limited choices - something I had just done with Elizabeth.

"Foster kids often feel out of control of their own lives. After all, what real decisions do they get to make? Give them several choices if you can. It will give them a feeling of power and control that they may have never felt they had before," the instructor had advised, and it had struck a chord with me. I could remember Hannah doing much the same thing with me in those first weeks and months I was in her house. In many ways, it helped me feel in control of at least some small aspect of my life. My wishes felt validated.

"I see. Well, that is what we have right now. Which one would you like the most?"

"I don't want any of those. We have macaroni and cheese. Or you can toast cheese sticks for me. I'll eat that," Elizabeth said coolly, her eyes steadfast, assessing.

The fostering classes had covered the potential of a child asking for something not offered and given tips on how to react. What they hadn't covered was a complete change in attitude. This was a side of our daughter I had literally never seen before.

"Elizabeth, that isn't a breakfast food. I am happy to give you macaroni and cheese for lunch, but right now, it is breakfast time, and breakfast is the most important meal of the day!" I smiled at her with a cheer I didn't quite feel, while staring at the expression on her face. The generally sweet disposition normally there was transformed into a discontented frown. It felt as if an alien had taken over my child's body and was speaking through her.

"I... want... *mac and cheese*!" A look of hatred flared in her eyes. Her tiny white teeth were set in a grimace.

Something in the deep, dark part of me reared up. It surged forward, a flare of anger. "Well, you aren't getting macaroni and cheese for breakfast and that's final!"

Her cheeks flushed, two red spots blooming across her pale white skin. "I hate you!" Elizabeth screamed and turned and ran out of the room, slamming the door behind her.

I started shaking. Part of me wanted to tell her I would give her the damned macaroni and cheese. Another part of me, however, wanted to shake her, slap her even, and return the hurtful words tenfold. Always the hurt, the anger, it roiled there. Usually far below the surface, sealed away in a black box where no one could ever see. It had come out a lot when I was young, in those first couple of years with Hannah and Andy. I hadn't understood it then, but thankfully Hannah had. She could see the hurt little girl behind the confrontation, the talking back, and the rejection. She had given me unconditional love, understanding, and patience.

I certainly hadn't been her hardest child to deal with. Andy and Hannah had fostered dozens of kids over the years, and I had met many of them as I grew up there in the house. Some would come to the door, long after they had aged out of the system, longer still since their stay with Andy and Hannah, and ask for help. Whether they stayed a night, a week, or even a month, I could see how much my adoptive parents cared. I think that seeing the others come back to what was, in some cases, the only safe place they had ever lived in, helped change my fear of rejection and allowed me to bond with them both.

You could have just given her macaroni and cheese for breakfast. In the bigger scheme of things, would it really have been so bad?

Give the kid an inch and she'll take a mile.

She's going to remember this. And she won't ever really love you. Not like she did Kate.

Kate was a better parent. More patient. Not damaged like you.

I shook my head, as if I could shake the voices loose, shake them out. I stood up and walked out the front door, my fingers dialing the phone, calling Jhon.

It rang three times before he answered. "Yes?" His voice sounded distracted, stressed.

"Are you busy?"

"Insanely so, and I have to be in a meeting right away. What is it?"

"It's nothing, really. I'm sorry I bothered you. It's uh, just a spat with Elizabeth over what to eat for breakfast. She said she hated me and ran off to her room." The last part came out in a rush.

I could hear the noise of the office recede as he closed the door to his office. "Oh hon, you know what they said in the classes."

"Yeah. Yeah, I know. She was just so *angry*. Uncharacteristically so. I just..."

I could hear the low, baritone voice of Jhon's boss intercede. "Jhon? Everyone else is in the meeting room."

"I'm sorry, babe. I gotta go." And with that, there was a click, and the line went dead.

I stared at my phone's black screen for a moment, unsure of what to do.

Get it together. Be a parent. Go tell the little brat she's going to eat what you tell her to.

You've mollycoddled her long enough. She needs to listen and behave, not try to manipulate her way around you and Jhon.

I hated all the voices. If they weren't telling me what a complete screw-up I was, they were casting doubt on Elizabeth. She was just an innocent little girl who had been through hell and back. Abandoned by her mother, surviving the murder of her adoptive parents and a house fire, and now trying her best to find her path. I had to be patient. I had to be kind. Consistent. Loving. I took a deep, cleansing breath of the cool air and slipped back into the house.

Elizabeth was perched on a stool at the breakfast bar, the macaroni and cheese leftovers from the day before open before her. Her mouth was bulging with a large mouthful. She turned and stared at me, then spat the half-masticated lump out into the open container.

"It tastes yucky when it's cold."

My mouth dropped open in shock.

"Go to your room, *now,*" I spluttered.

Elizabeth shrugged and slid off the stool. As she did, she muttered under her breath.

"What did you say?" I asked, feeling the anger slither through me, lighting up my own cheeks. I felt hot, flushed.

Elizabeth was halfway down the hallway. She stopped, turning to stare at me for a second. Then she smiled. It was the creepiest smile I had ever seen in my life.

"I said that you will be sorry." Then she turned away and continued down the hall, the door to her bedroom clicking closed behind her.

She didn't emerge for the rest of the morning. Our normal routine was a walk, or a visit to the playground with the local play group, but lately those get-togethers had been few and far between. Weather, illness, and a rise in spats between the kids had all contributed, and it had been well over a month since the last get-together. I frowned, realizing I hadn't seen anything in the group text in a while, which was odd.

I called Angela, Jemima's mom, and it went straight to voicemail. I left a short, cheery message. I hadn't seen her for over a month. Not since a disastrous group playdate had led to Jemima and another child falling from the play structure and nearly taking Elizabeth down with them. Elizabeth had been the only calm one amongst them, the other two wailing and sobbing loudly enough to draw gazes from all over the playground.

A few moments later, my phone rang, Angela's name flashing across the screen.

"Hey!" I said, smiling. "Long time, no talk!"

In the background, I could hear children playing and the sound of the morning train. The tracks ran close to the playground where we usually met. Angela's voice was cold, angry. "You need to stop calling me, Nichole. I mean it."

"I..." I swallowed, a cold tingling radiating up from my extremities. This had to be a bad joke. "What?"

"Oh please. Let's not play any more games. You've been calling late at night, saying nothing, just... breathing. Like you are some kind of stalker. Anthony tells me I should just ignore it, that eventually you will get on with your life, or whatever. But seriously, I'm sick and tired of it. Ever since I texted and told you what Elizabeth did to Jemima and Sadie... Bad enough you told me to fuck off, but the endless stalker calls? Really, this is just too much."

My mouth worked. It opened. It closed. But the words. I couldn't even make any words come out. Seconds later, I was staring at a blank screen and wondering what the hell to do.

I finally shook out of the funk. Checked my text messages, scanned back two months, and found nothing. What the hell was she talking about? What had Elizabeth supposedly done to Jemima and Sadie? And who had Angela texted? It certainly wasn't me. Whoever it was had told her to fuck off, which was weird and off-putting. Why not just tell her she had the wrong number? A stranger, obviously. It hadn't been me. I wouldn't have done that. Jhon wouldn't either.

I was a Luddite. It was well known. I had barely mastered sending texts recently, and as far as I could see, they were all still here. It certainly wasn't me who had sent a text to Angela. I stared at my phone.

Wait. Angela said I had called. Which I haven't. So if I look in my call history and don't find anything, I could send a screen shot of it, so that she sees it isn't me.

I began to comb through the call history. Nothing. Nothing. Nothing. *Wait...*

Her number appeared a week earlier, and a few days before that, and another week back. I wrote each instance down, then thought to tap on the circled 'i'.

February 28, 2018

1:15 AM Outgoing call

"What the hell?"
March 3, 2018
1:04 AM Outgoing call
March 8, 2018
2:01 AM Outgoing call
March 10, 2018
1:57 AM Outgoing call

The list went on and on. But always in the middle of the night, when Jhon, me, and Elizabeth were all asleep. It was impossible.

I set the phone down. I had looked at the list, returning to each call over and over on my phone until I practically had the dates and times memorized. All of them in the wee morning hours. None for longer than a minute. Someone in our house had been calling Angela. And it wasn't me. Unless I had suddenly started sleepwalking.

I checked the group chat. No one, absolutely no one, had posted in the group chat in over four weeks. Before that, barely a day would go by without someone posting. It was a small group, just five of us moms, but active. And yet, nothing for the past month. How had I not noticed? Had they simply cut me out and created a different group text that didn't have me in it?

I had to talk to Jhon. But he was in a meeting. Meetings. He had mentioned it yesterday after dinner. And considering the groundswell response to the last office opening in Peru, along with a new group of wealthy donors willing to invest millions into ULSC, those meetings would last all day.

Despite her behavior, Elizabeth sailed out of her bedroom at half-past eleven, smiling and happy.

"Can I have mac and cheese now, Mommy? I'm hungry."

The little girl I knew and loved was back. I stared at her for a moment, torn between addressing her behavior and letting it slide. She flashed a brilliant smile in my direction and my heart melted. She was still my sweet girl. This morning had been an aberration. It had to be.

What about what Angela said?

What happened to Jemima and Sadie on the playground?

Why were you cut from the mom's group chat?

Elizabeth isn't who you think she is.

I shook off the voices of dissent. They didn't make sense. What made sense was what was right in front of me. A little girl who needed me. A little girl I loved.

"Sure, sweetheart. Mac and cheese for lunch sounds yummy. Shall we have carrots and celery on the side? Or a banana?"

Elizabeth smiled wider. "Sure, Mommy. You choose. Then can we go out for ice cream?"

Don't you dare give that little brat ice cream after the way she behaved!

The road to hell is paved with good intentions. Yours are nothing but pitiful excuses to spoil a child into loving you. She'll never love you. Can't you see that?

"I think I could be talked into that."

Elizabeth's giggle as she climbed into a chair made my heart soar.

Our peace was short-lived.

Jhon returned home in a terrible mood. The office roll-out had faltered and failed without him there in Venezuela, and he had shouldered the blame. "I should have flown out there. I knew the staff was green, untested, and I should have been there."

He was wrapped up in his day, totally and completely, his mind still at the office.

"I want two scoops of ice cream for dessert," Elizabeth announced.

Jhon blinked as if he had just noticed her for the first time and zeroed in on the broccoli that remained on her plate, untouched.

"Eat that broccoli, and I'll make sure you have *one* scoop of ice cream."

"No." Her expression was openly defiant.

Jhon's eyebrows raised in shock, his mouth a round 'o' of surprise. He turned to look at me. I expect my face looked just as surprised.

"Excuse me, young lady?" I tried to sound stern, but I could hear my voice waver. I've never liked conflict, and after the morning's clashes, all I wanted was peace.

"I *said* I... want... ice... cream." She enunciated it slowly, as if she were speaking to village idiots. I gaped at her. What was happening here? Why was Elizabeth acting like this?

"Elizabeth, you had ice cream after lunch, remember?" I said gently, "We don't get to have dessert all the time, you know."

"*Ice... cream*!" Elizabeth said, glaring.

Jhon's ears began to redden, and two bright spots of red appeared on his cheeks. "Uh, no. That's not how it works, young lady. You will eat your broccoli *now*."

"Fine," Elizabeth said, pushing her seat away from the table. "I'll get it myself."

Jhon rose abruptly, the chair clattering to the floor behind him. Elizabeth marched over to the fridge and pried the door open. She could barely reach the freezer at the top, and I watched her open the refrigerator door and step inside it for the precious additional six-inch boost she needed to access the freezer. As she reached the cardboard container of ice cream, Jhon was there, removing her fingers from the container, while simultaneously trying to pick her up to return her to her seat at the table.

Elizabeth screamed wordlessly in anger. In the span of a second, she became a blur, a whirling dervish of kicking, screaming, and biting. Jhon swore as her fingernails raked a red slash across his arm.

"Elizabeth!" I tried to intercede as Jhon fought to control the wild creature in his grasp. Together, we fought to get control and move toward the bedroom. She bit me, hard, on the wrist and I yanked away, shocked at her violence. She was so tiny and I could not understand where this anger and hatred had come from, even as it manifested before me. The words that came out of her mouth were foul and her willingness to do violence in order to get her way was unprecedented. Jhon deposited her unceremoniously on her bed and slammed the door in her face with both of us on the other side, out of breath, hearts hammering.

She hit the door with a hard thump and I worried she would crack the cheap, hollow-core door with the force of the impact.

Jhon turned to me, his face flushed, his lip bloodied.

"What the hell was that about?" he asked. The door shuddered a second time. I could hear Elizabeth give a wordless growl on the other side.

"She's been like this for the past week, worse in the last couple of days."

Jhon stared at me. "And you didn't say anything?"

I couldn't look at him. Instead, I stared at the floor. "You've been preoccupied, and I thought if I just tried to be patient, it would pass. You know what they said about emotions in the classes. They come in waves.

Who knows why or when, and I was hoping she would just go back to her normal sweet self."

Another hard thump at the door. She muttered words I couldn't hear, then stomped away. A second later, I heard the bedsprings creak.

Jhon frowned, his mouth thinning, and walked away, back to the kitchen. I followed.

"What did she say?" I asked in a whisper.

"She said we would both be sorry," he whispered back tightly. His eyes searched mine. "Nichole, why haven't you talked to me about this?"

Go on, tell him, you little fuck-up. Tell him how you haven't paid any attention to the fact that you've been cut out of the mom group. Tell him about the phone call with Angela. And the weird outgoing calls over the past month or more. Tell him how you don't have a clue how to be a good mom, you've just been winging it, and now look at it. What a loser you are! Can't get anything right, can you?

I wanted to tear these voices out of my brain. I wished I could reach in and scoop them out, even if it meant removing a hunk of gray matter in the process. I struggled to form the words. When they did come out, they sounded whiny, weak, and desperate.

"I've tried, Jhon. But you're busy with work and I thought I could handle it. I just try to give her what she wants most of the time, and that's usually enough."

And I had. I'd basically given over control to a four-year-old. Looking back at the past three months, I'd slowly but surely ceded control to Elizabeth. I hadn't meant to do it. I'd just wanted her to be happy. And hadn't she had enough unhappy things in life, already? So she ate mac and cheese and ice cream. So what if she wanted two scoops of ice cream and no broccoli? Was it really that bad?

Yes! She's been manipulating you for weeks! For months! You aren't acting like a mother; you are acting like she's your best friend. You're letting her be in charge! She needs a good slap on the rear, that one.

God, how I hated the voices. Surely there was a happy medium somewhere between the authoritarian line the voices inside my head called for, and my permissive daily behaviors. All of a sudden, everything felt unbalanced and out of control. Tears gathered in my eyes. Why couldn't I get this right? How had I gotten so far off course? Elizabeth was a gem. So how had I managed to get it all so twisted up? I'd been too permissive, too easy, and somehow I'd spoiled her. What else could explain it?

Jhon pulled me close and hugged me. "Sweetheart, I'm so sorry. I've left all the parenting up to you, and we are in this together. It's just a phase. And you are a wonderful mom! Don't beat yourself up so much. As soon as this next rollout is complete, I'm going to pick up the slack, I promise."

Elizabeth didn't respond to my soft knock at her door half an hour later. I cracked the door and peered in to see a lump huddled under the covers. Asleep. Of course.

Sick, no doubt. Not surprising you didn't notice. All you care about is you.

I grimaced and resolved to call my therapist in the morning. I needed someone to talk to.

That night, Jhon and I turned in early, too stressed out and exhausted from the altercation to watch TV or read. We had no idea that in less than two hours we would be fighting for our lives.

Incident/Case #: 18-02521

Classification: Assault/Arson

Date: 2018-20-09

Location: Rush Creek, Raaen Road

Victim(s): Staunton, Jhon and Elizabeth

Suspect: Staunton, Nichole

Evidence ID#: 18-02521-017 (page out of handwritten journal)

The Moon. Of course. Especially after the visit from the social worker. The voices told me what to do, what to say. I made tea. Talked about the weather. Made nice. Admitted nothing. Damn that teacher!

I should have known better than to send her to school. The voices warned me, and I ignored them.

- N -

14. He's Coming

- Nichole -

September 18th, 2019 - Brisbane, Australia

"And then what happened?"

"That night, she tried to kill us. And she very nearly succeeded."

I can tell from the look in his eyes that Vincent didn't believe me.

I can't blame him. Some days it is hard for even me to believe, and I lived through it.

My stomach twists; my entire core aches from sitting in one place for so long, in an uncomfortable chair. Is it morning yet? It has to be. It was dark when they brought me here, but by now, outside, the sun has surely risen.

The world moves on while I sit here and talk and talk. I can see Vincent is waiting for me to go on, but my mouth is parched, my throat aches.

How long have I been here? How many hours have passed?

I think of Jhon and my heart skipped a beat. Will they even tell me if he was okay? If he is alive?

"Mrs. Staunton?" Vincent leans forward. I can smell his cologne, and behind that his familiar smell. Even a decade later, I recognize it. Skin knows skin. Body knows body. "Do you need something to drink? To eat?"

How solicitous. And perfunctory. How formal.

A sudden flash of us together in the basement of Larry Abbott's house off of St. John, kissing for the second time. Of all the places to run into Vincent Gallagher, I had not expected to see him over 8,000 miles away from Kansas City. The Vincent I knew hadn't dreamed of traveling the world. He had loved where he was. He was at home in Kansas City, alongside his large, extended family who were scattered all over the metro. I remember him telling me they had been there for more than four generations.

I saw it in his eyes, standing there, his back to the camera, his eyes holding a warning just as the note said it all. And I know, I *know*, he is breaking all kinds of rules by sitting here and questioning me himself. I've watched enough crime shows. Questioning a former lover, isn't that a conflict of interest?

I want to ask how he is here, how in all the gin joints in all the towns, in all the world, he walked into mine. I want to see him smile at the cheesy line. I want to hear him laugh. We'd had that, those moments, that connection, for a dozen years. A friendship and easy camaraderie that turned on its ear in high school, blossoming into something else. Growing into a love that we both believed would last forever.

He might not have been my first boyfriend, or my first kiss, but he had been my first lover. And long before that, my best friend. I had walked away from it — run, if I am being honest — so convinced I wasn't worthy, that I couldn't have that love, and that I didn't deserve it. I had run from Kansas City all the way to Seattle and never looked back. And now, here he was, sitting in front of me, an impossible feat, half a world away from where we'd started.

"Nichole?"

He is waiting for an answer, and I am lost in memories of a life I no longer live.

"Yes, please. A water would be nice."

"I'll be back in a moment."

I stand slowly, alone in the concrete room with cheap square carpet tiles. My sit bones ache. I reach back and try massaging my aching back, try to ignore how my legs tremble. I need to know that Jhon is going to be all right. I try to imagine what it will be like without him and simply can't. He is my rock, just as Vincent once was. My stomach clenches again, more of a stabbing pain this time, and I run a hand over my belly, feel for my unborn son, and try to summon some level of calm. After all, I have lucked out. If anything good can come of this disaster. This is Vincent, a man who *knows* me. At least he who *knew* who I was as a person back then. Ten years away from him, true, but we have been friends since I was six years old. He knows me better than I know myself. He knows the girl I had been and the woman I became. He saw my journey over twelve long years. And if I am to be completely honest, had I given him the opportunity, he would have stuck with me. I know he would have. I had been the one to break it off. I had ended it. I had thrown away someone who loved me because I had let the voices tell me I didn't deserve him.

And here he is, giving me the benefit of the doubt, trying to understand, and doing his best to protect me. I can see it so clearly. The voices are muttering, a low susurration of commentary that I am doing my best to ignore.

You left him and broke his heart.

He's moved on. Married. See the ring on his hand?

He's never going to believe you. Jhon is as good as dead and you'll be put in prison.

Your son will grow up without a mother.

I rub at a spot on my left temple where a headache has set in and I feel my stomach contract again. This time it hurts, the pain sharp and twisting, and all too familiar.

"Sweet boy, I need you to hang on," I whisper, feeling for him, praying that through all of this, he stays alive. Not like before, not like my little lost girl.

The door clicks and swings open. Vincent steps inside with a bottle of water and a glazed doughnut on a paper plate.

He sets them down on the metal table and sits down, his eyes never leave me. I wonder what he is thinking, then I briefly examine a paranoid thought that he has followed me, not just across the country from Kansas City to Seattle, but to a completely different country. Our eyes meet. I'm not ready to talk again. Not yet. He hasn't told them he knows me, so I'll play along.

"You're American," I state.

I watch an unreadable expression flit across his face. "Yes, I am. Born and raised in the heart of America. I emigrated out here six years ago."

"For your wife?" My eyes zero in on his wedding ring and he pulls his hand back down, out of sight.

"Something like that." His eyes flick to the CCTV on the wall behind him, warning me. Playtime is over, and we are being watched. I sit down again, reach for the water bottle.

"A doughnut. How ubiquitous," I quip, then pick it up and take a bite. Immediately, my stomach flips and twists. Another contraction knifes through it.

Shit.

I swallow the bite, then three more in quick succession, determined to ignore the obvious. I open the water bottle, gulp down the water, and revel in how it soothes my raw throat.

The water is soothing, but the doughnut has the opposite effect. In addition to the growing contractions, I now feel nauseous. A nasty combination of stress, discomfort, and reaction to the sugar has my body sweating and cold. The contractions began to intensify.

"I'd like to go back to your last statement, Mrs. Staunton. You stated that Elizabeth tried to kill you and your husband" — he consults his notes — "and this was on March 21st, 2018. Is that correct?"

"Actually, no, it was the 20th, while Elizabeth was still in control. Shortly before midnight," I answer, trying desperately to not react as my body quickly wrests control away from me. Of all the times to go into labor, this was not it. I struggle to formulate the words. "I didn't stop her. I couldn't. And neither could my husband. He was unconscious, and I had a broken leg."

Vincent frowns, his head angling to one side. I remember teasing him more than once that he looks like a confused dog when he does it. Another contraction hits and, worse, my mouth begins to salivate heavily. I stand up again, feeling desperation take over.

Vincent stands up as well. "Mrs. Staunton?"

"I..." I cast about for something, anything, but the room was empty, not even a trash can. The urgency is rising. "I think I'm going to be..."

My body erupts, betraying me utterly. The meager contents of my stomach empties into a great splat of chunks and saliva that spatter everywhere, including Vincent's shoes. Simultaneously, my waters break, cascading down my legs, wetting the jail uniform they had given me just hours before. The contractions knife through me and I wobble in place, shocked at their violence.

"Sick."

To his credit, Vincent doesn't return the favor. Instead, he turns on his heel and leaves the room, returning seconds later with a roll of paper towels, a trash can, and another bottle of water. He tears off a handful of towels and hands them to me. I wipe my mouth, coughing, and I suck in a breath as another contraction hits. Tears are running down my cheeks. I am standing in a puddle of water, my jail-issued pants damp, clinging to my legs.

"And you're in labor. I'm calling for transport to the hospital."

Damn, it hurt. All the memories of the first time came back. I tell myself this was different, but still, all I want right now is Jhon's hand in mine. Instead, I feel Vincent's hand on my shoulder. I remember his smell, his steadfast love, his attention and loyalty. In so many ways, Jhon and Vincent are cut from the same cloth. His familiar scent filled my nostrils, and I close my eyes. I am transported back to those lazy summer days swimming at Longview Lake, my body wrapped around his. I would tuck in close to him as we rode his motorcycle down the back roads. Hannah always worried about us taking highways. I remember making love to him, and the feel of his hands exploring my body. Part of me wants to cling to him, another part wants to kiss him, just to see if he still tastes the same. I remember losing the child we had made just weeks after learning I was pregnant. His hand holding mine a mere dozen days later at the funeral for Hannah and Andy. The bereft look on his face when I broke off our engagement and fled for the West Coast.

Another contraction knifes through me and the door opens. Two paramedics, a wheelchair at the ready.

I walk on my own two feet as far as the outer hallway before another contraction hits, and I teeter in place. The next thing I know, they are strapping me onto a gurney and the lights on the ceilings above are slipping past. Whatever birth plan I hoped for, it was shot to hell now. We had never counted on this. Not on Elizabeth breaking out of her room and attacking, and certainly not on our baby coming nearly three weeks early.

I huff and puff, cry and moan, and desperately wish I had an epidural. Epidurals, however, are reserved for those who aren't already in the *final* stage of labor before they arrive at the hospital. I know that isn't in the cards, not a chance. This baby is coming and there will be no compromise or delay.

The sun outside is bright, the air nippy, but it is that final half-hearted gasp of winter before the world down under turns to spring with open arms. I can smell spring coming. Just around the corner. A promise of life beginning anew, of safety for our little family. We were close, so very close. But not close enough.

As they load me in, all I can think of was the last time I was in labor and loaded into an ambulance. The panic rises in me, and I can feel my heart hammering in my chest as the contractions seem to blend into one continuous wrench of my insides. I hear that Scientologists gave birth silently, without medication. All I can think in this moment is that they are completely fucking insane. That or superhuman robots. There is no way, no way at all.

You're going to die.

Your baby is going to die.

What have they done with Elizabeth? Where have they put her? It will be your fault if she kills someone else. You swore you would never let that happen again.

I try to breathe the pain out, try not to scream. The female paramedic, her dark skin, broad face, and kinky brown hair clearly identify her as an Aborigine. She attaches a fetal heart rate monitor to my distended belly, humming gently as she does. It has a soothing effect, and I focus all of my intent on that.

"I have a 29-year-old female, in labor with an ETA of eight minutes. Requesting an OB team on site. Fetal heartrate of 150 BPM. Prep for a possible VBAC."

Tears course down my cheeks. It isn't just the pain, but the fear, God, the fear. That after all this, after coming so close to spring, we have fallen short. Jhon hurt, possibly dead, Elizabeth days from losing her hold, and her body's control falling to Isabel's gentle hand. Me, giving birth to a child who might never know his father or his mother, a child conceived in love, wanted and prayed for. Will I lose him too?

The Aborigine woman smiles at me and continues to hum. I focus on it, held it front and center. The hum fills me. I can hear the beeps leveling out, the agonizing pain from the contractions subsiding. Still there, but transmuted somehow, receding from the forefront of my brain as the humming replaces it.

And then I feel the ambulance stop. The doors open, the early morning sun bears down, the air crisp and clean. It is time. Time for me to meet my son. Time for nothing else but this, this ancient practice, one that billions have experienced before me and billions more will long after I am gone. The primal separation from a life intertwined to two separate lives. The gurney moves swiftly into the hospital and I feel everything change again. The need, the urgency that all the books had told me I would feel slams through me.

"I need to push," I pant, feeling it flow through me, bearing down whether they are ready for me to or not.

I feel the gurney accelerate, skidding around a corner, down another corridor, and the smell of everything changed. If life has a smell, a different odor, I have found it. Don't ask me to describe it, for I cannot. I only know that I am smelling the beginning of life. As if Theo has already entered the room.

I sit up on my elbows and push again, humming as I do. I think of the countless women who have come before me lining up, shadowy figures of support. I am one with them. I push again.

"The baby's crowning. Almost there, Nichole, just one more now..." The paramedic is gone, replaced by a nurse with a close-cropped shock of white hair. The hum remains.

I feel it build. This moment, this second, this life - the hum tells me to push, and I do, feeling the pull and push of him sliding out of me, leaving the safety of my womb for the capriciousness of the world at large. His shoulders catch momentarily, then turn, adjust, edge their way out, the rest of his body follows. Seconds later, what feels like an eternity but had to have only taken a second, perhaps two, I hear his cry.

My eyes open, no longer intent on the hum. It had centered me, gotten me through it, and brought my son into the world. I am thankful for it. My heart soars as I drink in the sight of him. His squashed little face, his red shock of hair and pale skin. Jhon's son. My son. I reach for him, desperate to hold him for as long as I can. Any moment they might take him away, might send me to jail.

The nurses see my jail uniform, but the look on my face, desperation and love and terror all rolled into one, must strike a nerve.

"Here you go," she says, speaking to my son, "Here's your mommy. I'm giving you to her right now." She places him gently in my arms, his body is still covered with the vernix paste that kept his body insulated and warm inside of the womb.

"Take a few minutes," she says to me. "Hold your child. He'll need to go to the nursery for now, but I hope we can bring him back soon."

"Thank you," I whisper, tears rolling down my cheeks. I wish that Jhon were here in this moment. Our son is perfect, and a replica of his father's newborn picture currently in storage back in Seattle.

He blinks at me with the foggy blue that most newborns are born with but few get to keep. He looks slightly befuddled, as if the world were loud and overly bright. It most certainly is overwhelming. His cries have stopped and one fist, closed tight, waves in the air as he settles into my arms. He is perfect. Isabel, Lizzie, Elsa - they will all love him.

If they get a chance to meet him.

I sigh. The voices won't give me a moment's peace. Not even now. Not with all that has happened.

They watch me closely. I feel the nurse's eyes on me, and I hear Vincent's voice in the corridor, although he does not come in. Not until the nurse says gently, "Nichole, I need to take him to the nursery now, and you need to eat and get some rest."

I nod, tears slip down my cheeks. The tray that they bring has a sandwich, including vegemite, on the side. I shudder. I have never understood how anyone could or would eat the stuff. I pick at the pudding, but the truth is that I have no appetite. I worry about Jhon, about our baby, and yes, even for Elizabeth and whoever has the misfortune of caring for her.

Two and a half more days until Isabel.

Sweet little Isabel. The fear that will flood through her in that moment of transition. It makes me ill to think of how she will feel if she can't see me, if she loses Jhon.

"You need to eat," a familiar voice says. I look up into Vincent's handsome face. "It will help bring your milk in. At least, that's what they told my wife."

"Is there any word on Jhon?" I ask, pushing the plate away. "Is he out of surgery?"

"Yes."

He says nothing more. There is so much I want to ask him, starting with how in the hell he is here in Australia. But so much more. Does he hate me? Can he forgive me? Is he happy? How many children does he have?

So many questions.

He draws closer, his hand on mine. I can still feel the electricity, the connection, that has always moved between us. Perhaps if we had stayed together, never parted, perhaps it would be different, and the connection dulled. But in this moment, despite us both being married, and me having just given birth, I feel it stirring inside of me. He deserves better from me. If I had it to do over, I wouldn't have left. I would have stayed.

The voices are so loud. *So* loud. And they have been wrong as well. I have deserved love. His love. Our love.

I recognize it, and a bittersweet tendril of sadness runs through me. We have moved on, each of us marrying someone else, and I can't unmake my decision. Nevertheless, I feel the weight of it pass between us.

"Nicky, they won't let me stay. Not today. So rest, and I'll be back tomorrow." He speaks quietly, his eyes straying to a nurse who has entered the room, his hand pulls away.

"We will continue this interview tomorrow, Mrs. Staunton," he says, louder, and nods to the nurse before exiting without a backward glance.

The tears slip down my cheeks again, my body shakes with exhaustion and hormones. In less than 24 hours, I have seen my husband nearly die, bludgeoned my daughter to stop the attack, nearly passed out trying to drag them both from the house while it was on fire, been arrested and interrogated by my ex-fiancé, and given birth to my son.

"Oh honey," the nurse clucks as her hand squeezes my shoulder. "You are exhausted and worn out from all of those hormones rushing through you. The doc wants you to eat and rest, and it looks like you aren't too keen on eating, so let's get you rested, all right?"

I nod. She adds something to the IV and I feel a heaviness roll through me.

"That's it. I'm going to set your bed back down, get you another blanket, and dim the lights."

My eyes are so heavy that, try as I might, I can't stop them from slipping shut, my body succumbing to the need for rest. My think of Jhon, fighting for his life. I think of Elizabeth and the promise of Isabel just days from appearing. I can only hope that all of attempts at a normal life haven't been lost. The sedative surges through me and I let my exhausted, aching body slip into the heavy stillness of sleep.

15. The Journal

- Vincent -

September 18th, 2019 - Brisbane, Australia

I walk away from Royal Brisbane and Women's Hospital, my memories are filled with Eli's birth four years ago. And not just that. Justine and I came here just seven short months ago to pick up our newborns, Jarrah and Jedda. That was before Justine asked for a trial separation, one that grew to include a divorce petition. There is something about seeing Nicky's newborn that moves something primal in me: the need to fix what I broke in my marriage, to reconnect with Justine, and be present for my children. God knows I have tried. Sometimes it seemed like the harder I try, the more Justine pulls away. Whatever she wants, it isn't me.

I push Justine out of my mind. I need to see the crime scene, or what is left of it. A twenty-minute drive and I arrive at the Staunton house. It is still smoking, and I can see Trevor Stevens, an investigator for the fire department, poking about.

He looks up and waves me over. "Vincent! You working this case?"

"I am. Good to see you back in action." Trevor was investigating a fire nearly a year earlier when a section of ground had caved in. We had learned later that the sole occupant of the house was a conspiracy nut. The Aussies didn't have as many of them as the U.S. did, but they still ran into the type down under. The guy had used a sledgehammer to break through the floor of his large walk-in closet and then burrowed under the ground, creating a tunnel to his fallout shelter. This had collapsed when the house caught fire and the firefighters turned thousands of gallons of water loose, much of it swamping the already unstable tunnel. Trevor had fallen over six feet, broken his femur in two places, and been hospitalized for a week. Months of rehab later, and here he was, back on the job, moving slower, but hell, he was upright.

"Thanks, mate. How's your latest set of ankle biters?"

I laugh. "The twins? Growing fast. So what do you know so far?"

Trevor scratches his nose and looks over his shoulder at the smoking ruin. "It started in the garage and looks and smells like petrol for an accelerant. Likely the can they used to fill the mower. It was on its side."

Half of the house is a blackened ruin, whereas the other half is smoke damaged. I nod toward the stairs, gaze up to the second level that includes the bedrooms. "Okay to go up?"

Trevor nods. "Stick to the right-hand side and don't go toward the larger master bedroom near the back. It's unstable."

No great surprise there. It sits directly over the garage and kitchen, whereas the two smaller bedrooms over the front half of the house look as if they were barely affected. The reek of smoke fills my nostrils as I make my way up the stairs and into what turns out not to be a child's bedroom but is instead Nicky and her husband Jhon's room. Drywall, buckled and brown from the torrent of water, looks on the edge of crumbling, the windows along the front are broken out.

The hallway leading to the master bedroom in the back is dim, but something head-height on the half-closed door catches my eye. A lock. A deadbolt? One that takes a key to operate from either side. It was on the outside of the door. Was that the door to Elizabeth's room? I glance at the two smaller bedrooms. No locks. The door to the master bedroom is open, and after my eyes adjust, I can see inside it. It is sparsely furnished. I can see a mattress on the floor in the left corner. Under the window sits a heavy desk with what looks like crayons and a pile of paper. The edge of a dresser shows on the right next to the door to the en suite bathroom.

The small bedroom next to Jhon and Nichole's room contains boxes and what appears to be a half-assembled crib. The baby's room. I peer again into what remains of the master suite. The window has a western exposure, and the sun's rays are intense as it slips toward the edge of the horizon, painting the sky with salmon and orange and yellow. We'd had a few wildfires spring up along the interior, and with it, breathtaking sunsets for the past two weeks. There is something about the view, though. Something not right. I stare at the window, and then back the other direction through the nursery window. Both are smoke and fire-damaged, and the flames have charred the curtains that are there in the master suite. But there is something else. I pull out my phone and take a photo of each room.

As I step over the threshold into the mid-sized bedroom positioned over the front of the house, I can see Nicky's touches everywhere, despite the fire and smoke damage. She always had a knack for it, a way of making a room welcoming and comfortable and stylish. I note she has arranged a small space on a tall dresser to display her sculptures. In a few steps, I cross the room to pick up one piece. It is of a child, elfin features, innocent, wide eyes. She has captured the child's innocence perfectly. Another, a girl not unlike the first, but with a riot of curls, a sprinkle of freckles across her face, and an almost calculating look in her eyes. It impresses me. The depth of expression, the level of detail. Nicky's abilities as an artist and sculptor were always impressive, but she has obviously honed her skills in the last decade. I Google her name and find a series of sculpture installations by her around the United States.

I set the figurine down and scan the room. I'm unsure what I am looking for. The tale she has told is so unbelievable that I struggle to reconcile it with the down-to-earth girl I knew, grew up with, and fell in love with. Somehow, I have to find something here, in this room, her room, Nicky's sanctuary. The place where she felt safest.

And why this room? Why not the master bedroom? I think of the lock on the outside of the door. Had they locked their daughter in there? Had they chosen that room so that she didn't have to leave to use the restroom? If so, did that mean they locked her in at all times?

My eyes survey the cramped bedroom. They stray to the bed. The bed where she makes love to her husband. A man who isn't me. A man as different from me as you could get.

I don't want to think about the feelings that seeing her again stirs in me, no more than I want to imagine her with another man. Her husband. Jhon. I glimpsed him through the large window in the ICU. Intubated, spatters of blood still marking his face, his arms. Bandages encasing his chest, abdomen, and arms. He is red-haired, freckled, slight of build. My thoughts stray back to Nicky. How did they met? Why did she choose him? What makes him better than me?

I open the nightstand drawer with a gloved hand. There is a bottle of prescription meds inside, nestled next to a set of nail clippers and tweezers. I reach in, pick it up, read the label... guanfacine. I recognize it. The doctors suggested that Eli might benefit from it in a few years. It lowers blood pressure, but it is also used to treat ADHD in children, which Eli had in spades. Nicky didn't mentioned having high blood pressure. Then again, perhaps she hadn't gotten around to it.

I look underneath the bed. The best insight to understanding a perp is in the belongings they keep close. And the underside of beds ranks pretty high up there. I notice a familiar small floral cardboard box under the bed. I kneel down, ignoring how the sodden carpet squishes and soaks my knees as I lever the box out from underneath the box springs. The sodden cardboard lid flops open to reveal documents, newspaper articles, and more. I shuffle through them. There is a newspaper article that details a house fire. The date matches it to the one that took her mother's life and nearly killed her as well. A birth certificate, one that shows Hannah and Andy as her parents. She showed it to me once, years after the adoption.

"The state changed my birth certificate when Hannah and Andy adopted me," she had said, her finger tracing Hannah's and Andy's names on the official document.

I know that now. We adopted the twins months before Justine and I separated, and Australia handled it much the same as the U.S. did. Our names replaced the twins' mother on the newly issued birth certificate.

I dig deeper, past photographs and grade cards. I can feel a larger object near the bottom. I wrest it out, ignore the cascade of old birthday cards that slip down further into the box as I grasp a huge clue.

I stare at the leather-bound journal in my hands, the initials NS are engraved on the thick leather cover. It reeks of the fire, but it is untouched. The pages are slightly yellowed, but that is to be expected. The box Nicky stored it in wasn't airtight, but miraculously, the journal seems undamaged. I gather the papers, add them to an evidence bag. The journal I slip into one of the deep pockets in my coat.

I can't say why I do it. Only that the same inner voice that warned me not to tell my boss that I knew Nichole better than anyone else in the world is now telling me not to enter the journal into evidence.

Not yet.

Not until I truly understood what was happening.

I look further and find nothing more. Nothing but smoke-damaged clothing and the delicate statuettes arranged on the dresser.

It is on the drive back that it hits me. That sense of not-quite-rightness from my view in the hallway. I stop to fill up the tank, grab a soda, and it becomes crystal-clear.

Elizabeth's window. It had thick metal bars mounted to the outside of the window. None of the other windows had bars. Only hers. A second-floor window at that. Combined with a lock on the *outside* of the door. A room designed to contain someone within it. But... why?

A few hours in the office, writing up my notes, and I head back to the sparse room for rent, ready to page through the journal.

I prop the two thin pillows up against the creaky headboard and dig in. I don't know how many times I read it. A dozen? It keeps me up all night. I stare at the pages, examine the writing, even entertain the thought that her husband has somehow created this in order to incriminate her.

Finally, I turn the light off in the cheap room for rent and settle back on the lumpy bed, my stomach churning. The journal changes everything.

Everything I thought I knew about Nichole, everything I thought I understood, is... wrong. What I just read, it isn't just unsettling; it is *damning*. I am seeing for myself the slow unraveling of a woman's grip on reality.

What caused this, and why? Did she really start the fire? Did she really attack and beat her husband and adoptive daughter while the house burned? It doesn't sit right with me. It seems so contrary to the Nicky I knew.

The only thing that makes little or no sense is the drugs. She wrote in the journal that she took sleeping pills, that she wanted to die, *intended* to die. Perhaps she changed her mind, lost her nerve, but I found no medications other than the blood pressure meds inside her nightstand.

Did she set fire to the place, try to kill them both, and then came to her senses? Maybe her story at the station of that little girl changing personalities is just her way of excusing it.

Damned if I haven't seen some crazy shit in the past decade of police work. My first big case down under, the one that propelled me to my current position even while fracturing my marriage, was the copycat Claremont serial killings in Perth. The case had been so similar to the Claremont killings that there had been talk of a possible second serial killer. One missed in the initial case. I had nearly been too late, too. The truth was right under my nose and I hadn't even seen it. The danger, well, that had been what bothered Justine the most. It was her worst nightmare come true. Getting the call. Learning that I had barely survived an encounter with the killer. We had moved over 4,000 kilometers to escape that infamy and it still hadn't mattered. My divorce from Justine would be final in two weeks.

I try to swallow past the hard lump in my throat. I shouldn't be working on this case. The journal is ample evidence of that fact. Chain of custody be damned. Seeing it there, taking and hiding it without a word to anyone. I had done so hoping I could understand Nicky's crazy tale.

But reading it, somehow makes my impulsive action worse. Far worse.

If I've learned anything, serving first as a beat cop and later as a detective here in Australia, it's that people are not simple. They aren't cut and dried, black or white. They're like onions. One layer after another of complexity, conflicting emotions and actions, a sum of their experiences. As much as I want to believe that I *knew* Nicky, I don't. Not really. The only ones we truly know are ourselves. Sometimes not even that is for sure. We view everything we see through the lens of our experiences, emotions, and motivations. I don't *want* to believe Nicky is capable of this, and that makes me the wrong person to handle this case. I have a personal stake in it.

When Andy and Hannah Mott died in that fire, it was as if a switch had been turned for Nicky. She'd changed. One day I was attending their funeral by her side, the next she was telling me we were over. She was gone before I could talk her out of it. I'd turned nineteen a week later, sitting in my room in my parents' house, staring at the promise ring I'd given her the year before, wondering what the hell I had done wrong.

How did we go from being in love, talking about marriage and a family, to her leaving me and moving over 1,500 miles away? We had our entire lives mapped out. A plan. We were, or so I thought, in love. But Andy and Hannah's deaths, on the heels of the miscarriage, it had been too much. I can see now how fragile Nicky was, how miserable she must have been. I thought too, for months, that she would come back. But she hadn't.

And now, if this journal is to be believed, and I know I am still fighting that reality, then Nicky is unhinged in a way I can not begin to understand. I groan, run my fingers through my hair and give up on sleep. I need to get to the office, take some notes. I'm sitting at my desk, telling myself I'd be better off getting the book entered into evidence when I hear a familiar voice.

"Vince, fancy a cuppa, mate?" Arno leans against my cubicle, his eyebrows raised. "You look like hell. Maureen'd take one look at you and say you look like a dog's breakfast. You working on that crazy sheila case? The pregnant one who tried to burn down her house and kill her husband and daughter?"

I nod and rub my eyes. They burn from lack of sleep. Right about now, a quart of coffee might not be enough.

"Yeah, coffee might help."

I shove a pile of papers over the journal, stand up, and walk with Arno down to the coffeepot in the hall. The hallway reeks of burned coffee and cigarettes. The back door of the station where the smokers hid their habits from the public is right next to the coffee nook. I pat my pocket reflexively searching for the cigarettes, even though I've been smoke-free for nearly three years.

The coffee is strong enough to burn holes in the cup's bottom. I blow on it and try to sip it. I should have waited. The dark brew scalds my tongue.

"Even preggers, that Nichole, she's something else," Arno muses. "Hard to believe a sheila as pretty as that has done what she has, trying to kill her husband and daughter. Don't you let her pull the wool over your eyes, now."

I force a grin onto my face. "No chance of that, my man."

Arno laughs and punches my arm. "Nah, you nabbed the copycat killer in Perth. He might've been ugly, but I know better than to think you'd get taken in by a pretty face. Hey, I didn't tell you about last weekend, did I?" Whatever he says next is lost as my mind slips back in time.

Sure, I'd nabbed that serial killer and nearly taken one in the gut while doing it. I still couldn't eat spicy food, thanks to the damage he did.

The powers that be would have written me up for not following procedure if it hadn't been for the full confession and fast-tracked conviction I had finagled. There had been words about Americans and cowboys and the rest, but I'd gotten my transfer to Brisbane and a promotion to detective. Likely, the chief just wanted to get rid of me. Who could blame him?

As far as the Staunton case, well, I know I'm definitely on the road to hell. I've told no one about my connection to Nicky. Just seeing her there in the interrogation room, alone, terrified, and pregnant - it had been impulsive to come in and, with my back to the camera, hold up the note I had scribbled on the napkin.

I'm a fool. And complicit as well if I don't come clean. The coffee's heat warms the cup to an uncomfortable level. It burns the tips of my fingers. Normally, I'd remember to bring my mug from my desk. But not today, not with most of my mind on the journal.

Those words, they were the ravings of a lunatic. I could break it down into better terms, sure. I could couch it in the psychological terms I had learned during my training classes, but crazy was crazy, no matter how you played it.

For the first time in decades, I wonder about Nichole's past, and her childhood before we met.

I have always known she was adopted, of course. Hell, everyone knew Andy and Hannah. They had fostered a long line of kids before Nichole. I remember my mom talking about it and speculating about Nichole's background. Mom was always a bit of a gossip, and she'd scurried over to see Hannah when Nicky first arrived at school. That I was her first friend had made it almost an imperative for my nosy mother. But Hannah Motts was close-mouthed about it, saying only that Nicky needed a new start and they were hoping to adopt.

I cast back in my memories. I remember the quiet girl she had been, withdrawn, shy. Over the years, I had asked, but she had never really answered. Whether that it wasn't something she wanted to talk about, or that the memories of her first six years of life were so hazy, I really did not know.

"Anyway, my mate's wearing these budgie smugglers and nothing else, drunk as a skunk, and all set to show what he's got to God and country." Arno's voice pulls me from my musings. "Hey, you even hearing me? You're a thousand miles away, aren't ya, mate? You okay?"

I blink. "Me? Yeah. Just not sleeping. Goddamn bed in the rented room has rocks in it."

Arno looked sympathetic. "Any chance she'll reconsider?"

Justine had filed for divorce for real this time, and I'd been out on my ass for the past two months, staying close to the station since I was there all the time anyway. Justine had never wanted to marry a cop. She'd made that clear. But then she'd gotten pregnant with Ninah and it'd made sense to get married. Hell, I'd even emigrated to Australia from the States to try to keep her happy. The Claremont case had meant a move here, to Brisbane, and I'd gotten off the beat and earned my detective badge. But it hadn't been enough. She'd lost her dad to the job, first with alcohol and finally by suicide.

"The things you see, that he saw, Vince, it messes with you," she'd said once. "You can't leave your work behind. You carry it, like an addict carries the monkey on his back."

Arno is waiting for an answer. I shrug. "She seems to have her mind made up."

He claps me on the shoulder, and a muscle twinges painfully in response. "Sorry to hear that, mate. Maureen's been on me to invite you both over. Haven't had the heart to tell her you broke up. She wants to know more about fostering and all that."

Maureen is a five-foot-tall spitfire of a woman. She can't have kids, or at least one of the two is shooting blanks. I've never gotten a for sure on where the problem lay. When Maureen invited us over for dinner, Justine was wrangling our two plus our new set of twins. Our little ones, ages five and four, respectively, had swarmed through the small flat that Arno and Maureen were renting. By the end of the evening, Arno looked shell-shocked. Maureen, well, she'd been over the moon and ready to dive into becoming a foster parent with or without her husband.

Justine loves being a mom. It doesn't matter whether she has given birth to them; she loves the kids. It is one thing I like about her the most. It is also the reason she objects to my job so much.

"I need to know you are going to be there, Vincent. I don't want them showing up at my door and telling me you caught a bullet when you should be at home playing catch with Eli."

Arno is waiting for a response. "I'll have Justine call her." The boiling heat from the cup is melting my fingers. I set it down and hunt in the upper cabinet for a cardboard sleeve, finding nothing. So much for safety. I eye the back door that led to the smoking area. The longing for a cigarette rises, clawing at me, even after all this time. I fight it down. "I'd better get back to it. I'm going to the hospital later to continue the interview."

"So she had that baby?" Arno asks, curious.

"Yep, eight pounds, three ounces. The kid has red hair like his pops."

Arno leans against the door and I shift the cup again, the fingers in my left hand uncomfortably hot. I imagine the heat melting my fingerprints smooth.

"They say all those pregnancy hormones really get women tied in knots. Betcha she tries some kind of defense like that."

I shrug, thinking that, so far, Nicky has claimed something far weirder. "I'm hoping the husband wakes up soon and we can talk to him."

Arno's eyebrows rise. "Damn, I thought he was a goner."

"Well, he won't be waking up today. He's got a skull fracture and swelling. He needed nearly half a liter of blood. They have him in a medically induced coma. But yeah, I'm going to want to find out what he remembers of last night. You never know, it could change everything."

Saying it somehow makes me hope for it. Maybe it had been him that went crazy and Nichole just defended herself. I could hope for a solution like that. Anything was possible when dealing with a domestic situation if things got heated.

I know I want to make excuses for her. Hell, even now, with the most damning evidence I can think of, I want to believe Nicky is innocent, that she isn't a monster. It reminds me yet again of how impossible this situation is, and how badly I have fucked up the chain of command.

I change hands again and blow on the damned coffee, sipping just enough to know it will burn my tongue and strip me of the ability to taste anything for days.

Arno shakes his head. "The crazy sheila's getting to you. Looks pretty open and shut to me. I'm off to wrap up that suicide from late last week. You let me know if you got time, and we'll grab lunch at Chez Nous."

I grin. The last time we stopped at Chez Nous, Arno had tried the falafel burger. His wife was on a health kick and messaged him constantly with suggestions. I'd watched him eat the whole thing with a sick look on his face.

Arno rolls his eyes at the look on my face. "I tried it, it sucked. I'm going back to the real beef ones, damn it."

"I hear you on that. Hey, catch you another time, Arno!"

I head back to my desk. Right now, I have to figure out what the hell to do with the journal and how to approach it when I talk to Nicky today. I look at the clock on my computer - three more hours until I can talk to her. They don't enforce visiting hours for police, but I know from experience the nursing staff prefers it. I don't need any flinty-eyed glares from them. I've had enough of that from Justine.

Instead, there is enough time for another read-through and a bite of breakfast at Shelden on Mary. I slip the journal into a file folder, tuck it under my arm, and head for the parking lot.

16. An Odd Feeling

- Vincent -

September 19th, 2019 - Brisbane, Australia

Sitting in the parking lot of Royal Brisbane Women's Hospital, I read through the journal one more time. It isn't full, not by any means. Instead, it is less than one-quarter filled. I reach for my notepad to take a few notes. My pen balks, leaving an ink stain, then clears. Seconds later, ink is smearing the side of my hand. Justine is right. I need to stop being a complete technophobe and join the 21st century. She gave me a Remarkable smart notebook for my birthday last year and it sits in the box, unused.

"Stop being a complete Luddite, Vince, and use the damn thing," she scolded me a month ago. She's right. This notebook is the latest of a stack. I spilled coffee on it last week and the writing on several pages has blurred together into an unrecognizable mess. I was lucky that time. I'd already transcribed my notes into the computer.

I write, the pen scratching on the paper.

- No dates listed

- Pills listed, no pills (other than blood pressure meds) found

- Uses letters instead of names, but letters match up

** E for Elizabeth?*

** N for Nichole?*

** J for Jhon?*

- Suspect stated therapist advised she begin journaling. Get therapist's name and confirm patient status.

I am staring at the list when my phone rings. I know without even looking at it that it is Justine. It plays a Darth Vader ringtone. A foster kid managed to bypass my password and install it on my phone last year. It has certainly made for plenty of laughs when the damned thing goes off in the middle of a meeting. I'll admit, I can't help smiling every time I hear it.

"Hey, what's up?"

"I've got a situation here." In the background, I can hear Ninah wailing like a banshee. "Ninah's hurt and the twins are both down for a nap. Eli will need lunch, and I've got a new one here as well. Can you come over? I just need to pop over to the urgent care. It'll take me two hours, tops."

Given the choice between staying with the kids or taking Ninah to the urgent care, I'd happily choose the former any day of the week. Our firstborn's wails were the only thing that made me bonkers. She rivaled an air raid siren in intensity. My skin was crawling just hearing it over the phone.

"Yeah, I'm on my way. Be there in twenty."

"Make it fifteen. There's got to be some perks to being an officer of the law." The phone beeps twice and goes silent.

Damned if she isn't willing to reap the benefits of the badge, even as she complains about the hours, the pay, and the danger. I sigh, snap my seatbelt back on, and pull out of the parking space. There is no point in questioning it; Justine is who she was.

As I drive, my foot heavy on the pedal, I think about the fresh-faced clerical assistant I met the first month out of police academy. Justine had decided to spend her first two years of university in America, staying with her aunt who had immigrated to the U.S. back in the '80s from Brisbane. She enrolled at UMKC and took a job at the East Patrol campus for the part-time income. It had been barely a year since the fire and Nicky's departure, and I had started to accept that she wasn't coming back. Justine had been cute, and I fell for her Aussie accent and odd quirks. Her first two years had turned into the full four, and she'd been seven months pregnant with Ninah when she collected her diploma, a brand-new wedding ring sparkling on her finger.

It was Ninah's birth that had set in motion Justine's homesickness for Brisbane. Our rental in a rough section of Northeast Kansas City hadn't helped. By the end of Ninah's fourth month, we were on a plane to Perth. I'd found a job there, shockingly, through an inter-departmental U.S./Aussie partnership, and it had meant Justine was finally back in Australia.

It hadn't been enough, though. Perth was a hell of a distance from Brisbane. Looking on the maps, Australia always seemed... small. It was, in fact, nearly three million square miles. It was wider from east to west than the United States. It took longer to fly from Perth to Brisbane than it did to fly from San Francisco to New York. The United States was larger by nearly a million square miles, but Australia wasn't nearly as tiny as the globes made it out to be.

Justine hadn't been satisfied with staying in Perth, not when her family was on the opposite side of the continent.

Our marriage, hell, our relationship, had always been a seesaw of ups and downs. Once we emigrated, it felt as if it had just headed straight down.

I turn onto the highway, making time. I drive the newest Chrysler 300, yet another perk I can credit back to nabbing the serial killer in Perth. The lights mounted in the rear window have the desired effect, even without a siren. Cars move left and right, emptying the lane in front of me for all but the most clueless.

As I pull into the cul-de-sac, I can see Justine's car is running. I can even hear Ninah's siren screams through the sealed glass windows. Impressive. Justine rolls hers down as she backs out. She has to raise her voice to be heard. "The twins are asleep, but they'll be awake soon and need lunch. Keep an eye on the new one. Her name is Elizabeth. She came in yesterday."

She pulls away and exits the cul-de-sac with a short squeal of tires before I can do much more than blow a kiss at my screaming daughter.

I park, leave the journal inside the car, along with my notebook. The last time I brought a notebook home with me, Eli spilled hot chocolate all over it.

At the tender age of four, my son is talented in two things - pissing off his older sister and a staggering amount of clumsiness. I am rather shocked it wasn't Eli on the way to the urgent care instead of Ninah. He has managed to break his big toe, two fingers, get three concussions, and a laceration on his left buttock that required stitches. All in the space of four short years.

My hand is on the doorknob when Justine's words hit me. A new one by the name of Elizabeth? What are the odds it is Nicky's girl? I walk inside and I can hear the twins crying from their bedroom, with no other kids in sight.

"Eli?"

The pounding of little feet in combat boots is almost instantaneous. "Daddy!"

My boy rounds the corner and is airborne, launching himself through space instead of running down the last half-flight of stairs.

"Oof!" I catch an elbow in the eye as Eli hurtles into my arms. His close-cropped dark hair smells of the orange blossom shampoo that Justine is so fond of. He is dressed in his standard fare of shorts, no shirt, and the biggest stomping boots ever made for a four-year-old boy. One boot is half-laced, the other not so much. He still smells of milk and fruit, likely from his breakfast.

He grabs my face with both hands, his nose a mere inch from mine, which causes everything to blur. "I missed you, Daddy, and the new girl isn't nice. I don't like her; make her go away!"

"I missed you too, Bud." I look around. The girl is nowhere in sight. "But we've talked about this before, Eli. It isn't nice to say that about people. She's probably scared, and when people are scared, that can make them seem not nice."

Eli raises an eyebrow and shakes his head in disappointment. He is a little young to be copping an otherworldly air, but here it is. "Daddy, she's *mean*. She hurt Ninah."

A voice speaks from behind me. "I didn't. She tripped. I *tried* to help her up, but she just screamed worse. *She* was mean to *me*."

I turn around and recognize her instantly from Nicky's description of her. She is small for her purported age of nearly six years. In fact, Eli is bigger than her, although this was not surprising, as he will likely have my height. She has precious red curls, a sprinkle of freckles that play across her nose and cheeks, and the brightest crayon-blue eyes I have ever seen. Nicky's adopted daughter was beautiful. For that matter, Elizabeth looks as if she could easily pass for Jhon and Nicky's biological child, based on the photos I've seen of Jhon. I can't help wondering if this, too, is Nicky's psychosis bleeding through. Could Elizabeth in fact be their natural daughter? Could Nicky be imagining all of this? I give the girl a once-over. She's incredibly calm and centered, considering what she has been through over the past 24 hours.

For most children who enter the foster system, even if it was only for a few days, it is a frightening transition. No matter what terrible place they have come from, they are not calm and collected. Before Justine asked me to move out, we had a steady stream of children coming and going. Justine pushed for a larger house for just this reason. She wanted plenty of children in her life and Eli's birth had been hard on her. Her heart wanted more, but her body fought pregnancy tooth and nail.

It hadn't been a hard decision to try fostering. Still, the parallels between Nicky's life and mine were nuts. What were the odds that Justine and I had chosen the same path that Nicky had?

The house has five large bedrooms, so we have room, plenty of it. The second largest has been set aside as a playroom, but that doesn't stop the toys from migrating, as toys will, into every corner of the house. One of them squeaks underfoot as I bend down to Elizabeth's level. Eli squirms in my grasp and hides his face in my chest.

"You must be Elizabeth. I'm Vincent."

She doesn't smile, but it doesn't matter. She was adorable. *This* is the child that Nicky claimed has tried to kill her and her husband? Staring at her, I can't make myself believe it.

I can hear the twins continuing to cry and I untangle Eli, who is clinging like a monkey to me. He misses me as much as I miss him. He is clingier than usual, but I've been gone for nearly four days, so it is understandable.

"Come on, buddy, let's go get the twins, eh?"

Eli takes a leaping run at the stairs and I smile at Elizabeth and follow him. After the short flight of steps, there is a large landing and then two sets of stairs, one leads to the master bedroom suite, and another down a longer hallway consisting of five doors. One is a closet, and the other four are bedrooms with connecting Jack and Jill bathrooms between them. For now, with the twins so small, they are in one room together. Later, Justine will likely keep Jarrah on the girls' side of the corridor and put Jedda over on Eli's side. I have little doubt Justine will want to continue to foster and adopt, with or without me. She is a great mum, and she always wanted a large family. It seems that my presence in the house is not necessary for that. Justine handles most of the parenting anyway, always has, since my hours are irregular and the job demanding.

The twins' room is painted in bright greens, and Justine moved them to separate cribs a month ago. It hasn't gone over well. They are used to sleeping together, front to front, typically, with Jedda's arm over his sister. According to the nurses at the hospital, Jedda is eight minutes older than his sister. Their mother, a full-blooded Aborigine, and a 14-year-old orphan with a history of running away from foster homes, showed no interest in them. She checked herself out of the hospital on the second day and disappeared. Without any other family coming forward, Jarrah and Jedda were fast-tracked, and Justine and I adopted them when they were three months old. Now seven months and change, they are each sitting in their cribs, howling, fat tears running down their cheeks, each sporting a long scratch that runs in a diagonal line across their dusky-skinned faces.

"What happened to you?" I ask. The scratches are fresh, a line of blood forming at the edges of each one. Jarrah howls, and Jedda, normally our Buddha baby, as I call him, is sobbing too. Have they done this to themselves? I imagine them reaching through the bars of their cribs, each scratching the other by accident.

"I *told* you she was mean, Daddy," Eli says, sliding over to Jarrah's crib on the left, while he eyes Elizabeth reproachfully. She stands in the doorway and stares at the wailing babies dispassionately.

"Eli, not everything is the new kid's fault." I reach in and pick up first Jarrah and then Jedda, one in each arm. Their cries subside, slowly, their tiny bodies lean against my shoulders, their free hands reaching for each other. If it had been my choice, I would have let them sleep in the same crib. Bedtimes are harder since they have been separated. I read that twins share a special bond, and that co-sleeping, up to and sometimes well into the teen years, was a normal practice, even with twins of the opposite sex. I maneuver their clasped hands around until I can see their fingernails. Sure enough, they are both sporting longish talons. Justine usually has me cut them. She suffered a seizure and cardiac arrest after Eli's birth, and it left her hands shaky. Yet another reason why birthing her own children was no longer recommended. I forgot the last time I was here, and now the twins have gone and hurt themselves. I have no doubt that Justine will not be pleased to see the scratches.

"Ah, there now, see, Eli? See their nails? They both need a good nail trimming. That's how they got scratched. Your mum asked me to cut their nails, and I plumb forgot."

Eli climbs up on the nearby rocker, teetering dangerously as he does so, in order to get a better look at the twins' fingernails. He casts a suspicious look back at Elizabeth, who remains silent and still in the doorway, then shrugs.

"I still don't like her."

I sigh. Kids are remarkably plain-spoken at times. "C'mon, everyone, I'll see if I can't roust up some grilled cheese sandwiches. Eli, you check the pantry for applesauce, and I'll get the twins in the playpen to take their bottles."

Down in the kitchen, I see that Justine has already set out the bottles of formula. The babies seem content to recline against the soft pillows that line the playpen and suck down their bottles as I get lunch together for the three of us. While the pan heats, I slice cheese and add some thin-sliced ham, then butter the outsides of the bread and pop them into the pan to toast while melting the cheese into a gooey goodness.

I am skilled at catching crooks and basic survival food - grilled cheese, pancakes, and the occasional grilling out. The kids love it, and Justine usually bitches that I haven't included fruits or vegetables. I dive into the fridge and find a couple of carrots to cut up and section into sticks.

"I don't like carrots," Elizabeth says, appearing at my side. She stares up at me. "They taste yucky."

"Well, if you don't eat them, how are you going to keep your keen eyesight?" I ask, wiggling my eyebrows at her. She blinks and tilts her head to one side. No smile. I fear I am losing my touch.

Eli, who is usually up my ass with a periscope, as well as maddeningly underfoot, is seated at the table. He eyes Elizabeth and frowns. "My daddy is a police detective. So you'd better be nice now. He puts bad people in jail."

"Eli, lay off the girl already," I growl at my son.

Elizabeth doesn't seem the least bit perturbed. Instead, she seems even more interested. She watches me prep the meal and put everything on plates. I see a shadow cross her face when I place two carrot sticks on her plate. She doesn't argue when I direct her to a chair across from Eli. She even takes a napkin from the middle of the table and tucks it into her lap. She eats the grilled cheese sandwich, along with the applesauce, and avoids the carrot sticks.

When the sandwich and applesauce is devoured, she slides the plate away from her. "I don't like carrots."

"Fine, you get away with it this one time," I say, taking the plate from her. "But I'm the pushover. Justine? Not so much."

She stares at me, silent, and I turn toward Eli. "You, young sir..."

He pops a carrot stick in his mouth. "I *like* carrots, Daddy."

"Fair enough, son."

"Are you my new daddy?" Elizabeth asks, suddenly.

One of the training classes we had taken had covered this in detail. I finish chewing, smile, and say, "Justine and I take care of kiddos, sometimes for a short time, and some become our forever kids. I'm not here to replace your mommy or daddy. I'm here to take care of you right now. Tomorrow will work itself out."

Elizabeth blinks and sits silently. She truly does look as if she were Jhon and Nicky's biological child. I swear that I see not only Jhon's red hair and freckles, but Nicky's eyes, the wavy curls of her hair, the way her mouth looks when she is pondering something. It just goes to show that we see similarities where we want to see them in children.

It is, however, enough of a similarity that I want to double-check the records later, when Justine returns and I am free to leave.

"You don't live here, though." Elizabeth's voice intrudes into my thoughts.

"No, I don't. Not right now." The thought occurs to me that I have the perfect opportunity to learn more about Elizabeth's side of things. It isn't how it is supposed to be conducted, though. Hell, I am already off the rails by talking to Nicky instead of telling the Chief that I know her and removing myself from the investigation.

Know her, huh, that is sure as hell some revisionist history on my part. I don't just know *her; I was* engaged *to her. I know right where that little mole on her left breast...*

"Why not?" Elizabeth seems to take to interrogation with skill and ease. Perhaps she has a future as a detective. Aren't I the one who is supposed to ask the questions?

"Hm?"

"Why don't you live here?"

I can feel Eli's eyes on me. The twins are too young to care. Ninah is wrapped up in her mother and Barbies, but Eli, Eli misses me more than words could express. I can see it in his eyes. He has been the most confused and hurt by our separation.

In truth, at times I question why I should stay with Justine. We love each other, but not in that knock you down, rip your heart out, and please don't ever leave me kind of way. Certainly not the love I had felt with Nicky. Her leaving, it broke me. Relationships are complicated things, and sometimes love is not enough. I was willing to keep going, especially for the kids, but Justine has other opinions. She told me to leave and so I had gone. Next month, she might want me back again. Our relationship had long been a seesaw of pushing and pulling apart.

"Justine and I are, erm, working things out right now. Sometimes, that means living apart until we can find a way to either be together or stay apart permanently."

That seems to satisfy Elizabeth. Or if it doesn't, she isn't interested in pursuing the topic. "I want to watch television now."

Eli is nearly done and Elizabeth slips from her seat, walks past the twins in their playpen and into the living room, where she climbs into a chair and reaches for the remote.

"She pinches me if I try to change the channel," Eli says mournfully, his eyes plead with me to intercede. "And this morning she threw my Lego people into the toilet and flushed them and then told Mommy I did it."

Eli's favorite toys are his Legos. He plays with them for hours on end. It is, honestly, the only time the boy sits still. He can't even watch television without contorting his body into a pretzel or climbing and diving into the couch cushions.

"What did Mommy say?" I ask.

"She was too busy with the twins and then Elizabeth pushed Ninah down the stairs and she got hurt and Mommy called you to come home. Daddy, I miss you. You need to come home and *she*" — he says, whispering while glaring at Elizabeth's back — "needs to go away!"

"Eli, stop. She's new and we've talked about how foster kids need a lot of patience and understanding because they are having a hard time," I counsel my son. "Be patient and try to get along."

Tears spring to his eyes. "You aren't listening to me. Mommy wouldn't listen either. I don't like that girl! She's *mean*!" He runs away from the table and disappears up the stairs.

The twins are doing well, and I check their diapers as I walk by. They are still working on their bottles, and will be for a few minutes, so I sit down on the couch near Elizabeth.

"So, do you prefer to be called Elizabeth? Or do your mommy or daddy call you by a nickname? Maybe Lizzie? Or Isabel?" I ask her.

A disgusted expression crosses her face as I mention the nicknames. It is gone in a flash. If I hadn't been looking for it, I would have missed it.

"No, just Elizabeth."

It strikes me as odd, how mature and reserved she behaves. She pulls up Netflix using the remote and is navigating through the children's section under Ninah's account. It appears that she can read. She not only stops on the individual titles, but presses the down button as well. I watch her lips move as she reads the words silently.

Impressive, but not unheard of. Ninah has been reading since before she entered her first year of school at age five. Eli is already recognizing a few sight words. She reads quickly, pausing at each description momentarily, before moving on to the next. She glances at me and then chooses *The Hollow*.

"That might be a little scary," I warn her. Ninah watched the first episode and was terrified by it.

"I'm not afraid."

"Okay, then."

After a few minutes, I head upstairs to talk to Eli. He is sitting on the floor of his room, a scowl on his face, pawing through his Legos.

"Hey, buddy, are you going to play with Legos?"

His lip quivers. "I can't find Captain Jack."

"I'm sure he's in there somewhere." I look at the mass of Lego pieces scattered on the carpet. How he can find anything in this disaster, I have zero idea. To me, they are just a mass of colors and shapes. My eyes ache just from looking.

Downstairs, I hear the twins begin to fuss. As usual, when one begins, the other has to join in. They feed off each other, a mid-range disgruntled cry quickly turns to a wail of dissatisfaction and misery. I know they will only get worse, but at the moment, Eli needs me. I try and help him look for his favorite Lego character.

"She took him, Daddy," Eli's voice quavers. "I told her he was my favorite and now I can't find him."

I frown and Eli glances up and sees it. His lip quivers and his eyes fill with tears. "You don't believe me!"

It isn't like Eli to be this way about another foster child. Eli is not only a classic klutz who runs into walls and falls down stairs, he is also our designated greeter. He has welcomed half a dozen kids into our home and tearfully waved goodbye to all but the twins. His heart is bigger than all of ours combined. I wonder if my absence from the family home is hitting him harder than either Justine or I could anticipate.

I open my mouth to ask him more, only to hear the front door open. Justine and Ninah have returned.

"Mommy!" Eli yells. He jumps up and bolts down the stairs.

Ninah is pale and sad, her leg wrapped in a large bandage. Her face has dried tear tracks and when she sees me, her lip quivers.

"Daddy." Her face crumples into fresh tears.

Justine hands her over to me. "She had to have ten stitches. I'm pretty sure everyone with a fifty-foot radius has significant hearing loss. My eardrums are humming like they did after you took me to the Granada in Lawrence to see *That One Guy*."

She smiles, though, as Ninah buries her face into my shirt, her tiny shoulders shaking. Justine's smile fades, however, when she sees the twins' faces.

"What happened?"

"They were like that when I went upstairs to get them out of bed." I pat Ninah on the back and she quiets, lays her head on my shoulder, no doubt exhausted from all of her screaming.

"With all of these scratches?" She picks up Jarrah. "She's *bleeding*, Vincent!"

I walk over. Now there wasn't just one scratch on each of their faces, instead there are dozens of scratches, several of them oozing blood.

"What the hell?" I cast around for a toy and find the culprit hidden beneath a blanket. A Lego. A Captain Jack Sparrow Lego, if I didn't miss my guess.

Justine looks livid. "Eli Olivander Gallagher! I've told you not to leave your Lego's lying about and this one is in the twins' playpen!"

Eli doesn't bother trying to argue his case. Instead, he turns to me, his eyes overflowing with tears. He runs to me, wraps his arms around my leg, and sobs. Just as Ninah had calmed, Eli's tears seem to ramp her up again.

"You take the twins," I say. "I'll get these two upstairs. I think they could use a lie-down right about now." Justine nods tightly, looking exhausted. "Are you okay?" I ask her.

"Yeah, I just didn't sleep well last night. Kept hearing weird noises. I'm just being paranoid, I guess." Justine flaps her hand at me. "Go on, take those two upstairs."

I spare a glance in Elizabeth's direction. Throughout Justine's return, and sobbing and tears from all other children in the house, Elizabeth sits perfectly still on the couch, watching *The Hollow* and ignoring all of us. She sits cross-legged, back straight, watching a show that had scared the bejeezus out of Ninah just a few months ago. Kids are different, though. I was a shining example of that. I was crazy for the *Goosebumps* books by R. L. Stine growing up. I lurch up the stairs, Eli and Ninah cling to me, still sobbing. It takes twenty minutes for me to calm them and get them to lie down in our, well, Justine's, bedroom. By the time I creep away, they are both fast asleep.

When I return downstairs, the twins are playing peacefully in their playpen, and I tilt my head toward the front door and beckon Justine to follow.

"I'm working on a case, and Elizabeth is involved," I say in an undertone.

Justine sighs. "Do I want to know?"

I wrestle with what to tell her. Nicky's story is compelling, if not half nuts, but the journal, the journal changes everything. "No, probably not. But I need you to let me know if there's anything off, anything out of the ordinary."

She raises her eyebrows, then frowns. "Tell me you are staying safe. No matter what happens between us, Vince, our kids need their father."

I take that in, say nothing for a moment. "How's Rocco these days?"

I regret it instantly. I should have kept my mouth shut. Fire blazes in her eyes. "You can just fuck right off, Vince."

I nod, salute, and walk away. It was stupid of me to take a potshot at her high school sweetheart. Never mind that Justine herself had said he was a dipshit more times than I can count.

I'd caught him a week ago there in our living room. Feet up, watching the television, his arm around Justine, when I had run by to drop off Ninah's backpack. Ninah had left it in my car the Friday before when I took her for ice cream. I guess I should have called first. Or even knocked. Old habits die hard. Needless to say, it hadn't gone well. I'd given him a glare and that had set Justine off. Bastard could've at least waited until the divorce before settling in, though.

It was time to return to the hospital to talk to Nicky before visiting hours were over.

17. The Rest of the Story

- Nichole -

September 20th, 2019 - Brisbane, Australia

The day wears on slowly. I slept over twelve hours straight after the birth, but now it feels as if everything is stuck in molasses. It doesn't help that I have a clear view of the clock and can watch as the seconds hand continues to tick, tick, tick around and around.

The nurses come and go. I've seen two shift changes. Earlier, I tried to leave my room, to go to the nursery and find Theo, but a police officer blocked my exit. I am clearly not free to leave this room. One look from the officer and a nurse hustled over and encouraged me to return to my bed.

"You'll need to stay here, in your room, Mrs. Staunton," the nurse said, her gaze firmly on the machines, the lights, the door. Anywhere she can look without meeting my eyes.

I feel bad for her. After all, she is used to catching babies, not dealing with someone accused of trying to kill her husband and child while also setting fire to her house.

When they bring me lunch and Vincent still hasn't shown up, my appetite disappears. He is the detective on the case, isn't he? If so, then where is he? Maybe he's heard enough of my story, decided I am bonkers, and informed his superiors of our shared history. I pick at my food and let my thoughts spiral, imagining what he must think.

He thinks you're nuts. He doesn't believe you. No one will believe you. Only Jhon knows the truth, and he might be dead.

If I'd heard the story I told Vincent, would I even believe it? Elizabeth hadn't been much more than three years old when Kate and Rob died. As many times as my mind returns to that fact since the events of early 2018, I still can't say the words or accept it. I can't find it in me to say the truth. A half-truth is easier. "When Kate and Rob died." Stripped of reality, stripped of substance, just the bare, mostly there facts. It doesn't touch on *how*. It certainly doesn't address the who of it either.

I think we shy away from reality, just as we shy away from responsibility, no matter how accountable we think we are. When you knock over a glass in a bar because you're a little tipsy and thick-fingered, you tell the server, "We need some napkins; my drink spilled." Not, "I need some napkins because I knocked over my drink."

It is as if the fears we have of getting our butts beaten, or worse, as children, never really leave us. It's never our fault.

Even now, after all I have seen, I can't say it out loud. The reality of it all. Kate and Rob didn't just die. It wasn't an accidental fire. It wasn't a gas leak or a hurricane or an act of God. They had died in their bed, yes. But their heads were bashed in long before the fire took the house and left Elizabeth sitting outside in the rain. Even now, as I try to force my brain to say the words, I can't. I can't even think about them. A tiny child like that. Even I didn't want to think about it. And I have seen her. Lived with her. Watched as Winter's Child emerged not once, but twice. I *know* what she is capable of.

A new nurse clucks at my mostly uneaten plate of food. "Not hungry? Not after all that hard work yesterday?"

I manage to shake my head and ask after my baby. "If I could just hold him for a few minutes?"

Just as with the nurse before, her eyes slide away from mine. She manages to plaster a bright smile on her face. It doesn't reach her eyes.

"I'll talk to the doctor and get back to you." She disappears out of the door and it swooshes closed.

That is nurse-speak for "Not today, maybe not ever."

I want to scream. I want to cry. But mostly, I just want to see Vincent's face. The postpartum blues are hitting, but I can't rouse myself enough to let the tears out. I just want someone to believe me. I want to know that my husband is alive, and that he is going to make it. And I want my baby in my arms. I even want Elizabeth. Well, maybe not Elizabeth herself, but Isabel, Lizzie, even Elsa. It feels like forever since I have seen them.

Each of them, each aspect, is so... *different*. I love Isabel's habit of twisting her hair around her finger and nibbling on her lower lip. Her shy, quiet ways are a balm after the fear and stress of winter. I imagine her tiny body nestled against mine, face hidden in my shirt. She will be here soon, so soon.

The thought that I might never see her again practically stops my heart. The heaviness in my chest robs me of all the happiness I feel over Theo's birth.

As I sit here in the hospital room, the clock ticks through the day. When dinner comes and goes, my spirits fall.

He doesn't believe you. He thinks you're crazy.

He thinks you tried to murder your family.

They're going to lock you up and throw away the key.

I hate the voices. I try everything I can think of to ignore them, to tell myself Vincent is just delayed, that he will be back.

But as the day wears on, as the sun slips down in the sky and darkness falls, I am out of hope. They won't even let me see my baby.

This is your life now. Enjoy the next day or two, because after that it will be a thin mat and iron bars. Your son will never know you. Your husband is probably dead, and they will blame it all on you.

I don't look up when I hear the door open. I lay on my side, back to the door. Vincent appears at my side silently.

"Hey. I thought you were asleep." He holds out a bottle of Royal Crown soda to me. It glistens, moist and cold.

I sit up with a start. "You remembered."

He grins. "How could I forget? It was the best way to get on your good side."

I take the bottle from him, my own smile fights to make an appearance. The loss and loneliness I have felt all day slides away, vanishing as I meet Vincent's gaze. I open the bottle and sip the soda. I close my eyes as the sweet rush of bubbly soda slides down my throat.

"I was afraid you weren't coming back," I say, focusing on the bottle of soda rather than his beautiful hazel eyes. I can feel the tears rising.

"I was here, in the parking lot, but I had to go home. Family stuff."

I try to smile. "You have kids."

He nods. "I do."

I watch his face as it transforms from the gentle lover I have known to the professional investigator he now is. His tone changes, and he points to a chair.

"May I sit?"

I nod, and he reaches inside his coat and pulls out a notebook and pen. My heart sinks a little. I want something else from this. A connection, maybe. A few words. An explanation, even. How in the world is he here in Brisbane? How?

Brisbane, Australia, is a half of a world away from Kansas City, Missouri. Is it coincidence? Or something more?

Paranoid much, Nichole?

Maybe he's out to get you, too.

Or maybe you're just hoping he's still in love with you and will somehow bail you out of this mess.

God, how I hate the voices in my head.

"How is your son?" he asks, his dark eyes and expressionless face a mystery.

Tears well up in my eyes. "I don't know. They say he's in the nursery."

Vincent frowns. "And you haven't seen him today?"

I can't speak. I just stare at a bead of condensation that slips down the side of the bottle in my hands. I shake my head, feel the splash of warmth juxtaposed on the icy coldness of the bottle.

"Nicky" — his hand reaches out and lifts my chin — "talk to me."

"I got up and tried to go see him. They said I couldn't leave."

"The officer stationed outside your door said that?"

"Yes." A sob breaks free. "I asked a nurse if I could see my baby and she said she had to talk to the doctor. That was hours ago."

"Wait, he's been in the nursery all day? Haven't they let you breastfeed him?"

I shake my head, my throat closed, the emotions running through me rob me of speech.

Vincent stands abruptly. "Give me a moment." He strides from the room.

I strain to hear but only catch bits and pieces of the conversation between Vincent and the other officer. Seconds into it, a third voice joins in. It sounds like one of the nurses.

"Staunton is detained, yes, but..."

"Right of the mother to bond with her child..."

"Immediately..."

"Presumption of innocence..."

"Rights of a nursing mother..."

"You will do this *now*."

Most of it is Vincent, with the others arguing in lowered voices. Vincent seems to not care whether he draws others' attention. I can't help but smile. He has been the same way the entire time I have known him. If a cause is righteous in Vincent's mind, then his voice is clear and *loud*. Even in elementary school, he was this way. I suddenly remember a classmate accused of pulling the fire alarm. Instead, it had been a girl in front of Vincent who had done it on a dare. Vincent was small for his age then, long before adolescence and growth spurts took him to his now lean six-foot-plus height. He had stood up to the teacher, back ramrod straight, quivering with anger, and pointed the culprit out. Even then, Vincent's sense of right and wrong was strong.

Is it any real surprise he ended up in law enforcement?

A few minutes later, Vincent re-enters the room, a small procession behind him. A nurse wheels in a bassinet, her eyes dart to meet mine, apprehension shows clearly on her face. Behind her is the officer posted outside of my door. His eyes survey the room, settle on mine briefly, and focus back on Vincent.

"Should I..." He leaves the rest of his question hanging there in the air, unanswered.

Vincent nods towards the door. "I'll be in here. You can go grab a bite to eat for the cafeteria shuts down for the night." He turns back towards me. "Mrs. Staunton, in order to have your baby inside of the room with you, we must have a peace officer present at all times." I nod, marveling at how easily he turns the professional façade on in front of others.

The nurse looks at Vincent and then at the departing police officer, her mouth agape.

Vincent pulls out his badge. "I can serve as that officer. And I will take personal responsibility for the safety of Baby Staunton, ma'am. If I need to step out, I'll let you know right away."

"Oh, of course, of course." The nurse seems flustered and embarrassed. She has obviously forgotten that Vincent is a police officer as well. She stands there for a moment, unmoving, and then says, "I'll be at the nurse's station should you need me."

The door shuts behind her with a quiet click.

Vincent guides the bassinet over and reaches in, lifting Theo up with an ease that tells me he has done this before and is well-versed in handling babies. Theo makes a gurgling sound and yawns wide as Vincent places him gently in my arms. He moves swiftly, catching the forgotten bottle of soda from where it was nestled by my side before it can spill.

"He's beautiful, Nicky."

I stare into Theo's eyes and feel a wave of love and emotion sweep through me. The child I never thought I could have is here, in my arms. But at what cost? And Elizabeth? What about her? And Jhon?

"What's his name?" Vincent asks, and I look up to see the boy I once loved standing in front of me. Why did I leave him? I deserved happiness. I deserved love.

Fool. You left him. You broke his heart.

You don't really expect him to still love you, do you? He has a family. He has a wife and children. He moved on.

My gaze falls to the baby in my arms.

"Nicky?"

I shake my head. "Sorry, I, um, his name is Theo." I can't meet Vincent's eyes. All I can see in that moment is the look on Jhon's face when he learned we were having a boy. My eyes fill with tears, and I can feel a headache gathering steam. "Vincent, can you tell me? Is Jhon alive? Is he okay? Is Elizabeth all right? Is she safe?"

Vincent sighs, walks around the bed to where the chair is, and sits. "I checked in on Jhon's status before I headed over. He's out of surgery, and stable. His heart stopped briefly during surgery, but they were able to revive him. The head trauma is the biggest concern right now. The doctors are watching closely for brain swelling, and he is still unconscious at this time."

I cry and stroke our son, wishing I could see Jhon, feel the touch of his hand, and tell him I love him.

"Can I see him?" I ask, even though I already know the answer.

Vincent shakes his head. "No." He leans forward, speaks softly, as if we can be overheard here, alone in the hospital room. "I would do almost anything for you, Nicky, but that I cannot do. I'm skating on thin ice here." He reaches out, runs a finger along Theo's baby-soft wisps of bright red hair. "Tell me everything. And I promise you, I will find you the best defense lawyer in the country."

My heart sinks. He doesn't believe me. He can't and say that. I don't need a defense lawyer. I haven't done anything wrong!

"You don't believe me."

Vincent closes his eyes and sighs again. "Nicky, would *you* believe the story you have told so far if *you* heard it?"

"It's *me*, Vincent. You were there when I crashed and burned on my first bike. You helped carry me back to Hannah and Andy. We memorized lines together for the school play in fifth grade. You *know* me." I feel a knot form in the back of my throat. My tongue feels thick, to the point I can barely speak.

"You know me, Vincent," I whisper. "You are the only one who really does."

He sits silent, his eyes search mine. I sense a question there. Not one that has to do with working a case or interrogating a suspect, but something far more personal.

I finally give voice to the reason I left him a decade ago. "I didn't think I deserved you."

A frown crosses his features at my words. "What?"

"After the fire. After I lost Hannah and Andy. After I lost our..." My jaw clamps down. Even now I can't give that terrible grief words. The loss still feels like it did in the days after the fire. Devastating. Overwhelming. "It felt as if all the terrible things my birth mother said to me were true. That I didn't deserve love, or happiness, or success. I didn't deserve to live. And I sure didn't deserve you. That's what I thought. That's why I left."

He turns away, stands up, and paces the room, shaking his head.

"I should have handed this off to someone else." He casts an agonized look my way. "From the second I saw you, the only thing I could think of was, 'I need to help her.' Because I couldn't believe that you had done what they were saying you did. But damn it, Nicky, you have to be honest with me."

"I am being honest with you, Vincent. I've never once, not in all of my life, lied to you. And I'm not about to start now." I stare into his eyes. "Please,

please. Let me finish the story. You haven't heard everything; you need to hear the rest. *Please.*"

In my arms, Theo stirs, then closes his eyes, his body warm and relaxed, close to me once again. He is where he needs to be, where I need him to be as well. I can't see Jhon, I have no idea where Elizabeth is, and my only lifeline is a man I had once planned on spending the rest of my life with.

Vincent shoots me a look, returns to the chair, and sits down. "I'll listen. But Nicky, at the end of this, I'm going to have to come clean with my boss. For you, for me, for the sake of the case. Tell me you understand."

I nod. "I understand. But you need to hear the rest of the story."

He leans back in his chair. "Okay. Yesterday, we were interrupted by you going into labor. You had just gotten to" — he consults his notes — "March 20th, 2018, at approximately midnight."

"Right before midnight," I correct. I take a deep breath. "I was convinced Jhon and I were going to die there on the floor of our rental house."

As I stare into Vincent's eyes, I push away a vivid memory of his hands against my naked skin. I remind myself yet again that what we had is gone. Ten years gone. The love isn't. I can feel it here, between us. But there is still so much to tell him. I open my mouth and begin to describe the moment I first saw Elizabeth change aspects right before my eyes.

Incident/Case #: 18-02521

Classification: Assault/Arson

Date: 2018-20-09

Location: Rush Creek, Raaen Road

Victim (s): Staunton, Jhon and Elizabeth

Suspect: Staunton, Nichole

Evidence ID#: 18-02521-018 (page out of handwritten journal)

Eight of Swords. The cards know my heart. They know me. I wanted a family, but what do I really have? A husband who promised to love me and isn't here. A child I cannot trust or find it in me to truly love. I am trapped and imprisoned. And there is no way out.

- N -

18. A New Beginning

- Nichole -

March 21st, 2018 - Seattle, Washington

If I were to put a finger on the moment it all changed and everything hit home for me, it was seeing the transformation for the first time. A changing of the guard, if you will. A brief second where one stepped back, however unwillingly, and the other came forward.

In that moment, she could have done it, she could have killed us both, and we would not have been able to stop her. How does a small child, one less than four years old, for heaven's sake, manage to come mere seconds away from killing two grown adults?

All I can tell you is that despite all the warning signs, despite everything, even Rob and Kate's deaths, the thought that Elizabeth could truly hurt us seemed impossible.

Life isn't a horror movie. The paranormal doesn't exist. Children don't go from innocence to psychopathic murderers in the space of a season. They don't.

I've looked back on that night hundreds of times since. I've examined it, and the days that led up to it, and all I can tell you is that Elizabeth could and would have killed us, but she ran out of time.

That cuckoo clock Jhon inherited from his grandparents chimed once, twice, and kept going until it reached twelve. I didn't move. I couldn't. Jhon was unconscious on the floor next to me. We didn't lift a hand to stop her because we weren't able. *She* stopped.

No. That isn't right.

I watched it. You can tell me I'm crazy, but I *saw* it. The clock chimed and Elizabeth froze in place, unmoving. Those teeth, so perfectly white and even, I bore the marks of them on one wrist, the skin already swelling and bruised. The eyes, glinting with madness and hatred. All of it slid away in that moment and Isabel emerged. She blinked, her face turning from dark victory to one of fear and uncertainty.

"Isabel." I guess I said it out loud. She blinked at me, and her blue eyes looked trusting, sweet - the monster had slipped away.

She looked down, saw the knife in her hand, and dropped it. It clattered to the floor and spun in place, rotating twice before slowing and stopping. I could see it, I could see *her*, she was back, our sweet little Isabel. Elizabeth, the one who had likely poisoned Clementine, who had stabbed Jhon and done her best to incapacitate me, and who had been seconds away from stabbing me - she had vanished. Isabel stood there in her place. She looked lost at first, then horrified. She glanced back up at my face, fear and anxiety warring for control, where only a moment before there had been no emotion other than the stuff of nightmares.

"Mommy?" Her eyes traveled over me. My right leg was twisted wrong, bruised and swelling, and likely broken. Jhon was beside me, moaning. Blood seeped from his head and arm.

I blinked, tried to focus, but I'd taken such a knock on the head that everything kept shifting from single to double-vision. I tried to move, but my leg wasn't having it. The waves of pain were pulsing through it, and on up through my butt and back. When I had fallen, I'd felt the crunch.

"Mommy." She edged closer, and I flinched as she reached out a hand to touch mine. Her touch was tentative, gentle. She met my eyes, and I felt as if I could be lost in the blue. "It wasn't *me*, Mommy."

"I... I know, baby." As if the doors of knowledge had finally been opened, I flew back in time, back to each change, each shift. Isabel's transition to Lizzie had happened overnight. So had Lizzie's transition to Elsa's and Elsa's to Elizabeth's. They'd damn well announced themselves, for God's sake, and I had been too dense to pick it up.

"It was Elizabeth." Her voice was soft, wavering with emotion. "I'm sorry, Mommy."

"You have nothing to be sorry about, Isabel." I paused and asked, just to be sure. "She's gone, right? And she's not coming back for a while?"

Isabel's tears spilled out of her eyes. "She's gone. She won't be back until it's cold again." She looked at my leg. "You're *hurt*. Daddy too."

"Isabel, when Elizabeth was here, where were you?"

Isabel looked at me, her lip quivering. "I go into a room with windows."

"A room with windows? So, you can see out? You can see what the others are doing?"

Isabel nodded.

"And you remember? Even if you aren't out of the room and here with me?

Isabel nodded again.

"But you can't stop her? Or the others? Have you ever tried?"

Isabel shrugged and shook her head. Fresh tears coursed down her cheeks. "I'm sorry, Mommy."

The changes were so obvious, *so* obvious. Why had I refused to see them? Would I have ever put it together if it hadn't been for seeing it now, here, with my own eyes? I felt stupid and confused. Slow.

This wasn't dissociative identity disorder. Or, at least, it wasn't any kind I had ever heard of. She shouldn't be able to remember if another identity was in charge of anything that had happened. Those who suffered from DID experienced blackouts.

I didn't completely understand it, but at that moment I realized I wasn't the mother of *one* child. I was the mother of *four*. They always appeared on the solstice or equinox. March 21st, June 21st, September 21st, and, God help me, December 21st.

One was dark and dangerous, yes, but the others were loving, kind - and they needed me. And somehow, somehow, now that I knew, I had to protect them. Spring, summer, fall, and winter - a child for each season. Winter's Child had gone away, yanked out of power by the clock striking midnight, and now here was Isabel, my sweet, shy little girl. In three more months, Lizzie would return, vivacious, fun-loving, with a heart of gold. Even Elsa, her anxiety and fear so well-founded. All three outweighed the one bad one.

I had to protect her. I had to protect *them*. I had to protect us all. Jhon stirred.

"Isabel, sweetheart, can you reach the paper towels?"

Isabel nodded. I could no longer think of her as Elizabeth. Moreover, I didn't want to. Elizabeth was the one child of four that I could honestly say I had no interest in ever seeing. I knew she was part and parcel of the rest, however. Four children, one body.

I must have closed my eyes. Lost consciousness for just one moment, maybe two. Isabel's presence next to me caused my eyes to fly open, and we both jumped. She was timid and frightened. As for me, well, I was damaged, in pain, and with the adrenaline of the past few hours coursing through me.

"I got the paper towels, Mommy."

"Thank you, sweetheart."

I took the knife. It was just in reach. I took it and wrapped it thickly in the paper towels, careful to make sure there was no blood seeping through.

"Sweetheart, I need you to hide this knife. But first, let me see your hands."

Isabel held them out to me, turning them one way and then the next. There were smears of blood, but they had already dried.

"Okay, good. I want you to hide it somewhere no one is going to find it, okay? Can you hide it behind the pots and pans?"

"Okay, Mommy."

She opened the cabinet door and peered inside. "Way back in there, sweetheart." I reached over to Jhon and shook him gently. He groaned, opened his eyes, and tried to shift. I heard him gasp in pain.

"Nichole, Elizabeth..." He stopped, and his eyes flew open, "Oh God..."

"Jhon, listen to me. It's Isabel."

"What?"

"I wouldn't have believed it if I hadn't seen it with my own eyes, but Elizabeth is gone and Isabel is here now."

He clutched his side and inched toward me, his eyes flicking back and forth between us.

"It's March 21st, Jhon. I watched her change as the clock struck midnight. I can't explain it any better than this, but I need you to hear me. At the stroke of midnight, Elizabeth went away and Isabel, well, Isabel emerged."

Jhon stared at me, his mouth agape. He shot a look at our child and then back at me. One of his pupils was dilated, the other not, a sure sign of a concussion, possibly a severe one. I needed to call 9-1-1. But first, we had to keep Isabel safe.

"Jhon, listen to me. We need to spin this right. We need medical care. You have a concussion, my leg is broken. If we tell them the truth, they will never believe us."

"Spin this?" he repeated. "She tried to *kill* us, Nichole." His gaze kept flitting back to Isabel.

Isabel stood there, her lip trembling, tears filling her big blue eyes.

"It wasn't me. It was *her*." She whispered it, her tiny voice cracking.

"Her," Jhon repeated. The knife wound needed treatment, and so did his concussion. And I was half-sitting, my leg twisted in the most unnatural position possible. We needed help. But before we got it, we needed a damned good explanation.

"It was *Elizabeth* who attacked us. And Isabel is here now. Isabel would never hurt us, Jhon. You know that." I reached for Isabel's hand. "Come here, sweetheart."

He flinched away as Isabel, avoiding my injured leg, leaned against me, curling her body up tight against my left side. Tears slipped down her cheeks and her face wore an anguished expression as she buried her face in my neck.

"I've been keeping a journal," I told Jhon as I ran a comforting hand over her curls. Part of me still wanted to flinch away, the memory of Elizabeth still hanging heavy in my mind. "The therapist suggested it. The changes, they have come on the equinox and the solstice. March 21st, June 21st, September 21st, and December 21st. She isn't Elizabeth right now, Jhon, she's Isabel. She's safe. *We're* safe." I felt Isabel nod into my neck, her tears wetting my shirt.

"I don't... I can't..." His voice fell away. He leaned over, turning away from me, and vomited, bile splashing against the table leg.

"Jhon, listen to me, please. We need help. We need to call 9-1-1, get our injuries treated, but we can't tell them about Elizabeth. They'll never believe us anyway."

Jhon heaved again, strings of drool hanging from his mouth. "Christ." He whispered it. "You know how crazy this sounds, right?"

"Yes, that's why we need to lie. All of us." Isabel trembled in my arms. "It was a home invasion. They were looking for money, but we didn't have any. They roughed us up after breaking in. Isabel, you hid under the bed."

"And when they ask us what these guys looked like?" Jhon asked, his voice strained, his skin a sheen of sweat. Shock was setting in. He needed treatment.

"They were dressed in black. With black ski masks and black gloves. And it all happened so fast we can't remember anything of value." I said it quickly, amazed at how easily the lies fell from my lips.

He wiped his mouth with the back of his hand. "They just walked in?"

"You went to take out the trash, and they jumped you. Then they came in through the unlocked door."

"Christ." He said it again and stared at Isabel. His eyes fell to the bloody tooth marks on my wrist. "What about your wrist?"

I looked down at my swelling wrist. There was no way I could get away with saying they bit me. It was far too small of a wound to have been inflicted by an adult mouth. My mind spun and my head ached. "Isabel was panicked and bit me when I tried to pull her out from under the bed and run out of the house with her. Then one of them grabbed me and threw me down the hallway. I fell wrong, broke my leg." I patted Isabel. "Baby girl, go get my phone from the bedroom."

She stood reluctantly and skittered away to fetch it. Jhon watched her go, leaned over, and whispered, "Nichole, are you *sure* about this?"

"I've never been more sure in my life, Jhon. If you had seen it, if you had seen Elizabeth leave and Isabel arrive, you would believe it too. Please, my love, trust me."

Isabel returned, her cheeks still wet, and handed me my phone. I met Jhon's eyes. "Can you stick to the story?"

"If you are sure you want me to," he answered after a moment's silence.

"I'm sure." I turned to Isabel and took her hand. "Isabel, sweetheart, lying is bad. But sometimes, very rare times, it is necessary. I need you to repeat what I've said or else they will take you away from us. And we don't want that, do we, Jhon?" He shook his head slowly, reluctantly, his eyes unreadable, dark. I turned back to Isabel. "You need to tell them you heard scary noises and hid under your bed. You didn't see anyone. Can you say that back to me?"

"I heard scary noises and hid under my bed. I didn't see anyone." Her tiny voice shook.

I smiled at her. "Good, that's good. I'm going to call 9-1-1 now."

We were separated first in the ambulance. Isabel had clung to me, terrified, as we had ridden in one together, while Jhon had been transported in the other.

At the hospital, a social worker took her by the hand and Isabel clung to my left hand with a death grip, until I reassured her that she was just going to be away for a few minutes. Once they had X-rayed my leg and wheeled me into the treatment room, I had asked for her to be brought back to me.

"She's terrified, and she needs me."

"Of course, Mrs. Staunton, of course." The nurse had reassured me and after the doctor set the leg and the cast was in place, a frizzy-haired matronly woman led her into the room.

"Mommy!" Isabel had pulled away from the social worker's grasp and buried her face in my side. I leaned down and pulled her up onto the bed, tears dripping into her curls. Isabel smelled of chocolate and cookies.

"Well now, there she is. Mommy's leg is all fixed up and soon all will be well, yes?" The older woman smiled warmly, and there was a gap between her top two teeth.

"May I see my husband?" I asked. "How is he?"

"He's speaking with the police at the moment, Mrs. Staunton, and he has a slight concussion, but it won't be long now."

Hours later, the sun was already well over the horizon as we made our way slowly out of the hospital. My lower right leg was in a cast, and the pain meds had taken most of the headache away but left me feeling loopy.

A police car sat waiting to take us to a hotel. A detective with the last name of Getz had taken both of our statements and spoken to Isabel while she was curled up at my side. She had repeated the lies I had told her to say, her tiny body trembling as she did. Detective Getz had nodded sympathetically and scratched a few notes in a small spiral-topped notepad.

I hadn't known it at the time, but there had been a rash of break-ins a few blocks over the past few weeks.

"Looks like they might be amping up, getting a bit more aggressive," Getz said, closing his notepad. "I can get one of our patrolmen to give you a ride back to your house, or a hotel, if you would prefer. We dusted for prints, and I apologize, but it leaves a bit of a mess."

As much as I loved our little rental house, I didn't want to see it at the moment. The memories were too fresh, too raw. All I could see when I closed my eyes was Elizabeth coming towards us with a butcher knife in her hand. I was bone-tired, woozy from the pain meds, and I wanted to just curl up and sleep until noon. Isabel was tucked against me, shadows of exhaustion pooling under her normally bright blue eyes, making her pale skin appear almost yellow. I didn't have to look at Jhon to know he felt the same way. We were all dead on our feet.

"Please take us to a hotel."

The officer nodded. "There's a Hyatt Regency off of Howell."

"Yes, thank you."

Isabel was sound asleep as Jhon carried her gingerly onto the elevator and up to our room. She didn't wake when he placed her gently on the couch and covered her with a small blanket. My armpits were already aching from leaning on the crutches. We were both bruised, battered, and exhausted.

Jhon closed the door to the bedroom once we were inside. I collapsed on the bed. The sheets smelled of lavender and, only faintly, of bleach.

"I'm exhausted," I muttered. "How about you?"

"Exhausted, yes. But I lied to that detective, Nichole." He ran his hand through his hair, wincing as his fingers found the lump where Elizabeth had hit him with the paperweight. "I'm not sure how I feel about any of this. How I feel about *her*." He nodded toward the outer room where Isabel lay sleeping. "This is fucking crazy, you know that, right?"

"If you had seen her, Jhon, you'd believe it too. I *saw* Elizabeth go away, and Isabel take control."

"You keep saying that. So what the hell does it even mean? Is it that dissociative identity thing you were talking about?"

I shrugged, "Maybe? I don't think so, but I'm not a psychologist. I don't know. From what I read, the different identities are unaware of each other, and they basically black out when another identity takes charge. Isabel is different. These shifts take place on the equinoxes and solstices. And Isabel says she can see everything that is happening but not control it when it isn't her season.

"I've been keeping track since September, and before that, actually. I went back and filled in the dates. I flew in from Peru on March 21st.

Remember how the caseworker said the foster parent reported having trouble with her? It was because *Elizabeth* was still in charge. When I flew in and Cara picked her up from the emergency placement and brought to me, she was already Isabel. And I remember the exact day that Lizzie came out because it was also the longest day of the year, June 21st. And then the first nightmare came on September 21st, and that's when Elsa emerged."

"All derivatives of Elizabeth," Jhon muttered.

"Isabel is meek, shy, easily frightened. Lizzie is happy, warm, effusive, and lovable," I added.

"Elsa is withdrawn, frightened," Jhon murmured, then paused. "And Elizabeth is a goddamn psychopath."

"We have to figure out a way to keep Elizabeth buried and let the others stay in control," I said thoughtfully, my mind focused on the problem. A moment of silence went by before I looked up and saw Jhon's face.

"You want to *keep* her?" He stared at me, a look of horror on his face.

"I want to keep Isabel, Lizzie, and Elsa," I fired back. "And if that means finding a way to deal with a psychopath for three months out of the year, then it's worth it. *They* are worth it."

"Nichole, we have no way of knowing when the psychopath aspect might come back. You are hypothesizing. It's nothing more than a guess. What if she comes back in a week or two, or a month? What then?"

"She won't, Jhon. Elizabeth can only come out between December 21st and March 20th. She's Winter's Child," I stated glibly, hoping I was on to something and not being a gullible idiot. "Trust me, you will see Lizzie come out on June 21st, and Elsa on September 21st. And when you do, you will understand why I'm so sure we can do this. We have nine months before Winter's Child comes back."

Jhon laid back on the bed. "I can't... I'm just too tired to talk about this anymore. I mean, I guess we will see what happens, but when we get back to the house, I'm putting a lock on her door. And one on ours, too."

I knew better than to try to argue. And besides, after all we had gone through, it made sense. I wanted to curl up against him like I usually did, but everything hurt and the cast on my leg felt awkward. Jhon reached out and laced his fingers into mine.

"I love you," he said simply.

"I love you, too." And within seconds, I was deeply asleep.

It wasn't until hours later, in the early afternoon, that we all woke up.

At first, Jhon kept his distance from Isabel. Who am I kidding? I did as well. But eventually, we both relaxed. She absolutely was the little, shy girl we remembered so vividly. And as the days passed, we took each day and relaxed little by little. We returned to our rental house, cleaned it up, and eventually my cast was removed. I still had to take it easy, and the leg felt weak, delicate, although it was likely my own nervousness more than anything.

I counted the days until June 21st. I was going to prove my theory.

Incident/Case #: 18-02521

Classification: Assault/Arson

Date: 2018-20-09

Location: Rush Creek, Raaen Road

Victim (s): Staunton, Jhon and Elizabeth

Suspect: Staunton, Nichole

Evidence ID#: 18-02521-019 (page out of handwritten journal)

I dream of making her scream. Or maybe it's the voices.

Not sure.

They whisper in my ears, and I find myself wondering what it would be like to give her a nice shove over the railing, watch the fear wash over her in that second when the ground is not beneath her feet and all safety has disappeared.

Will she scream? Or will she go silently?

- N -

19. A Theory Tested

- Nichole -

June 20th, 2018 - Seattle, Washington

We put Isabel to bed at 8 p.m. as we normally did. It had taken more than a month of Jhon watching her like a hawk, placing locks on the doors, and even adding a video monitor feed that recorded her every movement before he had relaxed and accepted that Elizabeth was really and truly gone. At least, for now.

My cast had been removed nearly six weeks before, and I had immersed myself in my projects three days a week when Isabel was in daycare. On the days that Isabel wasn't in daycare, we had practiced sculpting, and she showed a natural affinity for it, creating an array of animal sculptures that were strikingly accurate. I had reviewed my journal entries, even shown them to Jhon, and he had what I could only describe as a skeptical half-acceptance of my theory. Tonight, if my theory was right, Isabel would depart and Lizzie would emerge. We only had a few hours to wait.

"I've read those articles you found last week," Jhon said as he handed me my water bottle full of ice-cold water. "And it doesn't mention anything about seasons or even a specific date being a trigger for the change in personalities."

It was a well-worn topic by now. We had both pored over medical journals. I'd read about the classic cases of dissociative identity disorder, even watched the movie *Sybil* with Sally Field and I'd felt like an idiot the entire time. There was a feeling of not-quite-rightness to all of it. The more I reviewed my journal entries, the less I was sure about anything other than that we were dealing with four unique personalities who all seemed to reside in one body. With it boiled down to that simple description, four unique personalities, then the diagnosis seemed obvious, even if I was playing armchair psychiatrist. Despite this, I couldn't shake the feeling that dissociative identity disorder simply did not apply.

"After midnight, if Lizzie comes out and Isabel is gone, you will see it for yourself. Then, if you want, we can get another psychologist involved," I promised him. Jhon had been pushing for it, even as I argued that she was acting perfectly normal at the moment and no one would believe us. I still felt that way, but we had put our heads together and come up with a strategy. It had involved taking dozens of videos over the past few months to demonstrate baseline personality and behavior traits. One of the side effects of this was that I had been surprised to remember that Isabel liked foods, clothes, and even television shows and books that the others didn't. What I had assumed was just a change in tastes had been far different. And while some things she had outgrown — her Hello Kitty obsession had instead turned to Belle from *Beauty and the Beast* — her requests for grape jelly with her peanut butter sandwiches instead of strawberry had taken me by surprise.

I had written it all down. Jhon had raised his eyebrows when I pulled out a spiral-bound notebook and showed him. I had added four tabs:

- Spring - Isabel
- Summer - Lizzie
- Fall - Elsa
- Winter - Elizabeth

The spring tab was filled with lists. The others had tentative, half-written lists. Things I could remember, I wrote down. I hadn't exactly been keeping track of everything. But when a particular food like or dislike, or her clothing or color choices, had stood out in my memory, I had added them to the lists.

I wrote it all down. Anything I could remember. What clothes she preferred to wear — pretty much dresses all the time. What colors she chose, what foods she liked or disliked, and even the television shows and books that Isabel chose to watch or read.

Reading. That was another shock. How had I not noticed before Elizabeth appeared that the girls were able to read? Or had that developed over the winter? I wasn't sure, and Isabel became uncomfortable when I asked her too many questions about before.

Before.

Isabel used it first, and I simply followed suit. Isabel was here now. On that, we were all clear. I asked her once where Elizabeth had gone and Isabel had shrugged uneasily. "She's here. But she can only listen and watch."

"And the others? Is it the same way for Lizzie and Elsa?" Isabel had nodded, focusing on her Lego Friends build and seemed unwilling to say anything further. I couldn't help wondering if Lizzie would be more forthcoming. Isabel was shy, and obviously uncomfortable talking about the others, especially Elizabeth.

Before and After.

If tonight ended as I suspected it would, I certainly would miss Isabel's quiet ways. She was easy to care for, certainly. I also was curious to see just how many of her tastes would change when Lizzie took control.

"Shall we watch *Agents of S.H.I.E.L.D.*?" Jhon asked, interrupting my thoughts of a notebook tab filled with lists. "Season Five is on Netflix. I missed seeing it when it dropped in early December."

In early December, we were both sleep-deprived. By then, Elsa's nightmares were occurring several times in a night. We had been more in love with getting sleep any chance we could than watching television. And after the 21st, well, I still didn't like thinking about how awful it had become. By then, all that either of us could bear to watch were comedies and rom-coms.

"Sure." I didn't love *S.H.I.E.L.D.* as much as he did, but anything that would eat up the hours until midnight was appealing at the moment. I was too nervous to sleep, anyway. What if things switched up, and we suddenly had Elizabeth back? Or Elsa?

Jhon pulled me close to him on the sofa and turned the television on with his phone. The remote had been smashed to pieces in Elizabeth's assault right before Isabel appeared, and we hadn't bothered to get a replacement. It was a pain, really, but the screen was damaged too, pixels black and dead in the top right corner of the screen and I delayed, wondering if I shouldn't just replace the whole television. Maybe once I had finished the latest commission, a series of nature fairies for a local children's garden. Jhon's work paid the bills and necessities, and mine was quickly becoming the fun money. The last commission had paid for Christmas, and I had still managed to put nearly half of it in savings afterward. I smiled. Jhon's birthday was coming up. He would love one of the newer Roku televisions, and prices had been plummeting.

I itched to page through the notebook again, but I had already committed it to memory. I visualized the toys list, mentally parsing through it, thinking about Lizzie's obsession with coloring last year. Would she return to it? Perhaps ask for something other than the *Beauty and the Beast* activity books that Isabel seemed to enjoy so much?

It kept my brain occupied as the show droned on. I couldn't manage to concentrate on much of it past the premise that the group was transported to a space station through the monolith and discovered planetary wreckage is actually Earth, torn apart in some terrible cataclysm. Jhon's eyes were riveted to the screen, turning away from it in quiet moments to glance at me. We were both nervous, jumpy. Even though Jhon had maintained his wait-and-see stance for the past three months, I could tell he was as hopeful as I was that my theory would be proven right.

The hours crept by.

After the fourth episode concluded shortly after learning that Kasius was attempting to breed Inhumans, Jhon pressed a button on his phone and the screen went dark.

"We have still got twenty minutes until it's midnight."

He nodded. "I know." He took the notebook from my hand and set it on the coffee table. I slid closer and nestled my head against his chest, my fingers tracing the now-healed, but still red-edged scar on his arm. My cast had been removed nearly six weeks ago and my leg was nearly fully recovered. It wouldn't do to join a marathon or take up an extreme sport, but it only ached when I'd spent a day walking trails with Isabel or working on my sculptures.

Jhon wrapped his arms around me and I closed my eyes, comforted by his presence. It eased my fears significantly. Finally, Jhon spoke.

"What if she changes into Elizabeth?"

"She won't."

"How can you be so sure?" he persisted.

I shrugged. "I just am."

"And if we don't get Lizzie? What if we get Elizabeth back, instead?"

I sat up, met his eyes. "Jhon. Trust me. I know I'm right. It's June 20th, nearly midnight, nearly the 21st. Lizzie will come. Just wait a few more minutes and you will see."

He pulled away, sat up straighter, and dragged a hand across his face. He looked old for a moment, older than he should have. The stress and fear hadn't left us, not entirely, and I could see now how much it was affecting him. "It just sounds so impossible. Like we have stepped into a horror movie script. I wish I knew what to think."

"Just watch. You'll see." I looked up at his grandparents' cuckoo clock. The hands were nearly at midnight, just a few minutes to go. "Shall we wake her up now?"

Jhon stood up and headed for the hall, and I followed. As we stopped at her door, he reached for my hand. "Does she know what date it is?"

I shook my head. "No. I didn't want to discuss that with her, but honestly, I don't think it would matter. Telling time is still a challenge for her."

Jhon squeezed my hand. "Well, let's do this."

Her eyelashes fluttered in response to the door creaking open and the light shining in from the hallway as we both slipped into her room. She lay there, still tiny, even if she had grown a full size of clothing bigger and two shoe sizes in the past year. Her red curls spread across the yellow pillowcase and disappeared beneath the satin ruche sheet set of her *Beauty and the Beast* bedding. Her breathing changed, moving from a slow, rhythmic breathing to a shallower one as she slowly moved towards consciousness. Her eyelashes fluttered again and her lips twitched.

Her eyes blinked open, and she yawned. "Mommy?"

I smiled at her. My hands were sweaty and shaking with nervousness. "Hey, Isabel, sorry. I just wanted to check on you."

Her head dropped back onto the pillow. "Oh, okay, Mommy."

My heart plummeted. She hadn't reacted to the name, hadn't corrected me.

"Go back to sleep, sweetheart. Sweet dreams, Isabel." I slipped off of the bed gently, my chest aching, and moved towards the door. I had almost walked out of it when I heard her voice, heavy with sleep, mumble something.

"What did you say, baby?"

"I'm Lizzie," came her reply, with another jaw-cracking yawn. "Isabel's gone away now."

The air between Jhon and me crackled with energy as he shut the door softly, his eyes round and shocked.

"You didn't say anything to her? Coach her like you did after the attack?" he whispered, intense and distrustful.

"No!" I whispered back, affronted. "I promised you I wouldn't. I wanted to see how she would react. It wasn't scripted. I wouldn't do that, Jhon!"

Jhon bit his lip, stared at me, and glanced back at the closed door before ushering me down the hall to our bedroom where we could speak in normal voices. He sat down on the edge of the bed, shaking his head.

"Seriously, what the hell is going on here? What have we gotten ourselves into, Nichole?"

The last three months, we had tiptoed around this, and Jhon's questions hadn't changed. I had heard the phrase, "This is like something out of the *Twilight Zone*" too many times to count. I didn't blame him. I was right there with him. Fiction isn't reality. No matter how many science fiction shows or books I had read, this reality we were currently experiencing had no explanation. No matter how many Google searches I had done, no one with any lick of sanity was out there talking about the same thing. I had gone so far as to pay cash, and give a false name, and meet with two therapists. The moment I described our experiences, and pointed out that Elizabeth carried the memories of all of her personalities inside of her, was the moment I would see the look. The one that said that I was the problem. That I was the unhinged one. Careful questions. Like when the first one asked about my family history and whether I had ever suffered hallucinations or heard voices. The second had practically followed me out the door and I was thankful the main parking lot had been full and that I had instead parked at a Target two blocks away. I had certainly felt like the paranoid one as I walked as quickly as I could, my right leg aching in protest.

Now that my theory had been proven, and Lizzie, or Summer's Child, had made an appearance, it was time to figure out the rest of it. Specifically, how or what we would do in six months. I was terrified of Winter's Child. Nightmares of her returning woke me up at night. And the clock was ticking.

Summer would end and then it would be fall. Elsa would make an appearance.

Lizzie was the easiest to talk to about these changes. While she didn't understand them, and was frightened of Elizabeth as much as we were, she was the most willing to answer questions. Isabel, true to her nature, didn't want to talk about Elizabeth at all. It was simply too overwhelming for her. I felt bad even asking those few times in spring. The look of fear and sadness on her sweet little face was simply too much to bear. Lizzie was bubbly, but also more of a strong, down-to-earth personality. And while she frowned at the mention of Elizabeth, she was able to tell us clearly that all the personalities - Isabel, Elsa, and Elizabeth — were there but unable to come forward. "It's not their time," she said, shrugging. "They go to their rooms and can't come out. Not until it's their time. But when it isn't my time, I can see what the others are doing and saying. I can hear what they hear. See what they see."

This was completely at odds with any symptoms of dissociative identity disorder. And the half-dozen therapists we took Lizzie to were of no help. It was as if they were so focused on checking off the boxes, and either applying or rejecting the label, that they had nothing further to offer, except to turn their focus towards me. It was maddening and, as the months marched on, Jhon and I were both feeling the pressure. We couldn't go through another winter with Elizabeth, we just couldn't.

It was early August when a possible answer to our predicament presented itself.

"Jacob asked me to take the lead on the Paraguay office at the end of this month. For four weeks," Jhon said after Elizabeth was tucked into bed. "I told him it would only work if we could all go." He glanced at Elizabeth's closed door and then met my eyes. He had been turning down all travel for months. "He said he would look into it, but that it probably wouldn't be a problem. Just a quick there and back. What do you think?"

And then it dawned on me. In less than three weeks, it would be autumn here, but down in the southern hemisphere, it would be spring. My jaw dropped as the thought hit me like a freight train.

Jhon frowned in concern. "What is it?"

"We can test the theory."

"What do you mean?"

"The seasons. They are reversed in the southern hemisphere. And Paraguay is in the southern hemisphere. What if the personality changes are tied to seasons?"

"Okaaayyy," Jhon answered slowly.

"If we go down there at the end of the month, after the 21st, Elsa would go away. And Spring's Child, Isabel, would come out once we crossed the equator."

"Or we might get murdered on the plane ride down. Or murdered in our sleep today or tonight or next week if the psychopath comes out earlier than you expect." Jhon began to pace, his voice steadily rising.

"We didn't sign up for this, Nichole. It's one thing to hear the instructor tell us our foster child would pee in our shoes and all the rest, it's quite another to try to avoid being stabbed, hit with glass paperweights, tripped, and, oh God—" He stopped then, spun and faced me, his eyes widened. "She killed Kate and Rob, didn't she?"

I winced. It had taken him a while to put that together. I had my suspicions, which had seemed so nuts, so over-the-top, that I hadn't voiced them aloud. And then there was the fact that I honestly didn't want to know. I could ask Lizzie. Of all of them, she seemed the most able to handle the darkness. Perhaps it was because she was filled with light. And light overpowers darkness. I hesitated, though. I think that, more than anything, I didn't want to know. Asking her would mean an answer, and I didn't want to live with that truth. I didn't want to think of my sweet friend in those last moments of her life. She hadn't deserved to die like that.

The voices in my head certainly had given it some thought. They had plenty to say, even now, and I was doing my best to ignore the clamor.

You want to keep a psychopathic, murdering child?

She's going to kill you and Jhon, just like she killed Kate and Rob.

The priest tried to warn you, but you wouldn't listen.

Kate reached out to you for help and you ignored her.

I stared at the ground, trying to choose the right words.

"I think that *Elizabeth* killed them, yes. But not Isabel, or Lizzie, or Elsa. Kate and Rob died when *Elizabeth* was in control. Somehow, we have to find a way to take away her power, to prevent her aspect from manifesting."

Jhon just shook his head. "Nichole, this is all... this is too much."

"Tell them you can go down for a month. That's all they were asking for anyway. If it works, we can stay longer."

Jhon stared at me as if I was a stranger he could not recognize. "Why, Nichole? What if our covering up for her, our protection, is the wrong thing? What if they could, I don't know, treat her condition?"

"Jhon, there is no pill that will stop Elizabeth from being a psychopath. No amount of talk therapy, medication, or a... vaccine can treat this. There is *nothing*. Not a single therapist I met with even believed it was possible." My voice rose before I remembered that Lizzie would hear me and wake up. "But the others don't deserve this. They are all capable of love, of empathy. We just need to figure out how to contain Elizabeth, to stop her from coming out. If she is still Elsa and not Isabel, we still have at least two and a half months before Elizabeth comes out. That's enough time to return to the States, explain everything, and get her help. Even get her institutionalized if need be. At least during the three months when Winter's Child is in control." I reached out, grasping Jhon's hands tightly. "It doesn't harm anything to try, Jhon. And if it works, we can make it so that Winter's Child never gets another chance to hurt anyone ever again!"

Incident/Case #: 18-02521

Classification: Assault/Arson

Date: 2018-20-09

Location: Rush Creek, Raaen Road

Victim (s): Staunton, Jhon and Elizabeth

Suspect: Staunton, Nichole

Evidence ID#: 18-02521-020 (page out of handwritten journal)

Last night, I woke up E and asked her if she could hear the voices like me.

At first, she buried her head under the covers, pretended to sleep. Later, once she was awake, she swore she couldn't hear them.

Every time I told her to listen, she would. I could see she heard them. I KNOW she did.

And still she lied and insisted there was nothing. The voices are THERE. I know they are. And so does E. She knows, and she is LYING. My own child lying to me. And why?

Perhaps she likes to play mind games with me. Perhaps she is evil. Undeserving, unlovable, and manipulative - just like the voices say she is.

- N-

20. Just a Short Trip

- Nichole -

September 23rd, 2018 - Concepción, Paraguay

We landed in Paraguay on the 23rd of September. Elsa had appeared at exactly midnight two days before. We had waited for the new aspect to step forward, just as we had three months before. I had made sure Lizzie had a long nap during the day and although she was tired, this time she was awake when the change occurred. Jhon and I watched it happen, our eyes intent upon her. I could see it wash over her, this change. The way she held herself, the look in her eyes, everything. She was different. I spared a couple of glances over at Jhon, whose face remained inscrutable, and I wondered what he was thinking.

I can only imagine what you are thinking. It was crazy for me to even want a child knowing what she had done, not just to us, but to Kate and Rob, and likely to her own birth family. I wondered about her birth family constantly. The information from Children's Services had been sparse. Just a mother, no father in the picture. Had there ever been? My Google searches yielded me little or nothing. Whoever her mother had been, if she was even still alive, was scrubbed clean. I was an amateur, though. If only I could get a private detective on the case, but that took money we simply didn't have at the moment.

As crazy as it sounded to me, I saw her as four separate girls. How could I not? When the season changed, so did she. It wasn't just their personalities that were different; it was their interests as well.

I had spent countless hours reading *Beauty and the Beast* to Isabel in the spring. Or watching her play with Lego Friends and make the most delicate flowers out of clay as she diligently forged her own way in the creative arts.

Lizzie, however, she was obsessed with *Rapunzel* and watched the movie over and over, playing dress-up and, when tired out from a long day of play, would color in a stack of *Rapunzel*-themed coloring books.

And Elsa, true to her name, preferred *Frozen*-themed everything and painting with watercolors.

Elizabeth, well, she had shown an ability to sketch that was both impressive and terrifying. Her pictures were detailed, dark, graphic, and very unsettling.

And God help me, I loved them all, even in some odd fearful way, Elizabeth. I was terrified of her, and I was scared of the violence she was capable of, but I still loved her. I know it doesn't make sense. But she, they, shared my baby's birthday. She could have been her. And sometimes, it felt like she was. As if she came back to me. And maybe, maybe Winter's Child was the price for that return.

Elsa, when she appeared at midnight on September 21st, turned to me first, met my eyes, her beautiful blue ones tinged with that morose edge that only Elsa displayed, and smiled. "Hi Mommy."

Jhon shivered a little beside me. I know he saw it, too.

"Hey, sweetheart," I answered and smiled. I had already placed her Elsa blanket on the bed, even though we would have to leave it behind when we boarded the plane later in the day. I had packed both a thin Elsa throw in her carry-on along with a *Beauty and the Beast* one in my bag. I was hedging my bets but praying I was right. When we crossed the equator, would she change aspects? Would Isabel appear? I was hoping beyond hope that she would.

We tucked her into bed, and she smiled again at the Elsa comforter on her bed and snuggled under it. "Thank you, Mommy. I love it!"

Eight hours later, our first flight took off from Seattle, headed for Mexico City. We spent one day sightseeing before moving on to the second leg of our trip. Jhon hadn't had a vacation day in two years, and his boss Rocco had insisted we stay at a time-share that he and his wife Sharon had bought a few years previously.

"Little Elizabeth will love visiting the ocean," Sharon had texted me. "So much warmer than these chilly Seattle waters!"

Jhon had watched her like a hawk there in Mexico. We spent the day at one of the nicer beaches, just a short walk from the time-share. Elsa, normally rather reserved and dour, was unusually cheery. I slathered her in 50 SPF and she walked in the sand and built a sand castle with Jhon as I sunbathed. It was a perfect little respite before we boarded the next series of planes the next day mid-morning. Still tired, and a little sunburned, despite the repeated applications of sunscreen, she fell asleep immediately, curled up in her *Frozen* blanket that depicted Anna and Elsa and Olaf together, snowflakes falling all around them.

There wasn't any way of telling exactly when we would cross the equator, although I knew it would be early on in the first flight. An hour, possibly two. I watched her, my hand resting on her back, her chest slowly rising and falling, a tiny bit of drool at the corner of her mouth. She lay curled between us, the armrests pushed up out of between the chairs. Her head was nestled in my lap, her feet rested against Jhon's thigh.

I looked over at him. He was frowning slightly as he watched her. I wondered what he was thinking. And on cue, he looked up and caught my eye. His face held such sadness.

"I was thinking of Patricia," he said, reaching out to unfold the blanket and pull it over Elsa's leg.

Patricia. *Elizabeth.* Our baby. The memory of her struck me hard, again. The taste of grief filled my mouth. My hand stilled on Elsa's back. I had never told him that I thought of her as Elizabeth. Even now, with another child of the same name, born on the same day. What would she have looked like? I was sure that she would have looked exactly like the child that lay between us. It didn't have to make sense. It just was this feeling I couldn't let go of, the one that kept me loving her even when the darkness of winter appeared.

In the months following the stillbirth, we hadn't talked about it. Jhon and I could talk about the moon and the sun and the stars. We could examine political issues in depth, discuss global warming, the different aspects of his work and the people he worked with - everything but talk about our dead child. The words just fell away. The dreams we had, the plans we had made, they lay mute, unspoken, and I mourned that wedge of silence that lay between us.

I knew that he loved the child curled between us. I knew it was different from the feelings I had, the irrational belief that she was my lost child returned to me, although through a twist of fate and not without its price.

But he was also afraid of her. And who could blame him? I looked at her and marveled at the terrible magic of it all. How had it happened? How could four little girls, so different, so unique, reside in one body? What terrible thing had happened to her? Or had it? Was she born this way? I had more questions than answers, but I longed to wake her up from her dreams and see whether it was Elsa or Isabel who would emerge. Would I be proven right or wrong?

If I was wrong, we would have less than two months to take some kind of action. Action I didn't want to take but knew that Jhon would insist upon. Elizabeth, or Winter's Child, as I had come to call her in my thoughts, was dangerous, far more dangerous than either of us wanted to admit. Short of locking her up for three months, I didn't know what we would do, and I dreaded involving Children's Services or the authorities. They wouldn't believe us. No one would believe us, except possibly the priest, Father Daniels. And would they even believe him?

Yeah, sure, mention exorcism and see where it gets you.

The truth was, we would be hard-pressed to prove anything, and we had already lied to the authorities in the first place by telling them it was a break-in.

You were a fool and Jhon will end up hating you. Or worse, he'll end up dead. All because you had to be a mother. You. The girl who drove her own mother mad enough to set fire to your childhood home.

I could feel the pressure building in my skull, a headache forming. Who was I kidding? We would pass over the equator. Maybe we had already, and when we did, Elsa would wake up and the countdown to Elizabeth's arrival in less than three months would begin.

And as if on cue, her breathing shifted, and I could see she was rousing, moving from a deep sleep to a light doze. How often had I watched her sleep? Too many times to count. Especially in those first few months when the reality of her had been so magical, such a blessing, one I was sure I would wake from.

The noise in the cabin had risen as well as the stewardesses began to push the cart filled with drinks and snacks down the aisle. As our little girl roused, yawning and rubbing her eyes, the older stewardess, her warm brown eyes crinkling to match her wide smile, leaned in towards her, "Ay, dulce nina, estas despierta!"

Elizabeth blinked up at her and smiled tentatively in return.

"What is your name?" the stewardess asked in English. Her accent was heavy, but understandable.

"Mi nombre es Isabel," she answered. Jhon and I had been teaching her some Spanish in preparation for the trip and she had obviously remembered it. I heard Jhon suck in a breath as my own heart burst with joy. It had worked. My hunch had been right. It was August, and yet, Isabel, Spring's Child, had emerged.

I was practically vibrating with excitement. We had our answer. We had a solution.

Jhon recovered first. He smiled at the stewardess and reeled off a string of Spanish words I couldn't follow. Not yet at least, but I would learn. Oh yes, I would. I grinned like an idiot as he ordered a mango spritzer for me, juice for Isabel, and a beer for himself. My arm encircled Isabel's, my fingers reaching out to grip Jhon's. I was overwhelmed with feelings of joy, of hope for the future.

If we had to spend the next eight months in Paraguay and then return to Seattle in July, we would do it. Whatever it took.

With some careful planning, we could ensure that Winter's Child never emerged again.

Incident/Case #: 18-02521

Classification: Assault/Arson

Date: 2018-20-09

Location: Rush Creek, Raaen Road

Victim (s): Staunton, Jhon and Elizabeth

Suspect: Staunton, Nichole

Evidence ID#: 18-02521-021 (page out of handwritten journal)

I pulled The Tower card today.

Of course I did.

The voices are so loud. And they never, ever stop. Not even in my sleep.

-N-

21. Come Fall, Come Reek of Bone

- Nichole -

November 18, 2018 - Brisbane, Australia

We stayed in Paraguay for nearly two months. It had taken longer to establish the office than expected, as things often do when you are operating in a foreign country.

Between paperwork and staffing, and obtaining the necessary permits and more, it was well into November by the time the office was running smoothly and the first applicants were funded.

I had helped out in the office at first, and placed Isabel in a school suggested by the American consulate. Her shyness, though, and the knowledge we wouldn't be there forever, had caused me to reconsider and explore homeschooling her.

Isabel and Elsa would especially benefit from homeschooling, and I hoped that, by the time Lizzie made an appearance, I would have made enough friends through other American families living in the region to provide our most outgoing child with an adequate number of playmates. Of all of them, I felt she would be the most likely to suffer in any way from not being around the other children. Isabel and Elsa, while sweet, took some time to warm up to others.

The weather when we landed had been the perfect spring weather. Most of the time it remained in the mid to high 70s, but now that summer was nearly at its zenith, it never fell below 70 degrees at night and was exceeding 100 degrees during the day. Add to that the humidity and rain and it was exhausting. Add to that the stress I was feeling at returning to Seattle with just weeks to spare before Winter's Child emerged. I felt at my wits end. I think that Isabel could sense it.

Just as Jhon and I didn't speak of our stillborn baby, even now, Isabel and I did not speak of the other aspects, not even Lizzie or Elsa. It felt as if there were some kind of unspoken contract between us, that Isabel, or whichever aspect who was currently out, had the right to her life, the right to pretend, if only for this time, that there was no other. Or perhaps I just wanted to protect her as much as I could. Isabel was so gentle, so sweet, I couldn't bear bringing it up. She deserved happiness and these moments with me here in Paraguay.

We would go out early, before the sun's rays pierced the clouds and brought the thick, humid heat with it. The Playa de Concepcion off of the Paraguay River was a short walk from our apartment and also a short distance from the office that Jhon had established for ULSC. We would buy fruit and nuts and stop by the office for a late breakfast and Isabel would sculpt at a small table we had set up in a corner while I helped with paperwork. By the end of our stay, one of our first employees, Carina, a round-faced woman with huge brown eyes and a perpetual smile, had taken over my role entirely.

Jhon's anxiety had gone down instead of up. The change we had both seen in the plane after crossing the equator had cemented it for him. I was just as sure, but I couldn't help worrying about what we were going to do for the next few months. Would Jhon need to find a different job, one that allowed us to stay either here in Paraguay, or elsewhere in the southern hemisphere? We discussed returning to Peru, and Jhon had been rather tight-lipped about our options as he continued to work toward some kind of fix for our looming predicament. It was late evening at home, Isabel already tucked in and asleep, when Jhon let out a whoop of delight. He tossed his phone to one side and wrapped his arms around me, grinning wildly.

"Jacob wants us to go to Brisbane, Australia, for the next four months!"

"Are you serious?" I couldn't believe our luck. I counted through the months quickly in my head. "If he wants you back sooner than March 21st, you have some vacation time available, don't you?" We could spend Christmas with Lizzie and even see Elsa before we changed back to Isabel once we returned to Seattle in mid-to-late March. It was the perfect answer.

Jacob's offer to send us to Australia was just what we needed. And on the first of December, we flew to Brisbane and began looking for a home to rent instead of an apartment. Lizzie was so full of energy, the last thing I wanted was to live above other neighbors who might complain about her constant motion. If she wasn't on her feet and moving, she was asleep. There didn't seem to be any in-between. We spent two weeks in a cramped hotel room before finding a darling two-bedroom house in a quiet residential district on the edge of Brisbane. It was perfect for our little family.

I am sure this is the night we conceived Theo, though I would not realize this for nearly five months. And by then it was far too late.

When Lizzie emerged on December 21st, we greeted her at midnight. It had become a custom by then. We would say goodbye to the departing aspect. I would kiss her and tell her I would see her again soon. Jhon would give her a big hug, and we would watch as she changed over. It had taken us so long to get to this place, and I was so incredibly relieved, so thankful, that we had found a cure, if you will, to the darkness and danger that Winter's Child brought to everyone.

The thought of giving her up had never truly occurred to me. She was ours. Call it fate or karma or whatever, but she was my heart and soul and Jhon had come to believe it too. We belonged together. I couldn't imagine ever endangering any other family, either. They wouldn't understand, couldn't understand, just how dangerous Winter's Child could be, and I would never have been able to live with myself if another family had suffered the fate that Kate and Rob had.

Dear, sweet Kate. I wished I could go back in time and tell her the secret. Even if it meant that she would be Elizabeth's mother. More often though, I found myself wishing it had been me that had first been called, instead of Kate. Every time I saw Jhon and our daughter together, it cemented the conviction in me even more. She was meant to be with us. We belonged together.

By late February, I had some kind of nasty, recurring flu. Or so I thought. It continued into March, and we welcomed Elsa back on the 21st. I had enrolled Lizzie in several after-school programs so that her thirst for friendship of other age-mates could be properly sated. I wasn't sure if Elsa would want to continue, but I asked her and she seemed willing.

Elsa appeared happier somehow, less anxious, and I very nearly asked her about the other aspects. I still didn't know if they were able to speak to each other at all. And more specifically, if Winter's Child spoke to any of them. I couldn't help but wonder what Elizabeth, Winter's Child, thought of all of this. I was afraid to. The subject felt off limits, unapproachable. I guess that, no matter how much success we had seen, I was still afraid to break the spell. If we talked about Elizabeth, about Winter's Child, would that break the spell and allow her to emerge? Would saying her name give her power? It might seem silly, but I was rather paranoid about it. I had taken to referring to her as Winter's Child or simply *her* when Jhon and I discussed it in the quiet of our bedroom at night.

Mostly, though, I was enjoying being a mom. The sculptures would wait, her childhood would not. And I had found myself tired beyond all reason in the spaces in between homeschooling and shuttling Elsa to events. I was rather young for it, but my vision was blurring, and I set an appointment to see an optometrist in mid-June once we returned to Seattle. I was gaining weight too, and my wedding ring had to be removed and resized. It was odd, this weight gain, and my hands and face felt unreasonably plump. I tried to shake it off, eat more greens, and avoid the ubiquitous mac and cheese or peanut butter and jelly sandwiches that were Lizzie and Elsa's favorites for lunch.

It was safe to return to the United States now, but as always, delays at the ULSC Brisbane office had pushed off our return to mid-May. I wasn't worried. After all, we still had over a month before Winter's Child could return. Elsa's nightmares kept it in the forefront of our minds. Around us, the leaves were turning vibrant shades of oranges, reds, and yellows. The nights had begun to cool, and the days weren't so infernally hot. There were days when I dearly missed the chill of winter. I found myself dreaming of snow, of all of us in snow gear and skis. One night, I even dreamed we had a snowball fight. We would never have that with our child. The danger was far too great.

One evening, the temps dipped into the low-50s. We turned the heater on for the first time. It was May 5th, Cinco de Mayo, in the wee hours of the morning when Elsa's screams woke me. I pushed my sluggish brain and body out of bed, down the hall, and into her room. She was crying, shaking. "She's coming, Mommy. She's coming."

I gathered her into my arms. Even at five she was so tiny, so elfin of feature that I feared if I squeezed too hard she would break.

"Elsa, my love, we won't let that happen," I whispered to her, rocking her, trying to pour my love into her. "Daddy and I, we figured out a way around it. She's been gone for more than a year now. Maybe for good."

Elsa trembled in my arms. "No Mommy, she's in here. She's really, *really* mad too. She says she's coming, and that *she* knows a way around it. I'm scared."

Fear pierced my heart. Only for a moment. There were rules, after all. We had learned them. We understood them. Elizabeth couldn't change seasons. She was Winter's Child, after all. The plane tickets were purchased, and we had already notified the management company of our departure.

Elizabeth only wishes *she could come out.*

You better hope Elsa isn't right. Because if she is...

"It will be okay, sweetheart. I promise." I soothed her, my fingers gently smoothing her tangled curls, the other hand rubbing her back, humming softly as I did. We were okay, we were safe, and she would be fine. Eventually, I felt her body go limp, her breathing level out. I went back to bed and lay there thinking about her words for far too long before sleep finally stole my cycling thoughts away.

That morning, just a handful of hours later, I had the worst headache I had had in years. It settled behind my left eyeball, and I could feel it with every beat of my heart. Pain pulsated through my head and neck. Jhon had already left for work, determined to put in place a few more policies for the new team he had assembled and personally head the second wave of lending programs the ULSC was rolling out.

"Mommy? Are you feeling okay?" Elsa reached her tiny hand over and patted mine. I wasn't. Not at all. I sat up and felt a wave of nausea crash over me. I staggered as quickly as I could to the bathroom, barely making it, and was violently ill. It was hard to breathe, too. As if I couldn't catch my breath.

"Mommy?" Elsa patted my back as I crouched there on the cool tile floor. I looked over to see her sweet face pinched with worry, a flare of fear in her eyes.

"I've just got a nasty bug, sweetheart. I'll be okay with a little rest." I reached over and ran my fingers through her red riot of curls. They were mashed up on the left side more than the right. She had curled up on her left side, back to me, and nestled against me close last night after the nightmare.

I knew it would be better if I brushed her hair now, but the thought of doing anything but crawling back into bed felt overwhelming.

"Can you go get my phone, Elsa? I need to call Daddy." He would have to come home. No matter what he had left to do there in the office, I was far too ill. Exhaustion filled me. The act of even crouching there in front of the toilet felt impossible. I sagged against the porcelain tub and tried to catch my breath. Why was it so hard to breathe?

I slid farther down. My body felt so heavy, so tired, and the pain in my head blurred my vision. It tunneled now, turning dark and slipping away. I heard Elsa's voice at the end of it, far away, small. "Mommy? I've got the phone. Mommy? Mommy!" Her tiny hands shook me, but I couldn't respond, couldn't manage to form words. The darkness closed in.

Jhon told me later that Elsa managed to call the emergency services. How she knew it was 0-0-0 instead of 9-1-1, I have no idea. They arrived and found me unconscious on the bathroom floor and by then, she had called Jhon as well, crying so hard he had run out of a meeting without a word of explanation. He had been seconds behind the ambulance. This spoke volumes about the high rate of speed he must have driven. The office was nearly fifteen minutes' drive away from our home!

I woke, confused and frightened, to find myself in a hospital room, with machines beeping, an IV in my arm, and a nurse asking me when my due date was.

"Due date?" I answered, struggling to understand what had happened to me.

"Yes, dear." The nurse had a round, warm face. Her eyes were a pale green, and I could see she had lost a front tooth, and had it replaced with one that was more than slightly off-color. "I'm guessing around four months along, but you are barely showing and the doctor on call told me to ask your due date and obstetrician."

I blinked at her. Was I hallucinating? Was she?

"I can't be pregnant. I'm on the, um, the shot. I can't remember the name of it, but..."

She raised her eyebrows and looked surprised. "Oh dear. Hm." She plastered a bright smile on her face. "I'll be right back, dear. Don't you go anywhere!"

As if I could manage to go anywhere with an IV in my arm and machines and sensors plastered to my chest.

Before I could answer her, she bustled out of the room and into a busy hallway. I could tell I was in the heart of the emergency room, thanks to the brief flash of open door. Jhon appeared at the door a moment later, his face paler than usual.

He strode over to my bed and took my hands in his, his lips brushed my forehead. "Sweetheart, oh thank God, I was so scared."

"Where's Elsa?" I asked, my heart suddenly seizing in fear.

"She's in good hands. A social worker here at the hospital took her under her wing." He pulled away and I could see tears sparkling in his eyes. "They said your blood pressure spiked. It was 142/90! They've got it down, though."

"Jhon, that nurse asked me what my due date is."

He nodded. "I just was asked that as well. But you had the shot, that Depo, Depo-something. Didn't you?" He gave me a sideways glance.

You are pregnant. And he thinks you did it on purpose.

Maybe you did.

"I did get the shot, I did, I don't..." My voice petered out. I still felt like I was moving through thick molasses. The headache was still there, but receding. My mind, however, was spinning. How the hell could I be pregnant? I hadn't gotten the shot late. I'd made sure to get it from the doctor the American consulate had recommended there in Paraguay.

"I thought it was, like, I don't know, impossible to get pregnant with the shot," Jhon blurted and then clamped his lips together. I could see him struggling to understand it, just as much as I was. Finally, though, his face took on a hopeful smile. "It could be okay. It could be healthy and fine, Nichole."

I tried to smile back. I really did. But I couldn't. Because I understood what it meant.

High blood pressure?

Coupled with pre-eclampsia and an emergency C-section in my first pregnancy? What we had was a high-risk pregnancy. I started adding up the months of not feeling well. It had all started with nausea. I had thought it was the flu, but now that I looked back on the symptoms with the clearer eye of hindsight, the more I realized it hadn't been the flu at all. I was pregnant and had been for *months*. How had I not noticed? I had. There had been the weight gain, the change in energy levels, the nausea, and so much more. My mind had dismissed every single warning sign.

I lay there in the bed, struggling not to cry. I wanted this child, don't get me wrong. I wanted a baby more than I had ever wanted anything else in my life. But I knew, I *knew*, that the price for him was Winter's Child. There would be no flight to Seattle. Not now. Not until after the baby was born.

It was early afternoon until they were able to do an ultrasound. I lay there, barely breathing, as the ultrasound tech smeared the jelly on the wand, smiled brightly at us, and showed us the grainy image. I hoped that they would tell me I wasn't as far along, that I could fly away, no problem.

"Do you want to know the gender of your baby?" he asked and Jhon nodded quickly, a broad smile on his lips. I forced a smile onto my face as well. Jhon hadn't put it all together yet. He hadn't yet realized what this pregnancy meant, even if I had. I told myself it wasn't for sure, that the doctors still might be fine with traveling. Those hopes were hanging on by a thread, though. As soon as I had accepted the fact that I was pregnant, Elsa's nightmares, her talk of Elizabeth knowing a way around our switching of hemispheres, then it made an awful, terrifying sense.

"Let's see here. Oh, look, baby is sucking its thumb." He pointed, and I felt a surge of joy, despite my fears. "Turn for me now. Just a little. Someone is a tad shy, it seems."

Another moment ticked by and then suddenly I saw the baby twist and thrash his arms. In tandem, I felt a small flutter of movement. Nothing more than the kiss of butterfly wings inside of me.

"Well, Mom and Dad. It seems we are cooking up a son in there. Congratulations!" His fingers moved on the keyboard and words appeared on the screen.

HI, MOM AND DAD! I'M A BOY!!!

Jhon squeezed my hand, sucked a breath in, and smiled so widely it felt like the sun had come into the room. I managed a ghost of one in return.

"He's healthy?" I asked the doctor an hour later.

The woman smiled and nodded. "A little on the small side. But that's expected in a hypertensive, high-risk pregnancy. Just get plenty of rest, avoid stress, and you will be just fine."

Jhon stood beside me, his smile slipping. "High risk?"

The doctor nodded. "Yes. But I don't want you to worry, Mr. Staunton. I see plenty of hypertensive pregnancies go all the way to term with no further difficulties. Mrs. Staunton will need to be on bed rest and regular visits for the remainder of her pregnancy. We may want to induce early if her blood pressure doesn't respond to medication towards the end of her pregnancy, but other than that, you have a healthy baby boy on the way."

"We... we are due to return to the United States in two weeks," Jhon stammered.

The doctor's expression changed. "Oh no, that won't be possible, Mr. Staunton. As you may know, long plane flights can affect blood pressure. Even in first class, with the possibility of elevating the feet, I simply cannot endorse the risk."

"But we *have* to go..." Jhon whispered, his face draining of blood. He turned to look at Elsa, who had fallen asleep on the small sofa in the corner of the hospital room. He darted a glance at me.

The doctor frowned. "Mr. Staunton, I don't think you fully understand the nature of a high-risk pregnancy such as this. Now, if you are concerned about overstaying your visa, exigent circumstances like a high-risk pregnancy can easily be explained to immigration. I can personally vouch for you both. We have a social worker on staff who can help you prepare the necessary documentation."

"Thank you, Doctor, thank you so much." I forced a smile onto my face, a sick pool of dread forming in my stomach. Jhon looked ready to pass out, but there was no way to explain the situation to anyone. And I feared doing so anyway. No one was going to believe us. Instead, what Jhon and I needed to do was figure out how we were going to survive not just a high-risk pregnancy, but the return of Winter's Child.

Elsa had been right. *Elizabeth* was coming. And there was nothing we could do to escape that.

Incident/Case #: 18-02521

Classification: Assault/Arson

Date: 2018-20-09

Location: Rush Creek, Raaen Road

Victim (s): Staunton, Jhon and Elizabeth

Suspect: Staunton, Nichole

Evidence ID#: 18-02521-022 (page out of handwritten journal)

I've got to get control of myself. I've got to, I don't know, find a way to step back. Yesterday, I found myself wrapping my fingers around her throat. Pressing down. Stopping the air. She turned red. Started choking. The voices told me later that she was only pretending to choke, that she could breathe all along.

Still.

-N-

22. Darkest Before the Dawn

- Nichole -

September 17th, 2019 - Brisbane, Australia

We moved. That was the first order of business. We had already given notice to the management company, and we knew we needed a far different place. One we could secure, one that was remote and removed from neighbors.

I knew what Elizabeth was capable of. We both were. That first day back, after Elsa was tucked in and dreaming away under her *Frozen* comforter, her breathing soft and steady, we sat in the tiny living room.

Jhon brought me a cup of tea. "I think you'll like this flavor." He handed me the steaming cup. "It's Apricot Amaretto by Tea Forte." The hospital had given me a long list of dos and don'ts when it came to a hypertensive pregnancy. Removing caffeine from my diet had been one of them. I wasn't much of a soda drinker, but I did enjoy a cup of coffee in the morning and sometimes even at night. The caffeine, contrary to most others, didn't affect me or keep me awake. Still, I gave it up willingly. Whatever it took for a successful pregnancy.

I sipped it, expecting some watery, flavorless herbal tea. Instead, I was pleasantly surprised. Jhon had his own mug of tea. He grimaced. "Solidarity," he said as he raised the mug in salute and then took a cautious sip. "Huh, this isn't half bad."

"It's actually really good," I said as I took another sip and another. It was good to be back in familiar surroundings. I hated hospitals, especially since I usually ended up in one due to some kind of loss. First my mother, then our baby. I felt a gentle flutter in my abdomen. We were having a baby. Impossibly. And yet.

"We need to figure out..." We both spoke at the same time. I laughed, but Jhon didn't. His face was grave.

"Nichole, it's too dangerous. I can't protect us here. We have to consider..."

"No." I cut him off. "No, we are not giving her up. We can't. We owe it to Elsa and Isabel and Lizzie to make this work."

"Nichole, she damn near killed us last time."

"I remember. I was there."

His lips thinned, and he swallowed whatever he was going to say next.

"You could take Elsa back to the U.S. now. Isabel would come out, and I'd be home before Lizzie emerged," I offered, terrified at the thought of being alone and pregnant in a foreign country.

Jhon stared at me. "I'm not leaving your side. Not for an instant. You have to be on bed rest, anyway. There is no way I'm leaving you here."

I nodded. I figured he would feel that way, but I had felt it necessary to at least suggest an alternative.

"Well then, we need somewhere remote. We've already given notice here and we can find a bigger house in the outback, or at least far away from any neighbors. One that has at least one en suite bedroom."

He blinked, confused. "Why remote? Why en suite?"

"We need to lock her in, Jhon."

His eyes widened. "Lock... her... in?"

"And we might need to find a way to sedate her in case of emergency."

His jaw dropped open. "*What*?" He practically shouted it.

"Keep your voice down!" I hissed, glancing over my shoulder. The walls were thin. "Benadryl will do in a pinch. I'll buy extra next time I'm at the pharmacy."

Jhon's eyes were bugging out of his head. "Who are you and what have you done with my wife?"

I swallowed the last gulp of the delicious tea and set the mug down on the coffee table. "Jhon, we have to stay here. They won't allow me on a plane, and I could go into a hypertensive episode there over the middle of the Pacific Ocean and die." He winced at my words. I felt like a drama queen uttering it. Learning that I was pregnant had changed my entire view on things. "We *have* to be smart here. She's a five-year-old girl, but she's also a psychopath. If we want to survive winter, and carry our child full-term, we will need bars on the windows, locks on her doors, and somewhere where no one knows us. Where no one knows about *her*. Where no one can hear her scream bloody murder to get out."

He winced at the last sentence and ran his hand through his hair. "I don't know about this, Nichole."

"It's just for three months. Then Isabel will return, Theo will be full term, and we can return to Seattle, or stay until next May." I shrugged. "If you have a better plan, I'd love to hear it."

He stared at me. "Theo?"

I looked down at my hands. "I've always loved the name."

It wasn't the complete truth. Yes, I *had* always loved the name. It was just that I had imagined having a son and naming him Theo with another man. A man who I had left behind more than ten years ago. When we had begun dating, fallen in love, and gotten engaged, we had also gotten pregnant. For fourteen glorious weeks. Long enough for me to be sure we were having a boy. Long enough to share the news and pick out a name. Before the fire. Before losing Hannah and Andy.

"I love it." Jhon's voice brought me back from the past. He reached out and encompassed my hands in his. "Theo. Our son."

"We have to protect him, Jhon." I squeezed his hands in mine, gripping them tight. "No one will believe us. They won't understand. We *have* to do this."

It took a day or two for Jhon to come around, and a few more for us to finalize the details and find a house for rent. We needed something that wasn't in a subdivision. Somewhere no one would see us coming and going or wonder why Elsa was suddenly unavailable for playdates. As far as everyone except Jhon's boss and co-workers knew, we were returning to Seattle. And the house was far enough out of Brisbane, deep in the country. It would discourage any kind-hearted co-worker from randomly stopping by.

We lucked out thanks to an older couple forced to transition into assisted living after the wife fell and broke her hip. Their grown children were scattered to the winds and unprepared to return and handle packing it all up and selling the house. This meant, with a little negotiation and tact, we had a fully furnished house tucked into the countryside a solid thirty-minute drive from Brisbane. Situated nearly one quarter mile from the road, our nearest neighbors were mere specks on the horizon.

I hired a handyman to install the bars on the outside of Elsa's window and Jhon gave him some lame excuse about how she sleepwalked. Considering Elsa's petite curls barely made it over the bottom ledge of the window, I doubt he was convinced. Instead, he shrugged and muttered something about Americans going troppo. I paid him and Jhon tested them after we watched the man's vehicle kick up dust and disappear from sight around the bend.

The bars were solid. I doubted even Jhon could have dislodged them without taking the clapboard siding out, too. There was no way that Elizabeth would be able to get out through the window.

The lock we put on the door the next day. It was a little wonky and marred the door frame, but Jhon wasn't the handiest. He was better at interpersonal skills, not home improvement and security. The butterfly flutters grew to small kicks and movements, and my belly swelled. My pregnancy now seemed glaringly obvious. How had I not known? Not suspected? I felt ridiculous and foolish. The voices in my head were insidious, deprecating.

You were a blind fool. You should have noticed. Should have suspected. And now look at you.

You are going to get everyone killed. All because you didn't even notice what was happening to your body. How could you not know you were pregnant?

Jhon's boss, Jacob, had been more than understanding and accommodating. He even sent the necessary computer hardware and arranged to pay for internet to be installed so Jhon could work from home. Bed rest had been highly recommended by the hospital doctors and re-emphasized by the obstetrician we found on the outskirts of Brisbane. I hated the thought of it, but, really, what choice did we have?

We hadn't explained much to Elsa. It felt wrong, but I knew that the other aspects could hear and were aware of what was going on. I didn't want to give Elizabeth any kind of warning, although, really, it was obvious we were staying in Australia. If Elsa noticed that her window had bars and that the outside of the door now had a heavy-duty lock on it, she didn't say anything. She was subdued. Then again, that was normal fare for her. The nightmares had increased. It was as if the dread built in intensity over time.

At first, just a handful of nightmares. Then, by the final three weeks of Elsa's reign, they were nightly affairs.

My heart hurt for her. The horror she obviously felt, the fear; she was aware of what Elizabeth was capable of and felt utterly helpless to stop it. Each night, we would hear her cry out, and Jhon's feet would be on the floor in a flash. He was so worried about me and our baby that he insisted on getting up each night and bringing her to our bed instead of letting me go to her.

"Stay here. I'll bring her to you."

Holding her close, running my hand over her back, I waited for her tears to stop, her shaking to ease, and her breathing to slow. Call me crazy. I don't care, but I loved her desperately. She and Isabel and Lizzie were everything I wanted in a little girl, and I knew that if we could just get past this, through this one winter, I would do anything I had to do to make sure she never, ever had to watch Elizabeth come out again. To my mind, Elsa, Isabel, and Lizzie were Elizabeth's *victims* more than anything. They were the good and the light, and I looked forward to the years we would have together. I was absolutely certain we could have a good life, that we could help our child protect herself from the evil inside. I didn't understand how this had happened, and I wondered if I ever would. It mattered little, though. Compared to being the mother my sweet, red-haired little girl needed, that my unborn baby boy deserved, there was nothing else that was more important.

Each night, her sobs would ease and I would tell her the same thing. "It will be okay. We are safe. *You* are safe. Trust me, my sweet girl. I love you more than the moon and stars."

And every evening, as the days counted down, she would snuggle close, her body slowly drifting into sleep, her voice sleepy and slow. "I love you more than the moon and stars too, Mommy."

When June 20th arrived, Elsa was quiet and fearful all day. Nothing I said or did could shake her from her funk. The lessons ended that day. We wouldn't risk homeschooling Elizabeth, but I had filled the shelves with books and we had mounted a television high on the wall. Anything pointy, anything that could be used to stab or damage, was removed from the room. Jhon even disassembled the sturdy bed frame and placed a simple mattress on the floor. At midnight, Elizabeth would emerge. We had done everything we could think of to be ready for her.

As had become our custom, we stayed awake, all of us, for the transition. Normally, it was a moment of joy, for there were special quirks, individual charms in each aspect. I missed the love of sculpting that Isabel had, just as I found Elsa's obsession with chocolate chip pancakes endearing. I loved Isabel's gentleness and smiled in the face of Lizzie's exuberance and zest for life. Even Elsa was a joy, and I reveled in her attention to detail and delicate watercolors.

It wasn't a joyous occasion to see Elizabeth return, but it had become a custom, and I was determined to see it through. Elsa had glanced at the bed on the floor and her mouth had turned down at the corners, the upper lip trembling. My chest filled with guilt and sadness. I hated that she was sad and frightened. It wasn't fair. Not at all.

"It's two minutes till midnight," Jhon said. His hand reached for Elsa's and he held up his other hand towards me as I tried to step across the threshold. "Best to give Mommy a hug now, Elsa."

She nodded, her face crumpling, as I picked her up and hugged her tight against me. "I love you, sweetheart. Remember that." I pulled back so that I could see her face. Her eyes were filled with tears. I could feel mine welling up as well and, in that moment, I questioned everything. How could I have suggested doing this? Was I really going to lock up our little girl in a room for the next three months? What if we were wrong?

What if you have been making all of this up and you are crazy? Just like your mother was? What if this is all you, not her?

Elsa burrowed her face into my shoulder, tears soaking my shirt. "I'm scared."

"It's going to be okay, Elsa, I promise. You don't need to be scared. No one is going to hurt you."

"I'm scared for *you*, Mommy."

"One minute," Jhon said quietly. "Nichole, honey, it's time to put her down."

Elsa clung tighter. "She's really, really mad. She says, she says she's gonna..."

Jhon reached for her then and unwound her from me, and with that, the clock struck midnight. I've never seen anything like it, and I hoped to never see it again. Elizabeth reacted immediately. A blur of teeth, of kicking, fingernail-raking fury, and such anger and violence that it shook me to the core. I saw a head full of curls slam into the left side of his face. Jhon bellowed in shock and anger and instinctively thrust her away from us, towards the bed. She bounced against it and was on her feet instantly, closing the distance, her face transformed, twisted with hate. We slammed the door closed as Elizabeth launched herself at it and slammed into it hard enough to make the door shake.

"Jesus Christ!" Jhon slammed the key into the lock as I held the doorknob still. I could feel Elizabeth trying to turn it. For now, her strength fell short of mine. Jhon's hand was shaking so hard it took him several attempts before the deadbolt engaged. Then he fell back, clutching the left side of his face. A bruise was already gathering around his eye socket. He muttered a few more choice words before he slipped his arm around me. We backed down the hall slowly, our cramped bedroom at the far end of the hall. The door continued to rattle and shake, the doorknob turning one way and then another, and Elizabeth's shrieks of rage rolled through the air as if they were winged demons. No words, just *fury*. Theo rolled inside of me, woken, no doubt, by the ferocity of the encounter and the adrenaline now coursing through me.

I stood there for a moment, one hand on the door, the other on the bump that was Theo. The door stopped shaking, but I could feel her there, right on the opposite side.

"I... *hate*... you." She said it slowly and with such venom that my fingers grew cold and a shiver ran through my body. "Let... me... out."

I thought of Elsa. Here, just moments ago. The look in her eyes, the fear, it was still with me. I missed Elsa, and the others, already. The tears spilled over, tracking down my cheeks. Three months. We just had to make it three months. At that moment, it felt like forever. It felt insurmountable and overwhelming and so very, very depressing. I hated this. All of it. I wanted her back. Whether it was Elsa, or Isabel, or Lizzie. I just wanted them back. The guilt surged through me. It was my fault that we would be here through winter. My fault that Winter's Child was here with us now. My fault. All of it.

I stood there and let the tears flow. And finally, when I could catch a breath, when my voice was relatively steady, I said, "Good night, Elizabeth" and let Jhon guide me the rest of the way down the hall to our bedroom. Away from the sounds of Elizabeth screaming in a pure and unrelenting fury of one thwarted.

It wasn't easy. In fact, it was harder than hell to keep Elizabeth in that room. We had given her the master suite and taken a smaller room so that she wouldn't need to leave the room to take a bath or use the toilet. But that brought up other issues. Such as purposefully clogged toilets, water overflowing from the sink, and so much more.

Gone was the quiet plotting, the subterfuge and misdirection. Instead, we were inundated with the true face of the psychopath within. Worse, she was furious at being locked away for more than six months past her normal emergence.

I was beginning to see just how intelligent and dangerous she truly was. When we needed a plumber to visit and add shut-off valves on the main floor that would cut off the water supply to upstairs, we drugged her food. I know how terrible that sounds, but we were desperate. Afterwards, Jhon told her that if she plugged the plumbing or tried to swamp the bathroom, we would turn off the water. In response, she smeared feces all over the walls. We left it there for a full week and I feared it would turn from a pissing contest to a full-out war for control. But the smell was far worse for her, stuck in that room, than it was for us. After we drugged her again and washed the walls, she changed tactics.

I didn't think she had ever even *heard* the words that came out of her mouth, much less said them, but we were showered with obscenities for the next three days.

It was shocking, honestly. Elizabeth had been subtle, surreptitious, manipulative. She could put on a face that was guileless, innocent. I swear, looking back, I had thought myself a gullible fool, but she knew what she was doing. She knew how to manipulate others into giving her what she wanted. But that all changed with this manifestation. She had never been thwarted before. And frankly, she'd killed anyone who tried to stop her. The fact that she was well and truly trapped in the room enraged her.

She attacked Jhon every time he entered. She scratched and bit, kicked and clawed. She had time and opportunity to discover items that could become weapons that we had overlooked. A hairbrush blackened Jhon's eye, a tiny little knitting needle kit she had received for a birthday from one of Jhon's co-workers, unused and forgotten, had become a weapon. She buried it into the flesh of his hand, her strength fueled by the psychopathy.

In truth, if she had been any older, or any larger, we would have had no chance of keeping her in there. As it was, each interaction shook us to the core. And she tried everything - the whole range - from screaming and vicious attacks, to crying and pleading. I was especially sensitive to that. Once she even tried to pretend that Lizzie had made an appearance. It was the one and only time I entered the room, and I had an eye blackened in the process. I counted myself lucky it hadn't been worse.

For weeks after, Jhon hid the key, keeping it on his person at all times. We had groceries delivered to the outer gate, and no one, absolutely no one, was allowed near the house.

It was like a house of cards, temporary, rickety, and just barely holding on. Is it any wonder it ended like it did?

After nearly three months of daily attacks, every possible scenario, ones we hadn't imagined or thought to plan for, and at least a handful of near misses or escapes thwarted, things had calmed somewhat. If I thought for even a moment that Elizabeth had given up, I was about to find out how foolish that dream was.

It was late when Jhon must have heard her calling out. I hadn't heard her, but I had earplugs in to try to sleep. Instead, I woke as Jhon left the bed. Across the room, the digital clock read 11:15. My sleep, once deep and uninterrupted, had become a fragmented, inconstant thing. I was exhausted from the pregnancy, and from the blood pressure medication, which caused a wave of lethargy to roll through me within thirty minutes after taking the pill. Naps were common, but Theo was active, kicking and moving far more than our baby girl ever had. I was grateful for this. Believe me, I was. All I wanted was for him to make it, to be healthy, and for us to all get through the winter alive and well. But I felt as if I existed in a constant fog of exhaustion.

"Go back to sleep, I've got this," Jhon said, his voice muffled with the earplugs in my ears. I lay back down and I must have drifted off. Theo's kicks had kept me up until after ten and the oblivion of sleep called to me.

What felt like seconds later, I awoke again. Something had pulled me back out of the soft fuzzy comfort of sleep. I pulled first one earplug, and then the other from my ears. I wasn't entirely sure what I had heard, but it hadn't sounded like a normal nightly house sound. That thought alone brought me to full consciousness. Where was Jhon? What was I hearing?

Not just that, but there was a pungent smell. Not quite like a wood fire, but similar. I looked at the clock. It read 11:23. Jhon had gotten up at 11:15. Where was he? Why hadn't he come back to bed?

Eight minutes.

A lot can happen in eight minutes.

Had Jhon gone downstairs for a snack?

I listened, but there was nothing but the howl of the wind and rain falling outside. It had stormed for three days straight, and the entire world felt muddy and gray.

My mouth opened to call to Jhon. Then it closed. There was an odd smell. It smelled off, acrid, and irritating. Not like a bonfire so much as something that wakened a deep fear inside of me. My heart began to race. I felt Theo move, shifting inside of me.

I slipped out of bed as quietly as I could, wincing at the doorway where a loose board creaked briefly. I glanced down the hall. The door to Elizabeth's room stood open. A warm, red glow outside lit up the window at the far end of her room. Jhon was there, on the hall floor, a dark pool of what could only be blood slowly growing around him. And Elizabeth?

She was waiting for me. The second I stepped over the threshold, she swung something that looked like a baseball bat at my head. Her timing was off. She was expecting me to be tired, confused, unaware. She didn't expect me wide awake, and more than ready to defend myself and my unborn baby. I ducked, the bat slamming hard into my back as I shoved her away from me. I gasped at the spike of pain that spread across my lower shoulders. She wasn't even six years old, and small for her age, but she was stronger than she looked. She shrieked in rage, bouncing off of the door frame, and swung again. I absorbed the brunt of it with my left arm and shoulder and tried to wrench the bat from her, but she was too quick. I grabbed at the only thing I could, her hair, and yanked hard, feeling like a schoolyard bully as I did it. I had to disarm her, had to stop her, even as I hoped to not hurt her. Even now, I couldn't help but think of the others trapped in her body with her. Isabel. Lizzie. Elsa. They were the victims. Trapped inside, unable to control Elizabeth. I loathed the thought of hurting them. I felt myself holding back from hitting her with full force.

She swung again and the reality of my situation struck me full force as the bat slammed into my side, missing my belly by inches. If I wanted my baby and my husband to survive, I had to do whatever was possible to survive. To do anything less meant that one of us, possibly all, was going to die.

At the beginning of Elizabeth's reign, it had been so very hard for me to not react, to not feel bad, and to not engage. However, after multiple attacks, both physical and verbal, I had found a way to separate my emotions for the other aspects from Elizabeth. And while in the back of my mind, I was still worried about her and didn't want to hurt her, I was in full mama bear mode. I had a baby to protect, a husband to save, and I knew I had to stop Elizabeth.

I slapped her hard. Her head rocked back, her eyes widened in surprise. She attacked again, and I was half-standing, trying to move away from her and towards Jhon. I head-butted her, my belly weighing me down and she flew across the hallway, landing with a small grunt of surprise.

The burning smell had increased. Had she set the house on fire? Was that what she had done after murdering Kate and Rob in their sleep? And worse, it was spreading. As I defended myself against another attack, I could see the smoke creeping up the stairs. I blinked, my eyes beginning to burn. I spared a glance down the dark hallway at where Jhon lay, unmoving. Was he dead? Was I too late? Somehow, I had to get him out. Get me out. Elizabeth too, if I could stop her from attacking me long enough to subdue her. Otherwise, we were all going to die.

Elizabeth launched herself towards me again and I slapped her again. There was simply no time to contain her. I had to stop her attack, now. Her body went airborne, slamming into the far side of the hallway, and she bounced to her feet and flew at me again. This time I punched her. It happened before I even really registered the attack. Instinctual. Desperate.

Her body flew back, hitting the far wall again, but this time, she slid to the ground, limp, eyes closed.

"Oh God, oh God, oh God," a voice jabbered. A second later I realized the gibbering idiot was me. The burning smell was growing, the smoke acrid, burning. I began to cough. I had to get them both out of here.

Jhon's head wound was bleeding, but slower now. I felt for a pulse, coughing, with Theo writhing within me in tandem with my coughs. Jhon's pulse was slow but steady, and I felt a sense of short-lived relief wash over me. I had to get him out before the whole house went up in flames. Elizabeth too. I could carry her, but Jhon was far too heavy. His eyelids fluttered, and he came to, enough to see me and past me. His eyes widened in panic. The air felt displaced and I moved out of instinct. Just in time, and just enough that the bat slammed against my back, missing my skull by inches. Pain exploded, lining my sight with red. I don't know how I did it. I only know that seconds later, Elizabeth was the one on the floor, unconscious, and I was gripping the bat so hard my finger bones felt as if they would snap.

Jhon was barely able to sit up, and even in the gloom of the hallway I could see him wobble, trying desperately to stay upright.

"We have to get out. I think she set the house on fire." I gasped, then coughed as the smoke seemed to grow heavier.

Jhon said nothing, just groaned and managed to get on his hands and knees, his arms shaking, and the wound on his head had bled enough to make a gruesome slick of gore on the side of his face. He inched toward the stairs and I followed, dragging Elizabeth by her arm. At the top of the stairs, the smoke grew thicker and Jhon collapsed onto his stomach, his head pointing down the stairs. No amount of shaking could rouse him. I had to make a decision on which one to get out first. I chose Jhon. I knew he was heavier, and it would take longer, but if I took Elizabeth out first, she might wake up, attack again, and I was afraid we would all die.

I pulled Jhon out, trying not to let his head hit the stairs, but the pain from being hit in the back with the bat was so bad I could barely move. I dragged him out the front door and into the rain on the front lawn before returning to Elizabeth. I was worried she would wake up and attack us again, so I brought the bat with me out onto the lawn. It wasn't long after that before the fire department and police arrived.

We were all alive. But the second they saw that bat, I knew I couldn't claim another home invasion. I had to tell the truth and take the chance, however unlikely, that I would be believed. That our child had tried to kill us. That it wasn't the first time. And that she had killed before and would again if Elizabeth was ever able to take control. Somehow, I had to tell them the truth and hope beyond hope that I would be believed.

Incident/Case #: 18-02521

Classification: Assault/Arson

Date: 2018-20-09

Location: Rush Creek, Raaen Road

Victim (s): Staunton, Jhon and Elizabeth

Suspect: Staunton, Nichole

Evidence ID#: 18-02521-023 (page out of handwritten journal)

She's dead. I've killed her. I've killed her. I've killed her. Whoever reads this, you must know, I never meant to hurt her. It was the voices, always the voices, telling me she was evil, that she was plotting against me, that it was HER I should be afraid of. But now, with her lying there, so still, her forehead bloody, her body limp and boneless - I realize the truth. The truth is that it has always been me.

ME.

My fault, my wrongs, my listening to the voices instead of ignoring them. Me not taking my medications like the doctor said to.

J gone, and it's my fault. And E is gone now too. I don't deserve to live. I don't WANT to live. I set the fire and I've swallowed the pills. All I need to do now is wait.

-N-

23. But the Journal

- Vincent -

September 20th, 2019 - Brisbane, Australia

A nurse came to collect the baby after Nicky finished breastfeeding and held Theo for over an hour.

"I'll just take him back to the nursery now," she says, a bright smile on her face. It fades the moment she turns away from Nicky. She looks at me, opens her mouth, likely to mention visiting hours. I point to my notepad.

"I'm still taking a statement."

The nurse's lips compress into a frown, but she nods and leaves with a quick glance Nicky's way.

As Nicky's story resumes, all I can think of was the journal.

"Stop. Just... stop."

I hold up a hand. I can't take any more of it. The words Nicky wrote in the journal, the slow disintegration of self in the pages as she let go of her sanity further and further with each entry are unhinging me. Who am I kidding? The Nicky I knew, the girl I spent humid summers with, she is gone. My memories of her, of the first girl I ever fell in love with, didn't match this woman in front of me. She is a memory, a dream, lost in the decade since we last saw each other. I can hope for something different, I can continue to choose blindness, or I can accept what is blatantly obvious.

Nicky blinks at me, the hurt and confusion obvious on her face. In this moment, she seems so sane, so *normal*. Every moment I have spent with her in the past two days feels *normal,* despite the outlandish tale.

But it can't be. When I look at her, when I listen to her voice, all I can think of is the girl I knew. And this, this is exactly why I should have backed out of this case. I should have told the higher-ups about our shared history, and handed it over to Arno, anyone but me.

The things she has written. The abuse she has more than hinted at. If the journal was authentic, and I believe it is, then Nicky is crazier than I could have imagined. I should have swung by the station and entered it into evidence before heading here. No matter our shared history, some part of me wants to do my job, the part not won over by the earnest look in her eyes, her tears, her love of RC Cola and the that lost dream of marriage, children, and a life with her.

Some mental illnesses, schizophrenia in particular, often manifested in the late teens and early twenties. No matter how much I think I know Nicky, the person I remembered, the person I still loved, had been a teenager. Perhaps the mental illness coincided with her pregnancy... or had been exacerbated by it. Perhaps losing another child on top of all the other losses broke her.

I was desperate to see it as she must be. First, her biological parents had died. I know that much. She's never wanted to talk about it, but I had persisted one quiet spring night, not long after we had learned she was pregnant. She had told me that her father died when she was four, that she had few memories. Her mother had died in the house fire two years later. I hadn't pressed her for details. Even back then, twelve years after her mother's death, the memories haunted her. That was obvious.

I remember times when she would get quiet, withdrawn. Sometimes for days at a time. A couple of unpleasant episodes in her mid-teens had meant she stayed home sick, with Hannah asking me to pick up any shared homework for her. I look at her now, wan, still exhausted from giving birth, and my heart twinges at the memory.

And haven't I made it worse? I'm not blameless. Not then and certainly not now. I should have been responsible back then. I should have made sure I had a condom, or abstained. Instead, we'd found ourselves pregnant. Sure, we were in love. But at that young of an age, of course she lost the baby. Then, two weeks later, losing Hannah and Andy in the fire, it had been too much. I can see that now. I can see with the clarity of hindsight how much pressure and trauma Nicky had endured in such a short amount of time. Was it any wonder she had fled to the West Coast? The memories of everyone she lost was there in Kansas City. And that had outweighed the love we had together. Buried it beneath an avalanche of grief.

"You don't believe me." Her words cut through my thoughts, sharp, hurt.

"Would you believe it?" I ask her. I reach into my coat pocket and pull out the journal. It stinks of smoke, even inside of the plastic zippered evidence bag. "I found your journal, Nicky."

She stares at it. Blinks. Her lips part, then she frowns and bites her lip. "That's not my journal, Vincent."

I stare at her. Is she suffering from a psychotic break? Does she not recognize her own journal? Her own initials are carved into the leather!

"Where is Elizabeth, Vincent?" Nicky suddenly asks, her face pale, fearful. "Because wherever she is, those people, that family, they aren't safe." Her eyes track to a clock on the wall near the door. "Every time that Elizabeth has come out, the last days, the last hours especially, they are the most dangerous. It's as if she thinks she can wrest control back from the other aspects. Wrest it back, through violence, through blood. Wherever she is, Vincent, there are people in grave danger."

She is changing the subject. Creating a diversion. Look over here, at this, not the reality that was in front of her. And yet, a niggling doubt kept popping up. This is Nicky, after all. I've never seen psychosis present itself, not once. And my heart, which certainly isn't based on logic, is telling me there is something wrong here. That *I* am wrong. This isn't cut and dried. This isn't a simple story of a woman gone mad.

Is Nicky be telling the truth? Is this journal truly her *mother's*, not hers?

No, I have to focus on the journal. I have to make her see that she is confusing reality. The other option, that of a child capable of murder at the age of, what, five, almost six? It is impossible.

I shake my head. "You refer to a J in the journal. That stands for Jhon. And of course the E in the journal, that stands for Elizabeth."

Nicky shakes her head in return. "They changed my name, Vincent. Hannah and Andy. To protect me from the news reports, the rumors. They were afraid it would follow me forever, taint me. I didn't even know about the journal until after they passed. It was in a safe deposit box. My birth name is Evelyn, Evelyn Nichole Stone, and my father's name did start with a J. It was Jack Stone. He died in a car accident when I was four. My mother never really recovered from it."

I persist. "You mention art, a series you called The Children of Ruin."

"My mother was a painter. Only a few pieces are left. Sold pieces. Everything in the house, everything in her studio, was destroyed."

"There are the initials NS on the cover. Nichole Staunton."

Again, she shakes her head. "Nora Stone. It was my mother's name. Google it. My father worked the leather, engraved it with her initials, and gave it to her for their first anniversary. There was a note, well, a card, from him that said as much. It's in the box."

I persist.

"The journal mentions of this J; they waver back and forth. In one entry he is there, in another he's gone. And then back again."

Tears formed in her eyes. "My mom teetered on the edge of sanity after my dad died. And likely even before that. At least, that's how Hannah and Andy explained it to me when I was older, when I could better understand it all. My dad seemed to keep her balanced, mostly sane. But once he was gone, her mind went too. She wouldn't remember, from one day to the next, that he was gone. I remember her talking to the air, just as if he was there. Sometimes shouting, as if they were arguing."

She wipes at her tears. "She tried to kill me, Vincent. I never wanted to talk about it. I never wanted to even think about it. Even now, it hurts. Even now, I wish I could forget it all. But I can't. I loved her, but she scared me. Hannah and Andy gave me the first home I ever felt truly safe in."

Her words repeated in my mind. And I sat there, each of the details rotating through.

Nora Stone. *Not* Nichole Staunton. And it would explain so much, not just the odd mismatch of details that had caught my eye. No wonder Nicky hadn't wanted to talk about her mother, hadn't wanted to revisit the past at all. Especially if Nora had tried to kill her. And burned their house down around them.

The journal didn't belong to Nicky. It had belonged to her mother.

I had been so convinced. So sure.

"Vincent. Where is Elizabeth? Is she in a home? Is she around other children?"

I say nothing, my thoughts spinning. I glance at the clock. It is just approaching nine p.m.

The last days, the last hours especially, they are the most dangerous.

Elizabeth is at my home. With my family. With Justine. Eli and Ninah. The twins. Eli had tried to tell me. And I'd brushed him off. Thought they were being silly or overemotional. I told myself that kids get jealous, they misunderstand things. But now...

There are moments in our lives when we are faced with ice-cold, smack-you-in-the-face, reality. When the world as you know it isn't just a lie, it is an atrocity. My thoughts turn back to Robert Burris. And with the thought of him, my guts ache as if they are feeling the stab of the knife for the first time. He'd been my mentor, my first friend in Perth. He'd also been the copycat serial killer determined to re-create every single one of the Claremont serial killer's crimes. I'd figured it out, the clues falling into place, not so different from how they did now. Almost too late. I'd very nearly paid for that mistake with my life. The scar on my abdomen throbs again.

My face betrays me. My veins, my hands, feel as if they have suddenly turned to ice.

Nicky's eyebrows draw together. "Vincent? What's wrong?"

I can't speak. I think of Ninah's pale, drawn face. Of Eli, who looks so much like me. Justine calls him my mini-me. Of the twins. Even Justine. We've had our ups and downs. And if I am honest with myself, I knew our relationship was doomed from the get-go. I've never really gotten over Nicky. I don't think I ever will. I'm willing to bet money that Justine can sense it, even now, a decade later. Maybe she's never really moved on from Rocco, either, despite the man being a complete shit.

"Vincent, where is Elizabeth?" Nicky's eyes bore into me. The warmth of her hand feels blazing hot on mine. Behind her, the window shows nothing but darkness spliced with the occasional play of lightning.

The last hours especially. They are the most dangerous.

"Vincent, please talk to me!"

Nicky's voice broke through my racing thoughts and I stand, abruptly, the chair squeals in protest as the legs slide across the floor.

I force the words out of my mouth. "Justine. She's with Justine. And my children."

Nicky's face turns bloodless, her eyes fill with horror. "Oh... God."

The look on her face sets a thick wedge of fear into my throat. This is real. She is terrified for me, for my children. This is no psychosis. At least, not on her part.

I turn and run for the door. I barrel out of it, ignoring everyone and everything.

I have to get to my family.

I have to stop Elizabeth.

Behind me, I hear Nicky call out through the open door.

"Vincent, please don't hurt her. Please! Isabel comes at midnight!"

24. Raise the Darkness

- Vincent -

September 20th, 2019 - Brisbane, Australia

I drive. Fast. My phone, linked to the Bluetooth, rings. No one is picking up. It is the fourth try. Justine keeps her phone close to her most nights, but she has complained that the charge is running down quicker now that it is out of warranty. She'd have it on the charger in the kitchen.

My foot presses harder on the accelerator. It is late, but it is also a Friday night. The city isn't easy to get out of, the roads are congested. I barrel through two stop signs without slowing.

"Call South Bank," I bark, and hear the call go through on the second ring. I barely listen to the greeting before my mouth was in motion. "This is Detective Vincent Gallagher speaking. There is a 102 and possible 401 in progress at..." I swerve, swearing, as a car slows to a crawl in front of me. I spew out the address of our house in a frenzy as I pump the brakes, the car slewing sideways, tires squealing. I have to get home, somehow, some way.

I barely wait for the confirmation before I tap the button to disconnect.

"Call home."

The phone rings. Once, twice. The tires squeal as I take the on-ramp to the M3 at far too high of a speed. The vehicle shudders. Cars were moving out of the way now that I've thought to activate the lights. I stare at the clock. It is a few minutes past nine p.m. The children will be in bed, even Ninah, who is deep in a campaign to have her bedtime extended to 8:30. Justine and our eldest have been going round and round about it for weeks. Ninah will not be getting her way soon, if I knew Justine at all.

The twins are usually fast asleep by seven and don't wake for God or country until after six in the morning.

"You've reached Justine. Leave a message." The phone beeps, and I swear again as I wrench the wheel to the left, barely missing clipping an ancient

Yugo that is puttering along in the fast lane, the driver oblivious. I didn't think there was a single one of the late 70s era rattletraps left.

"Justine, pick up the phone. You need... you need to watch out for Elizabeth. She's... just... protect the kids. I'm..." I wrench the wheel again, slamming my hand down on the horn. "I'm on my way!"

My mind races. Who the hell can I call? Who can get to her faster than the police or me? Stan, our next-door neighbor? He wouldn't be prepared for what he was walking into. No one would. What if Justine was already dead? Or the kids?

My heart feels as if it is trying to hammer out of my chest. Another car. It warbles back and forth before escaping my lights by jolting to the right and nearly hitting another car. I speed up and slip into the vacancy it has left. I hit redial.

"You've just reached..."

I scream wordlessly, and the car rocks as I slam my finger down on the red button and disconnect the call. How could I have been so blind? That she has been there, with my children, my wife, in my home. I second-guessed Eli, dismissed him.

If anything happens to them, it is my fault. Of all the people I swore to protect, my family comes first.

I watch the needle on the odometer creep higher, the engine changing from a growl to a roar. The sign for the exit appears, and I know I have to slow down, have to focus on maintaining control of the car.

The exit is less than a mile away. Around me, cars scatter at the sight of my lights, pulling out of the way, onto the shoulder, anywhere they can to get away from me. I hit the brakes and take the turn, my speed twice what the hazard signs advise. The car shudders and bucks, but it stays on the pavement.

The lights are against me, and I hit my horn and fly through. Danger be damned. My family. My children. They need me.

Please don't let me be too late.

The tires squeal as I take each turn, now firmly in the heart of our neighborhood and close to home. At this time of night, and in this weather, there aren't many outside. The chill after the sun goes down, along with the torrential rain keeps all but the most dedicated runners and bikers inside, where they wait for spring.

The streetlights are on and the rain is an onslaught - fierce, almost angry. The house is dark as I approach. Only a flicker of light glows around the edges of the curtains in the front-facing living room. The motion sensor lights pop on as I jump out of the car, ignoring the headlights and the chime alert, that reminds me to turn them off. I need light, not darkness, and I leave them illuminating the front of the house through the downpour.

I shout out and pound on the door, as I dig in my pocket for my house key. The doorknob turns in my hand as I fumble to insert the key. Unlocked. I throw open the door, bring the haze of rain and wind inside with me, leave it open to the storm outside. There is no time, no time at all. I run toward the living room. The television has to be the source of the light I have seen, and as I step over the threshold, and peer into the dim interior, the screen changes from dark to light and illuminates a gory, horrifying tableau.

Rocco. He stares at me, unblinking, blood covering one side of his face, his body is slumped into a half-sitting, half-prone position. The blood is darkening, congealing, and as I advance closer, I can see he is clearly dead, his skull partially concave. I am no stranger to death. But here, in my home, a place where my children play, and where we have laughed, and loved, it feels especially horrifying.

Where are my children? Where is Justine? Outside, the storm rages, and the rain hammers against the house. Inside, it is silent except for the TV muttering into the empty living room. It speaks only to the dead.

My stomach clenches in fear and I turn toward the stairs and dark hallway above, taking them two at a time as I head upstairs towards the children's rooms.

At that moment, there is a blinding flash of light and an enormous crack split the sky outside and shakes the walls of the house, sending the inside into pitch-black as the streetlights and power to the house die. The lightning must have hit the substation a block away. I make my way by feel to Eli's room, the first on the left.

"Eli?" Another strobe of light hits and illuminates the room through the window. It is empty. I cross the room and move through the shared bathroom, into Ninah's room. Also empty.

They are likely in Justine's room. But is it all of them? Including Elizabeth? I spin on my heel and re-enter the pitch-black hallway. The master bedroom is at the opposite end of the house. I am so intent on getting to them as quickly as possible that I stumble over something on the floor there in the hall. I reach a hand down and feel rough fur. My fingers come away sticky with its blood. It is lying still, obviously dead, its body rapidly cooling. A dog? What the hell was a dog doing here? And then I remember Rocco, dead, in the living room. He has some mutt that he insists on bringing with him. Ninah mentioned it. She said Rocco didn't like to leave the dog alone at night because it would shit on the rug.

So he'd planned to stay over. Brought the dog. And now they were both dead.

Rocco had been a loser, and that was for sure. But he hadn't deserved to die. Neither had his dog. And my family sure as shit didn't deserve to die. That dog saved my life, though. If I hadn't tripped over it, if I hadn't stopped and bent down, the bat that came whistling mere inches over my head would have easily incapacitated, and likely killed me.

The first attempt misses. I reach out an arm to stop the second swing, hearing it more than I can see it. She is such a small wisp of a child, but she is also fast, and far stronger than I give her credit for. My left arm explodes with pain and I hear the bone snap. My entire arm, to the fingers, feels as if I have touched a live wire.

"Sonuva..." I roll away from the dead dog and hit the wall. The entire hallway remains pitch-black. Not a single doorway is open. And with the power off, I have to rely on other senses to defend myself against the attack. The bat comes down again, but I move, my arm screaming in agony, and reach for the bat with my uninjured right hand. My left dangles uselessly, misshapen, electric shocks of pain radiate up and down it.

"Daddy!"

The sound of Eli's voice calling out from the other side of the closed master bedroom door energizes me. I ignore the overwhelming pain from my now useless left arm. As the bat comes whistling toward me, I hiss at the pain of its impact with my right hand. Somehow, I manage to grab and wrench it away from my attacker. My next move is to flip the bat around and swing it hard. In some ways, not seeing anything but the darkness makes it easier to return the attack. I can't see her, can't see her picture-perfect red curls or crayon-blue eyes, and I am damned grateful. If I could, I would likely hesitate, held back. I can't help wondering if Rocco saw her coming with the bat. Had he even realized the danger he was in? Elizabeth's danger lay in her innocent appearance. Rocco had likely not realized the ferocity of the attack until it was too late. How many times had she hit him? And how could a little girl hit so damned hard?

The bat hits home, and she cries out. Wordless, but obviously in pain. I stop myself from hitting her again, and instead bound past her, intent on reaching my family. The door, however, isn't just shut, it's barricaded. I slam into it and groan in pain and frustration.

"Justine! Eli!" I can't even clutch my now-bruised shoulder after rebounding off of the door. The bat slips from my hands onto the floor.

The door is fractured, split nearly in half vertically, but it still holds.

"Daddy!" Eli calls out again. "Mommy's hurt!" I can hear Ninah sobbing and the twins' wails. Thank God they are safely inside. Relief floods through me, but it is only temporary.

A small, angry scream in my ear as Elizabeth leaps at me, her fingers claws that grab and pinch and twist my broken left arm. I hear a high scream of agony and realize it is coming from me. I lash out with my bruised right arm and hit her, hard. She goes down.

Somehow, with Eli and Ninah grunting and pulling, and me pushing, I get inside of the door. I shove the heavy dresser back against the door. Part of me feels stupid. Have I really just locked myself and my family inside of our master bedroom out of fear of a five-year-old girl? I bite back a scream in the next second as Eli and Ninah barrel into me, Ninah's shoulder brushes my badly injured arm. The room is dark, with only the flickers of lightning illuminating the room. There on the bathroom floor are the twins and halfway between, Justine groans faintly. She is curled on her side in the fetal position.

"Justine? Christ."

"That girl hit Rocco." Eli's lip quivers through a wash of tears. Ninah says nothing, just clings to me and sobs. "Ninah and me, we helped Mommy get the twins and Mommy was right behind us when she got hit."

I kneel by my wife and brush the hair away from her face. I can already see an enormous goose egg forming on the side of her head. Is her skull fractured? I check her pulse. It is slow, but steady, and she groans again.

"Vince?" Her eyes flutter open. "Oh God. Thank God it's you." She reaches for my hand and puts a hand up to her head. "The twins?"

"They're fine. Scared, but fine," I reassure her, my ears strain to hear any movement outside of the room. Is Elizabeth still out there? How soon until the police arrive? I can't hear sirens, but I knew it has to be soon, a few minutes at most.

"Rocco..." Justine's voice falters. "He..."

"Shh." I help her turn over and sit her up, propping her against the end of the bed as she lists to one side and moans in pain. "I need you to just stay with me here, okay?"

"Daddy," Eli whispers, "Something smells bad!"

The words have barely left his mouth when I smell it too. The smell of natural gas. A moment later, the smell has expanded to include an acrid burning odor. Something is on fire. I glance at the window. The builder set it high in the wall and I know there isn't any way to climb down and out. Jumping, at least for Justine, is impossible. Still, we have to get out. Somehow, I have to save my family.

25. We Keep Going

- Vincent -

February 8th, 2020 - Brisbane, Australia

Nicky stood outside of the cab at the entrance to the airline terminal. The summer sun beat down on us. A few yards away, Jhon jiggled their son, Theo, in his arms. The baby had lost the slack, unformed look of a newborn and plumped up in the nearly five months since his birth.

Elizabeth, or Lizzie, was all smiles and giggles as she waved two finger puppets, one on each hand, at her baby brother. Even now, months after that dark night, I found it hard to see her as anything but a danger.

That dark night, I had emerged from the master bedroom holding Justine. Eli and Ninah had each been carrying a twin, and the hallway had been thick with smoke. I had gotten lucky. My family had survived long enough that, long after the sirens blasted through the downpour, and we had all seen the inside of the hospital on that night, I had watched Elizabeth cede control to Isabel. Every part of her demeanor had changed. Until then, I wasn't sure what to believe. Seeing it with my own eyes, that had really driven it home for me. I had watched her change. The person in charge had gone away, the new one stepping into the void. Isabel was the antithesis of Elizabeth. The look of horror and fear on her face had said it all.

I had gotten to know Isabel rather well over the months that followed. And I had insisted on seeing Isabel cede over to Lizzie. It remained a disconcerting sight and not one I was likely to forget, no matter how benevolent the Isabel and Lizzie aspects were.

"Are you sure about this?" I asked Nicky.

Nicky gave a half-smile. "I think we wore out our welcome here, don't you?"

There had been questions. So many of them. It had not gone well. There had been... fallout.

"You have time, though. It's summer, and she... I..." My voice fell away. I didn't know what to say. Or even how to say it. Jhon was standing less than twelve feet away. Justine and I had patched things up enough to stay the course for now. Funny how my saving her life had changed her outlook on divorce.

"Vincent, we will be okay." Her eyes held a warning. She was married. And not to me. "Jhon needs to oversee some staffing changes in the Arequipa office now that he's back on his feet, and as soon as the seasons change, we'll head back to Seattle." She glanced at her family and a warm smile spread over her face. "We're safe now. We know what to do, and how to avoid Winter's Child ever coming back. And you can see how wonderful Lizzie is with Theo. Isabel too. I'm looking forward to seeing Elsa again."

She turned back and her eyes begged me to accept this, to understand it, but all I could see was blood and death. I remembered the sight of Rocco splayed on the couch, his skull staved in. The guy was an asshole, a jerk, and a wife-stealing snake, but he hadn't deserved that end. My arm ached, as if in a sympathetic response. Elizabeth's blow with the bat had fractured the ulna on my left arm in two places. The cast had come off months ago, but it still felt weak and vulnerable.

My eyes strayed back to the girl. She giggled and hopped from one foot to the other, her entire focus on Theo. Nicky's gaze followed mine.

"She gets a little manic with him sometimes, Lizzie does. She's just so much more... *active*... than Isabel or Elsa. But she means well. She hasn't hurt him, not once, Vince. I need for you to know that."

I turned away. I didn't want to look at the kid. If I had been able to, I would have told the entire truth, no matter what Nicky had said.

Call it dissociative identity disorder, call it psychopathy. The child was dangerous. It was only a matter of time until the rules that Nicky thought would work didn't. And I wanted to shake the sense into her. Elizabeth was dangerous. She was a murderer. She hadn't just killed Rocco. She killed her first set of adoptive parents and tried twice with Nicky and Jhon. And who knew what she had done to her own mother? I had no idea how or why they were willing to believe it wouldn't happen again.

"What will you do now, Vince?"

I shrugged. My personal history with Nicky, two houses in smoking ruins, and Rocco's family screaming bloody murder about a cover-up - it had all culminated in the higher-ups recommending I voluntarily retire from the police department.

"We can spin it any way you like, Gallagher," my boss had said, his face a mask, eyes dark, "But you're done here. We don't need American cowboys gumming up protocol and conducting investigations with women they've got a history with. You withheld evidence." He had shaken his head, stood up, and begun pacing the room. "Hell, I'll even write you a rec if you end up heading back to the States. People don't need to know about this little hiccup. Not when you've done a stand-up job everywhere else."

I knew a good thing when I saw it offered. The fact that I'd withheld the journal, that I'd said nothing about my personal history with Nicky, either of those on their own would have been enough to get me fired in the States. The only thing I had going for me in the higher-ups' eyes was my success nailing the Butcher of Perth. I submitted my resignation and cited a need for a change as the reason. They'd accepted it and even thrown in a decent severance package. I'd never serve on the Australian police force again, but true to his word, my boss had written a letter of recommendation that glowed bright enough to hurt my eyes when I read it.

"I might work as a private dick," I said as I shrugged. "Who knows?"

Nicky smiled, and I wanted nothing more than to kiss her. To tell her I loved her. That I'd never stopped loving her. Instead, I stood still and waited for the feeling to pass.

"In other words, we keep going, right?" She reached for my hand. It was warm. I remembered the first time she had held it so many years ago. We'd been fifteen and standing at the top of the Kessler Reservoir looking down into the depths of it, at the trees and graffiti, and the lookout tower. The summer sun had been high overhead, and she'd dared me to a race.

"First one to the top of the tower wins!" She'd dropped my hand, turned on her heel, and began running with me right behind her. She'd won. Maybe I'd even let her win. If only because I had dared a kiss there on the creaky metal platform that poked out from the scraggly trees and brush, under "SCREW!" scrawled in graffiti against the sun-warmed metal wall.

Our first kiss. I wish we could go back. Back in time, back to that beautiful summer day. I wanted to carry this knowledge with me, travel back in time, and change everything. If I had known then what I knew now, how different our lives could have been. I wouldn't have let her leave. Or maybe I would have followed her to Seattle. Should have. But it was too late for that now.

"Yeah," I said gruffly, staring down at her hand in mine, not trusting my voice to say more.

I thought I saw the glimmer of tears in her eyes when she hugged me goodbye. And I know I heard her whisper that she loved me. So quiet, but I heard it nonetheless.

Before I could say it back, she was walking away, taking Jhon's hand in her left, and Elizabeth's in her right, without another glance. I watched them walk away. Stood there until they disappeared into the crowd and deep into the bowels of the airport.

26. You Found Me

- Nichole -

June 27th, 2021 - Santa Cruz, California

My phone rang as I pulled into the parking lot. I glanced at the screen and saw that it was Vincent. Of course it was. Ever since he found her, Lizzie's birth mother, and sent me the information, he'd checked in every other day or so. He didn't come right out and say it. Oh no. He just asked what I was up to, how Lizzie was doing, and always asked for an update on Theo. I knew it for what it was. He was gently circling around the question. He just didn't come out and say it.

He never asked if I had gone to see her. But the question was there.

I'd sat on the information for nearly two months. I'd had my excuses, sure I had. The fact was, I was terrified. I wanted to believe a monster had hurt my child, fractured her psyche, and made her who she was. Perhaps I was also afraid that she was as she had been born: four separate aspects fused into one body. I questioned whether knowing who my daughter's mother was would help, or if it would just spawn more unanswerable questions. My curiosity, however, finally won out. In the end, I'd gathered up my courage, called her, told her who I was, and we arranged to meet up. That had been a week ago. And now the moment was almost here.

I parked and picked it up on the third ring.

"Hey."

His reply back was muted. Then again, it was the wee hours of the morning there. I couldn't help wondering if he had crept downstairs, maybe out to the chilly, unheated garage, to make the call. And despite it being over twelve years since we had been lovers, it felt a little wrong. There was our shared history standing there next to us. You don't stop loving someone, even when you break up. And it hadn't been Vincent's fault I couldn't cope, not at all.

In the past year, I'd thought about it a lot. I couldn't help but imagine how different my life would have been with Vincent. If we had stayed together.

The wife of a cop, always wondering if he would come back from his shift. I like to think I would have handled it better than Justine.

I'd been all in until two days after the funeral. Losing Andy and Hannah like that, a freak fire, the dryer lint sparking and sending the entire house up into flames while they slept, blissfully unaware until it was too late. I'd been ready to take on the mantle of the thin blue line because I knew how much he wanted it, how much he believed in giving back to the community. But when the prayers were said, and they had covered the two gentlest and loving people I had ever known over with six feet of dirt, something broke inside of me. The voices I had spent so many years covering over, even running from, had surfaced once again, reminding me I didn't get happily ever after. I got loss and death and loneliness. That was my reality, my future. Or at least, that is how it had felt.

"How are you?" he asked, just as he'd asked a dozen times, likely more. I wonder how Jhon would feel, knowing Vincent calls so often.

"I'm meeting her. In five minutes. For coffee." Why I added that, I did not know.

So yeah, I invited the mother of my sometimes-psychotic child to have coffee with me.

"I wish I were there. I *should* be there," he said, and I could hear his voice rise. He was concerned. I wonder if he had convinced himself that after knowing her name for two months and doing nothing, I would remain on the same course. Say nothing. Do nothing. Try to forget that my child killed Kate and Rob and would have killed me and Jhon and our unborn child too. And I had wanted to forget. But I couldn't.

"It's a public place, Vincent. I'll be okay."

It was a shame he was no longer a cop. After all he had been through with his wife, how much he had done to appease her, to save their marriage. That was my fault too. The department had found out about his connection to me and assumed the worst. Assumed I had manipulated him into helping me, that I had "contaminated the evidence." Or worse, that he had done it with forethought and planning. I tried to tell myself that it had worked out somewhat - it saved his marriage, not being a cop. Still. It was my fault he lost his job. I could only hope that Vincent and his wife would stay together. Now that his life wasn't in danger, now that she had seen for herself that it wasn't just *his* work that could endanger their family, but hers, perhaps she would be more understanding of him, more supportive. He deserved that much.

"Nicky, I..." He inhaled and I could hear it over the phone line.

I felt my guts twist. He had never gotten over me. I'd seen it in his eyes that night he had stood in the interrogation room with his back to the camera, a note in his hand that read, "Pretend you don't know me." I'd played along. His familiar face had been a lifeline, a buoy when I was sure I was going to drown. When he had shown up at the hospital that last time. When he had held my mother's journal in his hand, a look of sick horror on his face, I had known how fragile trust can be.

"I have to go, Vincent." I pressed the red button and ended the call. It wasn't healthy, these calls he made. And God forbid his wife should look at his phone records and see so many of them. She would think the worst.

I sat there in my rapidly warming car and fought back tears. Sadness for what could have been a longing for a simpler life, a wish that all the complexity and stress could melt away and I could be normal. But I never had been. Not with my mother, not even with Andy and Hannah, God rest their gentle souls. I was nursed back from a catatonic state by them. They'd loved me and done everything they could to heal my heart and soul. They'd even helped me learn to quiet the voices. The best parts of me were from those two people and the twelve beautiful years I had spent with them.

I breathed, in and out, in and out, and tried to form my questions. What did I want to ask her? What was I looking for? Would there even be closure? Or simply more questions to follow me into the future?

Two more deep breaths.

I saw a redhead in the diner window. That had to be her. The red was the same shade as Elizabeth's. I gathered my courage and got out of the car.

Moments later, there I was, sitting opposite of Lizzie's mother. I couldn't help but stare.

I'm not sure what I expected, but Gail Pazza wasn't it. She seemed particularly well put together, a nice suit, heels. Her hair was identical to

Lizzie's, only straight, no curls. The dark green of her suit reminded me of the jail uniform, and I winced inwardly. I haven't worn that color since. It brought back too many memories.

I imagined someone holed up in a trailer park, chain smoking Pall Mall cigarettes and swilling cheap vodka. Not a woman in a smart suit with crayon-blue eyes. A woman who looked me over and met my eyes.

Perhaps I watch too many movies.

She was older than I had expected. Late forties, if I didn't miss my guess. A few strands of silver graced her hair. Why had I expected someone younger? And why did older seem somehow worse? Some women find themselves pregnant, and they think they can hack it, but can't. Is that what happened to her? Had she, at her, dare I say it, advanced age, found she couldn't hack being a single mom?

"So you found me. Not even the State of Washington could do that. Then again, I don't think they tried very hard." Her tone was calm, and she gave me a brief smile.

"You aren't what I expected," I confessed.

She smiled again and shrugged. "Few people are."

She reached up and hooked her hair with her left pinkie finger, just as Elsa would do when she was nervous or anxious. Isabel too. Gail *was* nervous; she just hid it really well.

"Can I buy you a coffee?" I asked her and she shook her head.

"I can't have caffeine, not since they stitched me back together with a few feet less intestine."

I blinked. Vincent had struggled to find Elizabeth's mother, interviewing nearby neighbors and more. The state had known who she was. They just couldn't seem to find her. But how hard had they truly looked for a woman who had obviously abandoned her child?

"I'm sorry?"

"She stabbed me five times," Gail said, then slid up her right sleeve. I could see a silvery ragged scar. "One I deflected." She let the sleeve fall back down as she slid her left sleeve up to reveal another longer scar and slight bump. "This one chipped bone and stuck. I had to pull the knife out myself. The other three sliced and diced my small intestines. I was in the hospital for nearly two months."

I sat there, my mouth hanging open. "Are you saying Elizabeth stabbed you?"

Gail's answer was simple. "Yes."

I blinked, calculating the timeline in my head. They had found Elizabeth half-conscious, suffering from exposure, on the steps of Church of the Blessed Sacrament. "But she was only two years old. How is that possible?"

Gail sat back, frowning. "You said you were her foster mother, yes?"

"Adoptive mother, actually. We adopted Elizabeth nearly two years ago."

"And she has tried to kill you, didn't she?" Gail pressed.

"Well, yes, but..." Suddenly, I felt completely out of my depth. What had I been thinking, really? Had I thought she was some monster who needed to be punished? For somehow making her child into some terrible creature with four separate personalities?

You came because you wanted answers, the voices said. *So ask the questions and stop dithering about.*

"Gail, tell me how this all started."

The woman's composure cracked. "You won't believe me. No one ever has."

How familiar that sounded! Only Vincent had been willing to listen to me, to Jhon, and after all I had seen, I wanted to be the one to extend the same to someone else.

"Try me," I said, and I folded my hands in my lap to stop them from shaking.

And so she did.

Gail wrapped her hands around the Smart Water she had brought with her, cleared her throat, and met my eyes.

"I'd worked for Microsoft since my teens. I wasn't on the ground floor, but I was close, and I took my time and invested any additional funds I had in company stock and shares in Google, right before it went public. By 2012, my invested shares were worth millions. I quit my job and retired at thirty-seven, financially independent and looking for love. My biological clock was ticking so hard I was sure everyone could hear it when I walked by." She tossed her hair a bit, gave me a quick, sad smile. "By then, I had zero idea how to date. I'd kept my nose to the grindstone for half my life and every guy I met was basically looking for the same thing, friends with benefits or a long-term, child-free commitment."

Gail sighed. "Eventually I decided that if I really wanted to be a mother, I'd go it alone. How hard could it be?" She laughed then. It sounded bitter. "I had the funds. The house was paid off. And I could stay at home and care for a child and never have to work a day in my life again.

"I had a wonderful childhood, with dedicated and loving parents, and I was really looking forward to having a child of my own. I visited a fertility clinic, picked out a sperm donor, and began charting my cycles." Her fingers drew a circle on the table. They were long, tapered, and delicate. "I tried again and again. Three miscarriages over a two-year span. The clinic suggested I consider trying IVF, with another provider who specialized in geriatric pregnancies." She grimaced. "That's what they call it after age thirty-five, a geriatric pregnancy, as if I need a cane or a walker to get around. It made me feel like I had one foot in the grave."

She leaned back, stared at the battered tin ceiling of the diner, and sighed. "The IVF guy did it differently. First, there were the injections of hormones meant to rev up my reproductive cycles and encourage the seating of any embryos. Those had me going through all kinds of mood swings. Then he convinced me we needed to implant multiple embryos. Four in all. I had the procedure done in mid-March, 2013."

She steepled her hands under her chin, her gaze far away, back in her memories. "He told me to expect a success rate of 25-50%."

"So one or two of the four would likely take?" I asked.

Gail nodded. "Yes. Just under a week later, on the 21st of March, the scan showed that all four embryos were still there and growing. I got a little nervous. It was one thing to have one child and dream of perhaps one more down the line, but four at one time? Even as a dedicated, stay-at-home mom, that was a lot to take on all by myself. I asked the doctor what my options were, and he suggested we adopt a wait-and-see attitude. It was that or selective reduction and I'm Catholic. So I chose the wait and see route."

I took a sip of my coffee, and she did the same with her water.

"I went on with my life. Joined an expectant single moms' group." She laughed. "Apparently, I wasn't the only one out there looking to start a family at my age.

"The evening of June 21st, I woke up screaming. The pain coming from my abdomen was intense, a stabbing, almost ripping feel. I was certain that I was miscarrying. The pain was more intense than anything I had felt with any of my previous miscarriages. They scanned me at the hospital and told me that my three babies were fine. "Perfectly healthy, and all appeared to have a heartbeat." She laughed bitterly. "The woman said all the heartbeats sounded like a conga line, just thumping away."

"Three?" I repeated, frowning.

"I told them there were four, not three, and we scanned again. And again." She bit her lower lip. "The fourth embryo was just... *gone*. And God help me, I was relieved. I really was."

"Embryos don't just *disappear*," I protested.

"The fertility clinic wrote it off as a blighted ovum." She bared her teeth. "But the lack of an empty gestational sac stumped them. In the end, they couldn't explain it, so they just kept calling it that. And as I moved into my second trimester, I convinced myself that I would cope. I began interviewing au pairs and live-in nannies. I had the space and the money. It was workable, and I was ready for my triplets, eager to meet them in person. I had just learned that they were identical. And all female."

She paused and took another sip of her water. The server came by and filled up my coffee cup, and Gail waited until she walked away.

"The evening of September 20th, I was watching a movie on Netflix. *The City of God*. One of my neighbors had worked on the filming of it and he had described a particular scene that I wanted to see. It was exactly midnight when the same excruciating pain hit. This time, it was worse than before. So bad, in fact, that I called 9-1-1."

A dark rope of doom coiled through me. "They found only two on the ultrasound, didn't they?"

Her eyes, a vibrant crayon-blue, turned gray. It reminded me of the storm clouds that would occasionally descend upon Kansas City, the dark gray swirls warning of imminent violent weather.

"They couldn't explain it. Neither could the fertility doctor. It was the same as before. The baby was just... *gone*... not even an empty sac to prove she had ever existed. Except we had *seen* the fetuses, all three of them, and I had ultrasounds that showed them." She reached for the photo book and flipped to the front. A grainy image showed four distinct gestational sacs. I read the date printed along the top. March 21st, 2013. Another flip of the page and the scan showed only three gestational sacs. Above the image, the date, June 21st, 2013. The last flip of a page displayed another image, this time with two gestational sacs. The date read September 21st, 2013.

"What did the doctor say?" I asked, my stomach turning to acid at the thought of it all.

Another bitter laugh, her fingers returning to the invisible circle on the Formica table. "'Not everything on God's earth can be explained, Ms. Pazza,'" she said, using a pompous tone. "The idiot. I didn't know it then, didn't understand it, but later..." Her voice faded and she drew the circles on the table, four of them, all in a tight grouping. She gulped, looked up and met my eyes, and I could only imagine how it had felt, seeing the babies, having the ultrasounds to prove it, and there being no satisfactory answer.

"So I was having twins." She sighed, long and measured. "I prepared for them, settled on the perfect au pair who could help with diapering and middle of the night feedings. The scans showed my girls were growing, they were... *perfect*. Whenever I had an ultrasound, I would hold my breath, half-convinced they would tell me it had been a mistake and that there really were four of them. I pored over each grainy image. But it was just these two." She returned to the image in the baby book that read December 12th, 2013. The image showed the two babies melded together, tight. They were larger as well, obviously close to delivery.

"When I felt labor pains in the late afternoon of December 20th, I waited to drive to the hospital until the contractions were five minutes apart. It was nearly midnight by then. There in the maternity ward, the clock turned over to midnight, and the most horrific pain I had ever felt seized me. Worse than the first two times, far worse. The pain was like nothing I have ever felt. Getting stabbed felt like a walk in the park in comparison." She grimaced at the memory. "I actually passed out from the pain."

The server came by with coffee, but I shook my head no. I'd already had two cups. A third would make me shaky and irritable.

"When I came to, the room was full. They were waving those putrid smelling salts under my nose. I later learned that the fetal monitor they had set up went nuts at midnight, which panicked the doctor and nurses.

They had seen nothing like it. It was... pandemonium. All I knew was that the pain had subsided. Well, at least it returned to regular labor pains. Five minutes after midnight, Elizabeth was born. When the second child didn't follow, and there was no evidence of it in my womb, well..." Gail shook her head. "No one could explain it. And this time? No one even *tried*. It was so completely out of their wheelhouse, they literally could not believe it and, therefore, it didn't exist. I hadn't been pregnant with quadruplets, triplets, or even twins. Oh no. Only one baby, all along. That's what they tried to tell me. Even with the proof of more right there in front of them!"

"What did you do?" I asked.

"What could I do?" Gail said. "I named her Elizabeth, and I took her home."

Her fingers, which had paused, resumed drawing circles on the table, moving slowly at first, then faster.

"She was quiet, not responsive at all. I didn't really know any different. The au pair did. She mentioned it. A lot. Once Elizabeth turned three months, we both noticed significant changes. She was still quiet, but at least now she was responsive. Then at six months there was another change. This time it was significant, as if a switch had been flipped. She smiled for the first time, chortled, and blossomed into this adorable, sweet baby girl. At nine months, she changed again."

"Reserved, instead of happy and playful? Anxious?" I interjected. My guts ached; I knew too what came next. Gail nodded.

"And after that, the quiet, emotionless one came out on her first birthday."

"Isabel is the spring child, Lizzie is the summer, Elsa is the fall, and Elizabeth, well, she's winter," I added.

Gail nodded. "Yes."

"Do you think that Elizabeth... I don't even know how to say this without it sounding insane." I shook my head and began again, "Did she somehow *absorb* the others?"

Gail stared out of the window. "I've always thought of it as more of an act of eating them, but absorbing might be a better way to describe it." She looked down at her hands. The short, ragged nails. "I can't help wondering, if I had just stopped with her, if she would have been different."

Dread twisted my guts. "Wait. You had another child?"

Gail's face crumpled, her lip quivering. "I went to a different doctor, when Elizabeth was just a few months old. I was running out of time, but I hoped I could have just one more. Another child, close in age. I wanted Elizabeth to have what I never did. A sibling."

She reached for her water and I could see her fingers trembling.

"The implantation was successful and my son, Alexander, was born nine months later." She reached into her purse, pulled out a small photo book, and pushed it toward me. "He was beautiful, healthy, and I was so happy."

I opened up the photo book. Dozens of pictures of a tiny infant, with a faint shock of red hair on his head transformed into a smiling chubby boy. Like Elizabeth, his eyes were a startling crayon blue. The last pictures showed him standing, holding tight to a table on shaky legs.

"I loved him so much." Gail's voice quavered. "He was born four months after her first birthday. He was so different from her. More responsive, more affectionate."

"Gail, where is your son?" I asked, suddenly terrified. Why else would Elizabeth have ended up on the steps of that Catholic church?

Gail turned back toward me, her eyes glimmering with unshed tears. "Lake View Cemetery. I buried him next to my parents in the plot I was supposed to inherit. I wish they could have met him. They would... they would have loved him."

"Did Elizabeth..." I faltered. A truth, once spoken, cannot be unspoken. Did I really want to know that Elizabeth had killed her little brother as well? At the tender age of, what, two years of age?

Gail reached for a rough napkin as her tears spilled over and ran down her pale cheeks.

"They said it was SIDS, but it wasn't. I know it wasn't. Ninety percent of SIDS deaths are before the age of six months. Alexander was eleven months old. He died on March 18th, 2015, one month before his first birthday." She met my eyes, a look of desperation on her face. "You know what she is capable of."

"She killed Alexander and then she tried to kill me in January 2016. By then, I knew no one would ever believe the truth. After I got out of the hospital, I spiked her juice with Benadryl, waited until she was unconscious, and took her to the church." She stared at her hands. "I guess I thought maybe they could do something I couldn't. That they could make her good, or somehow exorcise the darkness from inside her. But I was wrong. As soon as I saw that first couple's names who died in the fire, and that she had survived, I knew. I knew she could never be fixed. Not by me, and not by anyone."

Afterwards, long after she had gotten up and walked away from the table, I sat there. I sat there until my coffee had grown cold and my butt ached from the metal straps of the chair. I would have been sitting there still if my phone hadn't rung.

It was Sue. We had been roommates in college in Seattle. She had returned to her home in Santa Cruz and married, had a child, and divorced - all in a year. When Vincent had told me where Gail was, and I had finally geared up the courage to meet with her, it had been a mini-vacation down to Santa Cruz with Lizzie as a girls' getaway excuse. I hadn't wanted to tell Jhon anything about Gail Pazza, not when we had finally settled into a life that worked for us: six months in the States and six months in South America. I had packed up Lizzie, left Theo with Jhon, and drove down the coast to see Sue and her daughter Lana.

"Nichole, honey, I need to take Lana to the doctor. She tripped and smacked her head on a rock and is just sobbing her heart out. I hate to interrupt your meeting, but..." Sue's voice petered out. Nichole could hear Sue's daughter in the background, screaming like a banshee.

"Oh, Sue, I'm so sorry I took so long. I'm five minutes out. I'll be there as quick as I can."

Sue's house was just two minutes away, and I pulled in as Sue was loading Lana into her minivan. A few feet away stood Lizzie, holding onto a cute stuffed bear from Build-A-Bear. Lana had one just like it, and from what Sue had said, loved it to pieces. Sue had said something about going to Build-A-Bear, but I had thought that we planned it for tomorrow, not today. I glanced at the digital clock on the car radio. Had I really been gone four hours? I would owe Sue big-time for the bear. Maybe I would take the girls to the Santa Cruz Boardwalk and give Sue some time to rest. Newly remarried and with another baby on the way, the bags under my friend's eyes reminded me of how tiring growing a baby could be.

Sue's look of irritation and relief at my arrival had me wondering if the two girls had had an altercation. Lana was still howling, and I hustled out of the car as she leaned in to buckle Lana in place.

"Oh, Nichole, thank goodness you're here. I need to get Lana to the ER. The cut is deep and it won't stop bleeding." She finished buckling Lana, slid the door shut, and turned back towards me, frowning as she whispered, "She says Elizabeth pushed her. I didn't see it, and she was helping Lana up, so..."

I told myself even my golden summer child would have difficult moments. My guts twisted in fear.

"I'm so sorry. Take care of Lana, and I promise I'll make it up to you, Sue." I gave her a quick hug before I hustled Lizzie to the car. I had closed her door after her, leaving her to put her seatbelt on, when a thought occurred to me. Something Sue had said didn't feel right. I walked around the car, leaned in through my open window. "Sweetheart, buckle yourself in. I'll be right back, okay?"

"Okay, Mommy."

I ran back to Sue, and up to her driver's side, knocking on the window just as her SUV began to roll backwards out of the driveway. Sue stopped and rolled her window down. Lana's shrieks rolled out of the window, a wave of misery.

"Nichole, I really need to get Lana to the ER." Sue looked stressed out, and I could see her wince with every shriek. No doubt she already had the beginning of a migraine, and the screaming was only making it worse.

"I know. Sue, I just had a question." I gulped past the lump of fear in my throat. "You called her Elizabeth, and I just wondered why."

Sue stared at me. "Seriously? Nichole, my child is bleeding. She swears up and down that Elizabeth pushed her, and you want to know why I call her by her name?"

"I just... we call her Lizzie. That's what she prefers... usually." It sounded lame coming out of my mouth. Usually, shit, that was an understatement. As long as Winter's Child didn't come out, the name Elizabeth was merely a string of letters on documents. It easily explained her other names away. We were humoring a child, in others' eyes, and they didn't need to know more than that.

Sue threw her hands up. "Well, Nichole, you know how kids are. She said she preferred Elizabeth, so that's what I called her. I really need to go."

"Sure, I totally understand. Hey, Lana," I said, trying to plaster a smile on my suddenly numb face, "I hope you feel better, sweetie! I'm sorry you got hurt." The minivan backed up, and Sue closed the window, muffling Lana's shrieks once again.

I wanted to follow them. The urge to run away, to escape, crashed over me.

Jhon was back home in Seattle. With Theo. Tiny, innocent Theo. I stared as the minivan backed up into the street, turned, and sped around the corner with a small squeal of tires.

I stared at the little girl in the backseat of my car. A little girl I had loved and cared for since we met for the first time at Rob and Kate's. She met my eyes and her mouth curved up in the smile I knew so well. My Lizzie, my daughter, a child we had worked so hard to save. Isabel was sweet, timid, and almost tentative. It tinged our time with her with relief, and a little patience went a long way. Elsa tried hard, despite her fear and anxiety. We loved her anyway. Lizzie lit the room up like the sun. She made us laugh. Theo adored her. All three of them were worthy of love, worthy of commitment. The only child we couldn't handle was Elizabeth. Winter's Child.

I walked back to my car. Surely Sue had heard it wrong. Gotten confused. She had to have. Besides... it was *summer.* Winter was in full force down under, but here in the northern hemisphere, it was summer. Theo would turn two years old in just two more months. We had *time*, loads of it, before we needed to make our escape down under for spring. There were worse fates than never-ending spring and summer. After a childhood spent in the Midwest with its cold, dry winters, I didn't mind missing out on those months. Not at all.

I slid into my seat and clipped my seatbelt on. I kept my voice chipper and bright. "My goodness, that must have been upsetting, sweetheart. What a sad end to what must have been a lovely day. I see Sue took you to Build-A-Bear. That must have been so much fun!"

"It was, Mommy. We had a very nice day," Lizzie chirped from her car seat. I turned on the blinker and waited for a car to pass before I pulled onto the road again.

"We didn't go to Build-A-Bear, though. Lana gave me hers, because we're best friends now."

I frowned. Something about this was all wrong. I drove on autopilot, each turn automatic as I turned onto the road, merged with traffic, and moved over to access Highway 1. Our Airbnb was a few stops away, nestled in the redwoods. Lizzie loved it.

Sue had talked about the bear. She said Lana went everywhere with it. Slept with it, ate with it, played with it. Yet there it sat, tucked into the crevice between the middle seat space and Lizzie's booster seat.

A feeling of wrongness grew, creeping up from my stomach, wrapping around my lungs and heart. It squeezed my throat. My mouth felt dry.

Elizabeth.

But how? It was *summer*. We had fixed this; we had figured out a workaround.

I stared into the rearview mirror as she looked up and smiled, all teeth. The sight of it turned my insides to jelly.

"I've missed you, Mommy. It's been a very long time."

My palms felt sweaty, my stomach clenching as the coffee rebelled in the pit of my stomach.

I pulled onto the highway and traffic thinned more the further we drove. My thoughts raced. All I could think of was Theo, back home in Seattle, with Jhon. My husband. My son. They didn't deserve this - they hadn't asked for this.

I'd been a fool. A dreamer. So sure that I had discovered a workaround. But Elizabeth was inevitable. She was the only one of the four embryos that had remained. It was *her* body the four girls resided in. Whatever fragments of the other three that were left, Elizabeth was in charge. And she had broken through, despite it being summer.

You know what you have to do.

My mother's voice broke through my haze of fear and horror. And with it, my resolve manifested.

"Did you bring me something back, Mommy?" Elizabeth asked. I glanced over at the remains of a half-eaten doughnut wrapped in a brown paper bag.

I forced a brightness I did not feel into my voice. "I sure did! It's there in the front seat."

"I'm hungry. I want it now."

Up ahead was a broad curve, with a section for parking and taking pictures. The fog had rolled in, however, and there was no one. No one parked, no oncoming traffic, and no one behind me. Beyond the parking was a steep cliff. Below that, rocks and pounding surf.

No one gets out of this life alive. You have a choice. Take her home and die alongside Theo and Jhon, or end it now.

I met her eyes in the rearview mirror. "Sure, sweetheart. Pop out of your seat and grab it if you like."

The bend in the road was approaching. I heard the seatbelt click. Felt Elizabeth brush past, reaching for the bag with the doughnut. I had to do this now. To save Theo and Jhon. My heart ached for Isabel, Lizzie, and Elsa - but still my foot pushed down further, accelerating toward the turnout, and the cliff beyond. The edge of the cliff grew closer. I closed my eyes.

27. Why Are You Here?

- Nichole -

December 21st, 2021 - Central California Women's Facility

I couldn't say no to the request. I don't know why. Perhaps I felt sentimental. After all, it was Elizabeth's birthday today. She would have been eight years old. In so many ways, the tiny stillborn child I had given birth to, and Elizabeth, and all her aspects, were the same in my mind. They had slowly assembled there together, becoming one. I had never held my baby, but I had held Elizabeth. I'd held Isabel, Lizzie, and Elsa. And I'd loved each one of them.

I thought of this as I walked down the long hall, through a series of checkpoints and steel doors, to the waiting room. I wondered what it was that he wanted, why he was really here.

I had nothing to offer him. I couldn't be a wife or a mother. I couldn't even be a lover. And what good is friendship behind walls such as these?

What Vincent and I had was long over, despite the way my body, heart, and mind reacted to his presence. Today of all days was especially hard. Perhaps that is why I didn't say no. I didn't want to sit in my cell and think of all the ways things had gone wrong. I didn't want to remember that it had all started eight years ago today.

He was seated when I walked into the visiting room, dressed in jeans and a T-shirt. A civilian now. He looked good. Thinner. Perhaps with a few more gray hairs springing up out of his temples, but good.

His mouth quirked up at the edges in a half-smile and I felt my body respond. I couldn't help the attraction - I had felt that way about him there in Brisbane and it had felt almost traitorous. Now, I recognized it for what it was. I had never stopped loving Vincent, even if I had married Jhon. I still loved him. I think I always will.

He stood and reached for me, pulling me into a hug as soon as I approached. It felt good and I let him hold me until one of the guards cleared his throat. I stepped away, the warmth of him lingered on my skin.

"How are you?" His voice was pitched low. "How's the leg?"

My left leg ached with a pain that never ceased. The chilly air of winter, no matter how temperate it was most of the year, had settled deep into my poorly healed bones and would not let go. I motioned to a table, and we both sat. I did my best not to show how much pain I was in. If only I had thought to remove my own seatbelt. I wouldn't be here. I'd be gone, right alongside Elizabeth.

"It's fine. I'm fine," I answered. "What are you doing here, Vincent?"

"I was up working a job in Seattle and I thought I'd visit Jhon and Theo." He cocked his head to one side, his gaze piercing. I felt like he could see every secret I was trying to hide. "It wasn't too far out of my way to come down and see you on the way back. I wanted to see how you are holding up."

"Jhon asked you to come see me, didn't he?" I had my suspicions the minute I saw Vincent's name on the visitor log request form. He hadn't taken my decision well, Jhon hadn't, but he hadn't really been given a choice. I'd refused to see him.

"Of course he did. He's worried, Nicky. Can you blame him? He loves you." He reached out and took my hand, and I felt a warm, familiar rush of desire and emotion surge over me. His voice dropped to a murmur. "God help me, I can't say I don't feel the same."

"I thought you and Justine might work it out."

His hand pulled away from mine.

"Some things can't be fixed, Nicky. You, of all people, should know that." He leaned back, blew out a breath, and shook his head.

"That said, she's here, believe it or not. We found a duplex outside of San Jose, well, a quadplex, but the other two will be rented out. We live next to each other, and we share custody of the kids." He shrugged. "We decided to stay married for immigration purposes. After, well, after Elizabeth, Justine just couldn't seem to settle there in Brisbane. Rocco's family filed a wrongful death lawsuit. Tried to say she'd killed him. It was a mess. She was open to options, and coming back here meant I could work as a detective, maybe even get back on the force someday, so here we are."

My heart hurt for him. Vincent was a good man. He deserved happiness and love. Not half-measures, not compromises. I couldn't help wondering if the location had been chosen because of me. Was he trying to rekindle what we had after all of these years?

I thought of Jhon's letters. So desperate, so sad. I couldn't stand to read any of them. I sent them back now, unopened. Refused his visits.

As if he could read my mind, Vincent's hand returned to cover mine. "Why won't you see him, Nicky?"

I stared down at his hand. No wedding ring. But the finger still showed a pale shadow where the band had been. "I... I don't want Theo here."

"Nicky..."

I waited for him to say more, but he didn't. And really, what was there to say? Tragedy, bad luck. That's what the news anchors had described it as. My defense attorney had played it up as an insanity defense. He had pointed to my troubled childhood with a mother who was mentally unhinged and had tried to kill me before burning the house down with her inside of it. And then, to lose two pregnancies, the second one to a stillbirth, had obviously damaged me in ways that most could not comprehend.

The trial had been on every news outlet nationwide. Reporters had camped outside of the small apartment that Jhon and Theo were staying at without me. Due to our frequent travels out of the country and the nature of the crime, I had been deemed a flight risk and was denied bail. At the time, I hadn't really cared. I was just disappointed I'd made it out of the crash alive. If I hadn't been confined to the infirmary in traction, I have no doubt they would have had me on suicide watch.

It hadn't lasted long. The seven-man, five-woman jury had convicted me of murder even without a body. I'd driven off a cliff, after all. Into the ocean. With a child improperly secured in the back seat and with my own seatbelt on. It didn't matter to them that I had been willing to die with her. I'd killed Elizabeth. A child. An innocent little girl who had been through enough trauma in her life already. It had shone a spotlight on foster care that hadn't been pretty or accurate.

Vincent finally spoke. "Kids are, well, they are adaptable. He misses you, Nicky. He's talking a blue streak and Jhon has pictures of you up everywhere.

At least, hell, I don't know, write to them. I know he can't get down to see you too often, but Theo needs to know who you are. He needs his mother."

I closed my eyes and wished I could close my ears as well. All I had ever wanted was a family. A husband, children to love who would love me back. It's all I had ever wanted.

"Why are you here, Vincent?" I asked as I opened my eyes and stared at him. My voice sounded sharp, defensive.

It was Vincent's turn to drop his gaze. To stare at the battered metal table beneath our clasped hands. "I want to see you get a new trial, Nicky."

"No."

His mouth tightened. So did his grip.

"Damn it, Nicky. You did what you had to at that moment. I talked to Gail Pazza. I have her permission to pull the medical data on her IVF treatment, on the scans they did on the fetuses."

"To what end, Vince?" I pulled my hands away. "It won't change anything."

"Elizabeth nearly killed her own mother, and the death of Kate and Rob Long is still an open case. We can prove it was Elizabeth by comparing the fingerprints taken from the scene against several of her personal items that Jhon still has."

My heart hurt thinking of Kate. Sweet Kate. She hadn't deserved to die like that.

"I can't, Vincent. I just can't go through it again."

"You were defending your family, Nicky. We could at the very least get it down to manslaughter. You could be out by the time Theo is done with elementary school, maybe sooner if we had a sympathetic judge and jury."

"No, Vincent. Just... no."

"Nicky..." He reached out and took my chin in his hand. "You aren't a bad person. You didn't deserve any of this. Let me help you."

I forced a smile to my lips and stood up. "Thank you for coming to see me, Vincent. It was very kind. Give my best to Justine and the kids."

"Nicky, please."

I turned away, trying my best not to limp as I walked back to the door and the guard. The uniformed guard, a new one I didn't recognize, ushered me through the door.

I didn't look back.

Epilogue

Ten Years Later

I watch the news on the battered old television. There she is, the woman who promised to love me and instead did her best to kill me. They say she's been a model prisoner. That my mother even came forward to testify on her behalf. Even the detective, the one whose harpy wife and kids I was stuck with for those few days in Australia, he testified as well.

They are billing it as the story of the decade. A child capable of murder. A woman defending her family. There are plenty of people on both sides. The news cameras show them protesting outside of the courtroom. On one side, the sycophants who are so sure I'm a monster. On the other, those convinced I'm an angel.

Laughable. Really.

I couldn't care less what they think.

That fateful day when I found a way out, past the other aspects, as Nichole referred to them, I nearly died. I realized nearly too late that Nichole meant to do me harm. And if I had gotten the chance to kill her first, I would have. But she'd been smart. And quick. Too quick.

Every one of the other three screamed as they saw the edge of the cliff approaching and the jagged rocks and surf below.

Free fall. That was the worst. Sometimes I dream about it. The impact knocked me out, just as it did her. At least, that's what Don says. He pulled us both out. Says God told him to take me away, and he did.

Don calls me his perfect angel. Says I changed his life. And he gives me whatever I want, which is how it should be. If the others had been like Don, they'd still be alive. It wasn't as if I was asking so much, really. They should have just given me what I wanted.

The new trial has dragged on for days. The testimony is riveting. The networks are having a field day analyzing the sensational claims. Still, I watch and I wait. I wanted her to spend the rest of her life in prison, but I also want the chance to kill her myself. I've spent a decade learning how to do it right. How to not get caught. Don helps me. He says I'm the angel of death and that I help release tortured souls from their bodies. It helps that these tortured souls are pimps and drug dealers with wads of cash in their pockets. Really, I'm doing the public a favor, don't you think?

The announcement scrolls across the screen. They are releasing her from prison. After just ten years. For murder! Never mind that I am still alive. They don't know that. No one does. No one can. Not if I want to get my way.

My chance will come. And I plan on exacting my revenge on every single one of them.

Author Note

Do you ever wonder what drives a story? Was it a single incident or one of many? How much of life lends itself to art?

Part of this book has come out of an exploration of mental health, including negative self-talk - the voices that all of us carry inside of us. Those quiet, dark moments when we sabotage ourselves, when we tell ourselves we aren't worthy of love or success or happiness.

May I stop here and say to you, that yes, you are worthy of love, success, and happiness? It's true. And success is such an elusive thing, really. One morning, while my family gathered for our shared moments of coffee and tea and milk (in the case of the little one), we dipped into a question of the day stack of cards. The card of the day asked, "If you knew that one thing was completely possible for you, what would you have it be?" I answered, "To be a world-renowned author."

My husband raised his eyebrows and said, "Wait a minute, aren't you already? Haven't people around the world read your books?"

Those words have stuck with me. It might not be the lucrative reality I hope for, but he wasn't wrong.

And so I say again - you and I, are absolutely worthy of love, success, and happiness. I don't have to know you to be certain that is true.

Back to *Winter's Child*. The rest of the premise came to me while I was attending mandatory training that would qualify us to adopt our foster daughter. Sitting there, I was suddenly struck with the idea of an adoption that goes horribly wrong. What if the beautiful, sunny child you think you are adopting has a hidden darkness? What if some part of that child is stunningly evil and beyond redemption?

The story would not let me go. It took a while of thinking on it and fleshing the story out before the timing was right, but you hold in your hands the result of my odd musings. I do hope you have enjoyed it. For the record, while it might seem to end on a cliffhanger, I do not plan on writing a sequel at this time. All too often we expect a story to be neatly wrapped up in a nice little package, but in real life, the story doesn't end in a happily ever after with that nice wedding kiss. There's life and diapers and getting old in there too.

Moreover, I wanted to leave the ending ambiguous. Who knows what might come down the pike in the years that follow?

I would love to make a series of paranormal thrillers. However, I have yet to think of *what* story to write next. These things can't be rushed, and I apologize for the delay if you are a fan of thrillers, and especially of this book, but it may be a while.

Note: I need to add here that my intent is *not* to turn people off from fostering or adopting! *Winter's Child* is a work of *fiction*. While we were warned during foster training that they would pee in our shoes, kill our family pets, set our house on fire, and never love us (we really were told that!), the exact opposite has been true. In my limited fostering experience, children are easy to love. Fostering them isn't any harder than parenthood in general. It's as easy as opening the door and opening your heart. The hard part is, and will always be, in saying goodbye.

If you are so inclined, consider genre-hopping and check out my dystopian, sci-fi, and even non-fiction and romance novels. You will find a list of all of my published works at the end of this book. I will repeat what others who have read my stories already know: if you like character-driven stories, you will likely enjoy the other genres I write in. Give them a chance — you never know what you might discover to be appealing!

And please, if it isn't too much trouble, I hope that you will leave a review. Reviews are social proof. They tell others that someone has 1) read this book, and 2) thought enough of it to write something about it. I don't know about you, but I usually check out the reviews on a book or other product before I click the buy button. I want to know I'm picking up a book worth reading. So if you think this book was worth reading, leave a review and tell *everyone*!

Thank you again for spending your valuable time to read this book. Send me an email at shuckchristine@gmail.com or drop me a message at any of the destinations listed below. You can find me at:

Facebook Author page: https://www.facebook.com/Christine.D.Shuck

Facebook Group (General Malcontent's Grumbles and Scribbles): https://www.facebook.com/groups/555880424837978

Instagram: https://www.instagram.com/christinedshuck/

Author Website: https://www.christineshuck.com[1]

1. https://www.christineshuck.com/

Acknowledgments

I don't know if it is appropriate to thank Covid, but I'll be the first to admit that it changed everything for me in early 2020. A trip to London for the Self-Publishing Show conference ended with us landing in Minneapolis to switch planes and learning that they were closing the borders and we were in the middle of a pandemic. Overnight, my short-term rental business dried up, and so did my fifteen-year-old cleaning business.

I did what I do best - I pivoted. I closed down the cleaning biz for good in July 2020 (this coincided with bringing home an adorable newborn foster son for five months), changed to a mid-term rental for several months, and decided to dig my heels in and start writing more than a book every two years or even a book a year. Apparently, a worldwide pandemic was exactly what I needed to start thinking *bigger*. Five more books and two years later, and my eyes are firmly set on the prize.

I'd like to thank Joanna Penn and her podcast, *The Creative Penn*. She keeps me going with weekly podcasts, and I especially appreciated her interview with Shawn Inmon and his tips on writing every single day. Jo, forgive me for cornering you in the loo in London in 2020 and halfway insulting you while nervously trying to tell you how much I liked your podcast. What can I say? I'm better off staying at home and not talking to anyone.

And while this should have been *first*, I would like to thank my family, especially my husband Dave, who puts up with my wacky ideas and having to cook most of the meals because I'm a workaholic. I love you, darling!

To Little Miss, who was in some very small way the inspiration for this book. Don't worry, she's *nothing* like Elizabeth! Fostering her these past four years has been a heck of a ride and that is for sure. We look forward to making her a permanent part of our family in the coming year.

To YumYum, our last foster baby and hopefully, soon-to-be forever son. You have rooted in our hearts a hope for tomorrow, and we love you more than words can express.

To the Little Prince, gone back to your dad after those five glorious months with us, I still miss you, sweet boy. I loved your smiles, your sweet baby giggles, and pretty much everything else. It's hard to believe you will soon be two years old. I thought of you on your birthday and pretty much every day since (thanks, Facebook Memories), and I can't tell you how much I miss holding you. I'll love you forever.

When people ask, I always say that fostering is easy. You open the door and you open your heart. It's the saying goodbye that is so very hard.

To Kerrie McLoughlin, copy-editor extraordinaire who keeps buying my books and spreading them around. You are fantastic and I wish we hung out more!

To Dani Rouse Holland, one of my most supportive fans on Facebook, love you!

Thanks to Brandy Hagemeister Pearson and Nataly Hocking for help with the perfect house location outside of Brisbane and other Australian know-how.

Thanks to Nicole Schumacher Hosier and Trauma Fiction on Facebook for the medical know-how!

Thanks to Jenny Brewer Dang for her knowledge of Seattle, Washington.

To everyone else who has put up with my infrequent posts over at *General Malcontent's Grumbles and Scribbles* on Facebook... thank you, thank you, thank you. Keep reading, keep commenting. I love to hear from you!

All Published Works

Christine writes cross-genre and her books can be found in e-book and in paperback through most book distributors.

Non-Fiction:

Get Organized, Stay Organized
The War on Drugs: An Old Wives Tale

Fiction Series:

WAR'S END

The Storm
A Brave New World
Tales of the Collapse

Gliese 581g

G581: The Departure
G581: Mars
G581: Earth

Chronicles of Liv Rowan

Fate's Highway a.k.a. Schicksal Turnpike

Benton Security Services

Hired Gun
Smoke and Steel

Children of Ruin

Winter's Child

Also by Christine D. Shuck

Benton Security Services

Hired Gun

Smoke and Steel

Chronicles of Liv Rowan

Fate's Highway

Gliese 581g

G581: The Departure

G581: Mars

G581: Earth

War's End

War's End: The Storm

War's End: A Brave New World

Tales of the Collapse

War's End Omnibus - Books 1-3

Standalone

The War on Drugs: An Old Wives Tale
Get Organized, Stay Organized
Winter's Child

Watch for more at christineshuck.com.

About the Author

Fueled by homemade coffee ice cream, a lifelong love of words, and armed with strong female (and male) characters I cross genres like the Ghostbusters crossed the streams in pursuit of the question.

"What is the question?" you ask.

The question is simple. It asks, "What would you do, if..."

What would you do if you were fifteen years old and the world as you knew it fell apart? Would you run? Would you fight? Would you survive? – Meet Jess and her brother Chris in the *War's End* series.

What would you do if you had a chance to live your life over? Not just once, but twice? – Meet Dean Edmonds in *Fate's Highway*

What would you do if everyone you loved was lost to a terrible virus and you faced the real possibility of the extinction of the human race in the dark void of space? – Meet Daniel Medry in *G581: The Departure*

What would you do if hitmen were after you and you had no idea why? – Meet Lila and Shane in *Hired Gun*

If I don't keep you turning pages late into the night, desperate to know what happens next, then I have failed at my job. I'm a Taurus and born in Missouri. That makes me bull-headed and stubborn to boot. I don't believe in failure or mistakes, only learning opportunities and clever conversation. There's not much I won't do to make you burn the midnight oil reading my words while you suffer sleep-deprivation the following day. It's my secret superpower.

Born in flyover country, I've also lived in Arizona and northern California. I am an eclectic mix of snark and oddball humor. My colorful metaphors would make a fishwife blush. I'm an incompetent gardener, a dreamer and doer, in love with old houses and shooting pool, and chief organizer of all thing's household and financial. Feed me tiramisu and I'm yours forever.

Find me on all major platforms by visiting Linktree: https://linktr.ee/christinedshuck

Read more at christineshuck.com.

CPSIA information can be obtained
at www.ICGtesting.com
Printed in the USA
BVHW022140021222
653365BV00003B/53

9 781955 150231